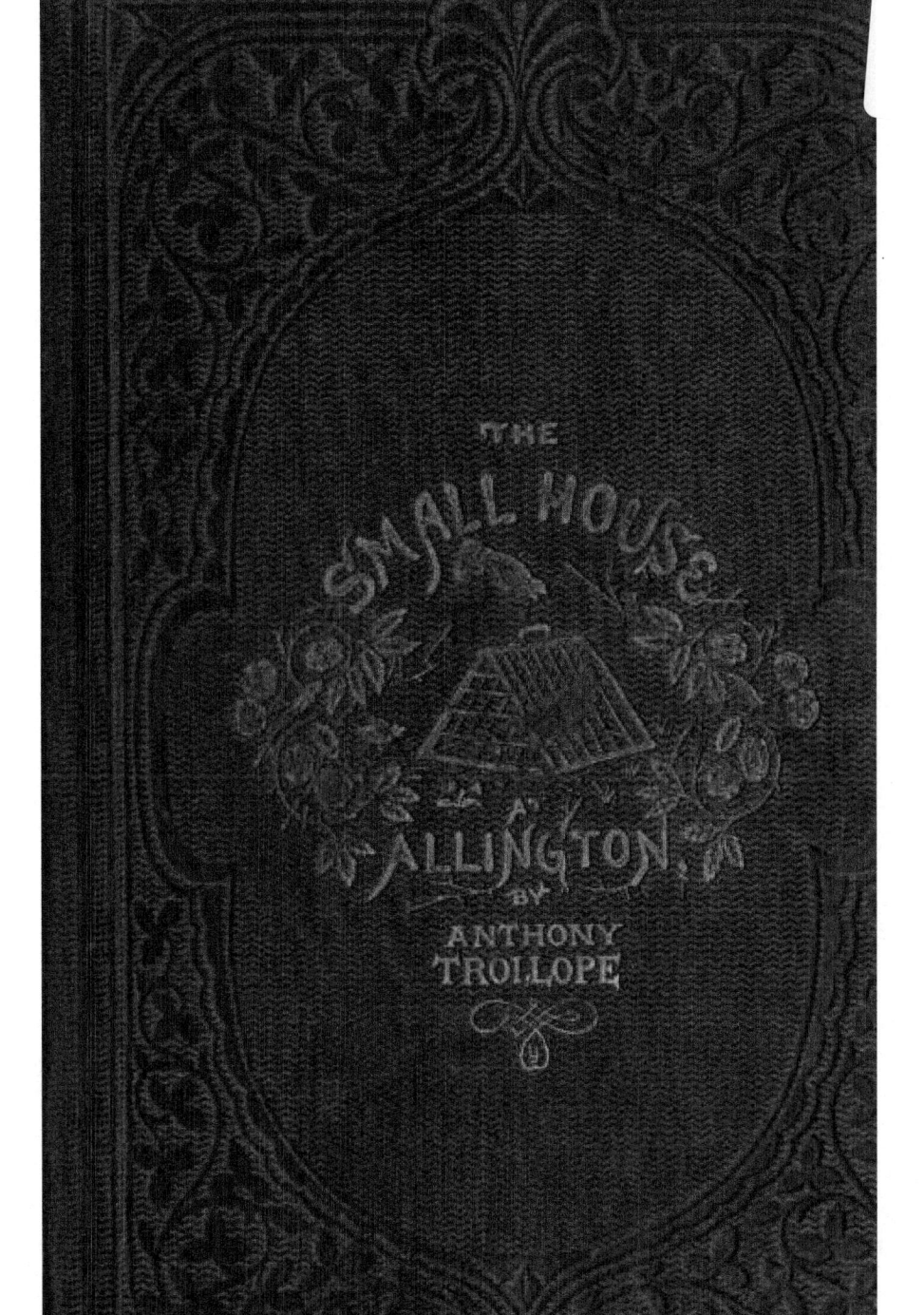

THE
SMALL HOUSE
AT
ALLINGTON.
BY
ANTHONY TROLLOPE

"WHY, ON EARTH, ON SUNDAY?"

THE

SMALL HOUSE AT ALLINGTON.

BY

ANTHONY TROLLOPE.

WITH EIGHTEEN ILLUSTRATIONS BY J. E. MILLAIS, R.A.

IN TWO VOLUMES.

VOL. II.

LONDON:
SMITH, ELDER AND CO., 65, CORNHILL.

M.DCCC.LXIV.

[The right of Translation is reserved.]

CONTENTS.

CHAP.		PAGE
I.	The Wounded Fawn	1
II.	Pawkins's in Jermyn Street	10
III.	"The Time will Come"	20
IV.	The Combat	32
V.	Væ Victis	40
VI.	"See, the Conquering Hero Comes"	52
VII.	An Old Man's Complaint	64
VIII.	Dr. Crofts is called in	72
IX.	Dr. Crofts is Turned out	83
X.	Preparations for the Wedding	95
XI.	Domestic Troubles	109
XII.	Lily's Bedside	118
XIII.	Fie, Fie	127
XIV.	Valentine's Day at Allington	139
XV.	Valentine's Day in London	148
XVI.	John Eames at his Office	160
XVII.	The New Private Secretary	172
XVIII.	Nemesis	181
XIX.	Preparations for Going	192
XX.	Mrs. Dale is Thankful for a Good Thing	202
XXI.	John Eames does Things which he Ought not to have Done	210
XXII.	The First Visit to the Guestwick Bridge	224
XXIII.	Loquitur Hopkins	234
XXIV.	The Second Visit to the Guestwick Bridge	243
XXV.	Not very Fie Fie after all	254
XXVI.	Showing how Mr. Crosbie became again a Happy Man	267
XXVII.	Lilian Dale Vanquishes her Mother	276
XXVIII.	The Fate of the Small House	286
XXIX.	John Eames becomes a Man	296
XXX.	Conclusion	306

TIE SMALL HOUSE AT ALLIMTOK

CHAPTER I. THE WOUNDED FAWN

NEARLY two months passed away, and it was now Christmas time at Allington. It may he presumed that there was no intention at either house that the mirth should he very loud. Such a wound as that received hy Lily Dale was one from which recovery could not he quick, and it was felt by all the family that a weight was upon them which made gaiety impracticable. As for Lily herself it may he said that she bore her misfortune with all a woman's courage. For the first week she stood up as a tree that stands against the wind, which is soon to be shivered to pieces because it will not bend. During that week her mother and sister were frightened by her calmness and endurance. She would perform her daily task. She would go out through the village, and appear at her place in church on the first Sunday. She would sit over her book of an evening, keeping back her tears; and would chide her mother and sister when she found that they were regarding her with earnest anxiety.

" Mamma, let it all be as though it had never been," she said.

" Ah, dear ! if that were but possible ! "

" God forbid that it should be possible inwardly," Lily replied. " But it is possible outwardly. I feel that you are more tender to me than you used to be, and that upsets me. If you would only scold me because I am idle, I should soon be better." But her mother could not speak to her as she perhaps might have spoken had no grief fallen upon her pet. She could not cease from those anxious tender glances which made Lily know that she was looked on as a fawn wounded almost to death.

At the end of the first week she gave way. " I won't get up, Bell," she said one morning, almost petulantly. " I am ill;—I had better lie here out of the way. Don't make a fuss about it. I'm stupid and foolish, and that makes me ill."

Thereupon Mrs. Dale and Bell were frightened, and looked into each other's blank faces, remembering stories of poor broken-hearted girls who had died because their loves had been unfortunate,—as small wax tapers whose lights are quenched if a breath of wind blows upon them too strongly. But then Lily was in truth no such slight taper as that. Nor was she the stem that must be broken because it will not bend. She bent herself to the blast during that week of illness, and then arose with her form still straight and graceful, and with her bright light unquenched.

After that she would talk more openly to her mother about her loss, openly and with a time appreciation of the misfortune which had befallen her; but with an assurance of strength which seemed to ridicule the idea of a broken heart. " I know that I can bear it, she said, " and that I can bear it without lasting unhappiness. Of course I shall always love him, and must feel almost as you felt when you lost my father."

In answer to this Mrs. Dale could say nothing. She could not speak out her thoughts about Crosbie, and explain to Lily that he was unworthy of her love. Love does not follow worth, and is not given to excellence ; nor is it destroyed by ill-usage, nor killed by blows and mutilation. "When Lily declared that she still loved the man who had so ill-used her, Mrs. Dale would be silent. Each perfectly understood the other, but on that matter even they could not interchange their thoughts with freedom.

" You must promise never to be tired of me, mamma," said Lily.

" Mothers do not often get tired of their children, whatever the children may do of their mothers."

" I'm not so sure of that when the children turn out old maids. And I mean to have a will of my own, too, mamma ; and a way also, if it be possible. When Bell is married I shall consider it a partnership, and I shan't do what I'm told any longer." " Forewarned will be forearmed." " Exactly; and I don't want to take you by surprise. For a year or two longer, till Bell is gone, I mean to be dutiful; but it would be very stupid for a person to be dutiful all their lives."

All of which Mrs. Dale understood thoroughly. It amounted to an assertion on Lily's part that she had loved once and could never love again; that she had played her game, hoping, as other girls hope, that she might van the prize of a husband; but that, having lost, she could never play the game again. It was that inward conviction on Lily's part which made her say such words to her mother. But Mrs. Dale would by no means allow herself to share this conviction. She declared to herself that time would cure Lily's wound, and that her child might yet be crowned by the bliss of a happy marriage. She would not in her heart consent to that plan in accordance with which Lily's destiny in life was to be regarded as already fixed. She had never really liked Crosbie as a suitor, and would herself have preferred John Eames, with all the faults of his hobbledehoyhood on his head. It might yet come to pass that John Eames' love might be made happy.

But in the meantime Lily, as I have said, had become strong in her courage, and recommenced the work of living with no lackadaisical self-assurance that because she had been made more unhappy than others, therefore she should allow herself to be more idle. Morning and night she prayed for him, and daily, almost hour by hour, she assured herself that it was still her duty to love him. It was hard, this duty of loving, without any power of expressing such love. But still she would do her duty.

" Tell me at once, mamma," she said one morning, " when you hear that the day is fixed for his marriage. Pray don't keep me in the dark."

" It is to be in February," said Mrs. Dale.

" But let me know the day. It must not be to me like ordinary days. But do not look unhappy, mamma; I am not going to make a fool of myself. I shan't steal off and appear in the church like a ghost." And then, having uttered her little joke, a sob came, and she hid her face on her mother's bosom. In a moment she raised it again. " Believe me, mamma, that I am not unhappy," she said.

After the expiration of that second week Mrs. Dale did write a letter to Crosbie :

I SUPPOSE (she said) it is right that I should acknowledge the receipt of your letter. I do not know that I have aught else to say to you. It would not become me as a woman to say what I think of your conduct, but I believe that your conscience will tell you the same things. If it do not, you must, indeed 1 , be hardened. I have promised my child that I will send to you a message from her. She bids me tell you that she has forgiven you, and that she does not hate you. May God also forgive you, and may you recover his love.

MART DALE.

I beg that no rejoinder may be made to this letter, either to myself or to any of my family.

The squire wrote no answer to the letter which he had received, nor did he take any steps towards the immediate punishment of Crosbie. Indeed he had declared that no such steps could be taken, explaining to his nephew that such a man could be served only as one serves a rat.

"I shall never see him," he said once again ; " if I did, I should not scruple to hit him on the head with my stick; but I should think ill of myself to go after him with such an object."

And yet it was a terrible sorrow to the old man that the scoundrel who had so injured him and his should escape scot-free. He had not forgiven Crosbie. No idea of forgiveness had ever crossed his mind. He would have hated himself had he thought it possible that he could be induced to forgive such an injury. "There is an amount of rascality in it, of low meanness, which I do not understand," he would say over and over again to his nephew. And then as he would walk alone on the terrace he would speculate within his own mind whether Bernard would take any steps towards avenging his cousin's injury. "He is right," he would say to himself; " Bernard is quite right. But when I was young I could not have stood it. In those days a gentleman might have a fellow out who had treated him as he has treated us. A man was satisfied in feeling that he had done something. I suppose the world is different now-a-days." The world is different ; but the squire by no means acknowledged in his heart that there had been any improvement.

Bernard also was greatly troubled in his mind. He would have had no objection to fight a duel wjth Crosbie, had duels in these days been possible. But he believed them to be no longer possible, — at any rate without ridicule. And if he could not fight the man, in what other way was he to punish him ? Was it not the fact that for such a fault the world afforded no punishment ? Was it not in the power of a man like Crosbie to amuse himself for a week or two at the expense of a girl's happiness for life, and then to escape absolutely without any ill effects to himself? "I shall be barred

out of my club lest I should meet him," Bernard said to himself, " but he will not be barred out." Moreover, there was a feeling within him that the matter would be one of triumph to Crosbie rather than otherwise. In having secured for himself the pleasure of his courtship with such a girl as Lily Dale, without encountering the penalty usually consequent upon such amusement, he would be held by many as having merited much admiration. He had sinned against all the Dales, and yet the suffering arising from his sin was to fall upon the Dales exclusively. Such was Bernard's reasoning, as he speculated on the whole affair, sadly enough,— wishing to be avenged, but not knowing where to look for vengeance. For myself I believe him to have been altogether wrong as to the light in which he supposed that Crosbie's falsehood would be regarded by Crosbie's friends. Men will still talk of such things lightly, professing that all is fair in love as it is in war, and speaking almost with envy of the good fortunes of a practised deceiver. But I have never come across the man who thought in this way with reference to an individual case. Crosbie's own judgment as to the consequences to himself of what he had done was more correct than that formed by Bernard Dale. He had regarded the act as venial as long as it was still to do, while it was still within his power to leave it undone; but from the moment of its accomplishment it had forced itself upon his own view in its proper light. He knew that he had been a scoundrel, and he knew that other men would so think of him. His friend Fowler Pratt, who had the reputation of looking at women simply as toys, had so regarded him. Instead of boasting of what he had done, he was as afraid of alluding to any matter connected with his marriage as a man is of talking of the articles which he has stolen. He had already felt that men at his club looked askance at him; and, though he was no coward as regarded his own skin and bones, he had an undefined fear lest some day he might encounter Bernard Dale purposely armed with a stick. The squire and his nephew were wrong in supposing that Crosbie was unpunished.

And as the winter came on he felt that he was closely watched by the noble family of De Courcy. Some of that noble family he had already learned to hate cordially. The Honourable John came up to town in November, and persecuted him vilely; insisted on having dinners given to him at Sebright's, of smoking throughout the whole afternoon in his future brother-in-law's rooms, and on borrowing his future brother-in-law's possessions; till at last Crosbie determined that it would be wise to quarrel with the Honourable John,—and he quarrelled with him accordingly, turning him out of his rooms, and telling him in so many words that he would have no more to do with him.

" You'll have to do it, as I did," Mortimer Gazebee had said to him ; " I didn't like it because of the family, but Lady Amelia told me that it must be so." Whereupon Crosbie took the advice of Mortimer Gazebee.

But the hospitality of the Gazebees was perhaps more distressing to him than even the importunities of the Honourable John. It seemed as though his future sister-in-law was determined not to leave him alone. Mortimer was sent to fetch him up for the Sunday afternoons, and he found that he was constrained to go to the villa in St. John's Wood, even in opposition to his own most strenuous will. He could not quite analyze the circumstances of his own position, but he felt as though he were a cock with his spurs cut off,—as a dog with his teeth drawn. He found himself becoming humble and meek. He had to acknowledge to himself that he was afraid of Lady Amelia, and almost even afraid of Mortimer Gazebee. He was aware that they watched him, and knew all his goings out and comings in. They called him Adolphus, and made him tame. That coming evil day in February was dinned into his ears. Lady Amelia would go and look at furniture for him, and talked by the hour about bedding and sheets. " You had better get your kitchen things at Tomkins'. They're all good, and he'll give you ten per cent, off if you pay him ready money, which of course you will, you know !" Was it for this that he had sacrificed Lily Dale ? for this that he had allied himself with the noble house of De Courcy ?

Mortimer had been at him about the settlements from the very first moment of his return to London, and had already bound him up hand and foot. His life was insured, and the policy was in Mortimer's hands. His own little bit of money had been already handed over to be tied up with Lady Alexandria's little bit. It seemed to him that in all the arrangements made the intention was that he should die off speedily, and that Lady Alexanclrina should be provided with a decent little income, sufficient for St. John's Wood. Things were to be so settled that he could not even spend the proceeds of his own money, or of hers. They were to go, under the fostering hand of Mortimer Gazebee, in paying insurances. If he would only die the day after his marriage, there would really be a very nice sum of

money for Alexandrina, almost worthy of the acceptance of an earl's daughter. Six months ago he would have considered himself able to turn Mortimer Gazebee round his finger on any subject that could be introduced between them. When they chanced to meet Gazebee had been quite humble to him, treating him almost as a superior being. He had looked down on Gazebee from a very great height. But now it seemed as though he were powerless in this man's hands.

But perhaps the countess had become his greatest aversion. She was perpetually writing to him little notes in which she gave him multitudes of commissions, sending him about as though he had been her servant. And she pestered him with advice which was even worse than her commissions, telling him of the style of life in which Alexandrina would expect to live, and warning him very frequently that such an one as he could not expect to be admitted within the bosom of so noble a family without paying very dearly for that inestimable privilege. Her letters had become odious to him, and he would chuck them on one side, leaving them for the whole day unopened. He had already made up his mind that he would quarrel with the countess also, very shortly after his marriage ; indeed, that he would separate himself from the whole family if it were possible. And yet he had entered into this engagement mainly with the view of reaping those advantages which would accrue to him from being allied to the De Courcys! The squire and his nephew were wretched in thinking that this man was escaping without punishment, but they might have spared themselves that misery.

It had been understood from the first that he was to spend his Christmas at Courcy Castle. From this undertaking it was quite out of his power to enfranchise himself: but he resolved that his visit should be as short as possible. Christmas Day unfortunately came on a Monday, and it was known to the De Courcy world that Saturday was almost a dies non at the General Committee Office. As to those three days there was no escape for him; but he made Alexandrina understand that the three Commissioners were men of iron as to any extension of those three days. " I must be absent again in February, of course," he said, almost making his wail audible in the words he used, " and therefore it is quite impossible that I should stay now beyond the Monday." Had there been attractions for him at Courcy Castle I think he might have arranged with Mr. Optimist for a week or ten days. " We shall be all alone," the countess wrote to him, " and I hope you will have an opportunity of learning more of our ways than you have ever really been able to do as yet." This was bitter as gall to him. But in this world all valuable commodities have their price ; and when men such as Crosbie aspire to obtain for themselves an alliance with noble families, they must pay the market price for the article which they purchase.

You'll all come up and dine with us on Monday," the squire said to Mrs. Dale, about the middle of the previous week.

" Well, I think not," said Mrs. Dale; " we are better, perhaps, as we are."

At this moment the squire and his sister-in-law were on much more friendly terms than had been usual with them, and he took her reply in good part, understanding her feeling. Therefore, he pressed his request, and succeeded.

"I think you're wrong," he said; "I don't suppose that we shall have a very merry Christmas. You and the girls will hardly have that whether you eat your pudding here or at the Great House. But it will be better for us all to make the attempt. It's the right thing to do. That's the way I look at it."

" I'll ask Lily," said Mrs. Dale.

" Do, do. Give her my love, and tell her from me that, in spite of all that has come and gone, Christmas Day should still be to her a day of rejoicing. We'll dine about three, so that the servants can have the afternoon."

"Of course we'll go," said Lily; "why not? We always do. And we'll have blind-man's-buff with all the Boyces, as we had last year, if uncle will ask them up." But the Boyces were not asked up for that occasion.

But Lily, though she put on it all so brave a face, had much to suffer, and did in truth suffer greatly. If you, my reader, ever chanced to slip into the gutter on a wet day, did you not find that the sympathy of the bystanders was by far the severest part of your misfortune ? Did you not declare to yourself that all might yet be well, if the people would only walk on and not look at you ? And yet you cannot blame those who stood and pitied you ; or, perhaps, essayed to rub you down, and assist you in the recovery of your bedaubed hat. You, yourself, if you see a man fall, cannot walk by as though nothing uncommon had happened to him. It was so with Lily. The people of Allington could not regard her with their ordinary eyes. They would look at her tenderly, knowing that she was a wounded fawn, and thus they aggravated the soreness of her wound.

Old Mrs. Heam condoled with her, telling her that very likely she would be better off as she was. Lily would not lie about it in any way. "Mrs. Hearn," she said, "the subject is painful to me." Mrs. Hearn said no more about it, but on every meeting between them she looked the things she did not say. "Miss Lily!" said Hopkins, one day, " Miss Lily!" and as he looked up into her face a tear had almost formed itself in his old eye—" I knew what he was from the first. Oh, dear!

oh, dear! if I could have had him killed!" " Hopkins, how dare you?" said Lily. "If you speak to me again in such a way, I will tell my uncle." She turned away from him; but immediately turned back again, and put out her little hand to him. " I beg your pardon," she said. " I know how kind you are, and I love you for it." And then she went away. " I'll go after him yet, and break the dirty neck of him," said Hopkins to himself, as he walked down the path.

Shortly before Christmas Day she called with her sister at the vicarage. Bell, in the course of the visit, left the room with one of the Boyce girls, to look at the last chrysanthemums of the year. Then Mrs. Boyce took advantage of the occasion to make her little speech. " My dear Lily," she said, "you will think me cold if I do not say one word to you. "No, I shall not," said Lily, almost sharply, shrinking from the finger that threatened to touch her sore. " There are things which should never be talked about "Well, well; perhaps so," said Mrs. Boyce. But for a minute or two she was unable to fall back upon any other topic, and sat looking at Lily with painful tenderness. I need hardly say what were Lily's sufferings under such a gaze ; but she bore it, acknowledging to herself in her misery that the fault did not lie with Mrs. Boyce. How could Mrs. Boyce have looked at her otherwise than tenderly ?

It was settled, then, that Lily was to dine up at the Great House on Christmas Day, and thus show to the Allington world that she was not to be regarded as a person shut out from the world by the depth of her misfortune. That she was right there can, I think, be no doubt; but as she walked across the little bridge, with her mother and sister, after returning from church, she would have given much to be able to have turned round, and have gone to bed instead of to her uncle's dinner.

CHAPTER II. PAWKINS'S IN JERMYN STREET.

THE show of fat beasts in London took place this year on the twentieth day of December, and I have always understood that a certain bullock exhibited by Lord De Guest was declared by the metropolitan butchers to have realized all the possible excellences of breeding, feeding, and condition. No doubt the butchers of the next half-century will have learned much better, and the Guestwick beast, could it be embalmed and then produced, would excite only ridicule at the agricultural ignorance of the present age ; but Lord De Guest took the praise that was offered to him, and found himself in a seventh heaven of delight. He was never so happy as when surrounded by butchers, graziers, and salesmen who were able to appreciate the work of his life, and who regarded him as a model nobleman. " Look at that fellow," he said to Eames, pointing to the prize bullock. Eames had joined his patron at the show after his office hours, looking on upon the living beef by gaslight. " Isn't he like his sire ? He was got by Lambkin, you know."

" Lambkin," said Johnny, who had not as yet been able to learn much about the Guestwick stock.

" Yes, Lambkin. The bull that we had the trouble with. He has just got his sire's back and fore-quarters. Don't you see ? "

" I daresay," said Johnny, who looked very hard, but could not see.

"It's very odd," exclaimed the earl, " but do you know, that bull has been as quiet since that day, as quiet as as anything. I think it must have been my pocket-handkerchief."

" I daresay it was," said Johnny ;" or perhaps the flies."

" Flies ! " said the earl, angrily. " Do you suppose he isn't used to flies ? Come away. I ordered dinner at seven, and it's past six now. My brother-in-law, Colonel Dale, is up in town, and he dines with us." So he took Johnny's arm, and led him off through the show, calling his attention as he went to several beasts which were inferior to his own.

And then they walked down through Portman Square and Grosvenor Square, and across Piccadilly to Jermyn Street. John Eames acknowledged to himself that it was odd that he should have an earl leaning on his arm as he passed along through the streets. At home, in his own life, his daily companions were Cradell and Amelia Roper, Mrs. Lupex and Mrs. Roper. The difference was very great, and yet he found it quite as easy to talk to the earl as to Mrs. Lupex.

" You know the Dales down at Allington, of course," said the earl.

" Oh, yes, I know them."

" But, perhaps, you never met the colonel."

" I don't think I ever did."

"He's a queer sort of fellow; very well in his way, hut he never does anything. He and my sister live at Torquay, and as far as I can find out, they neither of them have any occupation of any sort. He's come up to town now because we both had to meet our family lawyers and sign some papers, but he looks on the journey as a great hardship. As for me, I'm a year older than he is, but I wouldn't mind going up and down from Guestwick every day."

" It's looking after the bull that does it," said Eames.

" By George! you're right, Master Johnny. My sister and Crofts may tell me what they like, but when a man's out in the open air for eight or nine hours every day, it doesn't much matter where he goes to sleep after that. This is Pawkins's,—capital good house, but not so good as it used to be while old Pawkins was alive. SJiow Mr. Eames up into a bedroom to wash his hands."

Colonel Dale was much like his brother in face, but was taller, even thinner, and apparently older. "When Eames went into the sitting-room, the colonel was there alone, and had to take upon himself the trouble of introducing himself. He did not get up from his aim-chair, but nodded gently at the young man. " Mr. Eames, I believe ? I knew your father at Guestwick, a great many years ago ; " then he turned his face back towards the fire and sighed.

" It's got very cold this afternoon," said Johnny, trying to make conversation.

 It's always cold in London," said the colonel.

" If you had to be here in August you wouldn't say so."

" God forbid," said the colonel, and he sighed again, with his eyes fixed upon the fire. Eames had heard of the very gallant way in which Orlando Dale had persisted in running away with Lord De Guest's sister, in opposition to very terrible obstacles, and as he now looked at the intrepid lover, he thought that there must have been a great change since those days. After that nothing more was said till the earl came down.

Pawkins's house was thoroughly old-fashioned in all things, and the Pawkins of that day himself stood behind the earl's elbow when the dinner began, and himself removed the cover from the soup tureen. Lord De Guest did not require much personal attention, but he would have felt annoyed if this hadn't been done. As it was he had a civil word to say to Pawkins about the fat cattle, thereby shovdng that he did not mistake Pawkins for one of the waiters. Pawkins then took his lordship's orders about the wine and retired.

" He keeps up the old house pretty well," said the earl to his brother-in-law. " It isn't like what it was thirty years ago, but then everything of that sort has got worse and worse." .

" I suppose it has," said the colonel.

" I remember when old Pawkins had as good a glass of port as I've got at home,—or nearly. They can't get it now, you know."

" I never drink port," said the colonel. " I seldom take anything after dinner, except a little negus."

His brother-in-law said nothing, but made a most eloquent grimace as he turned his face towards his soup-plate. Eames saw it, and could hardly refrain from laughing. When, at half-past nine o'clock, the colonel retired from the room, the earl, as the door was closed, threw up his hands, and uttered the one word " negus ! " Then Eames took heart of grace and had his laughter out. *

The dinner was very dull, and before the colonel went to bed Johnny regretted that he had been induced to dine at Pawkins's. It might be a very fine thing to be asked to dinner with an earl, and John Eames had perhaps received at his office some little accession of dignity from the circumstance, of which he had been not unpleasantly aware ; but, as he sat at the table, on which there were four or five apples and a plate of dried nuts, looking at the earl, as he endeavoured to keep his eyes open, and at the colonel, to whom it seemed absolutely a matter of indifference whether his companions were asleep or awake, he confessed to himself that

'WON'T YOU TA.KK SOMK 11OKE WIN K ?'

the price he was paying was almost too dear. Mrs. Koper's tea-table was not pleasant to him, but even that would have been preferable to the black dinginess of Pawkins's mahogany, with ihe company of two tired old men, with whom he seemed to have no mutual subject of conversation. Once or twice he tried a word with the colonel, for the colonel sat with his eyes open looking at the fire. But he was answered with monosyllables, and it was evident to him that the colonel did not wish to talk. To sit still, with his hands closed over each other on his lap, was work enough for Colonel Dale during his after-dinner hours.

But the earl knew what was going on. During that terrible conflict between him and his slumber, in which the drowsy god fairly vanquished him for some twenty minutes, his conscience was always accusing him of treating his guests badly. He was very angry with himself, and tried to arouse himself and talk. But his brother-in-law would not help him in his efforts; and even Eames was not bright in rendering him assistance. Then for twenty minutes he slept soundly, and at the end of that he woke himself with one of his own snorts. " By George ! " he said, jumping up and standing on the rug, " we'll have some coffee; " and after that he did not sleep any more.

" Dale," said he, " won't you take some more wine ? "

" Nothing more," said the colonel, still looking at the fire, and shaking his head very slowly.

" Come, Johnny, fill your glass." He had already got into the way of calling his young friend Johnny, having found that Mrs. Eames generally spoke of her son by that name.

" I have been filling my glass all the time," said Eames, taking the decanter again in his hand as he spoke.

" I'm glad you've found something to amuse you, for it has seemed to me that you and Dale haven't had much to say to each other. I've been listening all the time."

" You've been asleep," said the colonel.

" Then there's been some excuse for my holding my tongue," said the earl. " By-the-by, Dale, what do you think of that fellow Crosbie?"

Eames' ears were instantly on the alert, and the spirit of dulness vanished from him.

" Think of him ? " said the colonel.

" He ought to have every bone in his skin broken," said the earl.

"So he ought," said Eames, getting up from his chair in his eagerness, and speaking in a tone somewhat louder than was perhaps becoming in the presence of his seniors. "So he ought, my lord. He is the most abominable rascal that ever I met in my life. I wish I was Lily Dale's brother." Then he sat down again, remembering that he was speaking in the presence of Lily's uncle, and of the father of Bernard Dale, who might be supposed to occupy the place of Lily's brother.

The colonel turned his head round, and looked at the young man with surprise. " I beg your pardon, sir," said Eames, " but I have known Mrs. Dale and your nieces all my life."

" Oh, have you ? " said the colonel. " Nevertheless it is, perhaps, as well not to make too free with a young lady's name. Not that I blame you in the least, Mr. Eames."

" I should think not," said the earl. "I honour him for his feeling. Johnny, my boy, if ever I am unfortunate enough to meet that man, I shall tell him my mind, and I believe you will do the same." On hearing this John Eames winked at the earl, and made a motion with his head towards the colonel, whose back was turned to him. And then the earl winked back at Eames.

" De Guest," said the colonel, " I think I'll go upstairs ; I always have a little arrowroot in my own room."

" I'll ring the bell for a candle," said the host. Then the colonel went, and as the door was closed behind him, the earl raised his two hands and uttered that single word, " negus ! " Whereupon Johnny burst out laughing, and coming round to the fire, sat himself down in the arm-chair which the colonel had left.

"I've no doubt it's all right," said the earl; " but I shouldn't like to drink negus myself, nor yet to have arrowroot up in my bedroom."

" I don't suppose there's any harm in it."

" Oh dear, no; I wonder what Pawkins says about him. But I suppose they have them of all sorts in an hotel."

" The waiter didn't seem to think much of it when he brought it."

" No, no. If he'd asked for senna and salts, the waiter wouldn't have showed any surprise. By-the-by, you touched him up about that poor girl."

" Did I, my lord ? I didn't mean it."

" You see he's Bernard Dale's father, and the question is, whether Bernard shouldn't punish the fellow for what he has done.

Somebody ought to do it. It isn't right that he should escape. Somebody ought to let Mr. Crosbie know what a scoundrel he has made himself."

" I'd do it to-morrow, only I'm afraid "

" No, no, no," said the earl; " you are not the right person at all. What have you got to do with it ? You've merely known them as family friends, but that's not enough."

" No, I suppose not," said Eames, sadly.

" Perhaps it's best as it is," said the earl. " I don't know that any good would be got by knocking him over the head. And if we are to be Christians, I suppose wo ought to be Christians."

" What sort of a Christian has he been ? "

" That's true enough; and if I was Bernard, I should be very apt to forget my Bible lessons about meekness."

" Do you know, my lord, I should think it the most Christian thing in the world to pitch into him; I should, indeed. There are some things for which a man ought to be beaten black and blue."

" So that he shouldn't do them again ? "

" Exactly. You might say it isn't Christian to hang a man."

" I'd always hang a murderer. It wasn't right to hang men for stealing sheep."

" Much better hang such a fellow as Crosbie," said Eames.

" Well, I believe so. If any fellow wanted now to curry favour with the young lady, what an opportunity he'd have."

Johnny remained silent for a moment or two before he answered. " I'm not so sure of that," he said, mournfully, as though grieving at the thought that there was no chance of currying favour with Lily by thrashing her late lover.

" I don't pretend to know much about girls," said Lord De Guest; "but I should think it would be so. I should fancy that nothing would please her so much as hearing that he had caught it, and that all the world knew that he'd caught it." The earl had declared that he didn't know much about girls, and in so saying, he was no doubt right.

" If I thought so," said Eames, " I'd find him out to-morrow."

" Why so ? what difference does it make to you ? " Then there was another pause, during which Johnny looked very sheepish. " You don't mean to say that you're in love with Miss Lily Dale ? "

" I don't know much about being in love with her," said Johnny, turning very red as he spoke. And then he made up his mind, in a

wild sort of way, to tell all the truth to his friend. Pawkins's port wine may, perhaps, have had something to do with the resolution. "But I'd go through fire and water for her, my lord. I knew her years before he had ever seen her, and have loved her a great deal better than he will ever love any one. When I heard that she had accepted him, I had half a mind to cut my own throat,—or else his." " Highty tighty," said the earl.

" It's very ridiculous, I know," said Johnny, " and of course she would never have accepted me." " I don't see that at all." " I haven't a shilling in the world." " Girls don't care much for that."

" And then a clerk in the Income-tax Office ! It's such a poor thing."

" The other fellow was only a clerk in another office." The earl living down at Guestwick did not understand that the Income-tax Office in the city, and the General Committee Office at Whitehall, were as far apart as Dives and Lazarus, and separated by as impassable a gulf.

" Oh, yes," said Johnny; "but his office is another kind of thing, and then he was a swell himself."

" By George, I don't see it," said the earl. " I don't wonder a bit at her accepting a fellow like that. I hated him the first moment I saw him; but that's no reason she should hate him. He had that sort of manner, you know. He was a swell, and girls like that kind of thing. I never felt angry with her, but I could have eaten him." As he spoke he looked as though he would have made some such attempt had Crosbie been present. " Did you ever ask her to have you ? " said the earl. " No; how could I ask her, when I hadn't bread to give her ? "

" And you never told her that you were in love with her,

I mean, and all that kind of thing."

" She knows it now," said Johnny ; " I went to say good-by to her the other day,—when I thought she was going to be married. I could not help telling her then."

" But it seems to me, my dear fellow, that you ought to be very much obliged to Crosbie;—that is to say, if you've a mind to "

"I know what you mean, my lord. I am not a bit obliged to him. It's my belief that all this will about kill her. As to myself, if I thought she'd ever have me "

Then he was again silent, and the earl could see that the tears were in his eyes.

" I think I begin to understand it," said the earl, " and I'll give you a bit of advice. You come down and spend your Christmas with me at Guestwick."

" Oh, my lord! "

" Never mind my-lording me, but do as I tell you. Lady Julia sent you a message, though I forgot all about it till now. She wants to thank you herself for what you did in the field."

" That's all nonsense, my lord."

"Very well; you can tell her so. You may take my word for this, too,—my sister hates Crosbie quite as much as you do. I think she'd ' pitch into him,' as you call it, herself, if she knew how. You come down to Guestwick for the Christmas, and then go over to Allington and tell them all plainly what you mean."

" I couldn't say a word to her now."

" Say it to the squire, then. Go to him, and tell him what you mean,—holding your head up like a man. Don't talk to me about swells. The man who means honestly is the best swell I know. He's the only swell I recognize. Go to old Dale, and say you come from me,—from Guestwick Manor. Tell him that if he'll put a little stick under the pot to make it boil, I'll put a bigger one. He'll understand what that means."

" Oh, no, my lord."

" But I say, oh, yes; " and the earl, who was now standing on the rug before the fire, dug his hands deep down into his trousers' pockets. "I'm very fond of that girl, and would do much for her. You ask Lady Julia if I didn't say so to her before I ever knew of your casting a sheep's-eye that way. And I've a sneaking kindness for you too, Master Johnny. Lord bless you, I knew your father as well as I ever knew any man; and to tell the truth, I believe I helped to ruin him. He held land of me, you know, and there can't be any doubt that he did ruin himself. He knew no more about a beast when he'd done, than than than that waiter. If he'd gone on to this day he wouldn't have been any wiser."

Johnny sat silent, with his eyes full of tears. What was he to say to his friend ?

" You come down with me," continued the earl, " and you'll find we'll make it all straight. I daresay you're right about not speaking to the girl just at present. But tell everything to the uncle, and then to the mother. And, above all things, never think that you're not good enough yourself. A man should never think that. My belief is that in life people will take you very much at your own reckoning. If you are made of dirt, like that fellow Crosbie, you'll be found out at last, no doubt. But then I don't think you are made of dirt."

" I hope not."

" And so do I. You can come down, I suppose, with me the day after to-morrow ? "

" I'm afraid not. I have had all my leave."

" Shall I write to old Buffle, and ask it as a favour."

" No," said Johnny; " I shouldn't like that. But I'll see to-morrow, and then I'll let you know. I can go down by the mail-train on Saturday, at any rate."

" That won't be comfortable. See and come with me if you can. Now, good-night, my dear fellow, and remember this,—when I say a thing I mean it. I think I may boast that I never yet went back from my word."

The earl as he spoke gave his left hand to his guest, and looking somewhat grandly up over the young man's head, he tapped his own breast thrice with his right hand. As he went through the little scene, John Eames felt that he was every inch an earl.

" I don't know what to say to you, my lord."

" Say nothing, not a word more to me. But say to yourself that faint heart never won fair lady. Good-night, my dear boy, good-night. I dine out to-morrow, but you can call and let me know at about six."

Eames then left the room without another wood, and walked out into the cold air of Jennyn Street. The moon was clear and bright, and the pavement in the shining light seemed to be as clean as a lady's hand. All the world was altered to him since he had entered Pawkins's Hotel. Was it then possible that Lily Dale might even yet become his wife ? Could it be true that he, even now, was in a position to go boldly to the Squire of Allington, and tell him what were his views with reference to Lily ? And how far would he be justified in taking the earl at his word ? Some incredible amount of wealth would be required before he could marry Lily Dale. Two or three hundred pounds a year at the very least ! The earl could not mean him to understand that any such sum as that would be made up with such an object! Nevertheless he resolved as he walked home

to Burton Crescent that he would go down to Guestwick, and that he would obey the earl's behest. As regarded Lily herself he felt that nothing could be said to her for many a long day as yet.

" Oh, John, how late you are!" said Amelia, slipping out from the back parlour as he let himself in with his latch key.

" Yes, I am;—very late," said John, taking his candle, and passing her by on the stairs without another word.

CHAPTER III. "THE TIME WILL COME."

" DID you hear that young Eames is staying at Guestwick Manor ?"

As these were the first words which the squire spoke to Mrs. Dale as they walked together up to the Great House, after church, on Christmas Day, it was clear enough that the tidings of

Johnny's visit, when told to him, had made some impression.

" At Guestwick Manor! " said Mrs. Dale. " Dear me! Do you hear that, Bell ? There's promotion for Master Johnny! "

" Don't you remember, mamma," said Bell, " that he helped his lordship in his trouble with the bull ? "

Lily, who remembered accurately all the passages of her last interview with John Eames, said nothing, but felt, in some sort, sore at the idea that he should be so near her at such a time. In some unconscious way she had liked him for coming to her and saying all that he did say. She valued him more highly after that scene than she did before. But now, she would feel herself injured and hurt if he ever made his way into her presence under circumstances as they existed.

" I should not have thought that Lord De Guest was the man to show so much gratitude for so slight a favour," said the squire. " However, I'm going to dine there to-morrow."

" To meet young Eames ? " said Mrs. Dale.

" Yes, especially to meet young Eames. At least, I've been very specially asked to come, and I've been told that he is to be there."

" And is Bernard going ? "

" Indeed I'm not," said Bernard. " I shall come over and dine with you."

A half-formed idea flitted across Lily's mind, teaching her to imagine for a moment that she might possibly be concerned in this arrangement. But the thought vanished as quickly as it came, merely leaving some soreness behind it. There are certain maladies which make the whole body sore. The patient, let him be touched on any point,—let him even be nearly touched, will roar with agony as though his whole body had been bruised. So it is also with maladies of the mind. Sorrows such as that of poor Lily's leave the heart sore at every point, and compel the sufferer to be ever in fear of new wounds. Lily bore her cross bravely and well; but not the less did it weigh heavily upon her at every turn because she had the strength to walk as though she did not bear it. Nothing happened to her, or in her presence, that did not in some way connect itself with her misery. Her uncle was going over to meet John Eames at Lord De Guest's. Of course the men there would talk about her, and all such talking was an injury to her.

The afternoon of that day did not pass away brightly. As long as the servants were in the room the dinner went on much as other dinners. At such times a certain amount of hypocrisy must always be practised in closely domestic circles. At mixed dinner-parties people can talk before Richard and William the same words that they would use if Richard and William were not there. People so mixed do not talk together their inward home thoughts. But when close friends are together, a little conscious reticence is practised till the door is tiled. At such a meeting as this that conscious reticence was of service, and created an effort which was salutary. When the door was tiled, and when the servants were gone, how could they be merry together ? By what mirth should the beards be made to wag on that Christmas Day ?

" My father has been up in town," said Bernard. " He was with Lord De Guest at Pawkins's."

" Why didn't you go and see him ? " asked Mrs. Dale.

" Well, I don't know. He did not seem to wish it. I shall go down to Torquay in February. I must be up in London, you know, in a fortnight, for good." Then they were all silent again for a few minutes. If Bernard could have owned the truth, he would have acknowledged that he had not gone up to London, because he did not yet know how to treat Crosbie when he should meet him. His thoughts on this matter threw some sort of shadow across poor Lily's mind, making her feel that her wound was again opened.

" I want him to give up his profession altogether," said the squire, speaking firmly and slowly. " It would be better, I think, for both of us that he should do so."

" Would it be wise at his time of life," said Mrs. Dale, " and when he has been doing so well ? "

" I think it would be wise. If he were my son it would be thought better that he should live here upon the property, among the people who are to become his tenants, than remain up in London, or perhaps be sent to India. He has one profession as the heir of this place, and that, I think, should be enough."

" I should have but an idle life of it down here," said Bernard.

" That would be your own fault. But if you did as I would have you, your life would not be idle." In this he was alluding to Bernard's proposed marriage, but as to that nothing further could be said in Bell's presence. Bell understood it all, and sat quite silent, with demure countenance;—perhaps even with something of sternness in her face.

"But the fact is," said Mrs. Dale, speaking in a low tone, and having well considered what she was about to say, "that Bernard is not exactly the same as your son."

" Why not ? " said the squire. " I have even offered to settle the property on him if he will leave the service."

"You do not owe him so much as ,you would owe your son; and, therefore, he does not owe you as much as he would owe his father."

" If you mean that I cannot constrain him, I know that well enough. As regards money, I have offered to do for him quite as much as any father would feel called upon to do for an only son."

" I hope you don't think me ungrateful," said Bernard.

"No, I do not; but I think you unmindful. I have nothing more to say about it, however;—not about that. If you should marry " And then he stopped himself, feeling that he could not go on in Bell's presence.

" If he should marry," said Mrs. Dale, " it may well be that his wife would like a house of her own."

" Wouldn't she have this house ? " said the squire, angrily. " Isn't it big enough? I only want one room for myself, and I'd give up that if it were necessary."

" That's nonsense," said Mrs. Dale.

" It isn't nonsense," said the squire.

" You'll be squire of Allington for the next twenty years," said

Mrs. Dale. " And as long as you are the squire, you'll be master of this house ; at least, I hope so. I don't approve of inonarchs abdicating in favour of young people."

" I don't think uncle Christopher would look at all well like Charles the Fifth," said Lily.

" I would always keep a cell for you, my darling, if I did," said the squire, regarding her with that painful, special tenderness. Lily, who was sitting next to Mrs. Dale, put her hand out secretly and got hold of her mother's, thereby indicating that she did not intend to occupy the cell offered to her by her uncle; or to look to him as the companion of her monastic seclusion. After that there was nothing more then said as to Bernard's prospects.

" Mrs. Hearn is dining at the vicarage, I suppose ? " asked the squire.

"Yes; she went in after church," said Bell. "I saw her go with Mrs. Boyce."

" She told me she never would dine with them again after dark in winter," said Mrs. Dale. " The last time she was there, the boy let the lamp blow out as she was going home, and she lost her way. The truth was, she was angry because Mr. Boyce didn't go with her."

" She's always angry," said the squire. " She hardly speaks to me now. When she paid her rent the other day to Jolliffe, she said she hoped it would do me much good; as though she thought me a brute for taking it."

" So she does," said Bernard.

" She's very old, you know," said Bell.

" I'd give her the house for nothing, if I were you, uncle," said Lily.

"No, my dear; if you were me you would not. I should be very wrong to do so. Why should Mrs. Hearn have her house for nothing, any more than her meat or her clothes ? It would be much more reasonable were I to give her so much money into her hand yearly; but it would be wrong in me to do so, seeing that she is not an object of charity; and it would be wrong in her to take it."

" And she wouldn't take it," said Mrs. Dale.

" I don't think she would. But if she did, I'm sure she would grumble because it wasn't double the amount. And if Mr. Boyce had gone home with her, she would have grumbled because he walked too fast."

"She is very old," said Bell, again.

" But, nevertheless, she ought to know better than to speak disparagingly of me to my servants. She should have more respect for herself." And the squire showed by the tone of his voice that he thought very much about it.

It was very long and very dull that Christmas evening, making Bernard feel strongly that he would be very foolish to give up his profession, and tie himself down to a life at Allington. Women are more accustomed than men to long, dull, unemployed hours ; and, therefore, Mrs. Dale and her daughters bore the tedium courageously. While he yawned, stretched himself, and went in and out of the room, they sat demurely, listening as the squire laid down the law on small matters, and contradicting him occasionally when the spirit of either of them prompted her specially to do so. " Of course you know much better than I do," he would say. " Not at all," Mrs. Dale would answer. "I don't pretend to know anything about it.

But " So the evening wore itself away; and when the squire

was left alone at half-past nine, he did not feel that the day had passed badly with him. That was his style of life, and he expected no more from it than he got. He did not look to find things very pleasant, and, if not happy, he was, at any rate, contented.

" Only think of Johnny Eames being at Guestwick Manor ! " said Bell, as they were going home.

" I don't see why he shouldn't be there," said Lily. " I would rather it should be he than I, because Lady Julia is so grumpy."

" But asking your uncle Christopher especially to meet him ! " said Mrs. Dale. " There must be some reason for it." Then Lily felt the soreness come upon her again, and spoke no further upon the subject.

We all know that there was a special reason, and that Lily's soreness was not false in its mysterious forebodings. Eames, on the evening after his dinner at Pawkins's, had seen the earl, and explained to him that he could not leave town till the Saturday evening; but that he could remain over the Tuesday. He must be at his office by twelve on Wednesday, and could manage to do that by an early train from Guestwick.

" Very well, Johnny," said the earl, talking to his young friend with the bedroom candle in his hand, as he was going up to dress. " Then I'll tell you what ; I've been thinking of it. I'll ask Dale to come over to dinner on Tuesday ; and if he'll come, I'll explain the whole matter to him myself. He's a man of business, and he'll understand. If he won't come, why then you must go over to Allington, and find him, if you can, on the Tuesday morning; or I'll go to him myself, which will be better. You mustn't keep me now, as I am ever so much too late."

Eames did not attempt to keep him, but went away feeling that the whole matter was being arranged for him in a very wonderful way. And when he got to Allington he found that the squire had accepted the earl's invitation. Then he declared to himself that there was no longer any possibility of retractation for him. Of course he did not wish to retract. The one great longing of his life was to call Lily Dale his own. But he felt afraid of the squire, that the squire would despise him and snub him, and that the earl would perceive that he had made a mistake when he saw how his client was scorned and snubbed. It was arranged that the earl was to take the squire into his own room for a few minutes before dinner, and Johnny felt that he would be hardly able to stand his ground in the drawing-room when the two old men should make their appearance together.

He got on very well with Lady Julia, who gave herself no airs, and made herself very civil. Her brother had told her the whole story, and she felt as anxious as he did to provide Lily with another husband in place of that horrible man" Crosbie. " She has been very fortunate in her escape," she said to her brother; " very fortunate." The earl agreed with this, saying that in his opinion his own favourite Johnny would make much the nicer lover of the two. But Lady Julia had her doubts as to Lily's acquiescence. " But, Theodore, he must not speak to Miss Lilian Dale herself about it yet a while."

"No," said the earl; " not for a month or so."

" He will have a better chance if he can remain silent for six months," said Lady Julia.

" Bless my soul! somebody else will have picked her up before that," said the earl. In answer to this Lady Julia merely shook her head. Johnny went over to his mother on Christmas Day after church, and was received by her and by his sister with great honour. And she gave him many injunctions as to his behaviour at the earl's table, even descending to small details about his boots and linen. But Johnny had already begun to feel at the Manor that, after all, people are not so very different in their ways of life as they are supposed to be. Lady Julia's manners were certainly not quite those of Mrs. Eoper; but she made the tea very much in the way in which it was made at Burton Crescent, and Eaines found that he could eat his egg, at any rate on the second morning, without any tremor in his hand, in spite of the coronet on the silver egg-cup. He did feel himself to be rather out of his place in the Manor pew on the Sunday, conceiving that all the congregation was looking at him ; but he got over this on Christmas Day, and sat quite comfortably in his soft comer during the sermon, almost going to sleep. And when he walked with the earl after church to the gate over which the noble peer had climbed in his agony, and inspected the hedge through which he had thrown himself, he was quite at home with his little jokes, bantering his august companion as to the mode of his somersault. But be it always remembered that there are two modes in which a young man may be free and easy with his elder and superior, the mode pleasant and the mode offensive. Had it been in Johnny's nature to try the latter, the earl's back would soon have been up at once, and the play would have been over. But it was not in Johnny's nature to do so, and therefore it was that the earl liked him.

At last came the hour of dinner on Tuesday, or at least the hour at which the squire had been asked to show himself at the Manor House. Eames, as by agreement with his patron, did not come down so as to show himself till after the interview. Lady Julia, who had been present at their discussions, had agreed to receive the squire; and then a servant was to ask him to step into the earl's own room. It was pretty to see the way in which the three conspired together, planning and plotting with an eagerness that was beautifully green and fresh.

" He can be as cross as an old stick when he likes it," said the earl, speaking of the squire; " and we must take care not to rub him the wrong way."

"I shan't know what to say to him when I come down," said Johnny.

"Just shake hands with him and don't say anything," said Lady Julia.

"I'll give him some port wine that ought to soften his heart," said the earl, "and then we'll see how he is in the evening."

Eames heard the wheels of the squire's little open carnage and trembled. The squire, unconscious of all schemes, soon found himself with Lady Julia, and within two minutes of his entrance was walked off to the earl's private room. "Certainly," he said, "certainly;" and followed the man-servant. The earl, as he entered, was standing in the middle of the room, and his round rosy face was a picture of good humour.

"I'm very glad you've come, Dale," said he. "I've something I want to say to you."

Mr. Dale, who neither in heart nor in manner was so light a man as the earl, took the proffered hand of his host, and bowed his head slightly, signifying that he was willing to listen to anything.

"I think I told you," continued the earl, "that young John Eames is down here; but he goes back to-morrow, as they can't spare him at his office. He's a very good fellow,—as far as I am able to judge, an uncommonly good young man. I've taken a great fancy to him myself."

In answer to this Mr. Dale did not say much. He sat down, and in some general terms expressed his good-will towards all the Earnes family.

"As you know, Dale, I'm a very bad hand at talking, and therefore I won't beat about the bush in what I've got to say at present. Of course we've all heard of that scoundrel Crosbie, and the way he has treated your niece Lilian."

"He is a scoundrel,—an unmixed scoundrel. But the less we say about that the better. It is ill mentioning a girl's name in such a matter as that."

"But, my dear Dale, I must mention it at the present moment. Dear young child, I would do anything to comfort her! And I hope that something may be done to comfort her. Do you know that that young man was in love with her long before Crosbie ever saw her?"

"What; John Eames!"

"Yes, John Eames. And I wish heartily for his sake that he had won her regard before she had met that rascal whom you had to stay down at your house."

"A man cannot help these things, De Guest," said the squire.

"No, no, no! There are such men about the world, and it is impossible to know them at a glance. He was my nephew's friend, and I am not going to say that my nephew was in fault. But I wish,—I only say that I wish,—she had first known what are this young man's feelings towards her."

"But she might not have thought of him as you do."

"He is an uncommonly good-looking young fellow; straight made, broad in the chest, with a good, honest eye, and a young man's proper courage. He has never been taught to give himself airs like a dancing monkey; but I think he's all the better for that."

"But it's too late, now, De Guest."

"No, no; that's just where it is. It mustn't be too late! That child is not to lose her whole life because a villain has played her false. Of course she'll suffer. Just at present it wouldn't do, I suppose, to talk to her about a new sweetheart. But, Dale, the time will come; the time will come;—the time always does come."

"It has never come to you and me," said the squire, with the slightest possible smile on his dry cheeks. The story of their lives had been so far the same; each had loved, and each had been disappointed, and then each had remained single through life.

"Yes, it has," said the earl, with no slight touch of feeling and even of romance in what he said. " We have retricked our beams in our own ways, and our lives have not been desolate. But for her,—you and her mother will look forward to see her married some day."

" I have not thought about it."

" But I want you to think about it. I want to interest you in this fellow's favour; and in doing so, I mean to be very open with you. I suppose you'll give her something ? "

" I don't know, I'm sure," said the squire, almost offended at an inquiry of such a nature.

" Well, then, whether you do or not, I'll give him something," said the earl. " I shouldn't have ventured to meddle in the matter had I not intended to put myself in such a position with reference to him as would justify me in asking the question." And the peer as he spoke drew himself up to his full height. " If such a match can be made, it shall not be a bad marriage for your niece in a pecuniary point of view. I shall have pleasure in giving to him; but I shall have more pleasure if she can share what I give."

" She ought to be very much obliged to you," said the squire.

" I think she would be if she knew young Eames. I hope the day may come when she will be so. I hope that you and I may see them happy together, and that you too may thank me for having assisted in making them so. Shall we go in to Lady Julia now ? " The earl had felt that he had not quite succeeded ; that his offer had been accepted somewhat coldly, and had not much hope that further good could he done on that day, even with the help of his best port wine.

" Half a moment," said the squire. " There are matters as to which I never find myself .able to speak quickly, and this certainly seems to be one of them. If you will allow me I will think over what you have said, and then see you again." " Certainly, certainly."

" But for your own part in the matter, for your great generosity and kind heart, I beg to offer you my warmest thanks." Then the squire bowed low, and preceded the earl out of the room.

Lord De Guest still felt that he had not succeeded. We may probably say, looking at the squire's character and peculiarities, that no marked success was probable at the first opening-out of such a subject. He had said of himself that he was never able to speak quickly in matters of moment; but he would more correctly have described his own character had he declared that he could not think of them quickly. As it was, the earl was disappointed; but had he been able to read the squire's mind, his disappointment would have been less strong. Mr. Dale knew well enough that he was being treated well, and that the effort being made was intended with kindness to those belonging to him; but it was not in his nature to be demonstrative and quick at expressions of gratitude. So he entered the drawing-room with a cold, placid face, leading Eames, and Lady Julia also, to suppose that no good had been done.

" How do you do, sir ?" said Johnny, walking up to him in a wild sort of manner,—going through a premeditated lesson, but doing it without any presence of mind.

" How do you do, Eames ? " said the squire, speaking with a very cold voice. And then there was nothing further said till the dinner was announced.

" Dale, I know you drink port," said the earl when Lady Julia left them. " If you say you don't like that, I shall say you know nothing about it."

" Ah! that's the '20," said the squire, tasting it.

" I should rather think it is," said the earl. " I was lucky enough to get it early, and it hasn't been moved for thirty years. I like to give it to a man who knows it, as you do, at the first glance. Now there's my friend Johnny there; it's thrown away upou him."

" No, my lord, it is not. I think it's uncommonly nice."

" Uncommonly nice ! So is champagne, or ginger-beer, or lollipops,—for those who like them. Do you mean to tell me you can taste wine with half a pickled orange in your mouth?"

"It'll come to him soon enough," said the squire.

"Twenty port won't come to him when he is as old as we are," said the earl, forgetting that by that time sixty port will be as wonderful to the then living seniors of the age as was his own pet vintage to him.

The good wine did in some sort soften the squire; but, as a matter of course, nothing farther was said as to the new matrimonial scheme. The earl did observe, however, that Mr. Dale was civil, and even kind, to his own young friend, asking a question here and there as to his life in London, and saying something about the work at the Income-tax Office.

"It is hard work," said Eames. "If you're under the line, they make a great row about it, send for you, and look at you as though you'd been robbing the bank; but they think nothing of keeping you till five."

"But how long do you have for lunch and reading the papers?" said the earl.

"Not ten minutes. We take a paper among twenty of us for half the day. That's exactly nine minutes to each; and as for lunch, we only have a biscuit dipped in ink."

"Dipped in ink!" said the squire.

"It comes to that, for you have to be writing while you munch it."

"I hear all about you," said the earl; "Sir Kaffle Buffle is an old crony of mine."

"I don't suppose he ever heard my name as yet," said Johnny. "But do you really know him well, Lord De Guest?"

"Haven't seen him these thirty years; but I did know him."

"We call him old Huffle Scuffle."

"Huffle Scuffle! Ha, ha, ha! He always was Huffle Scuffle; a noisy, pretentious, empty-headed fellow. But I oughtn't to say so before you, young man. Come, we'll go into the drawing-room."

"And what did he say?" asked Lady Julia, as soon as the squire was gone.

There was no attempt at concealment, and the question was asked in Johnny's presence.

"Well, he did not say much. And coming from him, that ought
to be taken as a good sign. He is to think of it, and let me see him again. You hold your head up, Johnny, and remember that you shan't want a friend on your side. Faint heart never won fair lady."

At seven o'clock on the following morning Eames started on his return journey, and was at his desk at twelve o'clock,—as per agreement with his taskmaster at the Income-tax Office.

THE SMALL HOUSE AT ALLINGTON.

CHAPTER IV. THE COMBAT.

I HAVE said that John Eames was at his office punctually at twelve; but an incident had happened before his arrival there very important in the annals which are now being told,— so important that it is essentially necessary that it should be described with some minuteness of detail.

Lord De Guest, in the various conversations which he had had with Eames as to Lily Dale and her present position, had always spoken of Crosbie with the most vehement abhorrence. "He is a damned blackguard," said the earl, and the fire had come out of his round eyes as he spoke. Now the earl was by no means given to cursing and swearing, in the sense which is ordinarily applied to these words. When he made use of such a phrase as that quoted above, it was to be presumed that he in some sort meant what he said; and so he did, and had intended to signify that Crosbie by his conduct had merited all such condemnation as was the fitting punishment for blackguardism of the worst description.

" He ought to have his neck broken," said Johnny.

" I don't know about that," said the earl. " The present times have become so pretty behaved that corporal punishment seems to have gone out of fashion. I shouldn't care so much about that, if any other punishment had taken its place. But it seems to me that a blackguard such as Crosbie can escape now altogether unscathed."

" He hasn't escaped yet," said Johnny.

" Don't you go and put your finger in the pie and make a fool of yourself," said the earl. If it had behoved any one to resent in any violent fashion the evil done by Crosbie, Bernard Dale, the earl's nephew, should have been the avenger. This the earl felt, but under these circumstances lie was disposed to think that there should be no such violent vengeance. " Things were different when I was young," he said to himself. But Eames gathered from the earl's tone that the earl's words were not strictly in accordance with his thoughts, and he declared to himself over and over again that Crosbie had not yet escaped.

He got into the train at Guestwick, taking a first-class ticket, because the earl's groom in livery was in attendance upon him. Had he been alone he would have gone in a cheaper carnage. Very weak in him, was it not ? little also, and mean ? My friend, can you say that you would not have done the same at his age ? Are you quite sure that you would not do the same now that you are double his age? Be that as it may, Johnny Eames did that foolish thing, and gave the groom in livery half-a-crown into the bargain.

" We shall have you down again soon, Mr. John," said the groom, who seemed to understand that Mr. Eames was to be made quite at home at the manor.

He went fast to sleep in the carriage, and did not awake till the train was stopped at the Barchester Junction.

" Waiting for the up-train from Barchester, sir," said the guard. " They're always late." Then he went to sleep again, and was aroused in a few minutes by some one entering the carriage in a great hurry. The branch train had come in, just as the guardians of the line then present had made up their minds that the passengers on the main line should not be kept waiting any longer. The transfer of men, women, and luggage was therefore made in great haste, and they who were now taking their new seats had hardly time to look about them. An old gentleman, very red about the gills, first came into Johnny's carriage, which up to that moment he had shared with an old lady. The old gentleman was abusing everybody, because he was hurried, and would not take himself well into the compartment, but stuck in the doorway, standing on the step.

" Now, sir, when you're quite at leisure," said a voice behind the old man, which instantly made Eames start up in his seat.

" I'm not at all at leisure," said the old man; " and I'm not going to break my legs if I know it."

" Take your time, sir," said the guard.

" So I mean," said the old man, seating himself in the corner nearest to the open door, opposite to the old lady. Then Eames saw plainly that it was Crosbie who had first spoken, and that he was getting into the carriage.Crosbie at the first glance saw no one but the old gentleman and the old lady, and he immediately made for the unoccupied corner seat. He was busy with his umbrella and his dressing-bag, and & little flustered by the pushing and hurrying. The carriage was actually in motion before he perceived that John Eames was opposite to him: Eames had, instinctively, drawn up his legs so as not to touch him. He felt that he had become very red in the face, and to tell the truth, the perspiration had broken out upon his brow. It was a great occasion,—great in its imminent trouble, and great in its opportunity for action. How was he to carry himself at the first moment of his recognition by his enemy, and what was he to do afterwards ?

It need hardly be explained that Crosbie had also been spending his Christmas with a certain earl of his acquaintance, and that he too was returning to his office. In one respect he had been much more fortunate than poor Eames, for he had been made happy with the smiles of his lady love. Alexandrina and the countess had fluttered about him softly, treating him as a tame chattel, now belonging to the noble house of De Courcy, and in this way he had been initiated into the inner domesticities of that illustrious family. The two extra men-servants, hired to wait upon Lady Dumbello, had vanished. The champagne had ceased to flow in a perennial stream. Lady Rosina had come out from her solitude, and had preached at him constantly. Lady Margaretta had given him some lessons in economy. The Honourable John, in spite of a late quarrel, had borrowed five pounds from him. The Honourable George had engaged to come and stay with his sister during the next May. The earl had used a father-in-law's privilege, and had called him a fool. Lady Alexandrina had told him more than once, in rather a tart voice, that this must be done, and that that must be done; and the countess had given him her orders as though it was his duty, in the course of nature, to obey every word that fell from her. Such had been his Christmas delights; and now, as he returned back from the enjoyment of them, he found himself confronted in the railway carriage with Johnny Eames!

The eyes of the two met, and Crosbie made a slight inclination of his head. To this Eames gave no acknowledgment whatever, but looked straight into the other's face. Crosbie immediately saw that

they were not to know eacli other, and was v/ell contented that it should be so. Among all his many troubles, the enmity of John Eames did not go for much. He showed no appearance of being disconcerted, though our friend had shown much. He opened his bag, and taking out a book was soon deeply engaged in it, pursuing his studies as though the man opposite was quite unknown to him. I will not say that his mind did not run away from his book, for indeed there were many things of which he found it impossible not to think; but it did not revert to John Eames. Indeed, when the carriages reached Paddington, he had in truth all but forgotten him; and as he stepped out of the carriage, with his bag in his hand, was quite free from any remotest trouble on his account.

But it had not been so with Eames himself. Every moment of the journey had for him been crowded with thought as to what he would do now that chance had brought his enemy within his reach. He had been made quite wretched by the intensity of his thinking ; and yet, when the carriages stopped, he had not made up his mind. His face had been covered with perspiration ever since Crosbie had come across him, and his limbs had hardly been under his own command. Here had come to him a great opportunity, and he felt so little confidence in himself that he almost knew that he would not use it properly. Twice and thrice he had almost flown at Crosbie's throat in the carnage, but he was restrained by an idea that the world and the police would be against him if he did such a thing in the presence of that old lady.

But when Crosbie turned his back upon him, and walked out, it was absolutely necessary that he should do something. He was not going to let the man escape, after all that he had said as to the expediency of thrashing him. Any other disgrace would be preferable to that. Fearing, therefore, lest his enemy should be too quick for him, he hurried out after him, and only just gave Crosbie time to turn round and face the carriages before he was upon him. " You confounded scoundrel! " he screamed out. " You confounded scoundrel! " and seized him by the throat, throwing himself upon him, and almost devouring him by the fury of his eyes.

The crowd upon the platform was not very dense, but there were quite enough of people to make a very respectable audience for this little play. Crosbie, in his dismay, retreated a step or two, and his retreat was much accelerated by the weight of Eames's attack. He endeavoured to free his throat from his foe's grasp ; but in that he failed entirely. For the minute, however, he did manage to escape-any positive blow, owing his safety in that respect rather to Eames's awkwardness than to his own efforts. Something about the police he was just able to utter, and there was, as a matter of course, an immediate call for a supply of those functionaries. In about three minutes three policemen, assisted by six porters, had captured our poor friend Johnny; but this had not been done quick enough for Crosbie's purposes. The bystanders, taken by surprise, had allowed the combatants to fall back upon Mr. Smith's book-stall, and there Eames laid his foe prostrate upon the newspapers, falling himself into the yellow shilling-novel depot by the over fury of his own energy; but as he fell, he contrived to lodge one blow with his fist in Crosbie's right eye,—one telling blow; and Crosbie had, to all intents and purposes, been thrashed.

" Con—founded scoundrel, rascal, blackguard ! " shouted Johnny, with what remnants of voice were left to him, as the police dragged him off. " If you only knew—what he's—done." But in the meantime the policemen held him fast.

As a matter of course the first burst of public sympathy went with Crosbie. He had been assaulted, and the assault had come from Eames. In the British bosom there is so firm a love of well-constituted order, that these facts alone were sufficient to bring twenty knights to the assistance of the three policemen and the six porters; so that for Eames, even had he desired it, there was no possible chance of escape. But he did not desire it. One only sorrow consumed him at present. He had, as he felt, attacked Crosbie, but had attacked him in vain. He had had his opportunity, and had misused it. He was perfectly unconscious of that happy blow, and was in absolute ignorance of the great fact that his enemy's eye was already swollen and closed, and that in another hour it would be as black as his hat.

" He is a con—founded rascal! " ejaculated Eames, as the policemen and porters hauled him about. " You don't know what he's done."

" No, we don't," said the senior constable; " but we know what you have done. I say, Bushers, where's that gentleman ? He'd better come along with us."

Crosbie had been picked up from among the newspapers by another policeman and two or three other porters, and was attended also by the guard of the train, who knew him, and knew that he had

-come up from Courcy Castle. Three or four hangers-on were standing also around him, together with a benevolent medical man who was proposing to him an immediate application of leeches. If he could have done as he wished, he would have gone his way quietly, allowing Eames to do the same. A great evil had befallen him, but he could in no way mitigate that evil by taking the law of the man who had attacked him. To have the thing as little talked about as possible should begins endeavour. What though he should have Eames locked up and fined, and scolded by a police magistrate ? That would not in any degree lessen his calamity. If he could have parried the attack, and got the better of his foe; if he could have administered the black eye instead of receiving it, then indeed he could have laughed the matter off at his club, and his original crime would have been somewhat glozed over by his success in arms. But such good fortune had not been his. He was forced, however, on the moment to decide as to what he would do.

" We've got him here in custody, sir," said Bushers, touching his hat. It had become known from the guard that Crosbie was somewhat of a big man, a frequent guest at Courcy Castle, and of repute and station in the higher regions of the Metropolitan world. " The magistrates will be sitting at Paddington, now, sir—or will be by the time we get there."

By this time some mighty railway authority had come upon the scene and made himself cognizant of the facts of the row, a stern official who seemed to carry the weight of many engines on his brow ; one at the very sight of whom smokers would drop their cigars, and porters close their fists against sixpences; a great man with an erect chin, a quick step, and a well-brushed hat powerful with an elaborately upturned brim. This was the platform-superintendent, dominant «ven over the policemen.

" Step into my room, Mr. Crosbie," he said. " Stubbs, bring that man in with you." And then, before Crosbie had been able to make up his mind as to any other line of conduct, he found himself in the superintendent's room, accompanied by the guard, and by the two policemen who conducted Johnny Eames between them.

" What's all this ? " said the superintendent, still keeping on his hat, for he was aware how much of the excellence of his personal dignity was owing to the arrangement of that article ; and as he spoke he frowned upon the culprit with his utmost severity. " Mr.

Crosbie, I am very sorry that you should have been exposed to such brutality on our platform."

" You don't know what he has done," said Johnny. " He is the most confounded scoundrel living. He has broken ' But then

he stopped himself. He was going to tell the superintendent that the confounded scoundrel had broken a beautiful young lady's heart; but he bethought himself that he would not allude more specially to Lily Dale in that hearing.

" Do you know who he is, Mr. Crosbie? " said the superintendent.

" Oh, yes," said Crosbie, whose eye was already becoming blue. " He is a clerk in the Income-tax Office, and his name is Eames. I believe you had better leave him to me."

But the superintendent at once wrote down the words " Income-tax Office—Earnes," on his tablet. " We can't allow a row like that to take place on our platform and not notice it. I shall bring it before the directors. It's a most disgraceful affair, Mr. Eames— most disgraceful."

But Johnny by this time had perceived that Crosbie's eye was in a state which proved satisfactorily that his morning's work had not been thrown away, and his spirits were rising accordingly. He did not care two straws for the superintendent or even for the policemen, if only the story could be made to tell well for himself hereafter. It was his object to have thrashed Crosbie, and now, as he looked at his enemy's face, he acknowledged that Providence had been good to him.

" That's your opinion," said Johnny.

" Yes, sir, it is," said the superintendent; " and I shall know how to represent the matter to your superiors, young man."

" You don't know all about it," said Eames; " and I don't suppose you ever will. I had made up my mind what I'd do the first time I saw that scoundrel there ; and now I've done it. He'd have got much worse in the railway carriage, only there was a lady there."

" Mr. Crosbie, I really think we had better take him before the magistrates."

To this, however, Crosbie objected. He assured the superintendent that he would himself know how to deal with the matter which, however, was exactly what he did not know. Would the superintendent allow one of the railway servants to get a cab for him, and to find his luggage ? He was very anxious to get home without being subjected to any more of Mr. Eames's insolence.

" You haven't clone with Mr. Eames's insolence yet, I can tell you. All London shall hear of it, and shall know why. If you have any shame in you, you shall be ashamed to show your face."

Unfortunate man ! Who can say that punishment—adequate punishment—had not overtaken him '? For the present, he had to sneak home with a black eye, with the knowledge inside him that he had been whipped by a clerk in the Income-tax Office ; and for the future—he was bound over to many Lady Alexandrina De Courcy !

He got himself smuggled off in a cab, without being forced to go again upon the platform—his luggage being brought to him by two assiduous porters. But in all this there was very little balm for his hurt pride. As he ordered the cabman to drive to Mount Street, he felt that he had ruined himself by that step in life which he had taken at Courcy Castle. Whichever way he looked he had no comfort.

the fellow! " he said, almost out loud in the cab ; but though he did with his outward voice allude to Eames, the curse in his inner thoughts was uttered against himself.

Johnny was allowed to make his way down to the platform, and there find his own carpet-bag. One young porter, however, came up and fraternized with him.

" You guve it him tidy just at that last moment, sir. But, laws, sir, you should have let out at him at fust. What's the use of clawing a man's neck-collar ? "

It was then a quarter past eleven, but, nevertheless, Earnes appeared at his office precisely at twelve.

CHAPTER Y. Y.E YICTIS.

CROSBIE had two engagements for that day; one being his natural engagement to do his work at his office, and the other an engagement, which was now very often becoming as natural, to dine at St. John's Wood with Lady Amelia Gazebee. It was manifest to him when he looked at himself in the glass that he could keep neither of these engagements. " Oh, laws, Mr. Crosbie," the woman of the house exclaimed when she saw him.

" Yes, I know," said he. " I've had an accident and got a black eye. What's a good thing for it ? "

Oh! an accident! " said the woman, who knew well that that mark had been made by another man's fist. " They do say that a bit of raw beef is about the best thing. But then it must be held on constant all the morning."

Anything would be better than leeches, which tell long-enduring tales, and therefore Crosbie sat through the greater part of the morning holding the raw beef to his eye.

But it was necessary that he should write two notes as he held it, one to Mr. Butterwell at his office, and the other to his future sister-in-law. He felt that it would hardly be wise to attempt any entire concealment of the nature of his catastrophe, as some of the circumstances would assuredly become known. If he said that he had fallen over the coal-scuttle, or on to the fender, thereby cutting his face, people would learn that he had fibbed, and would learn also that he had had some reason for fibbing. Therefore he constructed his notes with a phraseology that bound him to no details. To Butterwell he said that he had had an accident—or rather a row—and that he had come out of it with considerable damage to his frontispiece. Ho intended to be at the office on the next day, whether able to appear

decently there or not. But for the sake of decency lie thought it well to give himself that one half-day's chance. Then to the Lady Amelia he also said that he had had an accident, and had been a little hurt. " It is nothing at all serious, and affects only my appearance, so that I had better remain in for a day. I shall certainly be with you on Sunday. Don't let Gazebee trouble himself to come to me, as I shan't be at home after to-day." Gazebee did trouble himself to come to Mount Street so often, and South Audley Street, in which was Mr. Gazebee's office, was so disagreeably near to Mount Street, that Crosbie inserted this in order to protect himself if possible. Then he gave special orders that he was to be at home to no one, fearing that Gazebee would call for him after the hours of business—to make him safe and cany him off bodily to St. John's Wood.

The beefsteak and the dose of physic and the cold-water application which was kept upon it all night was not efficacious in dispelling that horrid, black-blue colour by ten o'clock on the following morning.

"It certainly have gone down, Mr. Crosbie ; it certainly have," said the mistress of the lodgings, touching the part affected with her finger. "But the black won't go out of them all in a minute; it won't indeed. Couldn't you just stay in one more day ? " " But will one day do it, Mrs. Phillips ? "

Mrs. Phillips couldn't take upon herself to say that it would. " They mostly come with little red streaks across the black before they goes away," said Mrs. Phillips, who would seem to have been the wife of a prize-fighter, so well was she acquainted with black eyes. " And that won't be till to-morrow," said Crosbie, affecting to be mirthful in his agony.

" Not till the third day;—and then they wears themselves out, gradual. I never knew leeches do any good."

He stayed at home the second day, and then resolved that he would go to his office, black eye and all. In that morning's newspaper he saw an account of the whole transaction, saying how

Mr. C of the office of General Committees, who was soon about to lead to the hymeneal altar the beautiful daughter of the Earl De, had been made the subject of a brutal personal attack on the platform of the Great Western Railway Station, and how he was confined to his room from the injuries which he had received. The paragraph went on to state that the delinquent had, as it was believed, dared to raise his eyes to the same lady, and that his audacity had been treated with scorn by eveiy member of the noble family in question. "It was, however, satisfactory to know," so said the newspaper, "that Mr. C had amply avenged himself, and had so flogged the young man in question, that he had been unable to stir from his bed since the occurrence."

On reading this Crosbie felt that it would be better that he should show himself at once, and tell as much of the truth as the world would be likely to ascertain at last without his telling. So on that third morning he put on his hat and gloves, and had himself taken to his office, though the red-streaky period of his misfortune had hardly even yet come upon him. The task of walking along the office passage, through the messengers' lobby, and into his room, was very disagreeable. Of course everybody looked at him, and of course he failed in his attempt to appear as though he did not mind it. " Boggs," he said to one of the men as he passed by, "just see if Mr. Butterwell is in his room," and then, as he expected, Mr. Butter-well came to him after the expiration of a few minutes.

" Upon my word, that is serious," said Mr. Butterwell, looking into the secretary's damaged face. " I don't think I would have come out if I had been you."

" Of course it's disagreeable," said Crosbie ; " but it's better to put up with it. Fellows do tell such horrid lies if a man isn't seen for a day or two. I believe it's best to put a good face upon it."

" That's more than you can do just at present, eh, Crosbie ? " And then Mr. Butterwell tittered. " But how on earth did it happen ? The paper says that you pretty well killed the fellow who did it."

" The paper lies, as papers always do. I didn't touch him at all."

" Didn't you, though ? I should like to have had a poke at him after getting such a tap in the face as that."

" The policemen came, and all that sort of thing. One isn't allowed to fight it out in a row of that kind as one would have to do on Salisbury heath. Not that I mean to say that I could lick the fellow. How's a man to know whether he can or not ? "

" How, indeed, unless he gets a licking,—or gives it ? But who was he, and what's this about his having been scorned by the noble family? "

" Trash and lies, of course. He had never seen any of the De Courcy people."

" I suppose the truth is, it was about that other eh, Crosbie '?

I knew you'd find yourself in some trouble before you'd done."

" I don't know what it was about, or why he should have made such a brute of himself. You have heard about those people at Allington ? "

" Oh, yes; I have heard about them."

" God knows, I didn't mean to say anything against them. They knew nothing about it."

" But the young fellow knew them ? Ah, yes, I see all about it. He wants to step into your shoes. I can't say that he sets about it in a bad way. But what do you mean to do ? "

" Nothing."

" Nothing! Won't that look queer ? I think I should have him before the magistrates."

" You see, Butterwell, I am bound to spare that girl's name. I know I have behaved badly."

" Well, yes ; I fear you have."

Mr. Butterwell said this with some considerable amount of decision in his voice, as though he did not intend to mince matters, or in any way to hide his opinion. Crosbie had got into a way of condemning himself in this matter of his marriage, but was very t anxious that others, on hearing such condemnation from him, should say something in the way of palliating his fault. It would be so easy for a friend to remark that such little peccadilloes were not altogether uncommon, and that it would sometimes happen in life that people did not know their own minds. He had hoped for some such benevolence from Fowler Pratt, but had hoped in vain. Butterwell was a good-natured, easy man, anxious to stand well with all about him, never pretending to any very high tone of feeling or of morals ; and yet Butterwell would say no word of comfort to him. He could get no one to slur over his sin for him, as though it were no sin,—only an unfortunate mistake; no one but the De Courcys, who had, as it were, taken possession of him and swallowed him alive.

" It can't be helped now," said Crosbie. " But as for that fellow who made such a brutal attack on me the other morning, he knows that he is safe behind her petticoats. I can do nothing which would not make some mention of her name necessary."

"Ah, yes; I see," said Butterwell. "It's very unfortunate; very. I don't know that I can do anything for you. Will you come before the Board to-day ? "

" Yes ; of course I shall," said Crosbie, who was becoming very-sore. His sharp ear had told him that all Butterwell's respect and cordiality were gone,—at any rate for the time. Bntterwell, though holding the higher official rank, had always been accustomed to treat him as though he, the inferior, were to be courted. He had possessed, and had known himself to possess, in his office as well as in the outside world, a sort of rank much higher than that which from his position he could claim legitimately. Now he was being deposed. There could be no better touchstone in such a matter than Butterwell. He would go as the world went, but he would perceive almost intuitively how the world intended to go. " Tact, tact, tact," as he was in the habit of saying to himself when walking along the paths of his Putney villa. Crosbie was now secretary, whereas a few months before he had been simply a clerk; but, nevertheless, Mr. Butterwell's instinct told him that Crosbie had fallen. Therefore he declined to offer any sympathy to the man in his misfortune, and felt aware, as he left the secretary's room, that it might probably be some time before he visited it again.

Crosbie resolved in his soreness that henceforth he would brazen it out. He would go to the Board, with as much indifference as to his black eye as he was able to assume, and if any one said aught to him he would be ready with his answer. He would go to his club, and let him who intended to show him any slight beware of him in his wrath. He could not turn upon John Earnes, but he could turn upon others if it were necessary. He had not gained for himself a position before the world, and held it now for some years, to allow himself to be crushed at once because he had made a mistake. If the world, his world, chose to go to war with him, he would be ready for the fight. As for Butterwell,—Butterwell the incompetent, Butterwell the vapid,—for Butterwell, who in every little official difficulty had for years past come to him, he would let Butterwell know what it was to be thus disloyal to one who had condescended to be his friend. He would show them all at the Board that he scorned them, and could be their master. Then, too, as he was making some other resolves as to his future conduct, he made one or two resolutions respecting the De Courcy people. He would make it known to them that he was not going to be their very humble servant. He would speak out his mind with considerable plainness ; and if upon that they should choose to break off this " alliance," they might do so; he would not break his heart. And as he leaned back in his arm-

cliair, thinking of all this, an idea made its way into his brain,—a floating castle in the air, rather than the image of a thing that might by possibility be realized ; and in this castle in the air he saw himself kneeling again at Lily's feet, asking her pardon, and begging that he might once more be taken to her heart.

" Mr. Crosbie is here to-day," said Mr. Butterwell to Mr. Optimist.

" Oh, indeed," said Mr. Optimist, very gravely; for he had heard all about the row at the railway station. " They've made a monstrous show of him."

" I am very sorry to hear it. It's so—so—so If it were

one of the younger clerks, you know, we should tell him that it was discreditable to the department."

" If a man gets a blow in the eye, he can't help it, you know. He didn't do it himself, I suppose," said Major Fiasco.

"I am well aware that he didn't do it himself," continued Mr. Optimist; " but I really think that, in his position, he should have kept himself out of any such encounter."

" He would have done so if he could, with all his heart," said the major. " I don't suppose he liked being thrashed any better than I should."

" Nobody gives me a black eye," said Mr. Optimist. " Nobody has as yet," said the major.

" I hope they never will," said Mr. Butterwell. Then, the hour for their meeting having come round, Mr. Crosbie came into the Board-room.

" We have been very sorry to hear of this misfortune," said Mr. Optimist, very gravely.

" Not half so sorry as I have been," said Crosbie, with a laugh. "It's an uncommon nuisance to have a black eye, and to go about looking like a prize-fighter."

"And like a prize-fighter that didn't win his battle, too," said Fiasco.

" I don't know that there's much difference as to that," said Crosbie. " But the whole thing is a nuisance, and, if you please, we won't say anything more about it."

Mr. Optimist almost entertained an opinion that it was his duty to say something more about it. Was not he the chief Commissioner., and was not Mr. Crosbie secretary to the Board ? Ought he, looking at their respective positions, to pass over without a word of notice

such a manifest impropriety as this ? Would not Sir Raffle Buffle have said something had Mr. Bntterwell, when secretary, come to the office with a black eye ? He wished to exercise all the full rights of a chairman ; but, nevertheless, as he looked at the secretary he felt embarrassed, and was unable to find the proper words. " H—m, ha, well; we'll go to business now, if you please," he said, as though reserving to himself the right of returning to the secretary's black eye, when the more usual business of the Board should be completed. But when the more usual business of the Board had been completed, the secretary left the room without any further reference to his eye.

Crosbie, when he got back to his own apartment, found Mortimer Gazebee waiting there for him.

" My dear fellow," said Gazebee, " this is a very nasty affair."

"Uncommonly nasty," said Crosbie; "so nasty that I don't mean to talk about it to anybody."

"Lady Amelia is quite unhappy." He always called her Lady Amelia, even when speaking of her to his own brothers and sisters. He was too well behaved to take the liberty of calling an earl's daughter by her plain Christian name, even though that earl's daughter was his own wife. " She fears that you have been a good deal hurt."

" Not at all hurt ; but disfigured, as you see."

" And so you beat the fellow well that did it ?"

" No, I didn't," said Crosbie, very angrily. " I didn't beat him at all. You don't believe everything you read in the newspapers; do you?"

"No, I don't believe everything. Of course I didn't believe about his having aspired to an alliance with Lady Alexandrina. That was untrue, of course." Mr. Gazebee showed by the tone of his voice that imprudence so unparalleled as that was quite incredible.

" You shouldn't believe anything ; except this,-—that I have got a black eye."

" You certainly have got that. Lady Amelia thinks you would be more comfortable if you would come up to us this evening. You can't go out, of course ; but Lady Amelia said, very good-naturedly, that you need not mind with her."

" Thank you, no ; I'll come on Sunday."

" Of course Lady Alexandrina will be very anxious to hear from her sister; and Lady Amelia begged me very particularly to press you to come."

 Thank you, no ; not to-day." "Why not?"

" Oh, simply because I shall be better at home." " How can you be better at home ? You can have anything that you want. Lady Amelia won't mind, you know."

Another beefsteak to his eye, as he sat in the drawing-room, a cold-water bandage, or any little medical appliance of that sort; these were the things which Lady Amelia would, in her domestic good nature, condescend not to mind !

" I won't trouble her this evening," said Crosbie. " Well, upon my word, I think you're wrong. All manner of stories will get down to Courcy Castle, and to the countess's ears; and you don't know what harm may come of it. Lady Amelia thinks she had better write and explain it; but she can't do so till she has heard something about it from you."

" Look here, Gazebee. I don't care one straw what story finds its way down to Courcy Castle."

" But if the earl were to hear anything, and be offended ?" " He may recover from his offence as he best likes." " My dear fellow ; that's talking wildly, you know." " What on earth do you suppose the earl can do to me ? Do you think I'm going to live in fear of Lord De Courcy all my life, because I'm going to marry his daughter ? I shall write to Alexandrina myself to-day, and you can tell her sister so. I'll be up to dinner on Sunday, unless my face makes it altogether out of the question." " And you won't come in time for church ?" " Would you have me go to church with such a face as this?" Then Mr. Mortimer Gazebee went, and when he got home he told his wife that Crosbie was taking things with a high hand. " The fact is, my dear, that he's ashamed of himself, and therefore tries to put a bold face upon it."

" It was very foolish of him throwing himself in the way of that young man,—very; and so I shall tell him on Sunday. If he chooses to give himself airs to me, I shall make him understand that he is very wrong. He should remember now that the way in which he conducts himself is a matter of moment to all our family." " Of course he should," said Mr. Gazebee. When the Sunday came the red-streaky period had arrived, but

had by no means as yet passed away. The men at the office had almost become used to it; but Crosbie, in spite of his determination to go down to the club, had not yet shown himself elsewhere. Of course he did not go to church, but at five he made his appearance at the house in St. John's Wood. They always dined at five on Sundays, having some idea that by doing so they kept the Sabbath better than they would have done had they dined at seven. If keeping the Sabbath consists in going to bed early, or is in any way assisted by such a practice, they were right. To the cook that semi-early dinner might perhaps be convenient, as it gave her an excuse for not going to church in the afternoon, as the servants' and children's dinner gave her a similar excuse in the morning. Such little attempts at goodness,—proceeding half the way, or perhaps, as in this instance, one quarter of the way, on the disagreeable path towards goodness,—are very common with respectable people, such as Lady Amelia. If she would have dined at one o'clock, and have eaten cold meat, one perhaps might have felt that she was entitled to some praise.

" Dear, dear, dear; this is very sad, isn't it, Adolphus ? " she said on first seeing him.

" Well, it is sad, Amelia," he said. He always called her Amelia, because she called him Adolphus; but Gazebee himself was never quite pleased when he heard it. Lady Amelia was older than Crosbie, and entitled to call him anything she liked; but he should have remembered the great difference in their rank. "It is sad, Amelia," he said. " But will you oblige me in one thing ? "

" What thing, Adolphus ? "

" Not to say a word more about it. The black eye is a bad thing no doubt, and has troubled me much ; but the sympathy of my friends has troubled me a great deal more. I had all the family commiseration from Gazebee on Friday, and if it is repeated again, I shall lie down and die."

" Shall 'oo die, uncle Dolphus, 'cause 'oo've got a bad eye ? " asked De Courcy Gazebee, the eldest hope of the family, looking up into his face.

" No, my hero," said Crosbie, taking the boy up into his arms, " not because I've got a black eye. There isn't veiy much harm in that, and you'll have a great many before you leave school. But because the people will go on talking about it."

" But aunt Dina on't like 'oo, if oo've got an ugly bad eye."

" But, Adolphus," said Lady Amelia, settling herself for an argument, " that's all very well, you know—and I'm sure I'm very sorry to cause you any annoyance, but really one doesn't know how to pass over such a thing without speaking of it. I have had a letter from mamma."

" I hope Lady De Courcy is quite well."

" Quite well, thank you. But as a matter of course she is very anxious ahout this affair. She had read what has been said in the newspapers, and it may be necessary that Mortimer should take it up, as the family solicitor."

" Quite out of the question," said Adolphus.

" I don't think I should advise any such step as that," saidGazebee.

"Perhaps not; very likely not. But you cannot be surprised, Mortimer, that my mother under such circumstances should wish to know what are the facts of the case."

" Not at all surprised," said Gazebee.

" Then once for all, I'll tell you the facts. As I got out of the train a man I'd seen once before in my life made an attack upon me, and before the police came up, I got a blow in the face. Now you know all about it."

At that moment dinner was announced. " Will you give Lady Amelia your arm ? " said the husband.

"It's a very sad occurrence," said Lady Amelia with a slight toss of her head, "and, I'm afraid, will cost my sister a great deal of vexation."

"You agree with De Courcy, do you, that aunt Dina won't like me with an ugly black eye?"

"I really don't think it's a joking matter," said the Lady Amelia. And then there was nothing more said about it during the dinner.

There was nothing more said about it during the dinner^but it was plain enough from Lady Amelia's countenance that she was not very well pleased with her future brother-in-law's conduct. She was very hospitable to him, pressing him to eat; but even in doing' t that she made repeated little references to his present unfortunate state. She told him that she did not think fried plum-pudding would be bad for him, but that she would recommend him not to drink port-wine after dinner. "By-the-by, Mortimer, you'd better.have some claret up," she remarked. "Adolphus shouldn't take anything that is heating."

VOL. ii. 24

"Thank you," said Crosbie. "I'll liave some brandy-and-water, if Gazebee will give it me."

"Brandy-and-water!" said Lady Amelia. Crosbie in truth, was not given to the drinking of brandy-and-water; but he was prepared to call for raw gin, if he were driven much further by Lady Amelia's solicitude.

At these Sunday dinners the mistress of the house never went away into the drawing-room, and the tea was always brought into them at the table on which they had dined. It was another little step towards keeping holy the first day of the week. When Lady Rosina was there, she was indulged with the sight of six or seven solid good books which were laid upon the mahogany as soon as the bottles were taken off it. At her first prolonged visit she had obtained for herself the privilege of reading a sermon; but as on such occasions both Lady Amelia and Mr. Gazebee would go to sleep,—and as the footman had also once shown a tendency that way,—the sermon had been abandoned. But the master of the house, on these evenings, when his sister-in-law was present, was doomed to sit in idleness, or else to find solace in one of the solid good books. But Lady Rosina just now was in the country, and therefore the table was left unfurnished.

"And what am I to say to my mother?" said Lady Amelia, when they were alone.

"Give her my kindest regards," said Crosbie. It was quite clear, both to the husband and to the wife, that he was preparing himself for rebellion against authority.

For some ten minutes there was nothing said. Crosbie amused himself by playing with the boy whom he called Dicksey, by way of a nickname for De Courcy.

"Mamma, he calls me Dicksey. Am I Dicksey? I'll call 'oo old Cross, and then aunt Dina on't like 'oo."

"I wish you would not call the child nicknames, Adolphus. It seems as though you would wish to cast a slur upon the one which he bears."

"I should hardly think that he would feel disposed to do that," said Mr. Gazebee.

"Hardly, indeed," said Crosbie.

"It has never yet been disgraced in the annals of our country by being made into a nickname," said the proud daughter of the house. She was probably unaware that among many of his associates her

fatlier had been called Lord De Curse'ye, from the occasional energy of his language. "And any 'such attempt is painful in my ears. I think something of my family, I can assure you, Adolphus, and so does my husband."

"A very great deal," said Mr. Gazebee.

"So do I of mine," said Crosbie. "That's natural to all of us. One of my ancestors came over with William the Conqueror. I think he was one of the assistant cooks in the king's tent."

"A cook!" said young De Courcy.

"Yes, my boy, a cook. That was the way most of our old families were made noble. They were cooks, or butlers to the kings —or sometimes something worse."

"But your family isn't noble?"

"No—I'll tell you how that was. The king wanted this cook to poison half-a-dozen of his officers who wished to have a way of their own; but the cook said, * No, my Lord King; I am a cook, not an executioner.' So they sent him into the scullery, and when they called all the other servants barons and lords, they only called him Cookey. They've changed the name to Crosbie since that, by

Mr. Gazebee was awestruck, and the face of the Lady Amelia became very dark. Was it not evident that this snake, when taken into their innermost bosoms that they might there warm him, was becoming an adder, and preparing to sting them? There was very little more conversation that evening, and soon after the story of the cook, Crosbie got up and went away to his own home.

CHAPTER VI. "SEE, THE CONQUERING HERO COMES."

JOHN EAMES had reached his office precisely at twelve o'clock, but when he did so he hardly knew whether he was standing on his heels or his head. The whole morning had been to him one of intense excitement, and latterly, to a certain extent, one of triumph. But he did not at all know what might be the results. Would he be taken before a magistrate and locked up? Would there be a row at the office? Would Crosbie call him out, and, if so, would it be incumbent on him to fight a duel with pistols? What would Lord De Guest say—Lord De Guest, who had specially warned him not to take upon himself the [duty of avenging Lily's wrongs? What would all the Dale family say of his conduct? And, above all, what would Lily say] and think? Nevertheless, the feeling of triumph was predominant; and now, at this interval of time, he was beginning to remember with pleasure the sensation of his fist as it went into Crosbie's eye.

During his first day at the office he heard nothing about the affair, nor did he say a word of it to any one. It was known in his room that he had gone down to spend his Christmas holiday with Lord De Guest, and he was treated with some increased consideration accordingly. And, moreover, I must explain, in order that I may give Johnny Eames his due, he was gradually acquiring for himself a good footing among the income-tax officials. He knew his work, and did it with some manly confidence in his own powers, and also with some manly indifference to the occasional frowns of the mighty men of the department. He was, moreover, popular— being somewhat of a radical in his official demeanour, and holding by his own rights, even though mighty men should frown. In truth, he was emerging from his hobbledehoyhood and entering upon his young-

AND YOU WJfiNT IN AT HIM ON THB STATION?'

manhood, having probably to go through much folly and some false sentiment in that period of his existence, but still with fair promise of true manliness beyond, to those who were able to read the signs of his character.

Many questions on that first day were asked him about the glories of his Christmas, but he had very little to say on the subject. Indeed nothing could have been much more commonplace than his Christmas visit, had it not been for the one great object which had taken him down to that part of the country, and for the circumstance with which his holiday had been ended. On neither of these subjects was he disposed to speak openly; but as he walked home to Burton Crescent with Cradell, he did tell him of the affair with Crosbie.

" And you went in at him on the station ? " asked Cradell, with admiring doubt.

" Yes, I did. If I didn't do it there, where was I to do it ? I'd said I would, and therefore when I saw him I did it." Then the whole affair was told as to the black eye, the police, and the superintendent. " And what's to come next ? " asked our hero.

" Well, he'll put it in the hands of a friend, of course; as I did with Fisher in that affair with Lupex. And, upon my word, Johnny, I shall have to do something of the kind again. His conduct last night was outrageous ; would you believe it "

" Oh, he's a fool."

" He's a fool you wouldn't like to meet when he's in one of his mad fits, I can tell you that. I absolutely had to sit up in my own bedroom all last night. Mother Koper told me that if I remained in the drawing-room she would feel herself obliged to have a policeman in the house. What could I do, you know ? I made her have a fire for me, of course."

" And then you went to bed."

" I waited ever so long, because I thought that Maria would want to see me. At last she sent me a note. Maria is so imprudent, you know. If he had found anything in her writing, it would have been terrible, you know,—quite terrible. And who can say whether Jemima mayn't tell ? "

" And what did she say ? "

" Come ; that's tellings, Master Johnny. I took very good care to take it with me to the office this morning, for fear of accidents."

But Eames was not so widely awake to the importance of his friend's adventures as lie might have been had he not been weighted with adventures of his own.

" I shouldn't care so much," said he, " about that fellow, Crosbie, going to a friend, as I should about his going to a police magistrate."

" He'll put it in a friend's hands, of course," said Cradell, with the air of a man who from experience was well up in such matters. " And I suppose you'll naturally come to me. It's a deuced bore to a man in a public office, and all that kind of thing, of course. But I'm not the man to desert my friend. I'll stand by you, Johnny, my boy."

" Oh, thank you," said Eames, " I don't think that I shall want that."

" You must be ready with a friend, you know."

" I should write down to a man I know in the country, and ask his advice," said Eames; " an older sort of friend, you know."

" By Jove, old fellow, take care what you're about. Don't let them say of you that you show the white feather. Upon my honour, I'd sooner have anything said of me than that. I would, indeed,— anything."

"I'm not afraid of that," said Eames, with a touch of scorn in his voice. " There isn't much thought about white feathers now-a-days,-—not in the way of fighting duels."

After that, Cradell managed to carry back the conversation to Mrs. Lupex and his own peculiar position, and as Eames did not care to ask from his companion further advice in his own matters, he listened nearly in silence till they reached Burton Crescent.

" I hope you found the noble earl well," said Mrs. Roper to him, as soon as they were all seated at dinner.

" I found the noble earl pretty well, thank you," said Johnny.

It had become plainly understood by all the Roperites that Barnes's position was quite altered since he had been honoured with the friendship of Lord De Guest. Mrs. Lupex, next to whom he always sat at dinner, with a view to protecting her as it were from the dangerous neighbourhood of Cradell, treated him with a marked courtesy. Miss Spruce always called him " sir." Mrs. Roper helped him the first of the gentlemen, and was mindful about his fat and gravy, and Amelia felt less able than she was before to insist upon the possession of his heart and affections. It must not be supposed that Amelia intended to abandon the fight, and allow the enemy to walk off with his forces; but she felt herself constrained to treat him with a deference that was hardly compatible with the perfect equality which should attend any union of hearts.

"It is such a privilege to be on visiting terms with the nobility," said Mrs. Lupex. " When I was a girl, I used to be very intimate "

" You ain't a girl any longer, and so you'd better not talk about it," said Lupex. Mr. Lupex had been at that little shop in Drury Lane after he came down from his scene-painting.

" My dear, you needn't be a brute to me before all Mrs. Eoper's company. If, led away by feelings which I will not now describe, I left my proper circles in marrying you, you need not before all the world teach me how much I have to regret." And Mrs. Lupex, putting down her knife and fork, applied her handkerchief to her eyes.

" That's pleasant for a man over his meals, isn't it ? " said Lupex, appealing to Miss Spruce. " I have plenty of that kind of thing, and you can't think how I like it."

" Them whom God has joined together, let no man put asunder," said Miss Spruce. " As for me myself, I'm only an old woman."

This little ebullition threw a gloom over the dinner-table, and nothing more was said on the occasion as to the glories of Eames's career. But, in the course of the evening, Amelia heard of the encounter which had taken place at the railway station, and at once perceived that she might use the occasion for her own purposes.

" John," she whispered to her victim, finding an opportunity for coming upon him when almost alone, "what is this I hear? I insist upon knowing. Are you going to fight a duel ? "

" Nonsense," said Johnny.

" But it is not nonsense. You don't know what my feelings will be, if I think that such a thing is going to happen. But then you are so hard-hearted ! "

" I ain't hard-hearted a bit, and I'm not going to fight a duel."

" But is it true that you beat Mr. Crosbie at the station ? "

" It is true. I did beat him."

" Oh, John ! not that I mean to say you were wrong, and indeed I honour you for the feeling. There can be nothing so dreadful as a young man's deceiving a young woman and leaving her after he has won her heart,—particularly when she has had his promise in plain words, or, perhaps, even in black and white." John thought of that horrid, foolish, wretched note which he had written. "And a poor girl, if she can't right hers'elf hy a hreach of promise, doesn't know what to do. Does she, John ? "

" A girl who'd right herself that way wouldn't be worth having."

" I don't know about that. When a poor girl is in such a position, she has to be said by her friends. I suppose, then, Miss Lily Dale won't bring a breach of promise against him."

This mention of Lily's name in such a place was sacrilege in the ears of poor Eames. " I cannot tell," said he, " what may be the intention of the lady of whom you speak. But from what I know of her friends, I should not think that she will be disgraced by such a proceeding."

" That may be all very well for Miss Lily Dale " Amelia said, and then she hesitated. It would not be well, she thought, absolutely to threaten him as yet,— not as long as there was any possibility that he might be won without a threat. " Of course I know all about it," she continued. " She was your L. D., you know. Not that I was ever jealous of her. To you she was no more than one of childhood's friends. Was she, Johnny ? "

He stamped his foot upon the floor, and then jumped up from his seat. " I hate all that sort of twaddle about childhood's friends, and you know I do. You'll make me swear that I'll never come into this room again."

" Johnny!"

" So I will. The whole thing makes me sick. And as for that Mrs. Lupex "

"If this is what you learn, John, by going to a lord's house, I think you had better stay at home with your own friends."

" Of course I had;—much better stay at home with my own friends. Here's Mrs. Lupex, and at any rate I can't stand her. So he went off, and walked round the Crescent, and down to the New Road, and almost into the Regent's Park, thinking of Lily Dale and of his own cowardice with Amelia Roper.

On the following morning he received a message, at about one o'clock, by the mouth of the Board-room messenger, informing him that his presence was required in the Board-room. " Sir Raffle Buffle has desired your presence, Mr. Eames."

" My presence, Tupper ! what for ?" said Johnny, turning upon the messenger almost with dismay.

" Indeed I can't say, Mr. Eames; but Sir Raffle Buffle has desired your presence in the Board-room."

Such a message as that in official life always strikes awe into the heart of a young man. And yet, young men generally come forth from such interviews without having received any serious damage, and generally talk about the old gentlemen whom they have encountered with a good deal of light-spirited sarcasm,—or chaff, as it is called in the slang phraseology of the day. It is that same ' majesty which doth hedge a king' that does it. The turkey-cock in his own farmyard is master of the occasion, and the thought of him creates fear. A bishop in his lawn, a judge on the bench, a chairman in the big room at the end of a long table, or a policeman with his bull's-eye lamp upon his beat, can all make themselves terrible by means of those appanages of majesty which] have been vouchsafed to them. But how mean is the policeman in his own home, and how few thought much of Sir Raffle Buffle as he sat asleep after dinner in his old slippers! How well can I remember the terror created within me by the air of outraged dignity with which a certain fine old gentleman, now long since gone, could rub his hands slowly, one on the other, and look up to the ceiling, slightly shaking his head, as though lost in the contemplation of my iniquities ! I would become sick in my stomach, and feel as though my ankles had been broken. That upward turn of the eye unmanned me so completely that I was speechless as regarded any defence. I think that that old man could hardly have known the extent of his own power.

Once upon a time a careless lad, having the charge of a bundle of letters addressed to the King,—petitions and such like, which in the course of business would not get beyond the hands of some lord-in-waiting's deputy assistant,—sent the bag which contained them to the wrong place ; to Windsor, perhaps, if the Court were in London ; or to St. James's, if it were at Windsor. He was summoned ; and the great man of the occasion contented himself with holding his hands up to the heavens as he stood up from his chair, and exclaiming twice, " Mis-sent the Monarch's pouch ! Mis-sent the Monarch's pouch!" That young man never knew how he escaped from the Board-room; but for a time he was deprived of all power of exertion, and could not resume his work till he had had six months' leave of absence, and been brought round upon rum and asses' milk. In that instance the peculiar use of the word Monarch had a power which the official magnate had never contemplated. The story is traditional; but I believe that the circumstance happened as lately as in the days of George the Third.

John Eames could laugh at the present chairman of the Income-tax Office with great freedom, and call him old Huffle Scuffle, and the like; but now that he was sent for, he also, in spite of his radical propensities, felt a little weak about his ankle joints. He knew, from the first hearing of the message, that he was wanted with reference to that affair at the railway station. Perhaps there might be a rule that any clerk should be dismissed who used his fists in any public place. There were many rules entailing the punishment of dismissal for many offences,—and he began to think that he did remember something of such a regulation. However, he got up, looked once around him upon his friends, and then followed Tupper into the Board-room.

" There's Johnny been sent for by old Scuffles," said one clerk.

" That's about his row with Crosbie," said another. " The Board can't do anything to him for that."

" Can't it ? " said the first. " Didn't young Outonites have to resign because of that row at the Cider Cellars, though his cousin, Sir Constant Outonites, did all that he could for him ?"

" But he was regularly up the spout with accommodation bills."

" I tell you that I wouldn't be in Eames's shoes for a trifle. Crosbie is secretary at the Committee Office, where Scuffles was chairman before he came here; and of course they're as thick as thieves. I shouldn't wonder if they didn't make him go down and apologize."

" Johnny won't do that," said the other.

In the meantime John Eames was standing in the august presence. Sir Baffle Buffle was throned in his great oak arm-chair at the head of a long table in a very large room; and by him, at the corner of the table, was seated one of the assistant secretaries of the office. Another member of the Board was also at work upon the .long table; but he was reading and signing papers at some distance from Sir Baffle, and paid no heed whatever to the scene. The assistant secretary, looking on, could see that Sir Baffle was annoyed by this want of attention on the part of his colleague, but all this was lost upon Eames.

" Mr. Eames ? " said Sir Raffle, speaking with a peculiarly harsh voice, and looking at the culprit through a pair of gold-rimmed glasses, which he perched for the occasion upon his big nose. " Isn't that Mr. Eames ? "

" Yes," said the assistant secretary, "this is Eames."

" All! "—and then there was a pause. " Come a little nearer, Mr. Eames, will you ? " and Johnny drew nearer, advancing noiselessly over the Turkey carpet.

" Let me see; in the second class, isn't he ? Ah! Do you know, Mr. Eames, that I have received a letter from the secretary to the Directors of the Great Western Eailway Company, detailing circumstances which,—if truly stated in that letter,—redound very much to your discredit ? "

" I did get into a row there yesterday, sir."

" Got into a row! It seems to me that you have got into a very serious row, and that I must tell the Directors of the Great Western Eailway Company that the law must be allowed to take its course."

" I shan't mind that, sir, in the least," said Eames, brightening up a little under this view of the case.

" Not mind that, sir ! " said Sir Raffle;—or rather, he shouted out the words at the offender before him. I am inclined to think that he overdid it, missing the effect which a milder tone might have attained. Perhaps there was lacking to him some of that majesty of demeanour and dramatic propriety of voice which had been so efficacious in the little story as to the King's bag of letters. As it was, Johnny gave a slight jump, but after his jump he felt better than he had been before. " Not mind, sir, being dragged before the criminal tribunals of your country, and being punished as a felon,—or rather as a misdemeanor,—for an outrage committed on a public platform! Not mind it! What do you mean, sir ? "

"I mean, that I don't think the magistrate would say very much about it, sir. And I don't think Mr. Crosbie would come forward."

"But Mr. Crosbie must come forward, young man. Do you suppose that an outrage against the peace of the Metropolis is to go unpunished because he may not wish to pursue the matter ? I'm afraid you must be very ignorant, young man."

" Perhaps I am," said Johnny.

" Very ignorant indeed,—very ignorant indeed. And are you aware, sir, that it would become a question with the Commissioners of this Board whether you could be retained in the service of this department if you were publicly punished by a police magistrate for such a disgraceful outrage as that ? "

Johnny looked round at the other Commissioner, but that gentleman did not raise his face from his papers.

" Mr. Eames is a very good clerk," whispered the assistant

secretary, but in a voice which made his words audible to Eames; " one of the best young men we have," he added, in a voice which was not audible.

" Oh,—ah ; very well. Now, I'll tell you what, Mr. Eames, I hope this will be a lesson to you,—a very serious lesson."

The assistant secretary, leaning back in his chair so as to be a little behind the head of Sir Baffle, did manage to catch the eye of the other Commissioner. The other Commissioner, barely looking round, smiled a little, and then the assistant secretary smiled also. Eames saw this, and he smiled too.

" Whether any ulterior consequences may still await the breach of the peace of which you have been guilty, I am not yet prepared to say," continued Sir Raffle. " You may go now."

And Johnny returned to his own place, with no increased reverence for the dignity of the chairman.

On the following morning one of his colleagues showed him with great glee the passage in the newspaper which informed the world that he had been so desperately beaten by Crosbie that he was obliged to keep his bed at this present time in consequence of the flogging that he had received. Then his anger was aroused, and he bounced about the big room of the Income-tax Office, regardless of assistant secretaries, head clerks, and all other official grandees whatsoever, denouncing the iniquities of the public press, and declaring his opinion that it would be better to live in Russia than in a country which allowed such audacious falsehoods to be propagated.

" He never touched me, Fisher; I don't think he ever tried ; but, upon my honour, he never touched me."

" But, Johnny, it was bold in you to make up to Lord De Courcy's daughter," said Fisher.

" I never saw one of them in my life."

" He's going it altogether among the aristocracy, now," said another ; "I suppose you wouldn't look at anybody under a viscount ? "

" Can I help what that thief of an editor puts into his paper ? Flogged! Huffle Scuffle told me I was a felon, but that wasn't half so bad as this fellow; " and Johnny kicked the newspaper across the room.

" Indict him for a libel," said Fisher.

" Particularly for saying you wanted to many a countess's daughter," said another clerk.

" I never heard such a scandal in my life," declared a third; " and then to say that the girl wouldn't look at you."

But not the less was it felt by all in the office that Johnny Eames was becoming a leading man among them, and that he was one with whom each of them would be pleased to be intimate.

And even among the grandees this affair of the railway station did him no real harm. It was known that Crosbie had deserved to be thrashed, and known that Eames had thrashed him. It was all very well for Sir Raffle Buffle to talk of police magistrates and misdemeanours, but all the world at the Income-tax Office knew very well that Eames had come out from that affair with his head upright, and his right foot foremost.

" Never mind about the newspaper," a thoughtful old senior clerk said to him. "As he did get the licking and you didn't, you can afford to laugh at the newspaper."

" And you wouldn't write to the editor ? "

" No, no; certainly not. No one thinks of defending himself to a newspaper except an ass;—unless it be some fellow who wants to have his name puffed. You may write what's as true as the gospel, but they'll know how to make fun of it."

Johnny therefore gave up his idea of an indignant letter to the editor, but he felt that he was bound to give, some explanation of the whole matter to Lord De Guest. The affair had happened as he was coming from the earl's house, and all his own concerns had now been made so much a matter of interest to his kind friend, that he thought that he could not with propriety leave the earl to learn from the newspapers either the facts or the falsehoods. And, therefore, before he left his office he wrote the following letter:—

Income-tax Office, December 29, 186—. MY LORD,

He thought a good deal about the style in which he ought to address the peer, never having hitherto written to him. He began, " My dear Lord," on one sheet of paper, and then put it aside, thinking that it looked over-bold.

MY LORD,

As you have been so very kind to me, I feel that I ought to tell you what happened the other morning at the railway station, as I was coming back from Guestwick. That scoundrel Crosbie got into the same carriage with me at the Barchester Junction, and sat opposite to me all the way up to London. I did not speak a word to him, or he to me; but when he got out at the

Paddington Station, I thought I ought not to let him go away, so I I

can't say that I thrashed him as I wished to do; but I made an attempt, and I did give him a black eye. A whole quantity of policemen got round us, and I hadn't a fair chance. I know you will think that I was wrong, and perhaps I was; but what could I do when he sat opposite to me there for two hours, looking as though he thought himself the finest fellow in all London ?

They've put a horrible paragraph into one of the newspapers, saying that I got so " flogged " that I haven't been able to stir since. It is an atrocious falsehood, as is all the rest of the newspaper account. I was not touched. He was not nearly so bad a customer as the bull, and seemed to take it all very quietly. I must acknowledge, though, that he didn't get such a beating as he deserved.

Your friend Sir K. B. sent for me 'this morning, and told me I was a felon. I didn't seem to care much for that, for he might as well have called me a murderer or a burglar; but I shall care very much indeed if I have made you angry with me. But what I most fear is the anger of some one else,—at Allington.

Believe me to be, my Lord,

Yours very much obliged and most sincerely,

JOHN EAMES.

" I knew he'd do it if ever lie got the opportunity," said the earl when he had read his letter; and he walked about his room striking his hands together, and then thrusting his thumbs into his waistcoat-pockets. " I knew he was made of the right stuff," and the earl rejoiced greatly in the prowess of his favourite. " I'd have done it myself if I'd seen him. I do believe I would."

Then he went back to the breakfast-room and told Lady Julia. " What do you think ? " said he ; " Johnny Eames has come across Crosbie, and given him a desperate beating."

" No ! " said Lady Julia, putting down her newspaper and spectacles, and expressing by the light of her eyes anything but Christian horror at the wickedness of the deed.

" But he has, though. I knew he would if he saw him."

" Beaten him ! Actually beaten him ! "

" Sent him home to Lady Alexandrina with two black eyes."

" Two black eyes ! What a young pickle ! But did he get hurt himself?"

"Not a scratch, he says."

" And what'll they do to him ? "

"Nothing. Crosbie won't be fool enough to do anything. A man becomes an outlaw when he plays such a game as he has played. Anybody's hand may be raised against him with impunity.

" SEE, THE CONQUERING HERO COMES." G3

He can't show his face, you know. He can't come forward and answer questions as to what he has done. There are offences which the law can't touch, but which outrage public feeling so strongly that any one may take upon himself the duty of punishing them. He has been thrashed, and that will stick to him till he dies."

" Do tell Johnny from me that I hope he didn't get hurt," said Lady Julia. The old lady could not absolutely congratulate him on his feat of arms, but she did the next thing to it.

But the earl did congratulate him, with a full open assurance of his approval.

" I hope," he said, " I should have done the same at your age, under similar circumstances, and I'm very glad that he proved less difficult than the bull. I'm quite sure you didn't want any one to help you with Master Crosbie. As for that other person at Allington, if I understand such matters at all, I think she will forgive you." It may, however, be a question whether the earl did understand such matters at all. And then he added, in a postscript: " When you write to me again,—and don't be long first, begin your letter, ' My dear Lord De Guest,'—that is the proper way."

CHAPTER VII. AN OLD MAN'S COMPLAINT.

" HAVE you been thinking again of what I was saying to you, Bell ? " Bernard said to his cousin one morning.

11 Thinking of it, Bernard? Why should I think more of it? I had hoped that you had forgotten it yourself."

"No," he said; "I am not so easy-hearted as that. I cannot look on such a thing as I would the purchase of a horse, which I could give up without sorrow if I found that the animal was too costly for my purse. I did not tell you that I loved you till I was sure of myself, and having made myself sure I cannot change at all."

" And yet you would have me change."

" Yes, of course I would. If your heart be free now, it must of course be changed before you come to love any man. Such change as that is to be looked for. But when you have loved, then it will not be easy to change you."

"But I have not."

" Then I have a right to hope. I have been hanging on here, Bell, longer than I ought to have done, because I could not bring myself to leave you without speaking of this again. I did not wish to seem to you to be importunate "

" If you could only believe me in what I say."

"It is not that I do not believe. I am not a puppy or a fool, to natter myself that you must be in love with me. I believe you well enough. But still it is possible that your mind may alter."

"It is impossible."

" I do not know whether my uncle or your mother have spoken to you about this."

" Such speaking would have no effect."

In fact, her mother had spoken to her, but she truly said that such speaking would have no effect. If her cousin could not win the battle by his own skill, he might have been quite sure, looking at her character as it was known to him, that he would not be able to win it by the skill of others.

" We have all been made very unhappy," he went on to say, "by this calamity which has fallen on poor Lily."

" And because she has been deceived by the man she did love, I am to make matters square by marrying a man I ," and then she paused. " Dear Bernard, you should not drive me to say words which will sound harsh to you."

" No words can be harsher than those which you have already spoken. But, Bell, at any rate, you may listen to me."

Then he told her how desirable it was with reference to all the concerns of the Dale family that she should endeavour to look favourably on his proposition. It would be good for them all, he said, especially for Lily, as to whom, at the present moment, their uncle felt so kindly. He, as Bernard pleaded, was so anxious at heart for this marriage, that he would do anything that was asked of him if he were gratified. But if he were not gratified in this, he would feel that he had ground for displeasure.

Bell, as she had been desired to listen, did listen very patiently. But when her cousin had finished, her answer was very short. " Nothing that my uncle can say, or think, or do, can make any difference in this," said she.

" You will think nothing, then, of the happiness of others."

" I would not marry a man I did not love, to ensure any amount of happiness to others ;—at least I know I ought not to do so. But I do not believe I should ensure any one's happiness by this marriage. Certainly not yours."

After this Bernard had acknowledged to himself that the difficulties in his way were great. " I will go away till next autumn," he said to his uncle.

" If you would give up your profession and remain here, she would not be so perverse."

" I cannot do that, sir. I cannot risk the well-being of my life on such a chance." Then his uncle had been angry with him, as well as with his niece. In his anger he determined that he would go again to his sister-in-law, and, after some unreasonable fashion, he resolved that it would become him to be very angry with her also, if she declined to assist him with all her influence as a mother.

" Why should they not both marry ?" he said to himself. Lord De Guest's offer as to young Eames had been very generous. As he had then declared, he had not been able to express his own opinion at once ; but on thinking over what the earl had said, he had found himself very willing to heal the family wound in the manner proposed, if any such healing might be possible. That, however, could not be done quite as yet. When the time should come, and he thought it might come soon,—perhaps in the spring, when the days should be fine and the evenings again long,—he would be willing to take his share with the earl in establishing that new household. To Crosbie he had refused to give anything, and there was upon his conscience a shade of remorse in that he had so refused. But if Lily could be brought to love this other man, he would be more open-handed. She should have her share as though she was in fact his daughter. But then, if he intended to do so much for them at the Small House, should not they in return do something also for him ?

So thinking, he went again to his sister-in-law, determined to explain his views, even though it might be at the risk of some hard words between them. As regarded himself, he did not much care for hard words spoken to him. He almost expected that people's words should be hard and painful. He did not look for the comfort of affectionate soft greetings, and perhaps would not have appreciated them had they come to him. He caught Mrs. Dale walking in the garden, and brought her into his own room, feeling that he had a better chance there than in her own house. She, with an old dislike to being lectured in that room, had endeavoured to avoid the interview, but had failed.

" So I met John Eames at the manor," he had said to her in the garden.

4 'Ah, yes; and how did he get on there? I cannot conceive poor Johnny keeping holiday with the earl and his sister. How did he behave to them, and how did they behave to him ? "

" I can assure you he was very much at home there."

" Was he, indeed ? Well, I hope it will do him good. He is, I'm sure, a very good young man ; only rather awkward."

" I didn't think him awkward at all. You'll find, Mary, that he'll do very well; —a great deal better than his father did."

" I'm sure I hope he may." After that Mrs. Dale made her attempt to escape; but the squire had taken her prisoner, and led her captive into the house. " Mary," he said, as soon as he had induced her to sit down, " it is time that this should be settled between my nephew and niece."

" I am afraid there will be nothing to settle."

" What do you mean;that you disapprove of it ?"

"By no means,personally. I should approve of it very strongly. But that has nothing to do with the question."

" Yes, it has. I beg your pardon, but it must have, and should have a great deal to do with it. Of course, I am not saying that anybody should now ever be compelled to many anybody."

" I hope not."

" I never said that they ought, and never thought so. But I do think that the wishes of all her family should have very great weight with a girl that has been well brought up."

"I don't know whether Bell has been well brought up; but in such a matter as this nobody's wishes would weigh a feather with her ; and, indeed, I could not take upon myself even to express a wish. To you I can say that I should have been very happy if she could have regarded her cousin as you wish her to do."

" You mean that you are afraid to tell her so ?"

" I am afraid to do what I think is wrong, if you mean that."

" I don't think it would be wrong, and therefore I shall speak to her myself."

" You must do as you like about that, Mr. Dale ; I can't prevent you. I shall think you wrong to harass her on such a inatter, and I fear also that her answer will not be satisfactory to you. If you choose to tell her your opinion, you must do so. Of course I shall think you wrong, that's all."

Mrs. Dale's voice as she said this was stern enough, and so was her countenance. She could not forbid the uncle to speak his mind to his niece, but she specially disliked the idea of any interference with her daughter. The squire got up and walked about the room,, trying to compose himself that he might answer her rationally, but without anger.

" May I go now ?" said Mrs. Dale.

"May you go ? Of course you may go if you like it. If you think that I am intruding upon you in speaking to you of the welfare of your two girls, whom I endeavour to regard as my own daughters, —except in this,.that I know they have never been taught to love me,—if you think that it is an interference on my part to show anxiety for their welfare, of course you may go."

" I did not mean to say anything to hurt you, Mr. Dale."

" Hurt me ! What does it signify whether I am hurt or not ? I have no children of my own, and of course my only business in life is to provide for my nephews and nieces. I am an old fool if I expect that they are to love me in return, and if I venture to express a wish I am interfering and. doing wrong ! It is hard,—very hard. I know well that they have been brought up to dislike me, and yet I am endeavouring to do my duty by them."

"Mr. Dale, that accusation has not been deserved. They have not been brought up to dislike you. I believe that they have both loved and respected you as their uncle ; but such love and respect will not give you a right to dispose of their hands."

"Who wants to dispose of their hands ?"

"There are some things in which I think no uncle,—no parent, —should interfere, and of all such things this is the chief. If after that you may choose to tell her your wishes, of course you can do so."

"It will not be much good after you have set her against me."

"Mr. Dale, you have no right to say such things to me, and you are very unjust in doing so. If you think that I have set my girls against you, it will be much better that we should leave Allington altogether. I have been placed in circumstances which have made it difficult for me to do my duty to my children; but I have endeavoured to»do it, not regarding my own personal wishes. I ana quite sure, however, that it would be wrong in me to keep them here, if I am to be told by you that I have taught them to regard you unfavourably. Indeed, I cannot suffer such a thing to be said to me."

All this Mrs. Dale said with an air of decision, and with a voice expressing a sense of injury received, which made the squire feel that she was very much in earnest.

"Is it not true," he said, defending himself, " that in all that relates to the girls you have ever regarded me with suspicion ? "

"No, it is not true." And then she corrected herself, feeling that there was something of truth in the squire's last assertion. " Certainly not with suspicion," she said. " But as this matter has gone so far, I will explain what my real feelings have been. In worldly matters you can do much for my girls, and have done much."

" And wish to do more," said the squire.

"I am sure you do. But I cannot on that account give up my place as their only living parent. They are my children, and not

yours. And even could I bring myself to allow you to act as their guardian and natural protector, they would not consent to such an arrangement. You cannot call that suspicion."

" I can call it jealousy."

" And should not a mother be jealous of her children's love ? "

During all this time the squire was walking up and down the room with his hands in his trousers pockets. And when Mrs. Dale had last spoken, he continued his walk for some time in silence.

" Perhaps it is well that you should "have spoken out," he said.

" The manner in which you accused me made it necessary."

" I did not intend to accuse you, and I do not do so now; but I think that you have been, and that you are, very hard to me,very hard indeed. I have endeavoured to make your children, and yourself also, sharers with me in such prosperity as has been mine. I have striven to add to your comfort and to their happiness. I am most anxious to secure their future welfare. You would have been very wrong had you declined to accept this on their behalf; but I think that in return for it you need not have begrudged me the affection and obedience which generally follows from such good offices."

" Mr. Dale, I have begrudged you nothing of this."

" I am hurt;I am hurt," he continued. And she was surprised by his look of pain even more than by the unaccustomed warmth of his words. " What you have said has, I have known, been the case all along. But though I had felt it to be so, I own that I am hurt by your open words."

" Because I have said that my own children must ever be my own?"

" Ah, you have said more than that. You and the girls have been living here, close to me, for—how many years is it now ?and during all those years there has grown up for me no kindly feeling. Do you think that I cannot hear, and see, and feel ? Do you suppose that I am a fool and do not know ? As for yourself you would never enter this house if you did not feel yourself constrained to do so for the sake of appearances. I suppose it is all as it should be. Having no children of my own, I owe the duty of a parent to my nieces; but I have no right to expect from them in return either love, regard, or obedience. I know I am keeping you here against your will, Mary. I won't do so any longer." And he made a sign to her that she was to depart.

As she rose from her seat her heart was softened towards him. In these latter day she had shown much kindness to the girls,—a kindness that was more akin to the gentleness of love than had ever come from him before. Lily's fate had seemed to melt even his sternness, and he had striven to be tender in his words and ways. And now he spoke as though he had loved the girls, and had loved them in vain. Doubtless he had been a disagreeable neighbour to his sister-in-law, making her feel that it was never for her personally that he had opened his hand. Doubtless he had been moved by an unconscious desire to undermine and take upon himself her authority with her own children. Doubtless he had looked askance at her from the first day of her marriage with his brother. She had been keenly alive to all this since she had first known him, and more keenly alive to it than ever since the failure of those efforts she had made to live with him on terms of affection, made during the first year or two of her residence at the Small House. But, nevertheless, in spite of all, her heart bled for him now. She had gained her victory over him, having fully held her own position with her children ; but now that he complained that he had been beaten in the struggle, her heart bled for him.

" My brother," she said, and as she spoke she offered him her hands, " it may be that we have not thought as kindly of each other as we should have done."

" I have endeavoured," said the old man. " I have endeavoured " And then he stopped, either hindered by some excess of emotion, or unable to find the words which were necessary for the expression of his meaning.

" Let us endeavour once again,both of us."

" What, begin again at near seventy! No, Mary, there is no more beginning again for me. All this shall make no difference to the girls. As long as I am here they shall have the house. If they marry, I will do for them what I can. I believe Bernard is much in earnest in his suit, and if Bell will listen to him, she shall still be welcomed here as mistress of Allington. What you have said shall make no difference;—but as to beginning again, it is simply impossible."

After that Mrs. Dale walked home through the garden by herself. He had studiously told her that that house in which they lived should be lent, not to her, but to her children, during his lifetime. He had positively declined the offer of her warmer regard. He had made

her understand that they were to look on each other almost as enemies; but that she, enemy as she was, should still be allowed the use of his munificence, because he chose to do his duty by his nieces !

" It will be better for us that we shall leave it," she said to herself as she seated herself .in her own arm-chair over the drawing-room fire.

CHAPTER VIII. DOCTOR CROFTS IS CALLED IN.

MRS. DALE had not sat long in her drawing-room before tidings were brought to her which for a wMle drew her mind away from that question of her removal. " Mamma," said Bell, entering the room, " I really do believe that Jane has got scarlatina." Jane, the parlour-maid, had been ailing for the last two days, but nothing serious had hitherto been suspected.

Mrs. Dale instantly jumped up. "Who is with her?" she asked.

It appeared from Bell's answer that both she and Lily had been with the girl, and that Lily was still in the room. Whereupon Mrs. Dale ran upstairs, and there was on the sudden a commotion in the house. In an hour or so the village doctor was there, and he expressed an opinion that the girl's ailment was certainly scarlatina. Mrs. Dale, not satisfied with this, sent off a boy to Guestwick for Dr. Crofts, having herself maintained an opposition of many years' standing against the medical reputation of the apothecary, and gave a positive order to the two girls not to visit poor Jane again. She herself had had scarlatina, and might do as she pleased. Then, too, a nurse was hired.

All this changed for a few hours the current of Mrs. Dale's thoughts : but in the evening she went back to the subject of her morning conversation, and before the three ladies went to bed, they held together an open council of war upon the subject. Dr. Crofts had been found to be away from Guestwick, and word had been sent on his behalf that he would be over at Allington early on the following morning. Mrs. Dale had almost made up her mind that the malady of her favourite maid was not scarlatina, but had not on that account relaxed her order as to the absence of her daughters from the maid's bedside.

" Let us go at once," said Bell, who was even more opposed to any domination on the part of her uncle than was her mother. In the discussion which had been taking place between them the whole matter of Bernard's courtship had come upon the carpet. Bell had kept her cousin's offer to herself as long as she had been able to do so ; but since her uncle had pressed the subject upon Mrs. Dale, it was impossible for Bell to remain silent any longer. " You do not want me to marry him, mamma ; do you ? " she had said, when her mother had spoken with some show of kindness towards Bernard. In answer to this, Mrs. Dale had protested vehemently that she had no such wish, and Lily, who still held to her belief in Dr. Crofts, was almost equally animated. To them all, the idea that their uncle should in any way interfere in their own views of life, on the strength of the pecuniary assistance which they had received from him, was peculiarly distasteful. But it was especially distasteful that he should presume to have even an opinion as to their disposition in marriage. They declared to each other that their uncle could have no right to object to any marriage which either of them might contemplate as long as their mother should approve of it. The poor old squire had been right in saying that he was regarded with suspicion. He was so regarded. The fault had certainly been his own, in having endeavoured to win the daughters without thinking it worth his while to win the mother. The girls had unconsciously felt that the attempt was made, and had vigorously rebelled against it. It had not been their fault that they had been brought to live in their uncle's house, and made to ride on his ponies, and to eat partially of his bread. They had so eaten, and so lived, and declared themselves to be grateful. The squire was good in his way, and they recognized his goodness ; but not on that account would they transfer to him one jot of the allegiance which as children they owed to their mother. When she told them her tale, explaining to them the words which their uncle had spoken that morning, they expressed their regret that he should be so grieved ; but they were strong in assurances to their mother that she had been sinned against, and was not sinning.

" Let us go at once," said Bell.

"It is much easier said than done, my dear."

" Of course it is, mamma; else we shouldn't be here now. What I mean is this,—let us take some necessary first step at once. It is clear that my uncle thinks that our remaining here should give him some right over us. I do not say that he is wrong to think so.

Perhaps it is natural. Perhaps, in accepting his kindness, we ought to submit ourselves to him. If that be so, it is a conclusive reason for. our going."

" Could we not pay him rent for the house," said Lily, " as Mrs. Hearn does ? You would like to remain here, mamma, if you could do that ? "

" But we could not do that, Lily. We must choose for ourselves a smaller house than this, and one that is not burdened with the expense of a garden. Even if we paid but a moderate rent for this place, we should not have the means of living here."

" Not if we lived on toast and tea ? " said Lily, laughing.

" But I should hardly wish you to live upon toast and tea; and indeed I fancy that I should get tired of such a diet myself."

" Never, mamma," said Lily. " As for me, I confess to a longing after mutton chops; but I don't think you would ever want such vulgar things."

" At any rate, it would be impossible to remain here," said Bell. " Uncle Christopher would not take rent from mamma ; and even if he did, we should not know how to go on with our other arrangements after such a change. No; we must give up the dear old Small House."

"It is a dear old house," said Lily, thinking, as she spoke, more of those late scenes in the garden, when Crosbie had been with, them in the autumn months, than of any of the former joys of her childhood.

" After all, I do not know that I should be right to move," said Mrs. Dale, doubtingly.

" Yes, yes," said both the girls at once. " Of course you will be right, mamma; there cannot be a doubt about it, mamma. If we can get any cottage, or even lodgings, that would be better than remaining here, now that we know what uncle Christopher thinks of it."

" It will make him very unhappy," said Mrs. Dale.

But even this argument did not in the least move the girls. They were very sorry that their uncle should be unhappy. They would endeavour to show him by some increased show of affection that their feelings towards him were not unkind. Should he speak to them they would endeavour to explain to him that their thoughts towards him were altogether affectionate. But they could not remain at Allington increasing their load of gratitude, seeing that he expected a certain payment which they did not feel themselves able to render.

" We should be robbing him, if we stayed here," Bell declared;— " wilfully robbing him of what he believes to be his just share of the bargain."

So it was settled among them that notice should be given to their uncle of their intention to quit the Small House of Allington.

And then came the question as to their new home. Mrs. Dale was aware that her income was at any rate better than that possessed by Mrs. Eames, and therefore she had fair ground for presuming that she could afford to keep a house at Guestwick. " If we do go away, that is what we must do," she said.

" And we shall have to walk out with Mary Eames, instead of Susan Boyce," said Lily. " It won't make so much difference after all."

" In that respect we shall gain as much as we lose," said Bell.

" And then it will be so nice to have the shops," said Lily, ironically.

" Only we shall never have any money to buy anything," said Bell.

" But we shall see more of the world," said Lily. " Lady Julia's carnage comes into town twice a week, and the Miss Gruffens drive about in great style. Upon the whole, we shall gain a great deal; only for the poor old garden. Mamma, I do think I shall break my heart at parting with Hopkins; and as to him, I shall be disappointed in mankind if he ever holds his head up again after I am gone."

But in truth there was very much of sadness in their resolution, and to Mrs. Dale it seemed as though she were managing matters badly for her daughters, and allowing poverty and misfortune to come upon them through her own fault. She well knew how great a load of sorrow was lying on Lily's heart, hidden beneath those little attempts at pleasantry which she made. When she spoke of being disappointed in mankind, Mrs. Dale could hardly repress an outward shudder that would betray her thoughts. And now she was consenting to take them forth from their comfortable home, from the luxury of their lawns and gardens, and to bring them to some small dingy corner of a provincial town,—because she had failed to make herself happy with her brother-in-law. Could she be right to give up all the advantages which they enjoyed at Allington,—advantages which had

come to them from so legitimate a source,—because her own feelings had been wounded? In all their future want of comfort, in the comfortless dowdiness of the new home to which she would remove them, would she not always blame herself for having brought them to that by her own false pride ? And yet it seemed to her that she now had no alternative. She could not now teach her daughters to obey their uncle's wishes in all things. She could not make Bell understand that it would be well that she should many Bernard because the squire had set his heart on such a marriage. She had gone so far that she could not now go back.

" I suppose we must move at Lady-day ? " said Bell, who was in favour of instant action. " If so, had you not better let uncle Christopher know at once ? "

" I don't think that we can find a house by that time."

" We can get in somewhere," continued Bell. " There are plenty of lodgings in Guestwick, you know." But the sound of the word lodgings was uncomfortable in Mrs. Dale's ears.

" If we are to go, let us go at once," said Lily. " "We need not stand much upon the order of our going."

" Your uncle will be very much shocked," said Mrs. Dale.

" He cannot say that it is your fault," said Bell.

It was thus agreed between them that the necessary information should be at once given to the squire, and that the old, well-loved house should be left for ever. It would be a great fall in a worldly point of view,—from the Allington Small House to an abode in some little street of Guestwick. At Allington they had been county people, raised to a level with their own squire and other squires by the circumstance of their residence ; but at Guestwick they would be small even among the people of the town. They would be on an equality with the Eameses, and much looked down upon by the Gruffens. They would hardly dare to call any more at Guestwick Manor, seeing that they certainly could not expect Lady Julia to call upon them at Guestwick. Mrs. Boyce no doubt would patronize them, and they could already anticipate the condolence which would be offered to them by Mrs. Heam. Indeed such a movement on their part would be tantamount to a confession of failure in the full hearing of so much of the world as was known to them.

I must not allow my readers to suppose that these considerations were a matter of indifference to any of the ladies at the Small House. To some women of strong mind, of highly-strung philosophic ten-

dencies, such considerations might have been indifferent. But Mrs. Dale was not of this nature, nor were her daughters. The good things of the world were good in their eyes, and they valued the privilege of a pleasant social footing among their friends. They were by no means capable of a wise contempt of the advantages which chance had hitherto given to them. They could not go forth rejoicing in the comparative poverty of their altered condition. But then, neither could they purchase those luxuries which they were about to abandon at the price which was asked for them.

" Had you not better write to my uncle ? " said one of the girls. But to this Mrs. Dale objected that she could not make a letter on such a subject clearly intelligible, and that therefore she would see the squire on the following morning. "It will be very dreadful," she said, " but it will soon be over. It is not what he will say at the moment that I fear so much as the bitter reproaches of his face when I shall meet him afterwards." So, on the following morning, she again made her way, and now without invitation, to the squire's study.

" Mr. Dale," she began, starting upon her work with some confusion in her manner, and hurry in her speech, " I have been thinking over what we were saying together yesterday, and I have come to a resolution which I know I ought to make known to you without a moment's delay."

The squire also had thought of what had passed between them, and had suffered much as he had done so ; but he had thought of it without acerbity or anger. His thoughts were ever gentler than his words, and his heart softer than any exponent of his heart that he was able to put forth. He wished to love his brother's children, and to be loved by them ; but even failing that, he wished to do good to them. It had not occurred to him to be angry with Mrs. Dale after that interview was over. The conversation had not gone pleasantly with him; but then he hardly expected that things would go pleasantly. No idea had occurred to him that evil could come upon any of the Dale ladies from the words which had then been spoken. He regarded the Small House as their abode and home as surely as the Great House was his own. In giving him his due, it must be declared that any allusion to their holding these as a benefit done to them by him had been very far from his thoughts. Mrs. Hearn, who held her cottage at half its real value, grumbled almost daily at him as her landlord ; but it never occurred to him that therefore he should raise her rent, or that in not doing so he was acting with special munificence. It had ever been to him a grumbling, cross-grained, unpleasant world ; and he did not expect from Mrs. Hearn, or from his sister-in-law, anything better than that to which he had ever been used.

" It will make me very happy," said he, "if it has any bearing on Bell's marriage with her cousin."

" Mr. Dale, that is out of the question. I would not vex you by saying so if I were not certain of it; but I know my child so well!"

" Then we must leave it to time, Mary."

" Yes, of course; but no time will suffice to make Bell change her mind. We will, however, leave the subject. And now, Mr. Dale, I have to tell you of something else ;—we have resolved to leave the Small House."

" Eesolved on what ?" said the squire, turning his eyes full upon her.

" We have resolved to leave the Small House."

" Leave the Small House! " he said, repeating her words ; " and where on earth do you mean to go ? "

" We think we shall go into Guestwick."

" And why ? "

" Ah, that is so hard to explain. If you would only accept the fact as I tell it to you, and not ask for the reasons which have guided me ! "

" But that is out of the question, Mary. In such a matter as that I must ask your reasons; and I must tell you also that, in my opinion, you will not be doing your duty to your daughters in carrying out such an intention, unless your reasons are very strong indeed."

" But they are very strong," said Mrs. Dale; and then she paused.

" I cannot understand it," said the squire. " I cannot bring myself to believe that you are really in earnest. Are you not comfortable there ? "

" More comfortable than we have any right to be with our means."

" But I thought you always did very nicely with your money. You never get into debt."

"No ; I never get into debt. It is not that, exactly. The fact is, Mr. Dale, we have no right to live there without paying rent; but we could not afford to live there if we did pay rent."

"Who has talked about rent ? " he said, jumping up from his chair. " Some one has been speaking falsehoods of me behind my back." No gleam of the real truth had yet come to him. No idea had reached his mind that his relatives thought it necessary to leave his house in consequence of any word that he himself had spoken. He had never considered himself to have been in any special way generous to them, and would not have thought it reasonable that tjiey should abandon the house in which they had been living, even if his anger against them had been strong and hot. " Mary," he said, " I must insist upon getting to the bottom of this. As for your leaving the house, it is out of the question. Where can you be better off, or so well ? As to going into Guestwick, what sort of life would there be for the girls ? I put all that aside as out of the question; but I must know what has induced you to make such a proposition. Tell me honestly,— has any one spoken evil of me behind my back ? "

Mrs. Dale had been prepared for opposition and for reproach; but there was a decision about the squire's words, and an air of masterdom in his manner, which made her recognize more fully than she had yet done the difficulty of her position. She almost began to fear that she would lack power to carry out her purpose.

" Indeed, it is not so, Mr. Dale."

" Then what is it ? "

" I know that if I attempt to tell you, you will be vexed, and will contradict me."

" Vexed I shall be, probably."

" And yet I cannot help it. Indeed, I am endeavouring to do what is right by you and by the children."

" Never mind me ; your duty is to think of them."

" Of course it is; and in doing this they most cordially agree with me."

In using such argument as that, Mrs.' Dale showed her weakness, and the squire was not slow to take advantage of it. " Your duty is to them," he said ; " but I do not mean by that that your duty is to let them act in any way that may best please them for the moment. I can understand that they should be run away with by some romantic nonsense, but I cannot understand it of you."

" The truth is this, Mr. Dale. You think that my children owe to you that sort of obedience which is due to a parent, and as long as they remain here, accepting from your hands so large a part of their

daily support, it is perhaps natural that you should think so. In this unhappy affair about Bell "

" I have never said anything of the kind," said the squire, interrupting her.

" No; you have not said so. And I do not wish you to think that I make any complaint. But I feel that it is so, and they feel it. And, therefore, we have made up our minds to go away."

Mrs. Dale, as she finished, was aware that she had not told her story well, but she had acknowledged to herself that it was quite out of her power to tell it as it should be told. Her main object was to make her brother-in-law understand that she certainly would leave his house, and to make him understand this with as little pain to himself as possible. She did not in the least mind his thinking her foolish, if only she could so carry her point as to be able to tell her daughters on her return that the matter was settled. But the squire, from his words and manners, seemed indisposed to give her this privilege.

" Of all the propositions which I ever heard," said he, " it is the most unreasonable. It amounts to this, that you are too proud to live rent-free in a house which belongs ^to your husband's brother, and therefore you intend to subject yourself and your children to the great discomfort of a very straitened income. If you yourself only were concerned I should have no right to say anything; but I think myself bound to tell you that, as regards the girls, everybody that knows you will think you to have been very wrong. It is in the natural course of things that they should live in that house. The place has never been let. As far as I know, no rent has ever been paid for the house since it was built. It has always been given to some member of the family, who has been considered as having the best right to it. I have considered your footing there as firm as my own here. A quarrel between me and your children would be to me a great calamity, though, perhaps, they might be indifferent to it. But if there were such a quarrel it would afford no reason for their leaving that house. Let me beg you to think over the matter again."

The squire could assume an air of authority on certain occasions, and he had done so now. Mrs. Dale found that she could only answer him by a simple repetition of her own intention; and, indeed, failed in making him any serviceable answer whatsoever. 1 know that you are very good to my girls," she said.

" I will say nothing about that," he answered; not thinking at

"LF.T MW BF.O YOU TO THINTT OVER TH-E MATTER AGAIN."

that moment of the Small House, but of the full possession which he had desired to give to the elder of all the privileges which should belong to the mistress of Allington,—thinking also of the means by which he was hoping to repair poor Lily's shattered fortunes. What words were further said had no great significance, and Mrs. Dale got herself away, feeling that she had failed. As soon as she was gone the squire arose, and putting on his great-coat, went forth with his hat and stick to the front of the house. He went out in order that his thoughts might be more free, and that he might indulge in that solace which an injured man finds in contemplating his injury. He declared to himself that he was very hardly used, so hardly used, that he almost began to doubt himself and his own motives. Why was it that the people around him disliked him so strongly,—avoided him and thwarted him in the efforts which he made for their welfare? He offered to his nephew all the privileges of a son,—much more indeed than the privileges of a son, merely asking in return that he would consent to live permanently in the house which was to be his own. But his nephew refused. " He cannot bear to live with me," said the old man to himself sorely. He was prepared to treat his nieces with more generosity than the daughters of the House of Allington had usually received from their fathers; and they repelled his kindness, running away from him, and telling him openly that they would not be beholden to him. He walked slowly up and down the terrace, thinking of this very bitterly. He did not find in the contemplation of his grievance all that solace which a grievance usually gives, because he accused himself in his thoughts rather than others. He declared to himself that he was made to be hated, and protested to himself that it would be well that he should die and be buried out of memory, so that the remaining Dales might have a better chance of living happily; and then as he thus discussed all this within his own bosom, his thoughts were very tender, and though he was aggrieved, he was most affectionate to those who had most injured him. But it was absolutely beyond his power to reproduce outwardly, with words and outward signs, such thoughts and feelings.

It was now very nearly the end of the year, but the weather was still soft and open. The air was damp rather than cold, and the lawns and fields still retained the green tints of new vegetation. As the squire was walking on the terrace Hopkins came up to him, and touching his hat, remarked that they should have frost in a day or two.

" I suppose we shall," said the squire.

" We must have the mason to the flues of that little grape-house, sir, before I can do any good with a fire there."

" Which grape-house ? " said the squire, crossly.

" Why, the grape-house in the other garden, sir. It ought to have been done last year by rights." This Hopkins said to punish his master for being cross to him. On that matter of the flues of Mrs. Dale's grape-house he had, with much consideration, spared his master during the last winter, and he felt that this ought to be remembered now. " I can't put any fire in it, not to do any real good, till something's done. That's sure."

" Then don't put any fire in it," said the squire.

Now the grapes in question were supposed to be peculiarly fine, and were the glory of the garden of the Small House. They were always forced, though not forced so early as those at the Great House, and Hopkins was in a state of great confusion.

" They'll never ripen, sir ; not the whole year through."

" Then let them be unripe," said the squire, walking about.

Hopkins did not at all understand it. The squire in his natural course was very unwilling to neglect any such matter as this, but would be specially unwilling to neglect anything touching the Small House. So Hopkins stood on the terrace, raising his hat and scratching his head. " There's something wrong amongst them," said he to himself, sorrowfully.

But when the squire had walked to the end of the terrace and had turned upon the path which led round the side of the house, he stopped and called to Hopkins.

" Have what is needful done to the flue," he said.

" Yes, sir; very well, sir. It'll only be re-setting the bricks. Nothing more ain't needful, just this winter."

" Have the place put in perfect order while you're about it," said the squire, and then he walked away.

CHAPTER IX.

DOCTOR CROFTS IS TURNED OUT.

" HAVE you heard the news, my dear, from the Small House ? " said Mrs. Boyce to her husband, some two or three days after Mrs. Dale's visit to the squire. It was one o'clock, and the parish pastor had come in from his ministrations to dine with his wife and children.

" What news ? " said Mr. Boyce, for he had heard none.

" Mrs. Dale and the girls are going to leave the Small House; they're going into Guestwick to live."

" Mrs. Dale going away; nonsense ! " said the vicar. " What on earth should take her into Guestwick ? She doesn't pay a shilling of rent where she is."

" I can assure you it's true, my dear. I was with Mrs. Hearn just now, and she had it direct from Mrs. Dale's own lips. Mrs. Heam said she'd never been taken so much aback in her whole life. There's been some quarrel, you may be sure of that."

Mr. Boyce sat silent, pulling off his dirty shoes preparatory to his dinner. Tidings so important, as touching the social life of his parish, had not come to him for many a day, and he could hardly bring himself to credit them at so short a notice.

" Mrs. Hearn says that Mrs. Dale spoke ever so firmly about it, as though determined that nothing should change her." ' " And did she say why ? "

" Well, not exactly. But Mrs. Hearn said she could understand there had been words between her and the squire. It couldn't be anything else, you know. Probably it had something to do with that man Crosbie."

" They'll be very pushed about money," said Mr. Boyce, thrusting his feet into his slippers.

" That's just what I said to Mrs. Hearn. And those girls have never been used to anything like real economy. What's to become

of them I don't know; " and Mrs. Boyce, as she expressed her sympathy for her dear friends, received considerable comfort from the prospect of their future poverty. It always is so, and Mrs. Boyce was not worse than her neighbours.

" You'll find they'll make it up before the time comes," said Mr. Boyce, to whom the excitement of such a change in affairs was-almost too good to be true.

" I am afraid not," said Mrs. Boyce ; " I'm afraid not. They are both so determined. I always thought that riding and giving the girls hats and habits was injurious. It was treating them as though they were the squire's daughters, and they were not the squire's daughters."

" It was almos't the same thing."

" But now we see the difference," said the judicious Mrs. Boyce. " I often said that dear Mrs. Dale was wrong, and it turns out that I was right. It will make no difference to me, as regards calling on them and that sort of thing."

" Of course it won't."

" Not but what there must be a difference, and a very great difference too. It will be a terrible come down for poor Lily, with the loss of her fine husband and all."

After dinner, when Mr. Boyce had again gone forth upon his labours, the same subject was discussed between Mrs. Boyce and her daughters, and the mother was very careful to teach her children that Mrs. Dale would be just as good a person as ever she had been, and quite as much a lady, even though she should live in a very dingy house at Guestwick; from which lesson the Boyce girls learned plainly that Mrs. Dale, with Bell and Lily, were about to have a fall in the world, and that they were to be treated accordingly.

From all this it will be discovered that Mrs. Dale had not given way to the squire's arguments, although she had found herself unable to answer them. As she had returned home she had felt herself to be almost vanquished, and had spoken to the girls with the air and tone of a woman who hardly knew in which course lay the line of her duty. But they had not seen the squire's manner on the occasion, nor heard his words, and they could not understand that their own purpose should be abandoned because he did not like it. So they talked their mother into fresh resolves, and on the following morning she wrote a note to her brother-in-law, assuring him that she had thought much of all that he had said, but again declaring that she regarded herself as bound in duty to leave the Small House. To this he had returned no answer, and she had communicated her intention to Mrs. Hearn, thinking it better that there should be no secret in the matter.

" I am sorry to hear that your sister-in-law is going to leave us," Mr. Boyce said to the squire that same afternoon.

" Who told you that ? " asked the squire, showing by his tone that he by no means liked the topic of conversation which the parson had chosen.

" Well, I had it from Mrs. Boyce, and I think Mrs. Hearu told her."

" I wish Mrs. Hearn would mind her own business, and not spread idle reports."

The squire said nothing more, and Mr. Boyce felt that he had been very unjustly snubbed.

Dr. Crofts had come over and pronounced as a fact that it was scarlatina. Village apothecaries are generally wronged by the doubts which are thrown upon them, for the town doctors when they come always confirm what the village apothecaries have said.

" There can be no doubt as to its being scarlatina," the doctor declared; "but the symptoms are all favourable."

There was, however, much worse coming than this. Two days afterwards Lily found herself to be rather unwell. She endeavoured to keep it to herself, fearing that she should be brought under the doctor's notice as a patient; but her efforts were unavailing, and on the following morning it was known that she had also taken the disease. Dr. Crofts declared that everything was in her favour. The weather was cold. The presence of the malady in the house had caused them all to be careful, and, moreover, good advice was at hand at once. The doctor begged Mrs. Dale not to be uneasy, but he was very eager in begging that the two sisters might not be allowed to be together. "Could you not send Bell into Guestwick,—to Mrs. Eames's ? " said he. But Bell did not choose to be sent to Mrs. Eames's, and was with great difficulty kept out of her mother's bedroom, to which Lily as an invalid was transferred.

" If you will allow me to say so," he said to Bell, on the second day after Lily's complaint had declared itself, " you are wrong to stay here in the house."

" I certainly shall not leave mamma, when she has got so much upon her hands," said Bell.

" But if you should be taken ill she would have more on her hands," pleaded the doctor.

" I could not do it," Bell replied. " If I were taken over to Guestwick, I should be so uneasy that I should walk back to Ailing-ton the first moment that I could escape from the house."

" I think your mother would be more comfortable without you."

" And I think she would be more comfortable with me. I don't ever like to hear of a woman running away from illness; but when a sister or a daughter does so, it is intolerable." So Bell remained, without permission indeed to see her sister, but performing various outside administrations which were much needed.

And thus all manner of trouble came upon the inhabitants of the Small House, falling upon them as it were in a heap together. It was as yet barely two months since those terrible tidings had come respecting Crosbie; tidings which, it was felt at the time, would of themselves be sufficient to crush them ; and now to that misfortune other misfortunes had been added,—one quick upon the heels of another. In the teeth of the doctor's kind prophecy Lily became very ill, and after a few days was delirious. She would talk to her mother about Crosbie, speaking of him as she used to speak in the autumn that was passed. But even in her madness she remembered that they had resolved to leave their present home ; and she asked the doctor twicje whether their lodgings in Guestwick were ready for them.

It was thus that Crofts first heard of their intention. Now, in these days of Lily's worst illness, he came daily over to Allingtou, remaining there, on one occasion, the whole night. For all this he would take no fee;—nor had he ever taken a fee from Mrs. Dale. " I wish you would not come so often," Bell said to him one evening, as he stood with her at the drawing-room fire, after he had left the patient's room; " you are overloading us with obligations." Oil that day Lily was over the worst of the fever, and he had been able to tell Mrs. Dale that he did not think that she was now in danger.

" It will not be necessary much longer," he said; " the worst of it is over."

1 ' It is such a luxury to hear you say so. I suppose we shall owe her life to you; but nevertheless "

" Oh, no ; scarlatina is not such a terrible thing now as it used to be."

" Then why should you have devoted your time to her as you have done ? It frightens me when I think of the injury we must have done you."

" My horse has felt it more than I have," said the doctor, laughing. " My patients at Guestwick are not so very numerous." Then, instead of going, he sat himself down. " And it is really true," he said, " that you are all going to leave this house ? "

" Quite true. We shall do so at the end of March, if Lily is well enough to he moved."

" Lily will he well long before that, I hope; not, indeed, that she ought to be moved out of her own rooms for many weeks to come yet."

" Unless we are stopped by her we shall certainly go at the end of March." Bell now had also sat down, and they both remained for some time looking at the fire in silence.

" And why is it, Bell ? " he said, at last. " But I don't know whether I have a right to ask."

" You have a right to ask any question about us," she said. " My uncle is very kind. He is more than kind ; he is generous. But he seems to think that our living here gives him a right to interfere with mamma. We don't like that, and, therefore, we are going."

The doctor still sat on one side of the fire, and Bell still sat opposite to him; but the conversation did not form itself very freely between them. " It is bad news," he said, at last.

" At any rate, when we are ill you will not have so far to come and see us."

" Yes, I understand. That means that I am ungracious not to congratulate myself on having you all so much nearer to me ; but I do not in the least. I cannot bear to think of you as living anywhere but here at Allington. Dales will be out of their place in a street at Guestwick."

" That's hard upon the Dales, too."

" It is hard upon them. It's a sort of offshoot from that very tyrannical law of noblesse oblige. I don't think you ought to go away from Allington, unless the circumstances are very imperative."

" But they are very imperative."

" In that case, indeed! " And then again he fell into silence.

" Have you never seen that mamma is not happy here ? " she said, after another pause. " For myself, I never quite understood it all before as I do now ; but now I see it."

" And I have seen it; —have seen at least what you mean. She has led a life of restraint ; but then, how frequently is such restraint the necessity of a life ? I hardly think that your mother would move on that account."

" No. It is on our account. But this restraint, as you call it, makes us unhappy, and she is governed by seeing that. My uncle is generous to her as regards money; but in other things, — in matters of feeling,—I think he has been ungenerous."

"Bell," said the doctor ; and then he paused.

She looked up at him, but made no answer. He had always called her by her Christian name, and they two had ever regarded each other as close friends. At the present moment she had forgotten all else besides this, and yet she had infinite pleasure in sitting there and talking to. him.

"I am going to ask you a question which perhaps I ought not to ask, only that I have known you so long that I almost feel that I am speaking to a sister."

"You may ask me what you please," said she.

"It is about your cousin Bernard."

"About Bernard!" said Bell.

It was now dusk; and as they were sitting without other light than that of the fire, she knew that he could not discern the colour which covered her face as her cousin's name was mentioned. But, had the light of day pervaded the whole room, I doubt whether Crofts would have seen that blush, for he kept his eyes firmly fixed upon the fire.

"Yes, about Bernard ? I don't know whether I ought to ask you."

"I'm sure I can't say," said Bell, speaking words of the nature of which she was not conscious.

"There has been a rumour in Guestwick that he and you "

"It is untrue," said Bell; "quite untrue. If you hear it repeated, you should contradict it. I wonder why people should say such things."

(' It would have been an excellent marriage; — all your friends must have approved it."

"What do you mean, Dr. Crofts ? How I do hate those words, ' an excellent marriage.' In them is contained more of wicked worldliness than any other words that one ever hears spoken. You want me to marry my cousin simply because I should have a great house to live in, and a coach. I know that you are my friend ; but I hate such friendship as that."

"I think you misunderstand me, Bell. I mean that it would have been an excellent marriage, provided you had both loved each other."

"No, I don't misunderstand you. Of course it would be an excellent marriage, if we loved each other. You might say the same if I loved the butcher or the baker. "What you mean is, that it makes a reason for loving him."

"I don't think I did mean that."

"Then you mean nothing."

After that, there were again some minutes of silence during which Dr. Crofts got up to go away. "You have scolded me very dreadfully," he said, with a slight smile, "and I believe I have deserved it for interfering "

"No ; not at all for interfering."

"But at any rate you must forgive me before I go."

"I won't forgive you at all, unless you repent of your sins, and alter altogether the wickedness of your mind. You will become very soon as bad as Dr. Gruffen."

"Shall I ? "

"Oh, but I will forgive you; for after all, you are the most generous man in the world."

"Oh, yes; of course I am. Well,—good-by."

"But, Dr. Crofts, you should not suppose others to be so much more worldly than yourself. You do not care for money so very much "

"But I do care very much."

"If you did, you would not come here for nothing day after day."

"I do care for money very much. I have sometimes nearly broken my heart because I could not get opportunities of earning it. It is the best friend that a man can have "

" Oh, Dr. Crofts ! "

" the best friend that a man can have, if it be honestly

come by. A woman can hardly realize the sorrow which may fall upon a man from the want of such a friend."

" Of course a man likes to earn a decent living by his profession; and you can do that."

" That depends upon one's ideas of decency."

"Ah! mine never ran veiy high. I've always had a sort of aptitude for living in a pigsty ;— a clean pigsty, you know, with nice fresh hean straw to lie upon. I think it was a mistake when they made a lady of me. I do, indeed."

" I do not," said Dr. Crofts.

" That's because you don't quite know me yet. I've not the slightest pleasure in putting on three different dresses a day. I do it very often because it comes to me to do it, from the way in which we have been taught to live. But when we get to Guestwick I mean to change all that; and if you come in to tea, you'll see me in the same brown frock that I wear in the morning,—unless, indeed, the morning work makes the brown frock dirty. Oh, Dr. Crofts ! you'll have it pitch-dark riding home under the Guestwick elms."

" I don't mind the dark," he said; and it seemed as though he hardly intended to go even yet.

" But I do," said Bell, " and I shall ring for candles." But he stopped her as she put her hand out to the bell-pull.

" Stop a moment, Bell. You need hardly have the candles before I go, and you need not begrudge my staying either, seeing that I shall be all alone at home."

" Begrudge your staying ! "

" But, however, you shall begrudge it, or else make me very welcome." He still held her by the wrist, which he had caught as he prevented her from summoning the servant.

" What do you mean ? " said she. " You know you are welcome to us as flowers in May. You always were welcome ; but now, when

you have come to us in our trouble At any rate, you shall never

say that I turn you out."

" Shall I never say so ? " And still he held her by the wrist. He had kept his chair throughout, but she was standing before him,—between him and the fire. But she, though he held her in this way, thought little of his words, or of his action. They had known each other with great intimacy, and though Lily would still laugh at her, saying that Dr. Crofts was her lover, she had long since taught herself that no such feeling as that would ever exist between them.

" Shall I never say so, Bell ? What if so poor a man as I ask for the hand that you will not give to so rich a man as your cousin Bernard ? "

She instantly withdrew her arm and moved back very quickly a

step or two across the rug. She did it almost with the motion which she might have used had he insulted her; or had a man spoken such words who would not, under any circumstances, have a right to speak them.

" Ah, yes ! I thought it would be so," he said. " I may go now, and may know that I have been turned out."

" What is it you mean, Dr. Crofts ? What is it you are saying ? Why do you talk that nonsense, trying to see if you can provoke me?"

" Yes ; it is nonsense. I have no right to address you in that way, and certainly should not have done it now that I am in your house in the way of my profession. I beg your pardon." Now he also was standing, but he had not moved from his side of the fireplace. "Are you going to forgive me before I go?"

" Forgive you for what ? " said she.

" For daring to love you; for having loved you almost as long as you can remember; for loving you better than all beside. This alone you should forgive; but will you forgive me for having told it?"

He had made her no offer, nor did she expect that he was about to make one. She herself had hardly yet realized the meaning of his words, and she certainly had asked herself no question as to the answer which she should give to them. There are cases in which lovers present themselves in so unmistakeable a guise, that the first word of open love uttered by them tells their whole story, and tells it without the possibility of a surprise. And it is generally so when the lover has not been an old friend, when even his acquaintance has been of modern date. It had been so essentially in the case of Crosbie and Lily Dale. When Crosbie came to Lily and made his offer, he did it with perfect ease and thorough self-possession, for he almost knew that it was expected. And Lily, though she had been flurried for a moment, had her answer pat enough. She already loved the man with all her heart, delighted in his presence, basked in the sunshine of his manliness, rejoiced in his wit, and had tuned her ears.to the tone of his voice. It had all been done, and the world expected it. Had he not made his offer, Lily would have been ill-treated;—though, alas, alas, there was future ill-treatment, so much heavier, in store for her! But there are other cases in which a lover cannot make himself known as such without great difficulty, and when he does do so, cannot hope for an immediate answer in his

favour. It is hard upon old friends that this difficulty should usually fall the heaviest upon them. Crofts had been so intimate with the Dale family that very many persons had thought it probable that he would marry one of the girls. Mrs. Dale herself had thought so, and had almost hoped it. Lily had certainly done both. These thoughts and hopes had somewhat faded away, but yet their former existence should have been in the doctor's favour. But now, when he had in some way spoken out, Bell started back from him and would not believe that he was in earnest. She probably loved him better than any man in the world, and yet, when he spoke to her of love, she could not bring herself to understand him.

" I don't know what you mean, Dr. Crofts; indeed I do not," she said.

" I had meant to ask you to be my wife ; simply that. But you shall not have the pain of making me a positive refusal. As I rode here to-day I thought of it. During my frequent rides of late I have thought of little else. But I told myself that I had no right to do it. I have not even a house in which it would be fit that you should live."

" Dr. Crofts, if I loved you,—if I wished to marry you "

and then she stopped herself.

" But you do not ? "

" No; I think not. I suppose not. No. But in any way no consideration about money has anything to do with it."

" But I am not that butcher or that baker whom you could love ? "

" No," said Bell; and then she stopped herself from further speech, not as intending to convey all her answer in that one word, but as not knowing how to fashion any further words.

" I knew it would be so," said the doctor.

It will, I fear, be thought by those who condescend to criticize this lover's conduct and his mode of carrying on his suit, that he was very unfit for such work. Ladies will say that he wanted courage, and men will say that he wanted wit. I am inclined, however, to believe that he behaved as well as men generally do behave on such occasions, and that he showed himself to be a good average lover. There is your bold lover, who knocks his lady-love over as he does a bird, and who would anathematize himself all over, and swear that his gun was distraught, and look about as though he thought the world was coming to an end, if he missed to knock over liis bird. And there is your timid lover, who winks his eyes when he fires, who has felt certain from the moment in which he buttoned on his knickerbockers that he at any rate would kill nothing, and who, when he hears the loud congratulations of his friends, cannot believe that he really did bag that beautiful winged thing by his own prowess. The beautiful winged thing which the timid man carries home in his bosom, declining to have it thrown into a miscellaneous cart, so that it may never be lost in a common crowd of game, is better to him than are the slaughtered hecatombs to those who kill their birds by the hundred.

But Dr. Crofts had so winked his eye, that he was not in the least aware whether he had winged his bird or no. Indeed, having no one at hand to congratulate him, he was quite sure that the bird had flown away uninjured into the next field. "No" was the only word which Bell had given in answer to his last sidelong question, and No is not a comfortable word to lovers. But there had been that in Bell's No which might have taught him that the bird was not escaping without a wound, if he had still had any of his wits about him.

"Now I will go," said he. Then he paused for an answer, but none came. "And you will understand what I meant when I spoke of being turned out."

"Nobody—turns you out." And Bell, as she spoke, had almost descended to a sob.

"It is time, at any rate, that I should go; is it not? And, Bell, don't suppose that this little scene will keep me away from your sister's bedside. I shall be here to-morrow, and you will find that you will hardly know me again for the same person." Then in the dark he put out his hand to her.

"Good-by," she said, giving him her hand. He pressed hers very closely, but she, though she wished to do so, could not bring herself to return the pressure. Her hand remained passive in his, showing no sign of offence; but it was absolutely passive,

"Good-by, dearest friend," he said.

"Good-by," she answered,—and then he was gone.

She waited quite still till she heard the front-door close after him, and then she crept silently up to her own bedroom, and sat herself down in a low rocking-chair over the fire. It was in accordance with a custom already established that her mother should remain with Lily till the tea was ready downstairs; for in these days of illness such dinners as were provided were eaten early. Bell, therefore, knew that she had still some half-hour of her own, during which she might sit and think undisturbed.

And what naturally should have been her first thoughts?—that she had ruthlessly refused a man who, as she now knew, loved her well, and for whom she had always felt at any rate the warmest friendship? Such were not her thoughts, nor were they in any way akin to this. They ran back instantly to years gone by,—over long years, as her few years were counted,—and settled themselves on certain halcyon days, in which she had dreamed that he had loved her, and had fancied that she had loved him. How she had schooled herself for those days since that, and taught herself to know that her thoughts had been over-bold! And now it had all come round. The only man that she had ever liked had loved her. Then there came to her a memory of a certain day, in which she had been almost proud to think that Crosbie had admired her, in which she had almost hoped that it might be so; and as she thought of this she blushed, and struck her foot twice upon the floor. "Dear Lily," she said to herself—"poor Lily!" But the feeling which induced her then to think of her sister had had no relation to that which had first brought Crosbie into her mind.

And this man had loved her through it all,—this priceless, peerless man,—this man who was as true to the backbone as that other man had shown himself to be false; who was as sound as the other man had proved himself to be rotten. A smile came across her face as she sat looking at the fire, thinking of this. A man had loved her, whose love was worth possessing. She hardly remembered whether or no she had refused him or accepted him. She hardly-asked herself what she would do. As to all that it was necessary that she should have many thoughts, but the necessity did not press upon her quite immediately. For the present, at any rate, she might sit and triumph;—and thus triumphant she sat there till the old nurse came in and told her that her mother was waiting for her below.

CHAPTER X. PREPARATIONS FOR THE WEDDING.

THE fourteenth of February was finally settled as the day on which Mr. Croshie was to be made the happiest of men. A later day had been at first named, the twenty-seventh or twenty-eighth haying been suggested as an improvement over the first week in March; but Lady Amelia had been frightened by Crosbie's behaviour on that Sunday evening, and had made the countess understand that there should be no unnecessary delay. " He doesn't scruple at that kind of thing," Lady Amelia had said in one of her letters, showing perhaps less trust in the potency of her own rank than might have been expected from her. The countess, however, had agreed with her, and when Crosbie received from his mother-in-law a very affectionate epistle, setting forth all the reasons which would make the fourteenth so much more convenient a day than the twenty-eighth, he was unable to invent an excuse for not being made happy a fortnight earlier than the time named in the bargain. His first impulse had been against yielding, arising from some feeling which made him think that more than the bargain ought not to be exacted. But what was the use to him of quarrelling ? What the use, at least, of quarrelling just then ? He believed that he could more easily enfranchise himself from the De Courcy tyranny when he should be once married than he could do now. WTien Lady Alexandrina should be his own he would let her know that he intended tq be her master. If in doing so it would be necessary that he should divide himself altogether from the De Courcys, such division should be made. At the present moment he would yield to them, at any rate in this matter. And so the fourteenth of February was fixed for the marriage.

In the second week in January Alexandria came up to look after her things ; or, in more noble language, to fit herself with becoming bridal appanages. As she could not properly do all this work alone, or even under the surveillance and with the assistance of a sister, Lady De Courcy was to come up also. But Alexandrina came first, remaining with her sister in St. John's Wood till the countess should arrive. The countess had never yet condescended to accept of her son-in-law's hospitality, but always went to the cold, comfortless house in Portman Square,—the house which had been the De Courcy town family mansion for many years, and which the countess would long since have willingly exchanged for some abode on the other side of Oxford Street; but the earl had been obdurate; his clubs and certain lodgings which he had occasionally been wont to occupy, were on the right side of Oxford Street; why should he change his old family residence? So the countess was coming up to Portman Square, not having been even asked on this occasion to St. John's Wood.

" Don't you think we'd tetter," Mr. Gazebee had said to his wife, almost trembling at the renewal of his own proposition.

" I think not, my dear," Lady Amelia had answered. " Mamma is not very particular; but there are little things, you know "

" Oh, yes, of course," said Mr. Gazebee; and then the conversation had been dropped. He would most willingly have entertained his august mother-in-law during her visit to the metropolis, and yet her presence in his house would have made him miserable as long as she remained there.

But for a week Alexandrina sojourned under Mr. Gazebee's roof, during which time Crosbie was made happy with all the delights of an expectant bridegroom. Of course he was given to understand that he was to dine at the Gazebees' every day, and spend all his evenings there ; and, under the circumstances, he had no excuse for not doing so. Indeed, at the present moment, his hours would otherwise have hung heavily enough upon his hands. In spite of his bold resolution with reference to his eye, and his intention not to be debarred from the pleasures of society by the marks of the late combat, he had not, since that occurrence, frequented his club very closely ; and though London was now again becoming fairly full, he did not find himself going out so much as had been his wont. The brilliance of his coming marriage did not seem to have added much to his popularity; in fact, the world,—his world,—was beginning to look coldly at him. Therefore that daily attendance at St. John's Wood was not felt to be so irksome as might have been expected.

A residence had been taken for the couple in a very fashionable row of buildings abutting upon the Bayswater-road, called Princess Koyal Crescent. The house was quite new, and the street being unfinished had about it a strong smell of mortar, and a general aspect of builders' poles and brickbats; but nevertheless, it was acknowledged to be a quite correct locality. From one end of the crescent a corner of Hyde Park could be seen, and the other abutted on a very handsome terrace indeed, in which lived an ambassador,— from South America,—a few bankers' senior clerks, and a peer of the realm. We know how vile is the sound of Baker Street, and how absolutely foul to the polite ear is the name of Fitzroy Square. The houses, however, in those purlieus are substantial, warm, and of good size. The house in Princess Royal Crescent was certainly not substantial, for in these days substantially-built houses do not pay. It could hardly have been warm, for, to speak the truth, it was even yet not finished throughout; and as for the size, though the drawing-room was a noble apartment, consisting of a section of the whole house, with a corner cut out for the staircase, it was very much cramped in its other parts, and was made like a cherub, in this respect, that it had no rear belonging to it. " But if you have no private fortune of your own, you cannot have everything," as the countess observed when Crosbie objected to the house because a closet under the kitchen-stairs was to be assigned to him as his own dressing-room.

When the question of the house was first debated Lady Amelia had been anxious that St. John's Wood should be selected as the site, but to this Crosbie had positively objected".

" I think you don't like St. John's Wood," Lady Amelia had said to him somewhat sternly, thinking to awe him into a declaration that he entertained no general enmity to the neighbourhood. But Crosbie was not weak enough for this.

"No; T do not," he said. "I have always disliked it. It amounts to a prejudice, I daresay. But if I were made to live here I am convinced I should cut my throat in the first six months."

Lady Amelia had then drawn herself up, declaring her sorrow that her house should be so hateful to him.

" Oh, dear, no," said he. "I like it very much for you, and VOL. n. 27 enjoy coming here of all things. I speak only of the effect which living here myself would have upon me."

Lady Amelia was quite clever enough to understand it all; but she had her sister's interest at heart, and therefore persevered in her affectionate solicitude for her brother-in-law, giving up that point as to St. John's Wood. Crosbie himself had wished to go to one of the new Pimlico squares down near Vauxhall Bridge and the river, actuated chiefly by consideration of the enormous distance lying between that locality and the northern region in which Lady Amelia lived; but to this Lady Alexandrina had objected strongly. If, indeed, they could have achieved Eaton Square, or a street leading out of Eaton Square,—if they could have crept on to the hem of the skirt of Belgravia,—the bride would have been delighted. And at first she was very nearly being taken in with the idea that such was the proposal made to her. Her geographical knowledge of Pimlico had not been perfect, and she had nearly fallen into a fatal error. But a friend had kindly intervened. "For heaven's sake, my dear, don't let him take you anywhere beyond Eccleston Square ! " had been exclaimed to her in dismay by a faithful married friend. Thus warned, Alexandrina had been firm, and now their tent was to be pitched in Princess Royal Crescent, from one end of which the Hyde Park may be seen.

The furniture had been ordered chiefly under the inspection, and by the experience, of the Lady Amelia. Crosbie had satisfied himself by declaring that she at any rate could get the things cheaper than he could buy them, and that he had no taste for such employment. Nevertheless, he had felt that he was being made subject to tyranny and brought under the thumb of subjection. He could not go cordially into this matter of beds and chairs, and, therefore, at last deputed the whole matter to the De Courcy faction. And for this there was another reason, not hitherto mentioned. Mr. Mortimer Gazebee was finding the money with which all the furniture was being bought. He, with an honest but almost unintelligible zeal for the De Courcy family, had tied up every shilling on which he could lay his hand as belonging to Crosbie, in the interest of Lady Alexandrina. He had gone to work for her, scraping here and arranging there, strapping the new husband down upon the grindstone of his matrimonial settlement, as though the future bread of his, Gazebee's, own children were dependent on the validity of his legal workmanship. And for this he was not to receive a penny, or gain any

advantage, immediate or ulterior. It came from his zeal,—his zeal for the coronet which Lord De Courcy wore. According to his mind an earl and an earl's belongings were entitled to such zeal. It was the theory in which he had been educated, and amounted to a worship which, unconsciously, he practised. Personally, he disliked Lord De Courcy, who ill-treated him. He knew that the earl was a heartless, cruel, bad man. But as an earl he was entitled to an amount of service which no commoner could have commanded from Mr. Gazebee. Mr. Gazebee, having thus tied up all the available funds in favour of Lady Alexandria's seemingly expected widowhood, was himself providing the money with which the new house was to be furnished. " You can pay me a hundred and fifty a year with four per cent, till it is liquidated," he had said to Crosbie; and Crosbie had assented with a grunt. Hitherto, though he had lived in London expensively, and as a man of fashion, he had never owed any one anything. He was now to begin that career of owing. But when a clerk in a public office marries an earl's daughter, he cannot expect to have everything his own way.

Lady Amelia had bought the ordinary furniture—the beds, the stair-carpets, the washing-stands, and the kitchen things. Gazebee had got a bargain of the dinner-table and sideboard. But Lady Alexandrina herself was to come up with reference to the appurtenances of the drawing-room. It was with reference to matters of costume that the countess intended to lend her assistance—matters of costume as to which the bill could not be sent in to Gazebee, and be paid for by him with five per cent, duly charged against the bridegroom. The bridal trousseau must be produced by De Courcy's means, and, therefore, it was necessary that the countess herself should come upon the scene. "I will have no bills, d'ye hear?" snarled the earl, gnashing and snapping upon his words with one specially ugly black tooth. " I won't have any bills about this affair." And yet he made no offer of ready money. It was very necessary under such circumstances that the countess herself should come upon the scene. An ambiguous hint had been conveyed to Mr. Gazebee, during a visit of business which he had lately made to Courcy Castle, that the milliner's bills might as well be pinned on to those of the furniture-makers, the crockery-mongers, and the like. The countess, putting it in her own way, had gently suggested that the fashion of the thing had changed lately, and that such an arrangement was considered to be the proper thing among people who lived

really in the world. But Gazebee was a clear-headed, honest man ; and he knew the countess. He did not think that such an arrangement could be made on the present occasion. "Whereupon the countess pushed her suggestion no further, but made up her mind that she must come up to London herself.

It was pleasant to see the Ladies Amelia and Alexandrina, as they sat within a vast emporium of carpets in Bond Street, asking questions of the four men who were waiting upon them, putting their heads together and whispering, calculating accurately as to extra twopences a yard, and occasioning as much trouble as it was possible for them to give. It was pleasant because they managed their large hoops cleverly among the huge rolls of carpets, because they were enjoying themselves thoroughly, and taking to themselves the homage of the men as clearly their due. But it was not so pleasant to look at Crosbie, who was fidgeting to get away to his office, to whom no power of choosing in the matter was really given, and whom the men regarded as being altogether supernumerary. The ladies had promised to be at the shop by half-past ten, so that Crosbie should reach his office at eleven—or a little after. But it was nearly eleven before they left the Gazebee residence, and it was very evident that half-an-hour among the carpets would be by no means sufficient. It seemed as though miles upon miles of gorgeous colouring were unrolled before them; and then when any pattern was regarded as at all practicable, it was unrolled backwards and forwards till a room was nearly covered by it. Crosbie felt for the men who were hauling about the huge heaps of material; but Lady Amelia sat as composed as though it were her duty to inspect every yard of stuff in the warehouse. " I think we'll look at that one at the bottom again." Then the men went to work and removed a mountain. "No, my dear, that green in the scroll-work won't do. It would fly directly, if any hot water were spilt." The man smiling ineffably, declared that that particular green never flew anywhere. But Lady Amelia paid no attention to him, and the carpet for which the mountain had been removed became part of another mountain.

" That might do," said Alexandrina, gazing upon a magnificent crimson ground through which rivers of yellow meandered, carrying with them in their streams an infinity of blue flowers. And as she spoke she held her head gracefully on one side, and looked down upon the carpet doubtingly. Lady Amelia poked it with her parasol as though to test its durability, and whispered something about

" THAT MTOHT DO."

yellows showing the dirt. Croshie took out his watch and groaned.

1 i It's a superb carpet, my lady, and about the newest thing we have. We put down four hundred and fifty yards of it for the Duchess of South Wales, at Cwddglwlch Castle, only last month. Nobody has had it since, for it has not been in stock." Whereupon Lady Amelia again poked it, and then got up and walked upon it. Lady Alexandrina held her head a little more on one side.

"Five and three?" said Lady Amelia.

"Oh, no, my lady; five and seven; and the cheapest carpet we have in the house. There is twopence a yard more in the colour; there is, indeed."

"And the discount?" asked Lady Amelia.

"Two and a half," my lady.

"Oh dear, no," said Lady Amelia. "I always have five per cent, for immediate payment—

quite immediate, you know." Upon which the man declared the question must be referred to his master. Two and a half was the rule of the house. Crosbie, who had been looking out of the window, said that upon his honour he couldn't wait any longer.

" And what do you think of it, Adolphus ?" asked Alexandrina.

" Think of what?"

" Of the carpet—this one, you know! "

" Oh—what do I think of the carpet ? I don't think I quite like all these yellow bands ; and isn't it too red ? I should have thought something brown with a small pattern would have been better. But, upon my word, I don't much care."

" Of course he doesn't," said Lady Amelia. Then the two ladies put their heads together for another five minutes, and the carpet was chosen—subject to that question of the discount. " And now about the rug," said Lady Amelia. But here Crosbie rebelled, and insisted that he must leave them and go to his office. " You can't want me about the rug," he said. " Well, perhaps not," said Lady Amelia. But it was manifest that Alexandrina did not approve of being thus left by her senior attendant.

The same thing happened in Oxford Street with reference to the chairs and sofas, and Crosbie began to wish that he were settled, even though |he should have to dress himself in the closet below the kitchen-stairs. He was learning to hate the whole household in St. John's Wood, and almost all that belonged to it. He was intro-

duced there to little family economies of which hitherto he had known nothing, and which were disgusting to him, and the necessity for which was especially explained to him. It was to men placed as he was about to place himself that these economies were so vitally essential,—to men who with limited means had to maintain a decorous outward face towards the fashionable world. Ample supplies of butchers' meat and unlimited washing-bills might be very well upon fifteen hundred a year to those who went out but seldom, and who could use the first cab that came to hand when they did go out. But there were certain things that Lady Alexandrina must do, and therefore the strictest household economy became necessary. Would Lily Dale have required the use of a carriage, got up to look as though it were private, at the expense of her husband's beefsteaks and clean shirts ? That question and others of that nature were asked by Crosbie'within his own mind, not unfrequently.

But, nevertheless, he tried to love Alexandrina, or rather to persuade himself that he loved her. If he could only get her away from the De Courcy faction, and especially from the Gazebee branch of it, he would break her of all that. He would teach her to sit triumphantly in a street cab, and to cater for her table with a plentiful hand. Teach her !—at some age over thirty ; and with such careful training as she had already received ! Did he intend to forbid her ever again to see her relations, ever to go to St. John's Wood, or to correspond with the countess and Lady Margaretta? Teach her, indeed ! Had he yet to learn that he could not wash a blackamoor white ? —that he could not have done so even had he himself been well adapted for the attempt, whereas he was in truth nearly as ill adapted as a man might be ? But who could pity him ? Lily, whom he might have had in his bosom, would have been no blackamoor!

Then came the time of Lady De Courcy's visit to town, and Alexandrina moved herself off to Portman Square. There was some apparent comfort in this to Crosbie, for he would thereby be saved from those daily dreary journeys up to the north-west. I may say that he positively hated that windy corner near the church, round which he had to walk in getting to the Gazebee residence, and that he hated the lamp which guided him to the door, and the very door itself. This door stood buried as it were in a wall, and opened on to a narrow passage which ran across a so-called garden, or front yard, containing on each side two iron receptacles for geraniums, painted to look like Palissy ware, and a naked female on a pedestal. No spot in London was, as he thought, so cold as the bit of pavement immediately in front of that door. And there he would be kept five, ten, fifteen minutes, as he declared,—though I believe in niy heart that the time never exceeded three,—while Eichard was putting off the trappings of his work and putting on the trappings of his grandeur.

If people would only have their doors opened to you by such assistance as may come most easily and naturally to the work! I stood lately for some minutes on a Tuesday afternoon at a gallant portal, and as I waxed impatient a pretty maiden came and opened it. She was a pretty maiden, though her hands and face and apron told tales of the fire-grates. " Laws, sir," she said, " the visitors' day is Wednesday ; and if you would come then, there would be the man in livery ! " She took my card with the corner of her apron, and did just as well as the man in livery; but what would have happened to her had her little-speech been overheard by her mistress ?

Crosbie hated the house in St. John's Wood, and therefore the coming of the countess was a relief to him. Portman Square was easily to be reached, and the hospitalities of the countess would not be pressed upon him so strongly as those of the Gazebees. When he first called he was shown into the great family dining-room, which looked out towards the back of the house. The front windows were, of course, closed, as the family was not supposed to be in London. Here he remained in the room for some quarter of an hour, and then the countess descended upon him in all her grandeur. Perhaps he had never before seen her so grand. Her dress was very large, and rustled through the broad doorway, as if demanding even a broader passage. She had on a wonder of a bonnet, and a velvet mantle that was nearly as expansive as her petticoats. She threw her head a little back as she accosted him, and he instantly perceived that he was enveloped in the fumes of an affectionate but somewhat contemptuous patronage. In old days he had liked the countess, because her manner to him had always been flattering. In his intercourse with her he had been able to feel that he gave quite as much as he got, and that the countess was aware of the fact. In all the circumstances of their acquaintance the ascendancy had been with him, and therefore the acquaintance had been a pleasant one. The countess had been a good-natured, agreeable woman, whose rank and position had made her house pleasant to him ; and

therefore lie had consented to shine upon her with such light as he had to give. Why was it that the matter was reversed, now that there was so much stronger a. cause for good feeling between them ? He knew that there was such change, and with hitter internal uphraidings he acknowledged to himself that this woman was getting the mastery over him. As the friend of the countess he had been a great man in her eyes ;—in all her little words and looks she had acknowledged his power; but now, as her son-in-law, he was to become a very little man,—such as was Mortimer Gazebee !

" My dear Adolphus," she said, taking both his hands, " the day is coming very near now; is it not ? "

" Very near, indeed," he said.

" Yes, it is very near. I hope you feel yourself a happy man.,"

" Oh, yes, that's of course."

" It ought to be. Speaking very seriously, I mean that it ought to be a matter of course. She is everything that a man should desire in a wife. I am not alluding now to her rank, though of course you feel what a great advantage she gives you in this respect."

Crosbie muttered something as to his consciousness of having drawn a prize in the lottery ; but he so muttered it as not to convey to the lady's ears a proper sense of his dependent gratitude. "I know of no man more fortunate than you have been," she continued ; " and I hope that my dear girl will find that you are fully aware that it is so. I think that she is looking rather fagged. You have allowed her to do more than was good for her in the way of shopping."

" She has done a good deal, certainly," said Crosbie.

" She is so little used to anything of that kind ! But of course, as things have turned out, it was necessary that she should see to these things herself."

" I rather think she liked it," said Crosbie.

" I believe she will always like doing her duty. We are just going now to Madame Millefranc's, to see some silks;—perhaps you would wish to go with us ?"

Just at this moment Alexandrina came into the room, and looked as though she were in all respects a smaller edition of her mother. They were both well-grown women, with handsome, large figures, and a certain air about them which answered almost for beauty. As to the countess, her face, on close inspection, bore, as it was entitled to do, deep signs of age ; but she so managed her face that any such close inspection was never made ; zftid her general appearance for her time of life was certainly good. Very little more than this could be said in favour of her daughter.

" Oh dear, no, mamma," she said, having heard her mother's last words,. "He's the worst person in a shop in the world. He likes nothing, and dislikes nothing. Do you, Adolphus ? "

" Indeed I do. I like all the cheap things, and dislike all the dear things."

" Then you certainly shall not go with us to Madame Mille-franc's," said Alexandrina.

" It would not matter to him there, you know, my dear," said the countess, thinking perhaps of the suggestion she had lately made to Mr. Gazebee.

On this occasion Crosbie managed to escape, simply promising to return to Portman Square in the evening after dinner. " By-the-by, Adolphus," said the countess, as he handed her into the hired carriage which stood at the door, " I wish you would go to Lambert's, on Ludgate Hill, for me. He has had a bracelet of mine for nearly three months. Do, there's a good creature. Get it if you can, and bring it up this evening."

Crosbie, as he made his way back to his office, swore that he would not do the bidding of the countess. He would not trudge off into the city after her trinkets. But at five o'clock, when he left his office, he did go there. He apologized to himself by saying that he had nothing else to do, and bethought himself that at the present moment his lady mother-in-law's smiles might be more convenient than her frowns. So he went to Lambert's, on Ludgate Hill, and there learned that the bracelet had been sent down to Courcy Castle full two months since.

After that he dined at his club, at Sebright's. He dined alone, sitting by no means in bliss with his half-pint of sherry on the table before him. A man now and then came up and spoke to him, one a few words, and another a few, and two or three congratulated him as to his marriage; but the club was not the same thing to him as it had formerly been. He did not stand in the centre of the rug, speaking indifferently to all or any around him, ready with his joke, and loudly on the alert with the last news of the day. How easy it is to be seen when any man has fallen from his pride of place, though the altitude was ever so small, and the fall ever so slight. Where is the man who can endure such a fall without showing it in his face, in his voice, in his step, and in every motion of every limb ? Crosbie

knew that he had fallen, and showed that he knew it by the manner in which he ate his mutton chop.

At half-past eight he was again in Portman Square, and found the two ladies crowding over a small fire in a small back^drawing-room. The furniture was all covered with brown holland, and the place had about it that cold comfortless feeling which uninhabited rooms always produce. Crosbie, as he had walked from the club up to Portman Square, had indulged in some serious thoughts. The kind of life which he had hitherto led had certainly passed away from him. He could never again be the pet of a club, or indulged as one to whom all good things were to be given without any labour at earning them on his own part. Such for some years had been his good fortune, but such could be his good fortune no longer. Was there anything within his reach which he might take in lieu of that which he had lost ? He might still be victorious at his office, having more capacity for such victory than others around him. But such success alone would hardly suffice for him. Then he considered whether he might not even yet be happy in his own home,—whether Alexandrina, when separated from her mother, might not become such a wife as he could love. Nothing softens a man's feelings so much* as failure, or makes him turn so anxiously to an idea of home as buffetings from those he meets abroad. He had abandoned Lily because his outer world had seemed to him too bright to be deserted. He would endeavour to supply her place with Alexandrina, because his outer world had seemed to him too harsh to be supported. Alas ! alas ! a man cannot so easily repent of his sins, and wash himself white from their stains!

When he entered the room the two ladies were sitting over the fire, as I have stated, and Crosbie could immediately perceive that the spirit of the countess was not serene. In fact there had been a few words between the mother and child on that matter of the trousseau, and Alexandrina had plainly told her mother that if she were to be married at all she would be married with such garments belonging to her as were fitting for an earl's daughter. It was in vain that her mother had explained with many circumlocutional phrases, that the fitness in this respect should be accommodated rather to the plebeian husband than to the noble parent. Alexandrina had been very firm, and had insisted on her rights, giving the countess to understand that if her orders for finery were not complied with, she would return as a spinster to Courcy, and prepare herself for partnership with Rosina.

11 My dear," said the countess, piteously, " you can have no idea of what I shall have to go through with your father. And, of course, you could get all these things afterwards."

" Papa has no right to treat me in such a way. And if he would not give me any money himself, he should have let me have some of my own."

" Ah, my dear, that was Mr. Gazebee's fault."

" I don't care whose fault it was. It certainly was not mine. I won't have him to tell me "—him was intended to signify Adolphus Croshie— " that he had to pay for my wedding-clothes."

" Of course not that, my dear."

" No ; nor yet for the things which I wanted immediately. I'd much rather go and tell him at once that the marriage must be put off."

Alexandrina of course carried her point, the countess reflecting with a maternal devotion equal almost to that of the pelican, that the earl could not do more than kill her. So the things were ordered as Alexandrina chose to order them, and the countess desired that the bills might be sent in to Mr. Gazebee. Much self-devotion had been displayed by the mother, but the mother thought that none had been displayed by the daughter, and therefore she had been very cross with Alexandrina.

Crosbie, taking a chair, sat himself between them, and in a very good-humoured tone explained the little affair of the bracelet. " Your ladyship's memory must have played you false," said he, with a smile.

"My memory is very good," said the countess; "very good indeed. If Twitch got it, and didn't tell me, that was not my fault." Twitch was her ladyship's lady's-maid. Crosbie, seeing how the land lay, said nothing more about the bracelet.

After a minute or two he put out his hand to take that of Alexandrina. They were to be married now in a week or two, and such a sign of love might have been allowed to him, even in the presence of the bride's mother. He did succeed in getting hold of her fingers, but found in them none of the softness of a ^response. "Don't," said Lady Alexandrina, withdrawing her hand; and the tone of her voice as she spoke the word was not sweet to his ears. He remembered at the moment a certain scene which took place one evening at the little bridge at Allington, and Lily's voice, and Lily's words, and Lily's passion, as he caressed her: "Oh, my love, my love, my love !"

" My dear," said the countess, " they know how tired I am. I wonder whether they are going to give us any tea." Whereupon Crosbie rang the bell, and, on resuming his chair, moved it a little farther away from his lady-love. .

Presently the tea was brought to them by the housekeeper's assistant, who did not appear to have made herself very smart for the occasion, and Crosbie thought that he was de trop. This, however, was a mistake on his part. As he had been admitted into the family, such little matters were no longer subject of care. Two or three months since, the countess would have fainted at the idea of such a domestic appearing with a tea-tray before Mr. Crosbie. Now, however, she was utterly indifferent to any such consideration. Crosbie was to be admitted into the family, thereby becoming entitled to certain privileges,—and thereby also becoming subject to certain domestic drawbacks. In Mrs. Dale's little household there had been no rising to grandeur; but then, also, there had never been any bathos of dirt. Of this also Crosbie thought as he sat with his tea in his hand.

He soon, however, got himself away. When he rose to go Alexandrina also rose, and he was permitted to press his nose against her cheekbone by way of a salute.

" Good-night, Adolphus," said the countess, putting out her hand to him. "But stop a minute; I know there is something I want you to do for me. But you will look in as you go to your office to-morrow morning."

CHAPTER XI. DOMESTIC TKOUBLES.

WHEN Crosbie was making his ineffectual inquiry after Lady De Courcy's bracelet at Lambert's, John Eames was in the act of entering Mrs. Roper's front door in Burton Crescent.

"Oh, John, where's Mr. Cradell ? " were the first words which greeted him, and they were spoken by the divine Amelia. Now, in her usual practice of life, Amelia .did not interest herself much as to the whereabouts of Mr. Cradell.

" Where's Caudle ? " said Eames, repeating the question. " Upon my word, I don't know. I walked to the office with him, but I haven't seen him since. We don't sit in the same room, you know."

" John ! " and then she stopped.

" What's up now ? " said John.

" John ! That woman's off and left her husband. As sure as your name's John Eames, that foolish fellow has gone off with her."

" What, Caudle ? I don't believe it."

" She went out of this house at two o'clock in the afternoon, and has never been back since." That, certainly, was only four hours from the present time, and such an absence from home in the middle of the day was but weak evidence on which to charge a married woman with the great sin of running off with a lover. This Amelia felt, and therefore she went on to explain. "He's there upstairs in the drawing-room, the very picture of disconsolateness."

"Who,—Caudle?"

"Lupex is. He's been drinking a little, I'm afraid; but he's very unhappy, indeed. He had an appointment to meet his wife here at four o'clock, and when he came he found her gone. He rushed up into their room, and now he says she has broken open a box he had and taken off all his money."

" But he never had any money."

" He paid mother some the day before yesterday."

" That's just the reason he shouldn't have any to-day."

" She certainly has taken things she wouldn't have taken if she'd merely gone out shopping or anything like that, for I've been up in the room and looked about it. She'd three necklaces. They weren't much account; but she must have them all on, or else have got them in her pocket."

" Caudle has never gone off with her in that way. He may be a fool "

" Oh, he is, you know. I've never seen such a fool about a woman as he has been."

" But he wouldn't be a party to stealing a lot of trumpery trinkets, or taking her husband's money. Indeed, I don't think he has anything to do with it." Then Eames thought over the circumstances of the day, and remembered that he had certainly not seen Cradell since the morning. It was that public servant's practice to saunter into Eames's room in the middle of the day, and there consume bread and cheese and beer,—in spite of an assertion which Johnny had once made as to crumbs of biscuit bathed in ink. But on this special day he had not done so. "I can't think he has been such a fool as that," said Johnny.

" But he has," said Amelia. " It's dinner-time now, and where is he ? Had he any money left, Johnny ? "

So interrogated Eames disclosed a secret confided to him by his friend which no other circumstances would have succeeded in dragging from his breast.

" She borrowed twelve pounds from him about a fortnight since, immediately after quarter-day. And she owed him money, too, before that."

"Oh, what a soft! " exclaimed Amelia; " and he hasn't paid mother a shilling for the last two months ! "

" It was his money, perhaps, that Mrs. Roper got from Lupex the day before yesterday. If so, it comes to the same thing as far as she is concerned, you know."

" And what are we to do now ? " said Amelia, as she went before her lover up-stairs. " Oh, John, what will become of me if ever you serve me in that way ? What should I do if you were to go off with another lady ? "

" Lupex hasn't gone off," said Eames, who hardly knew what to say when the matter was brought before him with so closely personal a reference.

" But it's the same thing," said Amelia. "Hearts is divided. Hearts that have been joined together ought never to be divided; ought they ? " And then she hung upon his arm just as they got to the drawing-room door.

"Hearts and darts are all my eye," said Johnny. "My belief is that a man had better never marry at all. How d'you do, Mr. Lupex ? Is anything the matter ? "

Mr. Lupex was seated on a chair in the middle of the room, and was leaning with his head over the back of it. So despondent was he in his attitude that his head would have fallen off and rolled on to the floor, had it followed the course which its owner seemed to intend that it should take. His hands hung down also along the back legs of the chair, till his fingers almost touched the ground, and altogether his appearance was pendent, drooping, and wobegone. Miss Spruce was seated in one corner of the room, with her hands folded in her lap before her, and Mrs. Roper was standing on the rug with a look of severe virtue on her brow,— of virtue which, to judge by its appearance, was very severe. Nor was its severity intended to be exercised solely against Mrs. Lupex. Mrs. Eoper was becoming very tired of Mr. Lupex also, and would not have been unhappy if he also had run away,—leaving behind him so much of his property as would have paid his bill.

Mr. Lupex did not stir when first addressed by John Eames, but a certain convulsive movement was to be seen on the back of his head, indicating that this new arrival in the drawing-room had produced a fresh accession of agony. The chair, too, quivered under him, and his fingers stretched themselves nearer to the ground and shook themselves.

"Mr. Lupex, we're going to dinner immediately," said Mrs. Eoper. "Mr. Eames, where is your friend, Mr. Cradell?"

"Upon my word I don't know," said Eames.

"But I know," said Lupex, jumping up and standing at his full height, while he knocked down the chair which had lately supported him. "The traitor to domestic bliss! I know. And wherever he is, he has that false woman in his arms. Would he were here!"

And as he expressed the last wish he went through a motion with his hands and arms which seemed intended to signify that if that unfortunate young man were in the company he would pull him in pieces and double him up, and pack him close, and then despatch his remains off, through infinite space, to the Prince of Darkness. "Traitor," he exclaimed, as he finished the process. "False traitor! Foul traitor! And she too!" Then, as he thought of this softer side of the subject, he prepared himself to relapse again on to the chair. Finding it on the ground he had to pick it up. He did pick it up, and once more flung away his head over the back of it, and stretched his finger-nails almost down to the carpet. %

"James," said Mrs. Eoper to her son, who was now in the room, "I think you'd better stay with Mr. Lupex while we are at dinner. Come, Miss Spruce, I'm very sorry that you should be annoyed by this kind of thing."

"It don't hurt me," said Miss Spruce, preparing to leave the room. "I'm only an old woman."

"Annoyed!" said Lupex, raising himself again from his chair, not perhaps altogether disposed to remain upstairs while the dinner, for which it was intended that he should some day pay, was being eaten below. "Annoyed! It is a profound sorrow to me that any lady should be annoyed by my misfortunes. As regards Miss Spruce, I look upon her character with profound veneration."

"You needn't mind me; I'm only an old woman," said Miss Spruce.

"But, by heavens, I do mind!" exclaimed Lupex; and hurrying forward he seized Miss Spruce by the hand. "I shall always regard

age as entitled" But the special privileges which Mr. Lupex would have accorded to age were never made known to the inhabitants of Mrs. Roper's boarding-house, for the door of the room was again opened at this moment, and Mr. Cradell entered.

"Here you are, old fellow, to answer for yourself," said Eames.

Cradell, who had heard something as he came in at the front door, but had not heard that Lupex was in the drawing-room, made a slight start backwards when he saw that gentleman's face. "Upon my word and honour," he began;—but he was able to carry his speech no further. Lupex, dropping the hand of the elderly lady whom he revered, was upon him in an instant, and Cradell was shaking beneath his grasp like an aspen leaf,—or rather not like an

aspen leaf, unless an aspen leaf when shaken is to be seen with its eyes shut, its mouth open, and its tongue hanging out.

"Come, I say," said Eames, stepping forward to his friend's assistance; "this won't do at all, Mr. Lupex. You've been drinking. You'd better wait till to-morrow morning, and speak to Cradell then," "To-morrow morning, viper," shouted Lupex, still holding his prey, but looking back at Eames over his shoulder. Who the viper was had not been clearly indicated. "When will he restore to me my wife? When will he restore to me my honour?"

"Upon-on-on-on my—" It was for the moment in vain that poor Mr. Cradell endeavoured to asseverate his innocence, and to stake his honour upon his own purity as regarded Mrs. Lupex. Lupex still held to his enemy's cravat, though Eames had now got him by the arm, and so far impeded his movements as to hinder him from proceeding to any graver attack.

"Jemima, Jemima, Jemima!" shouted Mrs. Koper. "Run for the police; run for the police!" But Amelia, who had more presence of mind than her mother, stopped Jemima as she was making to one of the front windows. "Keep where you are," said Amelia. "They'll come quiet in a minute or two. And Amelia no doubt was right. Calling for the police when there is a row in the house is like summoning the water-engines when the soot is on fire in the kitchen chimney. In such cases good management will allow the soot to burn itself out, without aid from the water-engines. In the present instance the police were not called in, and I am inclined to think that their presence would not have been advantageous to any of the party.

"Upon-my-honour—I know nothing about her," were the first words which Cradell was able to articulate, when Lupex, under Eames's persuasion, at last relaxed his hold.

Lupex turned round to Miss Spruce with a sardonic grin. "You hear his words,—this enemy to domestic bliss,—Ha, ha! man, tell me whither you have conveyed my wife!"

"If you were to give me the Bank of England I don't know," said Cradell.

"And I'm sure he does not know," said Mrs. Roper, whose suspicions against Cradell were beginning to subside. But as her suspicions subsided, her respect for him decreased. Such was the case also with Miss Spruce, and with Amelia, and with Jemima. They had all thought him to be a great fool for running away with Mrs. Lupex, but now they were beginning to think him a poor creature because he had not done so. Had he committed that active folly he would have been an interesting fool. But now, if, as they all suspected, he knew no more about Mrs. Lupex than they did, he would be a fool without any special interest whatever.

"Of course he doesn't," said Eames.

"No more than I do," said Amelia.

"His very looks show him innocent," said Mrs. Roper.

"Indeed they do," said Miss Spruce.

Lupex turned from one to the other as they thus defended the man whom he suspected, and shook his head at each assertion that was made. "And if he doesn't know who does?" he asked. "Haven't I seen it all for the last three months? Is it reasonable to suppose that a creature such as she, used to domestic comforts all her life, should have gone off in this way, at dinner-time, taking with her my property and all her jewels, and that nobody should have instigated her; nobody assisted her! Is that a story to tell to such a man as me! You may tell it to the marines!" Mr. Lupex, as he made this speech, was walking about the room, and as he finished it he threw his pocket-handkerchief with violence on to the floor. "I know what to do, Mrs. Roper," he said. "I know what steps to take. I shall put the affair into the hands of my lawyer to-morrow morning." Then he picked up his handkerchief and walked down into the dining-room.

"Of course you know nothing about it?" said Eames to his friend, having run upstairs for the purpose of saying a word to him while he washed his hands.

"What,—about Maria? I don't know where she is, if you mean that."

"Of course I mean that. What else should I mean? And what makes you call her Maria?"

"It is wrong. I admit it's wrong. The word will come out, you know."

"Will come out! I'll tell you what it is, old fellow, you'll get yourself into a mess, and all for nothing. That fellow will have you up before the police for stealing his things"

"But, Johnny"

"I know all about it. Of course you have not stolen them, and of course there was nothing to steal. But if you go on calling her Maria you'll find that he'll have a pull on you. Men don't call other men's wives names for nothing."

"Of course we've been friends," said Cradell, who rather liked this view of the matter.

"Yes,— yon have been friends! She's diddled yon out of your money, and that's the beginning and the end of it. And now, if you go on showing off your friendship, you'll be done out of more money. You're making an ass of yourself. That's the long and the short of it."

"And what have you made of yourself with that girl? There are worse asses than I am yet, Master Johnny." Eames, as he had no answer ready to this counter attack, left the room and went downstairs. Cradell soon followed him, and in a few minutes they were all eating their dinner together at Mrs. Roper's hospitable table.

Immediately after dinner Lupex took himself away, and the conversation upstairs became general on the subject of the lady's departure.

"If I was him I'd never ask a question about her, but let her go," said Amelia. :

"Yes; and then have all her bills following you, wherever you went," said Amelia's brother.

"I'd sooner have her bills than herself," said Eames.

"My belief is, that she's been an ill-used woman," said Cradell. "If she had a husband that she could respect and have loved, and all that sort of thing, she would have been a charming woman."

"She's every bit as bad as he is," said Mrs. Roper.

"I can't agree with you, Mrs. Roper," continued the lady's champion. "Perhaps I ought to understand her position better than any one here, and"

"Then that's just what you ought not to do, Mr. Cradell," said Mrs. Roper. And now the lady of the house spoke out her mind with much maternal dignity and with some feminine severity. "That's just what a young man like you has no business to know. What's a married woman like that to you, or you to her; or what have you to do with understanding her position? When you've a wife of your own, if ever you do have one, you'll find you'll have trouble enough then without anybody else interfering with you. Not but what I believe you're innocent as a lamb about Mrs. Lupex; that is, as far as any harm goes. But you've got yourself into all this trouble by meddling, and was like enough to get yourself choked upstairs by that man. And who's to wonder when you go on pretending to be in love with a woman in that way, and she old enough

to be your mother? What would your mamma say if she saw you at it?"

"Ha, ha, ha!" laughed Cradell.

"It's all very well your laughing, but I hate such folly. If I see a young man in love with a young woman, I respect him for it;" and then she looked at Johnny Eames. "I respect him for it,—even though he may now and then do things as he shouldn't. They most of 'em does that. But to see a young man like you, Mr. Cradell, dangling after an old married woman, who doesn't know how to behave herself; and all just because she lets him to do it;—ugh!— an old broomstick with a petticoat on would do just as well! It makes me sick to see it, and that's the truth of it. I don't call it manly; and it ain't manly, is it, Miss Spruce ? "

" Of course I know nothing about it," said the lady to whom the appeal was thus made. " But a young gentleman should keep himself to himself till the time comes for him to speak out,— begging your pardon all the same, Mr. Cradell."

" 1 don't see what a married woman should want with any one after her but her own husband," said Amelia.

" And perhaps not always that," said John Eames.

It was about an hour after this when the front-door bell was rung, and a scream from Jemima announced to them all that some critical moment had arrived. Amelia, jumping up, opened the door, and then the rustle of a woman's dress was heard on the lower stairs. " Oh, laws, ma'am, you have given us sich a turn," said Jemima. " We all thought you was run away."

" It's Mrs. Lupex," said Amelia. And in two minutes more that ill-used lady was in the room.

" Well, my dears," said she, gaily, " I hope nobody has waited dinner."

" No; we didn't wait dinner," said Mrs. Roper, very gravely.

"And where's my Orson? Didn't he dine at home? Mr. Cradell, will you oblige me by taking my shawl ? But perhaps you had better not. People are so censorious ; ain't they, Miss Spruce ? Mr. Eames shall do it'; and everybody knows that that will be quite safe. Won't it, Miss Amelia ? "

" Quite, I should think," said Amelia. And Mrs. Lupex knew that she was not to look for an ally in that quarter on the present occasion. Eames got up to take the shawl, and Mrs. Lupex went on.

" And didn't Orson dine at home ? Perhaps they kept him down

at the theatre. But I've been thinking all day what fun it would be when he thought his bird was flown."

" He did dine at home," said Mrs. Eoper; " and he didn't seem to like it. There wasn't much fun, I can assure you."

" Ah, wasn't there, though ? I believe that man would like to have me tied to his button-hole. I came across a few friends,— lady friends, Mr. Cradell, though two of them had their husbands; so we made a party, and just went down to Hampton Court. So my gentleman has gone again, has he ? That's what I get for gadding about myself, isn't it, Miss Spruce ?"

Mrs. Roper, as she went to bed that night, made up her mind that, whatever might be the cost and trouble of doing so, she would lose no further time in getting rid of her married guests.

CHAPTER XII. LILY'S BEDSIDE.

LILY DALE'S constitution was good, and her recovery was retarded by no relapse or lingering debility ; but, nevertheless, she was forced to keep her bed for many days after the fever had left her. During all this period Dr. Crofts came every day. It was in vain that Mrs. Dale begged him not to do so ; telling him in simple words that she felt herself bound not to accept from him all this continuation of his unremunerated labours now that the absolute necessity for them was over. He answered her only by little jokes, or did not answer her at all; but still he came daily, almost always at the same hour, just as the day was waning, so that he could sit for a quarter of an hour in the dusk, and then ride home to Guestwick in the dark. At this time Bell had been admitted into her sister's room, and she would always meet Dr. Crofts at Lily's bedside; but she never sat with him alone, since the day on which he had offered her his love with half-articulated words, and she had declined it with words also half articulated. She had seen him alone since that, on the stairs, or standing in the hall, but she had not remained with him, talking to him after her old fashion, and no further word of his love had been spoken in speech either half or wholly articulate.

Nor had Bell spoken of what had passed to any one else. Lily would probably have told both her mother and sister instantly ; but then no such scene as that which had taken place with Bell would have been possible with Lily. In whatever way the matter might have gone with her, there would certainly have been some clear tale to tell when the interview was over. She would have known whether or no she loved the man, or could love him, and would have given him some true and intelligible answer. Bell had not done so, but had given him an answer which, if true, was not intelligible, and if intelligible was not true. And yet, when she had gone away to think

over what had passed, she had been happy and satisfied, and almost triumphant. She had never yet asked herself whether she expected anything further from Dr. Crofts, nor what that something further might be,—and yet she was happy!

Lily had now become pert and saucy in her bed, taking upon herself the little airs which are allowed to a convalescent invalid as compensation for previous suffering and restraint. She pretended to much anxiety on the subject of her dinner, and declared that she would go out on such or such a day, let Dr. Crofts be as imperious as he might. " He's an old savage, after all," she said to her sister, one evening, after he was gone, " and just as bad as the rest of them."

" I do not know who the rest of them are," said Bell, " but at any rate he's not very old."

" You know what I mean. He's just as grumpy as Dr. Gruffen, and thinks everybody is to do what he tells them. Of Course, you take his part."

" And of course you ought, seeing how good he has been."

" And of course I should, to anybody but you. I do like to abuse him to you."

"Lily, Lily!"

" So I do. It's so hard to knock any fire out of you, that when one does find the place where the flint lies, one can't help hammering at it. What did he mean by saying that I shouldn't get up on Sunday ? Of course I shall get up if I like it."

" Not if mamma asks you not ? "

" Oh, but she won't, unless he interferes and dictates to her. Oh, Bell, what a tyrant he would be if he were married ! "

" Would he ? "

" And how submissive you would be, if you were his wife ! It's a thousand pities that you are not in love with each other;—that is, if you are not."

" Lily, I thought that there was a promise between us about that."

" Ah! but that was in other days. Things are all altered since that promise was given,—all the world has been altered." And as she said this the tone of her voice was changed, and it had become almost sad. " I feel as though I ought to be allowed now to speak about anything I please."

" You shall, if it pleases you, my pet."

" You see how it is, Bell; I can never again have anything of my own to talk about."

120 THE SMALL HOUSE AT ALLINGTON.

" Oh, my darling, do not say that."

" But it is so, Bell; and why not say it ? Do you think I never say it to myself in the hours when I am all alone, thinking over it— thinking, thinking, thinking. You must not,—you must not grudge to let me talk of it sometimes."

" I will not grudge you anything ;—only I cannot believe that it must be so always."

" Ask yourself, Bell, how it would be with you. But I sometimes fancy that you measure me differently from yourself."

" Indeed I do, for I know how much better you are."

" I am not so much better as to be ever able to forget all that. I know I never shall do so. I have made up my mind about it clearly and with an absolute certainty."

" Lily, Lily, Lily! pray do not say so."

"But I do say it. And yet I have not been very mopish and melancholy; have I, Bell ? I do think I deserve some little credit, and yet, I declare, you won't allow me the least privilege in the world."

" What privilege would you wish me to give you ? "

" To talk about Dr. Crofts."

" Lily, you are a wicked, wicked tyrant." And Bell leaned over her, and fell upon her, and kissed her, hiding her own face in the" gloom of the evening. After that it came to be an accepted understanding between them that Bell was not altogether indifferent to Dr. Crofts."

" You heard what he said, my darling," Mrs. Dale said the next day, as the three were in the room together after Dr. Crofts was gone. Mrs. Dale was standing on one side of the bed, and Bell on the other, while Lily was scolding them both. " You can get up for an hour or two to-morrow, but he thinks you had better not go out of the room.

" What would be the good of that, mamma ? I am so tired of looking always at the same paper. It is such a tiresome paper. It makes one count the pattern over and over again. I wonder how you ever can live here."

" I've got used to it, you see."

" I never can get used to that sort of thing; but go on counting, and counting, and counting. I'll tell you what I should like; and I'm sure it would be the best thing, too."

" And what would you like ? " said Bell.

1 'Just to get up at nine o'clock to-morrow, and go to church as though nothing had happened. Then, when Dr. Crofts came in the evening, you would tell him I was down at the school."

" I wouldn't quite advise that," said Mrs. Dale.

" It would give him such a delightful start. And when he found I didn't die immediately, as of course I ought to do according to rule, he would he so disgusted."

" It would be very ungrateful, to say the least of it," said Bell.

" No, it wouldn't, a bit. He needn't come, unless he likes it. And I don't believe he comes to see me at all. It's all very well, mamma, your looking in that way ; but I'm sure it's true. And I'll tell you what I'll do, I'll pretend to be bad again, otherwise the poor man will be robbed of his only happiness."

" I suppose we must allow her to say what she likes till she gets well," said Mrs. Dale, laughing. It was now nearly dark, and Mrs. Dale did not see that Bell's hand had crept under the bedclothes, and taken hold of that of her sister. " It's true, mamma," continued Lily, " and I defy her to deny it. I would forgive him for keeping me in bed if he would only make her fall in love with him."

" She has made a bargain, mamma," said Bell, " that she is to say whatever she likes till she gets well."

" I am to say whatever I like always ; that was the bargain, and I mean to stand to it."

On the following Sunday Lily did get up, but did not leave her mother's bedroom. There she was, seated in that half-dignified and half-luxurious state which belongs to the first getting up of an invalid, when Dr. Crofts called. There she had eaten her tiny bit of roast mutton, and had called her mother a stingy old creature, because she would not permit another morsel; and there she had drunk her half glass of port wine, pretending that it was very bad, and twice worse than the doctor's physic ; and there, Sunday though it was, she had fully enjoyed the last hour of daylight, reading that exquisite new novel which had just completed itself, amidst the jarring criticisms of the youth and age of the reading public.

" I am quite sure she was right in accepting him, Bell," she said, putting down the book as the light was fading, and beginning to praise the story.

" It was a matter of course," said Bell. " It always is right in the novels. That's why I don't like them. They are too sweet."

" That's why I do like them, because they are so sweet. A sermon is not to tell you what you are, but what you ought to be; and a novel should tell you not what you are to get, but what you'd like to get."

" If so, then, I'd go back to the old school, and have the heroine really a heroine, walking all the way up from Edinburgh to London, and falling among thieves; or else nursing a wounded hero, and describing the battle from the window. We've got tired of that; or else the people who write can't do it now-a-days. But if we are to have real life, let it be real."

"No, Bell, no ! " said Lily. " Real life sometimes is so painful." Then her sister, in a moment, was down on the floor at her feet, kissing her hand and caressing her knees, and praying that the wound might be healed.

On that morning Lily had succeeded in inducing her sister to tell her all that had been said by Dr. Crofts. All that had been said by herself also, Bell had intended to tell; but when she came to this part the story, her account was very lame. " I don't think I said anything," she said. " But silence always gives consent. He'll know that," Lily had rejoined. " No, he will not; my silence didn't give any consent; I'm sure of that. And he didn't think that it did." " But you didn't mean to refuse him ? " "I think I did. I don't think I knew what I meant; and it was safer, therefore, to look no, than to look yes. If I didn't say it, I'm sure I looked it." " But you wouldn't refuse him now ? " asked Lily. "I don't know," said Bell. "It seems as though I should want years to make up my mind ; and he won't ask me again."

Bell was still at her sister's feet, caressing them, and praying with all her heart that that wound might be healed in due time, when Mrs. Dale came in and announced the doctor's daily visit. " Then I'll go," said Bell.

" Indeed you won't," said Lily. " He's coming simply to make a morning call, and nobody need run away. Now, Dr. Crofts, you need not come and stand over me with your watch, for I won't let you touch my hand except to shake hands with me ; " and then she held her hand out to him. "And all you'll know of my tongue you'll learn from the sound."

" I don't care in the least for your tongue."

" I dare say not, and yet you may some of these days. I can speak out, if I like it; can't I, mamma ?"

" I should think Dr. Crofts knows that by this time, my dear."

" I don't know. There are some things gentlemen are very slow to learn. But you must sit down, Dr. Crofts, and make yourself comfortable and polite; for you must understand that you are not master here any longer. I am out of bed now, and your reign is over."

" That's the gratitude of the world, all through," said Mrs. Dale.

" Who is ever grateful to a doctor ? He only cures you that he may triumph over some other doctor, and declare, as he goes by Dr. Gruffen's door, * There, had she called you in, she'd have been dead before now; or else would have been ill for twelve months.' Don't you jump for joy when Dr. Gruffen's patients die ? "

" Of course I do—out in the market-place, so that everybody shall see me," said the doctor.

" Lily, how can you say such shocking things ? " said her sister.

Then the doctor did sit down, and they were all very cosy together over the fire, talking about things which were not medical, or only half medical in their appliance. By degrees the conversation came round to Mrs. Eames and to John Eames. Two or three days since Crofts had told Mrs. Dale of that affair at the railway station, of which up to that time she had heard nothing. Mrs. Dale, when she was assured that young Eames had given Crosbie a tremendous thrashing— the tidings of the affair which had got themselves substantiated at Guestwick so described the nature of the encounter— could not withhold some meed of applause.

" Dear boy! " she said, almost involuntarily. " Dear boy! it came from the honesty of his heart!" And then she gave special injunctions to the doctor—injunctions which were surely unnecessary —that no word of the matter should be whispered before Lily.

" I was at the manor, yesterday," said the doctor, " and the earl would talk about nothing but Master Johnny. He says he's the finest fellow going." Whereupon Mrs. Dale touched him with her foot, fearing that the conversation might be led away in the direction of Johnny's prowess.

"I am so glad," said Lily. " I always knew that they'd find John out at last."

" And Lady Julia is just as fond of him," said the doctor.

" Dear me!" said Lily. " Suppose they were to make up a match!"

" Lily, how can you be so absurd ?"

" Let me see; what relation would lie be to us? He would certainly be Bernard's uncle, and uncle Christopher's half brother-in-law. Wouldn't it be odd ? "

" It would rather," said Mrs. Dale.

" I hope he'll be civil to Bernard. Don't you, Bell ? Is he to give up the Income-tax Office, Dr. Crofts ?"

" I didn't hear that that was settled yet." And so they went on talking about John Eames.

" Joking apart," said Lily, " I am very glad that Lord De Guest has taken him by the hand. Not that I think an earl is better than anybody else, but because it shows that people are beginning to understand that he has got something in him. I always said that they who laughed at John would see him hold up his head yet." All which words sank deep into Mrs. Dale's mind. If only, in some coming time, her pet might be taught to love this new young hero ! But then would not that last heroic deed of his militate most strongly against any possibility of such love !

" And now I may as well be going," said the doctor, rising from his chair. At this time Bell had left the room, but Mrs. Dale was still there.

" You need not be in such a hurry, especially this evening," said Lily.

" Why especially this evening."

" Because it will be the last. Sit down again, Doctor Crofts. I've got a little speech to make to you. I've been preparing it all the morning, and you must give me an opportunity of speaking it."

" I'll come the day after to-morrow, and I'll hear it then."

" But I choose, sir, that you should hear it now. Am I not to be obeyed when I first get up on to my own throne ? Dear, dear Dr. Crofts, how am I to thank you for all that you have done ?"

" How are any of us to thank him ?" said Mrs. Dale.

" I hate thanks," said the doctor. " One kind glance of the eye is worth them all, and I've had many such in this house."

" You have our hearts' love, at any rate," said Mrs. Dale.

" God bless you all!" said he, as he prepared to go.

" But I haven't made my speech yet," said Lily. " And to tell the truth, mamma, you must go away, or I shall never be able to make it. It's very improper, is it not, turning you out, but it shall only take three minutes." Then Mrs. Dale, with some little joking word, left the room; but, as she left it, her mind was hardly at ease.

Ought she to have gone, leaving it to Lily's discretion to say what words she might think fit to Dr. Crofts ? Hitherto she had never doubted her daughters—not even their discretion ; and therefore it had been natural to her to go when she was bidden. But as she went downstairs she had her doubts whether she was right or no.

11 Dr. Crofts," said Lily, as soon as they were alone. " Sit down there, close to me. I want to ask you a question. What was it you said to Bell when you were alone with her the other evening in the parlour ? "

The doctor sal for a moment without answering, and Lily, who was watching him closely, could see by the light of the fire that he had been startled—had almost shuddered as the question was asked him.

" What did I say to her ?" and he repeated her words in a very low voice. " I asked her if she could love me, and be my wife."

" And what answer did she make to you ? "

" What answer did she make ? She simply refused me."

" No, no, no; don't believe her, Dr. Crofts. It was not so;— I think it was not so. Mind you, I can say nothing as coming from her. She has not told me her own mind. But if you really love her, she will be mad to refuse you."

" I do love her, Lily; that at any rate is true."

" Then go to her again. I am speaking for myself now. I cannot afford to lose such a brother as you would be. I love you so dearly that I cannot spare you. And she,—I think she'll learn to love you as you would wish to be loved. You know her nature, how silent she is, and averse to talk about herself. She has confessed nothing to me but this,—that you spoke to her and took her by surprise. Are we to have another chance ? I know how wrong I am to ask such a question. But, after all, is not the truth the best ? "

" Another chance ! "

" I know what you mean, and I think she is worthy to be your wife. I do, indeed; and if so, she must be very worthy. You won't tell of me, will you now, doctor ? "

" No; I won't tell of you."

"And you'll try again?"

"Yes; I'll try again."

" God bless you, my brother! I hope,—I hope you'll be my brother." Then, as he put out his hand to her once more, she

raised her head towards him, and he, stooping down, kissed her forehead. " Make mamma come to me," were the last words she spoke as he went out at the door.

" So you've made your speech," said Mrs. Dale.

" Yes, mamma."

" I hope it was a discreet speech."

" I hope it was, mamma. But it has made me so tired, and I believe I'll go to bed. Do you know I don't think I should have done much good down at the school to-day ? "

Then Mrs. Dale, in her anxiety to repair what injury might have been done to her daughter by over-exertion, omitted any further mention of the farewell speech.

Dr. Crofts as he rode home enjoyed but little of the triumph of a successful lover. " It may be that she's right," he said to himself; " and, at any rate, I'll ask again." Nevertheless, that " No " which Bell had spoken, and had repeated, still sounded in his ears harsh and conclusive. There are men to whom a peal of noes rattling about their ears never takes the sound of a true denial, and others to whom the word once pronounced, be it whispered ever so softly, comes as though it were an unchangeable verdict from the supreme judgment-seat.

CHAPTER XIII. FIE, FIE !

WILL any reader remember the loves,—no, not the .loves; that word is so decidedly ill-applied as to be incapable of awakening the remembrance of any reader; but the flirtations—of Lady Dumbello and Mr. Plantagenet Palliser? Those flirtations, as they had been carried on at Courcy Castle, were laid bare in all their enormities to the eye of the public, and it must be confessed that if the eye of the public was shocked, that eye must be shocked very easily.

But the eye of the public was shocked, and people who were particular as to their morals said very strange things. Lady De Courcy herself said very strange things indeed, shaking her head, and dropping mysterious words; whereas Lady Clandidlem spoke much more openly, declaring her opinion that Lady Dumbello would be off before May. They both agreed that it would not be altogether bad for Lord Dumbello that he should lose his wife, but shook their heads very sadly when they spoke of poor Plantagenet Palliser. As to the lady's fate, that lady whom they had both almost worshipped during the days at Courcy Castle,—they did not seem to trouble themselves about that.

And it must be admitted that Mr. Palliser had been a little imprudent,—imprudent, that is, if he knew anything about the rumours afloat,—seeing that soon after his visit at Courcy Castle he had gone down to Lady Hartletop's place in Shropshire, at which the Dum-bellos intended to spend the winter, and on leaving it had expressed his intention of returning in February. The Hartletop people had pressed him very much,—the pressure having come with peculiar force from Lord Dumbello. Therefore it is reasonable to suppose that the Hartletop people had at any rate not heard of the rumour.

Mr. Plantagenet Palliser spent his Christmas with his uncle, the Duke of Omnium, at Gatherum Castle. That is to say, he reached the castle in time for dinner on Christmas eve, and left it on the morning after Christmas day. This was in accordance with the usual practice of his life, and the tenants, dependants, and followers of the Omnium interest were always delighted to see this manifestation of a healthy English domestic family feeling between the duke and his nephew. But the amount of intercourse on such occasions between them was generally trifling. The duke would smile as he put out his right hand to his nephew, and say,— " Well, Plantagenet,—very busy, I suppose ?" The duke was the only living being who called him Plantagenet to his face, though there were some scores of men whó talked of Planty Pal behind his back. The duke had been the only living being so to call him. Let us hope that it still was so, and that there had arisen no feminine exception, dangerous in its nature and improper in its circumstances.

" Well, Plantagenet," said the duke, on the present occasion, " very busy, I suppose ? "

"Yes, indeed, duke," said Mr. Palliser. "When a man gets the harness on him he does not easily get quit of it."

The duke remembered that his nephew had made almost the same remark at his last

Christmas visit.

"By-the-by," said the duke, "I want to say a word or two to you before you go."

Such a proposition on the duke's part was a great departure from his usual practice, but the nephew of course undertook to obey his uncle's behests.

" I'll see you before dinner to-morrow," said Plantagenet. "Ah, do," said the duke. "I'll not keep you five minutes.'* And at six o'clock on the following afternoon the two were closeted together in the duke's private room.

" I don't suppose there is much in it," began the duke, " but people are talking about you and Lady Dumbello."

" Upon my word, people are very kind." And Mr. Palliser bethought himself of the fact,—for it certainly was a fact,—that people for a great many years had talked about his uncle and Lady Dumbello's mother-in-law.

"Yes; kind enough; are they not? You've just come from Hartlebury, I believe." Hartlebury was the Marquis of Hartletop's seat in Shropshire.

" Ah, I'm sorry for that. Not that I mean, of course, to interfere with your arrangements. You will acknowledge that I have not often clone so, in any matter whatever."

" No; you have not," said the nephew, comforting himself with an inward assurance that no such interference on his uncle's part could have been possible.

"But in this instance it would suit me, and I really think it would suit you too, that you should be as little at Hartlebury as possible. You have said that you would go there, and of course you will go. But if I were you, I would not stay above a day or two."

Mr. Plantagenet Palliser received everything he had in the world from his uncle. He sat in Parliament through his uncle's interest, and received an allowance of ever so many thousand a year which his uncle could stop to-morrow by his mere word. He was his uncle's heir, and the dukedom, with certain entailed properties, must ultimately fall to him, unless his uncle should marry and have a son. But by far the greater portion of the duke's property was unentailed; the duke might probably live for the next twenty years or more ; and it was quite possible that, if offended, he might marry and become a father. It may be said that no man could well be more dependent on another than Plantagenet Palliser was upon his uncle; and it may be said also that no father or uncle ever troubled his heir with less interference. Nevertheless, the nephew immediately felt himself aggrieved by this allusion to his private life, and resolved at once that he would not submit to such surveillance.

" I don't know how long I shall stay," said he ; " but I cannot say that my visit will be influenced one way or the other by such a rumour as that."

" No ; probably not. But it may perhaps be influenced by my request." And the duke, as he spoke, looked a little savage.

" You wouldn't ask me to regard a report that has no foundation."

"I am not asking about its foundation. Nor do I in the least wish to interfere with your manner in life." By which last observation the duke intended his nephew to understand that he was quite at liberty to take away any other gentleman's wife, but that he was not at liberty to give occasion even for a surmise that he wanted to take Lord Dumbello's wife. " The fact is this, Plantagenet. I have for many years been intimate with that family. I have not many intimacies, and shall probably never increase them. Such friends VOL. IT.

as I have, I wish to keep, and you will easily perceive that any such report as that which I have mentioned, might make it unpleasant for me to go to Hartlebury, or for the Hartlehury people to come here." The duke certainly could not have spoken plainer, and Mr. Palliser understood him thoroughly. Two such alliances between the two families could not be expected to run pleasantly together, and even the rumour of any such second alliance might interfere with the pleasantness of the former one.

" That's all," said the duke.

" It's a most absurd slander," said Mr. Palliser.

"I dare say. Those slanders always are absurd; but what can we do ? We can't tie up people's tongues." And the duke looked as though he wished to have the subject considered as finished, and to be left alone.

"But we can disregard them," said the nephew, indiscreetly.

" You may. I have never been able to do so. And yet, I believe, I have not earned for myself the reputation of being subject to the voices of men. You think that I am asking much of you ; but you should remember that hitherto I have given much and have asked nothing. I expect you to oblige me in this matter."

Then Mr. Plantagenet Palliser left the room, knowing that he had been threatened. What the duke had said amounted to this. If you go on dangling after Lady Dumbello, I'll stop the seven thousand a year which I give you. I'll oppose your next return at Silverbridge, and I'll make a will and leave away from you Matching and The Horns, a beautiful little place in Surrey, the use of which had been already offered to Mr. Palliser in the event of his marriage ; all the Littlebury estate in Yorkshire, and the enormous Scotch property. Of my personal goods, and money invested in loans, shares, and funds, you shall never touch a shilling, or the value of a shilling. And, if I find that I can suit myself, it may be that I'll leave you plain Mr. Plantagenet Palliser, with a little first cousin for the head of your family.

The full amount of this threat Mr. Palliser understood, and, as he thought of it, he acknowledged to himself that he had never felt for Lady Dumbello anything like love. No conversation between them had ever been wanner than that of which the reader has seen a sample. Lady Dumbello had been nothing to him. But now,— now that the matter had been put before him in this way, might it not become him, as a gentleman, to fall in love with so very leantifula woman, whose name had already been linked with his own ? We all know that story of the priest, who, hy his question in the confessional, taught the ostler to grease the horses' teeth. " I never did yet," said the ostler, " hut I'll have a try at it." In this case, the duke had acted the part of the priest, and Mr. Palliser, before the night was over, had almost become as ready a pupil as the ostler. As to the threat, it would ill become him, as a Palliser and a Plantagenet to regard it. The duke would not marry. Of all men in the world he was the least likely to spite his own face by cutting off his own nose; and, for the rest of it, Mr. Palliser would take his chance. Therefore he went down to Hartlebury early in February, having fully determined to be very particular in his attentions to Lady Dumbello.

Among a houseful of people at Hartlebury, he found Lord Porlock, a slight, sickly, worn-out looking man, who had something about his eye of his father's hardness, but nothing in his mouth of his father's ferocity.

" So your sister's going to be married ? " said Mr. Palliser.

" Yes. One has no right to be surprised at anything they do, when one remembers the life their father leads them."

"I was going to congratulate you."

"Don't do that."

"I met him at Courcy, and rather liked him."

Mr. Palliser had barely spoken to Mr. Crosbie at Courcy, but then in the usual course of his social life he seldom did more than barely speak to anybody.

"Did you?" said Lord Porlock. "For the poor girl's sake I hope he's not a ruffian. How any man should propose to my father to marry a daughter out of his house, is more than I can understand. How was my mother looking?"

"I didn't see anything amiss about her."

"I expect that he'll murder her some day." Then that conversation came to an end.

Mr. Palliser himself perceived,—as he looked at her he could not but perceive,—that a certain amount of social energy seemed to enliven Lady Dumbello when he approached her. She was given to smile when addressed, but her usual smile was meaningless, almost leaden, and never in any degree flattering to the person to whom it was accorded. Very many women smile as they answer the words which are spoken to them, and most who do so flatter by their smile. The thing is so common that no one thinks of it. The flattering pleases, but means nothing. The impression unconsciously taken simply conveys a feeling that the woman has made herself agreeable, as it was her duty to do,— agreeable, as far as that smile went, in some very infinitesimal degree. But she has thereby made her little contribution to society. She will make the same contribution a hundred times in the same evening. No one knows that she has flattered anybody; she does not know it herself; and the world calls her an agreeable woman. But Lady Dumbello put no flattery into her customary smiles. They were cold, unmeaning, accompanied by no special glance of the eye, and seldom addressed to the individual. They were given to the room at large; and the room at large, acknowledging her great pretensions, accepted them as sufficient. But when Mr. Palliser came near to her she would turn herself slightly, ever so slightly, on her seat, and would allow her eyes to rest for a moment upon his face. Then when he remarked that it had been rather cold, she would smile actually upon him as she acknowledged the truth of his observation. All this Mr. Palliser taught himself to observe, having been instructed by his foolish uncle in that lesson as to the greasing of the horses' teeth.

But, nevertheless, during the first week of his stay at Hartlebury, he did not say a word to her more tender than his observation about the weather. It is true that he was very busy. He had undertaken to speak upon the address, and as Parliament was now about to be opened, and as his speech was to be based upon statistics, be was full of figures and papers. His correspondence was pressing, and the day was seldom long enough for his purposes. He felt that the intimacy to which he aspired was hindered by the laborious routine of his life; but nevertheless he would do something before he left Hartlebury, to show the special nature of his regard. He would say something to her, that should open to her view the secret of—shall we say his heart? Such was his resolve, day after day. And yet day after day went by, and nothing was said. He fancied that Lord Dumbello was somewhat less friendly in his manner than he had been, that he put himself in the way and looked cross; but, as he declared to himself, he cared very little for Lord Dumbello's looks.

"When do you go to town?" he said to her one evening.

"Probably in April. "Ve certainly shall not leave Hartlebury before that."

"Ah, yes. You stay for the hunting."

"Yes; Lord Dumbello always remains here through March. He may run up to town for a day or two."

"How comfortable! I must be in London on Thursday, you know."

"When Parliament meets, I suppose?"

"Exactly. It is such a bore; but one has to do it."

"When a man makes a business of it, I suppose he must."

"Oh, dear, yes; it's quite imperative." Then Mr. Palliser looked round the room, and thought he saw Lord Dumbello's eye fixed upon him. It was really very hard work. If the truth must be told, he did not know how to begin. What was he to say to her? How was he to commence a conversation that should end by being tender? She was very handsome certainly, and for him she could look interesting; but for his very life he did not know how to begin to say anything special to her. A liaison with such a woman as Lady Dumbello,—platonic, innocent, but nevertheless very intimate,— would certainly lend a grace to his life, which, under its present circumstances, t was rather dry. He was told,—told by public rumour which had reached him through his uncle,—that the lady was willing. She certainly looked as though she liked him; but how was he to begin? The art of startling the House of Commons and frightening the British public by the voluminous accuracy of his statistics he had already learned; but what was he to say to a pretty woman?"

"You'll be sure to be in London in April?"

This was on another occasion.

"Oh, yes; I think so."

"In Carlton Gardens, I suppose."

"Yes; Lord Dumbello has got a lease of the house now."

"Has he, indeed? Ah, it's an excellent house. I hope I shall be allowed to call there sometimes."

"Certainly,—only I know you must be so busy."

"Not on Saturdays and Sundays."

"I always receive on Sundays," said Lady Dumbello. Mr. Palliser felt that there was nothing peculiarly gracious in this. A permission to call when all her other acquaintances would be there, was not much; but still, perhaps, it was as much as he could expect to obtain on that occasion. He looked up and saw that Lord Dumbello's eyes were again upon him, and that Lord Dumbello's brow was black. He began to doubt whether a country house, where all the people were thrown together, was the best place in the world for such manoeuvring. Lady Dumbello was very handsome, and he liked to look at her, but he could not find any subject on which to interest her in that drawing-room at Hartlebury. Later in the evening he found himself saying something to her about the sugar duties, and then he knew that he had better give it up. He had only one day more, and that was required imperatively for his speech. The matter would go much easier in London, and he would postpone It till then. In the crowded rooms of London private conversation would be much easier, and Lord Dumbello wouldn't stand over and look at him. Lady Dumbello had taken his remarks about the sugar very kindly, and had asked for a definition of an ad valorem duty. It was a nearer approach to a real conversation than he had ever before made; but the subject had been unlucky, and could not, in his hands, be brought round to anything tender; so he resolved to postpone his gallantry till the London spring should make it easy, and felt as he did so, that he was relieved for the time from a heavy weight.

"Good-by, Lady Dumbello," he said, on the next evening. "I start early to-morrow morning."

"Good-by, Mr. Palliser."

As she spoke she smiled ever so sweetly, but she certainly had not learned to call bim Plantagenet as yet. He went up to London and immediately got himself to work. The accurate and voluminous speech came off with considerable credit to himself,—credit of that quiet, enduring kind which is accorded to such men. The speech was respectable, dull, and correct. Men listened to it, or sat with their hats over their eyes, asleep, pretending to do so; and the Daily Jupiter in the morning had a leading article about it, which, however, left the reader at its close altogether in doubt whether Mr. Palliser might be supposed to be a great financial pundit or no. Mr. Palliser might become a shining light to the moneyed world, and a glory to the banking interests ; he might be a future Chancellor of the Exchequer. But then again, it might turn out that, in these affairs, he was a mere ignis fatuus, a blind guide,—a man to be laid aside as very respectable, but of no depth. Who, then, at the present time, could judiciously risk his credit by declaring whether Mr. Palliser understood his subject or did not understand it ? We are not content in looking to our newspapers for all the information that earth and human intellect can afford; but we demand from them

what we might demand if a daily sheet could come to us from the world of spirits. The result, of course, is this,—that the papers do pretend that they have come daily from the world of spirits ; but the oracles are very doubtful, as were those of old.

Plantagenet Palliser, though he was contented with this article, felt, as he sat in his chambers in the Albany, that something else was wanting to his happiness. This sort of life was all very well. Ambition was a grand thing, and it became him, as a Palliser and a future peer, to make politics his profession. But might he not spare an hour or two for Amaryllis in the shade ? Was it not hard, this life of his ? Since he had been told that Lady Dumbello smiled upon him, he had certainly thought more about her smiles than had been good for his statistics. It seemed as though a new vein in his body ha^d been brought into use, and that blood was running where blood had never run before. If he had seen Lady Dumbello before Dumbello had seen her, might he not have married her ? Ah! in such case as that, had she been simply Miss Grantly, or Lady Griselda Grantly, as the case might have been, he thought he might have been able to speak to her with more ease. As it was, he certainly had found the task dinicult, down in the country, though he had heard of men of his class doing the same sort of thing all his life. For my own part, I believe, that the reputed sinners are much more numerous than the sinners.

As he sat there, a certain Mr. Fothergill came in upon him. Mr. Fothergill was a gentleman who managed most of his uncle's ordinary affairs,—a clever fellow, who knew on which side his bread was buttered. Mr. Fothergill was naturally anxious to stand well with the heir; but to stand well with the owner was his business in life, and with that business he never allowed anything to interfere. On this occasion Mr. Fothergill was very civil, complimenting his future possible patron on his very powerful speech, and predicting for him political power with much more certainty than the newspapers which had, or had not, come from the world of spirits. Mr. Fothergill had come in to say a word or two about some matter of business. As all Mr. Palliser's money passed through Mr. Fothergill's hands, and as his electioneering interests were managed by Mr. Fothergill, Mr. Fothergill not unfrequently called to say a necessary word or two. "When this was done he said another word or two, which might be necessary or not, as the case might be.

" Mr. Palliser," said he, " I wonder you don't think of marrying, I hope you'll excuse me."

Mr. Palliser was by no means sure that he would excuse him, and sat himself suddenly upright in his chair in a manner that was intended to exhibit a first symptom of outraged dignity. But, singularly enough, he had himself been thinking of marriage at that moment. How would it have been with him had he known the beautiful Griselda before the Dumbello alliance had been arranged ? Would he have married her ? Would he have been comfortable if he had married her ? Of course he could not marry now, seeing that he was in love with Lady Dumbello, and that the lady in question, unfortunately, had a husband of her own; but though he had been thinking of marrying, he did not like to have the subject thus roughly thrust before his eyes, and, as it were, into his very lap by his uncle's agent. Mr. Fothergill, no doubt, saw the first symptom of outraged dignity, for he was a clever, sharp man. But, perhaps, lie did not in truth much regard it. Perhaps he had received instructions which he was bound to regard above all other matters.

" I hope you'll excuse me, Mr. Palliser, I do, indeed; but I say it because I am half afraid of some,—some,—some diminution of good feeling, perhaps, I had better call it, between you and your uncle. Anything of that kind would be such a monstrous pity."

" I ana not aware of any such probability."

This Mr. Palliser said with considerable dignity; but when the words were spoken he bethought himself whether he had not told a fib.

" No ; perhaps not. I trust there is no such probability. But the duke is a very determined man if he takes anything into his head ;and then he has so much in his power."

" He has not me in his power, Mr. Fothergill."

" No, no, no. One man does not have another in his power in this country,not in that way; but then you know, Mr. Palliser, it would hardly do to offend him ; would it ? "

" I would rather not offend him, as is natural. Indeed, I do not wish to offend any one."

" Exactly so; and least of all the duke, who has the whole property in his own hands. We may say the whole, for he can marry to-morrow if he pleases. And then his life is so good. I don't know a stouter man of his age, anywhere."

" I'm very glad to hear it."

" I'm sure you are, Mr. Palliser. But if lie were to take offence, you know ? "

" I should put up with it."

" Yes, exactly; that's what you would do. But it would be worth while to avoid it, seeing how much he has in his power."

" Has the duke sent you to me now, Mr. Fothergill ? "

" No, no, no, nothing of the sort. But he dropped words the other day which made me fancy that he was not quite,quite, quite at ease about you. I have long known that he would be very glad indeed to see an heir born to the property. The other mom-ing,I don't know whether there was anything in it, but I fancied he was going to make some change in the present arrangements. He did not do it, and it might have been fancy. Only think, Mr. Palliser, what one word of his might do ! If he says a word, he never goes back from it." Then, having said so much, Mr. Fothergill went his way.

Mr. Palliser understood the meaning of all this very well. It was not the first occasion on which Mr. Fothergill had given him advice,—advice such as Mr. Fothergill himself had no right to give him. He always received such counsel with an air of half-injured dignity, intending thereby to explain to Mr. Fothergill that he was intruding. But he knew well whence the advice came ; and though, in all such cases, he had made up his mind not to follow such counsel, it had generally come to pass that Mr. Palliser's conduct had more or less accurately conformed itself to Mr. Fothergill's advice. A word from the duke might certainly do a great deal! Mr. Palliser resolved that in that affair of Lady Durnbello he would follow his own devices. But, nevertheless, it was undoubtedly true that a word from the duke might do a great deal!

We, who are in the secret, know how far Mr. Palliser had already progressed in his iniquitous passion before he left Hartlebury. Others, who were perhaps not so well informed, gave him credit for a much more advanced success. Lady Clandidlem, in her letter to Lady De Courcy, written immediately after the departure of Mr. Palliser, declared that, having heard of that gentleman's intended matutinal departure, she had confidently expected to learn at the breakfast-table that Lady Dumbello had flown with him. From the tone of her ladyship's language, it seemed as though she had been robbed of an anticipated pleasure by Lady Dumbello's prolonged sojourn in the

halls of her husband's ancestors. " I feel, however, quite convinced," said Lady Clandidlem, " that it cannot go on longer than the spring. I never yet saw a man so infatuated as Mr. Palliser. He did not leave her for one moment all the time he was here. No one but Lady Hartletop would have permitted it. But, you know, there is nothing so pleasant as good old family friendships."

CHAPTER XIV. VALENTINE'S DAY AT ALLINGTON.

LILY had exacted a promise from her mother before her illness, and during the period of her convalescence often referred to it, reminding her mother that that promise had been made, and must be kept. Lily was to be told the day on which Crosbie was to be married. It had come to the knowledge of them all that the marriage was to take place in February. But this was not sufficient for Lily. She must know the day.

And as the time drew nearer,—Lily becoming stronger the while, and less subject to medical authority,—the marriage of Crosbie and Alexandrina was spoken of much more frequently at the Small House. It was not a subject which Mrs. Dale or Bell would have chosen for conversation; but Lily would refer to it. She would begin by doing so almost in a drolling strain, alluding to herself as a forlorn damsel in a play-book; and then she would go on to speak of his interests as a matter which was still of great moment to her. But in the course of such talking she would too often break down, showing by some sad word or melancholy tone how great was the burden on her heart. Mrs. Dale and Bell would willingly have avoided the subject, but Lily would not have it avoided. For them it was a very difficult matter on which to speak in her hearing. It was not permitted to them to say a word of abuse against Crosbie, as to whom they thought that no word of condemnation could be sufficiently severe ; and they were forced to listen to such excuses for his conduct as Lily chose to manufacture, never daring to point out how vain those excuses were.

Indeed, in those days Lily reigned as a queen at the Small House. Ill-usage and illness together falling into her hands had given her such power, that none of the other women were able to withstand it. Nothing was said about it; but it was understood by them all, Jane

and the cook included, that Lily was for the time paramount. She was a dear, gracious, loving, brave queen, and no one was anxious to rebel;—only that those praises of Crosbie were so very bitter in the ears of her subjects. The day was named soon enough, and the tidings came down to Allington. On the fourteenth of February, Crosbie was to be made a happy man. This was not known to the Dales till the twelfth, and they would willingly have spared the knowledge then, had it been possible to spare it. But it was not so, and on that evening Lily was told.

During these days, Bell used to see her uncle daily. Her visits were made with the pretence of taking to him information as to Lily's health; but there was perhaps at the bottom of them a feeling that, as the family intended to leave the Small House at the end of March, it would be well to let the squire know that there was no enmity in their hearts against him. Nothing more had been said about their moving,—nothing, that is, from them to him. But the matter was going on, and he knew it. Dr. Crofts was already in treaty on their behalf for a small furnished house at Guestwick. The squire was very sad about it,— very sad indeed. When Hopkins spoke to him on the subject, he sharply desired that faithful gardener to hold his tongue, giving it to be understood that such things were not to be made matter of talk by the Allington dependants till they had been officially announced. With Bell during these visits he never alluded to the matter. She was the chief sinner, in that she had refused to marry her cousin, and had declined even to listen to rational counsel upon the matter. But the squire felt that he could not discuss the subject with her, seeing that he had been specially informed by Mrs. Dale that his interference would not be permitted ; and then he was perhaps aware that if he did discuss the subject with Bell, ho would not gain much by such discussion. Their conversation, therefore, generally fell upon Crosbie, and the tone in which he was mentioned in the Great House was very different from that assumed in Lily's presence.

" He'll be a wretched man," said the squire, when he told Bell of the day that had been fixed.

" I don't want him to be wretched," said Bell. " But I can hardly think that he can act as he has done without being punished."

" He will be a wretched man. He gets no fortune with her, and she will expect everything that fortune can give. I believe, too, that she is older than he is. I cannot understand it. Upon my word, I

cannot understand how a man can be such a knave and such a fool. Give my love to Lily. I'll see her to-morrow or the next day. She's well rid of him; I'm sure of that;—though I suppose it would not do to tell her so."

The morning of the fourteenth came upon them at the Small House, as conies the morning of those special days which have been long considered, and which are to be long remembered. It brought with it a hard, bitter frost, a black, biting frost, such a frost as breaks the water-pipes, and binds the ground to the hardness of granite. Lily, queen as she was, had not yet been allowed to go back to her own chamber, but occupied the larger bed in her mother's room, her mother sleeping on a smaller one.

" Mamma," she said, " how cold they'll be ! " Her mother had announced to her the fact of the black frost, and these were the first words she spoke.

" I fear their hearts will be cold also," said Mrs. Dale. She ought not to have said so. She was transgressing the acknowledged rule of the house in saying any word that could be construed as being inimical to Crosbie or his bride. But her feeling on the matter was too strong, and she could not restrain herself.

"Why should their hearts be cold? Oh, mamma, that is a terrible thing to say. Why should their hearts be cold ? "

" I hope it may not be so."

" Of course you do ; of course we all hope it. He was not cold-hearted, at any rate. A man is not cold-hearted, because he does not know himself. Mamma, I want you to wish for their happiness."

Mrs. Dale was silent for a minute or two before she answered this, but then she did answer it. "I think I do," said she. " I think I do wish for it."

" I am very sure that I do," said Lily.

At this time Lily had her breakfast upstairs, but went down into the drawing-room in the course of the morning.

" You must be very careful in wrapping yourself as you go downstairs," said Bell, who stood by the tray on which she had brought up the toast and tea. " The cold is what you would call awful."

" I should call it jolly," said Lily, " if I could get up and go out. Do you remember lecturing me about talking slang the day that he first came ? "

"Did I, my pet?"

"Don't you remember, when I called him a swell? Ah, dear! so he was. That was the mistake, and it was all my own fault, as I had seen it from the first."

Bell for a moment turned her face away, and beat with her foot against the ground. Her anger was more difficult of restraint than was even her mother's, and now, not restraining it, but wishing to hide it, she gave it vent in- this way.

"I understand, Bell. I know what your foot means when it goes in that way; and you shan't do it. Come here, Bell, and let me teach you Christianity. I'm a fine sort of teacher, am I not? And I did not quite mean that."

"I wish I could learn it from some one," said Bell. "There are circumstances in which what we call Christianity seems to me to be hardly possible."

"When your foot goes in that way it is a very unchristian foot, and you ought to keep it still. It means anger against him, because he discovered before it was too late that he would not be happy,— that is, that he and I would not be happy together if we were married."

"Don't scrutinize my foot too closely, Lily."

"But your foot must bear scrutiny, and your eyes, and your voice. He was very foolish to fall in love with me. And so was I very foolish to let him love me, at a moment's notice,—without a thought as it were. I was so proud of having him, that I gave myself up to him all at once, without giving him a chance of thinking of it. In a week or two it was done. Who could expect that such an engagement should be lasting?"

"And why not? That is nonsense, Lily. But we will not talk about it."

"Ah, but I want to talk about it. It was as I have said, and if so, you shouldn't hate him because he did the only thing which he honestly could do when he found out his mistake."

"What; become engaged again within a week!"

"There had been a very old friendship, Bell; you must remember that. But I was speaking of his conduct to me, and not of his conduct to" And then she remembered that that other lady might at this very moment possess the name which she had once been so proud to think that she would bear herself. "Bell," she said, stopping her other speech suddenly, "at what o'clock do people get married in London?"

"Oh, at all manner of hours,—any time before twelve. They will be fashionable, and will be married late."

"You don't think she's Mrs. Crosbie yet, then?"

"Lady Alexandrina Crosbie," said Bell, shuddering.

"Yes, of course; I forgot. I should so like to see her. I feel such an interest about her. I wonder what coloured hair she has. I suppose she is a sort of Juno of a woman,—very tall and handsome. I'm sure she has not got a pug-nose like me. Do you know what I should really like, only of course it's not possible;—to be godmother to his first child."

"Oh, Lily!"

"I should. Don't you hear me say that I know it's not possible? I'm not going up to London to ask her. She'll have all manner of grandees for her godfathers and godmothers. I wonder what those grand people are really like."

"I don't think there's any difference. Look at Lady Julia."

"Oh, she's not a grand person. It isn't merely having a title. Don't you remember that he told us that Mr. Palliser is about the grandest grandee of them all. I suppose people do learn to like them. He always used to say that he had been so long among people of that sort, that it would be very difficult for him to divide himself off from them. I should never have done for that kind of thing; should I?"

" There is nothing I despise so much as what you call that kind of thing."

" Do you ? I don't. After all, think how much work they do. He used to tell me of that. They have all the governing in their hands, and get very little money for doing it."

" Worse luck for the country."

" The country seems to do pretty well. But you're a radical, Bell. My belief is, you wouldn't be a lady if you could help it."

" I'd sooner be an honest woman."

"And so you are,—my own dear, dearest, honest Bell,—and the fairest lady that I know. If I were a man, Bell, you are just the girl that I should worship."

" But you are not a man ; so it's no good."

" But you mustn't let your foot go astray in that way; you mustn't, indeed. Somebody said, that whatever is, is right, and I declare I believe it."

" I'm sometimes inclined to think, that whatever is, is wrong."

" That's because you're a radical. I think I'll get up now, Bell ; only it's so frightfully cold that I'm afraid."

" There's a beautiful fire," said Bell.

" Yes ; I see. But the fire won't go all around me, like the bed does. I wish I could know the very moment when they're at the altar. It's only half-past ten yet."

" I shouldn't be at all surprised if it's over."

" Over! What a word that is ! A thing like that is over, and then all the world cannot put it back again. "What if he should be unhappy after all ? "

" He must take his chance," said Bell, thinking within her own mind that that chance would be a very bad one.

" Of course he must take his chance. Well,—I'll get up now." And then she took her first step out into the cold world beyond her bed. " We must all take our chance. I have made up my mind that it will be at half-past eleven."

When half-past eleven came, she was seated in a large easy chair over the drawing-room fire, with a little table by her side, on which a novel was lying. She had not opened her book that morning, and had been sitting for some time perfectly silent, with her eyes closed, and her watch in her hand.

" Mamma," she said at last, " it is over now, I'm sure."

" What is over, my dear ? "

" He has made that lady his wife. I hope God will bless them, and I pray that they may be happy." As she spoke these words, there was an unwonted solemnity in her tone which startled Mrs. Dale and Bell.

" I also will hope so," said Mrs. Dale. " And now, Lily, will it not be well that you should turn your mind away from the subject, and endeavour to think of other things ? "

" But I can't, mamma. It is so easy to say that; but people can't choose their own thoughts."

"They can usually direct them as they will, if they make the effort."

" But I can't make the effort. Indeed, I don't know why I should. It seems natural to me to think about him, and I don't suppose it can be very wrong. When you have had so deep an interest in a person, you can't drop him all of a sudden." Then there was again silence, and after a while Lily took up her novel. She made that effort of which her mother had spoken, but she made it altogether in vain. " I declare, Bell," she said, " it's the greatest rubbish I ever attempted to read." This was specially ungrateful, because Bell had recommended the book. " All the books have got to be so stupid ! I think I'll read Pilgrim's Progress again."

" What do you say to Robinson Crusoe ? " said Bell.

" Or Paul and Virginia ? " said Lily. "But I believe I'll have Pilgrim's Progress. I never can understand it, but I rather think that makes it nicer."

" I hate books I can't understand," said Bell. " I like a book to be clear as running water, so that the whole meaning may be seen at once."

" The quick seeing of the meaning must depend a little on the reader, must it not ? " said Mrs. Dale.

" The reader mustn't be a fool, of course," said Bell.

"But then so many readers are fools," said Lily. "And yet they get something out of their reading. Mrs. Crump is always poring over the Revelations, and nearly knows them by heart. I don't think she could interpret a single image, but she has a hazy, misty idea of the truth. That's why she likes it,—because it's too beautiful to be understood; and that's why I like Pilgrim's Progress." After which Bell offered to get the book in question.

" No, not now," said Lily. " I'll go on with this, as you say it's so grand. The personages are always in their tantrums, and go on as though they were mad. Mamma, do you know where they're going for the honeymoon ? "

" No, my dear."

" He used to talk to me about going to the lakes." And then there was another pause, during which Bell observed that her mother's face became clouded with anxiety. " But I won't think of it any more," continued Lily; " I will fix my mind to something." And then she got up from her chair. " I don't think it would have been so difficult if I had not been ill ? "

" Of course it would not, my darling."

" And I'm going to be well again now, immediately. Let me see: I was told to read Carlyle's History of the French Revolution, and I think I'll begin now." It was Crosbie who had told her to read the book, as both Bell and Mrs. Dale were well aware. " But I must put it off till I can get it down from the other house."

" Jane shall fetch it, if you really want it," said Mrs. Dale.

" Bell shall get it, when she goes up in the afternoon; will you, Bell ? And I'll try to get on with this stuff in the meantime." Then again she sat with her eyes fixed upon the pages of the hook. " I'll tell you what, mamma,—you may have some comfort in this: that when to-day's gone by, I shan't make a fuss ahout any other day."

" Nohody thinks that you are making a fuss, Lily."

" Yes, hut I am. Isn't it odd, Bell, that it should take place on Valentine's day ? I wonder whether it was so settled on purpose, because of the day. Oh, dear, I used to think so often of the letter that I should get from him on this day, when he would tell me that I was his valentine. Well; he's got another—valen—tine—now." So much she said with articulate voice, and then she broke down, bursting out into convulsive sobs, and crying in her mother's arms as though she would break her heart. And yet her heart was not broken, and she was still strong in that resolve which she had made, that her grief should not overpower her. As she had herself said, the thing would not have been so difficult, had she not been weakened by illness.

" Lily, my darling ; my poor, ill-used darling."

" No, mamma, I won't be that." And she struggled grievously to get the better of the hysterical attack which had overpowered her. "I won't be regarded as ill-used; not as specially ill-used. But I am your darling, your own darling. Only I wish you'd beat me and thump me when I'm such a fool, instead of pitying me. It's a great mistake being soft to people when they make fools of themselves. There, Bell; there's your stupid book, and I won't have any more of it. I believe it was that that did it." And she pushed the book away from her.

After this little scene she said no further word about Crosbie and his bride on that day, but turned the conversation towards the prospect of their new house at Guestwick. «

"It will be a great comfort to be nearer Dr. Crofts; won't it, Bell?"

" I don't know," said Bell.

" Because if we are ill, he won't have such a terrible distance to come ? "

" That will be a comfort for him, I should think," said Bell, very demurely.

In the evening the first volume of the French Revolution had been procured, and Lily stuck to her reading with laudable per-

severance ; till at eight her mother insisted on her going to bed, queen as she was.

" I don't believe a bit, you know, that the king was such a bad man as that," she said.

"I do," said Bell.

"Ah, that's because you're a radical. I never will believe that kings are so much worse than other people. As for Charles the First, he was about the best man in history."

This was an old subject of dispute; but Lily on the present occasion was allowed her own way,—as being an invalid.

CHAPTEE XV. VALENTINE'S DAY IN LONDON.

THE fourteenth of February in London was quite as black, and cold, and as wintersome as it was at Allington, and was, perhaps, somewhat more melancholy in its coldness. Nevertheless Lady Alexan-drina De Courcy looked as bright as bridal finery could make her, when she got out of her carriage and walked into St. James's church at eleven o'clock on that morning.

It had been finally arranged that the marriage should take place in London. There were certainly many reasons which would have made a marriage from Courcy Castle more convenient. The De Courcy family were all assembled at their country family residence, and could therefore have been present at the ceremony without cost or trouble. The castle too was warm with the warmth of life, and the pleasantness of home would have lent a grace to the departure of one of the daughters of the house. The retainers and servants were there, and something of the rich mellowness of a noble alliance might have been felt, at any rate by Crosbie, at a marriage so celebrated. And it must have been acknowledged, even by Lady De Courcy, that the house in Portman Square was very cold,—that a marriage from thence would be cold, — that there could be no hope of attaching to it any honour and glory, or of making it resound with fashionable eclat in the columns of the Morning Post. But then, had they been married in the country, the earl would have been there ; whereas there was no probability of his travelling up to London for the purpose of being present on such an occasion.

The earl was very terrible in these days, and Alexandrina, as she became confidential in her communications with her future husband, spoke of him as of an ogre, who could not by any means be avoided in all the concerns of life, but whom one might shun now and again by some subtle device and careful arrangement of favourable circumstances. Crosbie had more than once taken upon himself to hint that he did not specially regard the ogre, seeing that for the future he could keep himself altogether apart from the malicious monster's dominions.

"He will not come to me in our new home," he had said to his love, with some little touch of affection. But to this view of the case Lady Alexandrina had demurred. The ogre in question was not only her parent, hut was also a noble peer, and she could not agree to any arrangement by which their future connection with the earl, and with nobility in general, might be endangered. Her parent, doubtless, was an ogre, and in his ogreship could make himself very terrible to those near him; but then might it not be better for them to be near to an earl who was an ogre, than not to be near to any earl at all. She had therefore signified to Crosbie that the ogre must be endured.

But, nevertheless, it was a great thing to be rid of him on that happy occasion. He would have said very dreadful things,—things so dreadful that there might have been a question whether the bridegroom could have borne them. Since he had heard of Crosbie's accident at the railway station, he had constantly talked with fiendish glee of the beating which had been administered to his son-in-law. Lady De Courcy in taking Crosbie's part, and maintaining that the match was fitting for her daughter, had ventured to declare before her husband that Crosbie was a man of fashion, and the earl would now ask, with a loathsome grin, whether the bridegroom's fashion had been improved by his little adventure at Paddington. Crosbie, to whom all this was not repeated, would have preferred a wedding in the country. But the countess and Lady Alexandrina knew better.

The earl had strictly interdicted any expenditure, and the countess had of necessity construed this as forbidding any unnecessary expense. " To marry a girl without any immediate cost was a thing which nobody could understand," as the countess remarked to her eldest daughter.

" I would really spend as little as possible," Lady Amelia had answered. "You see, mamma, there are circumstances about it which one doesn't wish to have talked about just at present. There's the story of that girl,—and then that fracas at the station. I really think it ought to be as quiet as possible." The good sense of Lady Amelia was not to be disputed, as her mother acknowledged. But

then if the marriage were managed in any notoriously quiet way, the very notoriety of that quiet would be as dangerous as an attempt at loud glory. " But it won't cost as much," said Amelia. And thus it had been resolved that the wedding should be very quiet.

To this Crosbie had assented very willingly, though he had not relished the manner in which the countess had explained to him her views.

" I need not tell you, Adolphus," she had said, "how thoroughly satisfied I am with this marriage. My dear girl feels that she can be happy as your wife, and what more can I want ? I declared to her and to Amelia that I was not ambitious, for their sakes, and have allowed them both to please themselves."

" I hope they have pleased themselves," said Crosbie.

"I trust so; but nevertheless,—I don't know whether I make myself understood ? "

" Quite so, Lady De Courcy. If Alexandrina were going to marry the eldest son of a marquis, you would have a longer procession to church than will be necessary when she marries me."

" You put it in such an odd way, Adolphus."

" It's all right so long as we understand each other. I can assure you I don't want any procession at all. I should be quite contented to go down with Alexandrina, arm in arm, like Darby and Joan, and let the clerk give her away."

We may say that he would have been much better contented could he have been allowed to go down the street without any encumbrance on his arm. But there was no possibility now for such deliverance as that.

Both Lady Amelia and Mr. Gazebee had long since discovered the bitterness of his heart and the fact of his repentance, and Gazebee had ventured to suggest to his wife that his noble sister-in-law was preparing for herself a life of misery.

" He'll become quiet and happy when he's used to it," Lady Amelia had replied, thinking, perhaps, of her own experiences.

" I don't know, my dear; he's not a quiet man. There's something in his eye which tells me that he could be very hard to a woman."

" It has gone too far now for any change," Lady Amelia had answered.

" Well; perhaps it has."

" And I know my sister so well; she would not hear of it. I

really think they will do very well when they become used to each other."

Mr. Gazebee, who also had had his own experiences, hardly dared to hope so much. His home had been satisfactory to him, because he had been a calculating man, and having made his calculation correctly was willing to take the net result. He had done so all his life with success. In his house his wife was paramount,—as he very well knew. But no effort on his wife's part, had she wished to make such effort, could have forced him to spend more than two-thirds of his income. Of this she also was aware, and had trimmed her sails accordingly, likening herself to him in this respect. But of such wisdom, and such trimmings, and such adaptability, what likelihood was there with Mr. Crosbie and Lady Alexandrina?

"At any rate, it is too late now," said Lady Amelia, thus concluding the conversation.

But nevertheless, when the last moment came, there was some little attempt at glory. Who does not know the way in which a lately married couple's little dinner-party stretches itself out from the pure simplicity of a fried sole and a leg of mutton to the attempt at clear soup, the unfortunately cold dish of round balls which is handed about after the sole, and the brightly red jelly, and beautifully pink cream, which are ordered, in the last agony of ambition, from the next pastry cook's shop?

" We cannot give a dinner, my dear, with only cook and Sarah."

It has thus begun, and the husband has declared that he has no such idea. " If Phipps and Dowdney can come here and eat a bit of mutton, they are very welcome; if not, let them stay away. And you might as well ask Phipps's sister ; just to have some one to go with you into the drawing-room."

" I'd much rather go alone, because then I can read,"—or sleep, we may say.

But her husband has explained that she would look friendless in this solitary state, and therefore Phipps's sister has been asked. Then the dinner has progressed down to those costly jellies which have been ordered in a last agony. There has been a conviction on the minds of both of them that the simple leg of mutton would have been more jolly for them all. Had those round balls not been carried about by a hired man; had simple mutton with hot potatoes been handed to Miss Phipps by Sarah, Miss Phipps would not have simpered with such unmeaning stiffness when young Dowdney spoke to

her. They would have been much more jolly. " Have a bit more mutton, Phipps; and where do you like it ? " How pleasant it sounds ! But we all know that it is impossible. My young friend had intended this, but his dinner had run itself away to cold round balls and coloured forms from the pastrycook. And so it was with the Crosbie marriage.

The bride must leave the church in a properly appointed carriage, and the postboys must have wedding favours. So the thing grew; not into noble proportions, not into proportions of true glory, justifying the attempt and making good the gala. A well-cooked rissole, brought pleasantly to you, is good eating. A gala marriage, when everything is in keeping, is excellent sport. Heaven forbid that we should have no gala marriages. But the small spasmodic attempt, made in opposition to manifest propriety, made with an inner conviction of failure,—that surely should be avoided in marriages, in dinners, and in all affairs of life.

There were bridesmaids and there was a breakfast. Both Mar-garetta and Rosina came up to London for the occasion, as did also a first cousin of theirs, one Miss Gresham, a lady whose father lived in the same county. Mr. Gresham had married a sister of Lord De Courcy's, and his services were also called into requisition. He was brought up to give away the bride, because the earl,— as the paragraph in the newspaper declared,—was confined at Courcy Castle by his old hereditary enemy, the gout. A fourth bridesmaid also was procured, and thus there was a bevy, though not so large a bevy as is now generally thought to be desirable. There were only three or four carriages at the church, but even three or four were something. The weather was so frightfully cold that the light-coloured silks of the ladies carried with them a show of discomfort. Girls should be very young to look nice in light dresses on a frosty morning, and the bridesmaids at Lady Alexandria's wedding were not very young. Lady Rosina's nose was decidedly red. Lady Margaretta was very wintry, and apprently very cross. Miss Gresham was dull, tame, and insipid; and the Honourable Miss O'Flaherty, who filled the fourth place, was sulky at finding that she had been invited to take a share in so very lame a performance.

But the marriage was made good, and Crosbie bore up against his misfortunes like a man. Montgomerie Dobbs and Fowler Pratt both stood by him, giving him, let us hope, some assurance that he was not absolutely deserted by all the world,—that he had not given

liimself up, bound hand and foot, to the De Courcys, to be dealt with in all matters as they might please. It was that feeling which had been so grievous to him,—and that other feeling, cognate to it, that if he should ultimately succeed in rebelling against the De Courcys, he would find himself a solitary man.

"Yes; I shall go," Fowler Pratt had said to Montgomerie Dobbs. " I always stick to a fellow if I can. Crosbie has behaved like a blackguard, and like a fool also; and he knows that I think so. But I don't see why I should drop him on that account. I shall go as he has asked me."

" So shall I," said Montgomerie Dobbs, who considered that he would be safe in doing whatever Fowler Pratt did, and who remarked to himself that after all Crosbie was marrying the daughter of an earl.

Then, after the marriage, came the breakfast, at which the countess presided with much noble magnificence. She had not gone to church, thinking, no doubt, that she would be better able to maintain her good humour at the feast, if she did not subject herself to the chance of lumbago in the church. At the foot of the table sat Mr. Gresham, her brother-in-law, who had undertaken to give the necessary toast and make the necessary speech. The Honourable John was there, saying all manner of ill-natured things about his sister and new brother-in-law, because he had been excluded from his proper position at the foot of the table. But Alexandrina had declared that she would not have the matter entrusted to her brother. The Honourable George would not come, because the countess had not asked his wife.

" Maria may be slow, and all that sort of thing," George had said; " but she is my wife. And she had got what they haven't. Love me, love my dog, you know." So he had stayed down at Courcy,—very properly as I think.

Alexandrina had wished to go away before breakfast, and Crosbie would not have cared how early an escape had been provided for him ; but the countess had told her daughter that if she would not wait for the breakfast, there should be no breakfast at all, and in fact no wedding; nothing but a simple marriage. Had there been a grand party, that going away of the bride and bridegroom might be very well; but the countess felt that on such an occasion as this nothing but the presence of the body of the sacrifice could give any reality to the festivity. So Crosbie and Lady Alexandrina Crosbie

heard Mr. Gresham's speech, in which he prophesied for the young couple an amount of happiness and prosperity almost greater than is compatible with the circumstances of humanity. His young friend Crosbie, whose acquaintance he had been delighted to make, was well known as one of the rising pillars of the State. Whether his future career might be parliamentary, or devoted to the permanent Civil Service of the country, it would be alike great, noble, and prosperous. As to his dear niece, who was now filling that position in life which was most beautiful and glorious for a young woman,—she could not have done better. She had preferred genius to wealth,—so said Mr. Gresham,—and she would find her fitting reward. As to her finding her fitting reward, whatever her preferences may have been, there Mr. Gresham was no doubt quite right. On that head I myself have no doubt whatever. After that Crosbie returned thanks, making a much better speech than nine men do out of ten on such occasions, and then the thing was over. No other speaking was allowed, and within half an hour from that time, he and his bride were in the post-chaise, being carried away to the Folkestone railway station; for that place had been chosen as the scene of their honeymoon. It had been at one time intended that the journey to Folkestone should be made simply as the first stage to Paris, but Paris and all foreign travelling had been given up by degrees.

" I don't care a bit about France,—we have been there so often," Alexandrina said.

She had wished to be taken to Naples, but Crosbie had made her understand at the first whispering of the word, that Naples was quite out of the question. He must look now in ajl things to money. From the very first outset of his career he must save a shilling wherever a shilling could be be saved. To this view of life no opposition was made by the De Courcy interest. Lady Amelia had explained to her sister that they ought so to do their honeymooning that it should not cost more than if they began keeping house at once. Certain things must be done which, no doubt, were costly in their nature. The bride must take with her a well-dressed lady's-maid. The rooms at the Folkestone hotel must be large, and on the first floor. A carriage must be hired for her use while she remained ; but every shilling must be saved the spending of which would not make itself apparent to the outer world. Oh, deliver us from the poverty of those who, with small means, affect a show of wealth! There is no whitening equal to that of sepulchres whited as they are whited !

By the proper administration of a slight bribe Crosbie secured for himself and his wife a compartment in the railway carriage to themselves. And as he seated himself opposite to Alexandrina, having properly tucked her up with all her bright-coloured trappings, he remembered that he had never in truth been alone with her before. He had danced with her frequently, and been left with her for a few minutes between the figures. He had flirted with her in crowded drawing-rooms, and had once found a moment at Courcy Castle to tell her that he was willing to marry her in spite of his engagement with Lilian Dale. But he had never walked with her for hours together as he had walked with Lily. He had never talked to her about government, and politics, and books, nor had she talked to him of poetry, of religion, and of the little duties and comforts of life. He had known the Lady Alexandrina for the last six or seven years ; but he had never known her,—perhaps never would know her,—as he had learned to know Lily Dale within the space of two months.

And now that she was his wife, what was he to say to her ? They two had commenced a partnership which was to make of them for the remaining term of their lives one body and one flesh. They were to be all-in-all to each other. But how was he to begin this all-in-all partnership ? Had the priest, with his blessing, done it so sufficiently that no other doing on Crosbie's own part was necessary ? There she was, opposite to him, his very actual wife,—bone of his bone ; and what was he to say to her ? As he settled himself on his seat, taking over his own knees a part of a fine fur rug trimmed with scarlet, with which he had covered her other mufflings, he bethought himself how much easier it would have been to talk to Lily. And Lily would have been ready with all her ears, and all her mind, and all her wit, to enter quickly upon whatever thoughts had occurred to him. In that respect Lily would have been a wife indeed,—a wife that would have transferred herself with quick mental activity into her husband's mental sphere. Had he begun about his office Lily would have been ready for him, but Alexandrina had never yet asked him a single question about his official life. Had he been prepared with a plan for to-morrow's happiness Lily would have taken it up eagerly, but Alexandrina never cared for such trifles.

" Are you quite comfortable ? " he said, at last.

" Oh, yes, quite, thank you. By-the-by, what did you do with my dressing-case ? "

And that question she did ask with some energy.

" It is under you. You can have it as foot-stool if you like it."

" Oh, no ; I should scratch it. I was afraid that if Hannah had it, it might be lost." Then again there was silence, and Crosbie again considered as to what he would next say to his wife.

"We all know the advice given us of old as to what we should do under such circumstances; and who can be so thoroughly justified in following that advice as a newly-married husband ? So he put out his hand for hers and drew her closer to him.

" Take care of my bonnet," she said, as she felt the motion of the railway carriage when he kissed her. I don't think he kissed her again till he had landed her and her bonnet safely at Folkestone. How often would he have kissed Lily, and how pretty would her bonnet have been when she reached the end of her journey, and how delightfully happy would she have looked when she scolded him for bending it! But Alexandrina was quite in earnest about her bonnet; by far too much in earnest for any appearance of happiness.

So he sat without speaking, till the train came to the tunnel.

" I do so hate tunnels," said Alexandrina.

He had half intended to put out his hand again, under some mistaken idea that the tunnel afforded him an opportunity. The whole journey was one long opportunity, had he desired it; but his wife hated tunnels, and so he drew his hand back again. Lily's little fingers would have been ready for his touch. He thought of this, and could not help thinking of it.

He had The Times newspaper in his dressing-bag. She also had a novel with her. Would she be offended if he took out the paper and read it ? The miles seemed to pass by very slowly, and there was still another hour down to Folkestone. He longed for his Times, but re'solved at last, that he would not read unless she read first. She also had remembered her novel; but by nature she was more patient than he, and she thought that on such a journey any reading might perhaps be almost improper. So she sat tranquilly, with her eyes fixed on the netting over her husband's head.

At last he could stand it no longer, and he dashed off into a conversation, intended to be most affectionate and serious.

" Alexandrina," he said, and his voice was well-tuned for the tender serious manner, had her ears been alive to such tuning. "Alexandrina, this is a very important step that you and I have taken to-day.

" Yes; it is, indeed," said she.

" I trust we shall succeed in making each other happy."

" Yes ; I hope we shall."

" If we hoth think seriously of it, and remember that that is our chief duty, we shall do so."

" Yes, I suppose we shall. I only hope we shan't find the house very cold. It is so new, and I am so subject to colds in my head. Amelia says we shall find it very cold; but then she was always against our going there."

" The house will do very well," said Crosbie. And Alexandrina could perceive that there was something of the master in his tone as he spoke.

" I am only telling you what Amelia said," she replied.

Had Lily been his bride, and had he spoken to her of their future life and mutual duties, how she would have kindled to the theme! She would have knelt at his feet on the floor of the carriage, and, looking up into his face, would have promised him to do her best,— her best,—her very best. And with what an eagerness of inward resolution would she have determined to keep her promise. He thought of all this now, but he knew that he ought not to think of it. Then, for some quarter of an hour, he did take out his newspaper, and she, when she saw him do so, did take out her novel.

He took out his newspaper, but he could not fix his mind upon the politics of the day. Had he not made a terrible mistake? Of what use to him in life would be that thing of a woman that sat opposite to him? Had not a great punishment come upon him, and had he not deserved the punishment? In truth, a great punishment had come upon him. It was not only that he had married a woman incapable of understanding the higher duties of married life, but that he himself would have been capable of appreciating the value of a woman who did understand them. He would have been happy with Lily Dale; and therefore we may surmise that his unhappiness with Lady Alexandrina would be the greater. There are men who, in marrying such as Lady Alexandrina De Courcy, would get the article best suited to them, as Mortimer Gazebee had done in marrying her sister. Miss Griselda Grantly, who had become Lady Dumbello, though somewhat colder and somewhat cleverer than Lady Alexandrina, had been of the same sort. But in marrying her Lord Dumbello had got the article best suited to him;—if only the ill-natured world would allow him to keep the article. It was in this that Crosbie's failure had been so grievous,—that he had seen and

approved the better course, but had chosen for himself to walk in that which was worse. During that week at Courcy Castle,—the week which he passed there immediately after his second visit to Allington,—he had deliberately made up his mind that he was more fit for the bad course than for the good one. The course was now before him, and he had no choice but to walk in it.

It was very cold when they got to Folkestone, and Lady Alex-andrina shivered as she stepped into the private-looking carriage which had been sent to the station for her use.

" We shall find a good fire in the parlour at the hotel," said Crosbie.

" Oh, I hope so," said Alexandrina, " and in the bedroom too."

The young husband felt himself to be offended, but he hardly knew why. He felt himself to be offended, and with difficulty induced himself to go through all those little ceremonies the absence of which would have been remarked by everybody. He did his work, however, seeing to all her shawls and wrappings, speaking with good-nature to Hannah, and paying special attention to the dressing-case.

" What time would you like to dine? " he asked, as he prepared to leave her alone with Hannah in the bedroom.

" Whenever you please; only I should like some tea and bread-and-butter presently."

Crosbie went into the sitting-room, ordered the tea and bread-and-butter, ordered also the dinner, and then stood himself up with his back to the fire, in order that he might think a little of his future career.

He was a man who had long since resolved that his life should be a success. It would seem that all men would so resolve, if the matter were simply one of resolution. But the majority of men, as I take it, make no such resolution, and very many men resolve that they will be unsuccessful. Crosbie, however, had resolved on success, and had done much towards carrying out his purpose. He had made a name for himself, and had acquired a certain fame. That, however, was, as he acknowledged to himself, departing from him. He looked the matter straight in the face, and told himself that his fashion must be abandoned; but the office remained to him. He might still rule over Mr. Optimist, and make a subservient slave of Butterwell. That must be his line in life now, and to that line he would endeavour to be true. As to his wife and his home,—he would look to them for Ms breakfast, and perhaps his dinner. He would have a comfortable arm-chair, and if Alexandrina should become a mother, he would endeavour to love his children; but above all things he would never think of Lily. After that he stood and thought of her for half an hour.

" If you please, sir, my lady wants to know at what time you have ordered dinner."

" At seven, Hannah."

" My lady says she is very tired, and will lie down till dinnertime."

" Very well, Hannah. I will go into her room when it is time to dress. I hope they are making you comfortable downstairs ? "

Then Crosbie strolled out on the pier in the dusk of the cold winter evening.

CHAPTER XVI. JOHN EAMES AT HIS OFFICE.

ME. CKOSBIE and his wife went upon their honeymoon tour to Folkestone in the middle of February, and returned to London about the end of March. Nothing of special moment to the interests of our story occurred during those six weeks, unless the proceedings of the young married couple by the sea-side may be thought to have any special interest. With regard to those proceedings I can only say that Crosbie was very glad when they were brought to a close. All holiday-making is hard work, but holiday-making with nothing to do is the hardest work of all. At the end of March they went into their new house, and we will hope that Lady Alexandrina did not find it very cold.

During this time Lily's recovery from her illness was being completed. She had no relapse, nor did anything occur to create a new-fear on her account. But, nevertheless, Dr. Crofts gave it as his opinion that it would be inexpedient to move her into a fresh house at Lady-day. March is not a kindly month for invalids; and therefore with some regret on the part of Mrs. Dale, with much impatience on that of Bell, and with considerable outspoken remonstrance from Lily herself, the squire was requested to let them remain through the month of April. How the squire received this request, and in what way he assented to the doctor's reasoning, will be told in the course of a chapter or two.

In the meantime John Eames had continued his career in London without much immediate satisfaction to himself, or to the lady who boasted to be his heart's chosen queen. Miss Amelia Roper, indeed, was becoming very cross, and in her ill temper was playing a game that was tending to create a frightful amount of hot water in Burton Crescent. She was devoting herself to a flirtation with Mr. Cradell,

not only under the immediate eyes of Johnny Eanies, but also under those of Mrs. Lupex. John Eames, the blockhead, did not like it. He was above all things anxious to get rid of Amelia and her claims ; so anxious, that on certain moody occasions he would threaten himself with diverse tragical terminations to his career in London. He would enlist. He would go to Australia. He would blow out his brains. He would have " an explanation " with Amelia, tell her that she was a vixen, and proclaim his hatred. He would rush down to Allington and throw himself in despair at Lily's feet. Amelia was the bugbear of his life. Nevertheless, when she flirted with Cradell, he did not like it, and was ass enough to speak to Cradell about it.

" Of course I don't care," he said, " only it seems to me that you are making a fool of yourself."

" I thought you wanted to get rid of her."

" She's nothing on earth to me ; only it does, you know "

' " Does do what ? " asked Cradell.

" Why, if I was to be fal-lalling with that married woman, you wouldn't like it. That's all about it. Do you mean to marry her ? "

" What!—Amelia ? "

" Yes; Amelia."

" Not if I know it."

" Then if I were you I would leave her alone. She's only making a fool of you."

Eames' advice may have been good, and the view taken by him of Amelia's proceedings may have been correct; but as regarded his own part in the affair, he was not wise. Miss Roper, no doubt, wished to make him jealous ; and she succeeded in the teeth of his aversion to her and of his love elsewhere. He had no desire to say soft things to Miss Roper. Miss Roper, with all her skill, could not extract a word pleasantly soft from him once a week. But, nevertheless, soft words to her and from her in another quarter made him uneasy. Such being the case, must we not acknowledge that John Eames was still floundering in the ignorance of his hobbledehoy-hood ?

The Lupexes at this time still held their ground in the Crescent, although repeated warnings to go had been given them. Mrs. Roper, though she constantly spoke of sacrificing all that they owed her, still hankered, with a natural hankering, after her money. And as each warning was accompanied by a demand for payment, and usually, produced some slight subsidy on account, the thing went on from week to week; and at the beginning of April Mr. and Mrs. Lupex were still boarders at Mrs. Roper's house.

Eames had heard nothing from Allington since the time of his Christmas visit, and his subsequent correspondence with Lord De Guest. In his letters from his mother he was told that game came frequently from Guestwick Manor, and in this way he knew that he was not forgotten by the earl. But of Lily he had heard not a word,— except, indeed, the rumour, which had now become general, that the Dales from the Small House were about to move themselves into Guestwick. When first he learned this he construed the tidings as favourable to himself, thinking that Lily, removed from the grandeur of Allington, might possibly be more easily within his reach; but, latterly, he had given up any such hope as, that, and was telling himself that his friend at the Manor had abandoned all idea of making up the marriage. Three months had already elapsed since his visit. Five months had passed since Crosbie had surrendered his claim. Surely such a knave as Crosbie might be forgotten in five months! If any steps could have been taken through the squire, surely three months would have sufficed for them ! It was very manifest to him that there was no ground of hope for him at Allington, and it would certainly be well for him to go off to Australia. He would go to Australia, but he would thrash Cradell first for having dared to interfere with Amelia Roper. That, generally, was the state of his mind during the first week in April.

Then there came to him a letter from the earl which instantly effected a great change in all his feelings; which taught him to regard Australia as a dream, and almost put him into a good humour with Cradell. The earl had by no means lost sight of his friend's interests at Allington; and, moreover, those interests were now backed by an ally who in this matter must be regarded as much more powerful than the earl. The squire had given in his consent to the Earnes alliance.

The earl's letter was as follows :—

MY DEAR JOHN, Guestwick Manor, April 7, 18 —

I TOLD you to write to me again, and you haven't done it. I saw your mother the other day, or else you might have been dead for anything I knew. A young man always ought to write letters when he is told to do so. [Eames, when he had got so far, felt himself rather aggrieved by this rebuke, knowing that he had abstained from writing to his patron simply from an unwillingness to intrude upon him with his letters. " By Jove, I'll write to him every week of his life, till he's sick of me," Johnny said to himself when he found himself thus instructed as to a young man's duties.]

And now I have got to tell you a long story, and I should like it much better if you were down here, so that I might save myself the trouble; but you would think me ill-natured if I were to keep you .waiting. I happened to meet Mr. Dale the other day, and he said that he should be very glad if a certain young lady would make up her mind to listen to a certain young friend of mine. So I asked him what he meant to do about the young lady's fortune, and he declared himself willing to give her a hundred a year during his life, and to settle four thousand pounds upon her after his death. I said that I would do as much on my part by the young man; but as two hundred a year, with your salary, would hardly give you enough to begin with, I'll make mine a hundred and fifty. You'll be getting up in your office soon, and with five hundred a year you ought to be able to get along; especially as you need not insure your life. I should live somewhere near Bloomsbury Square at first, because I'm told you can get a house for nothing. After all, what's fashion worth? You can bring your wife down here in the autumn, and have some shooting. She won't let you go to sleep under the trees, I'll be bound. „ .

But you must look after the young lady. You will understand that no one has said a word to her about it; or, if they have, I don't know it. You'll find the squire on your side, that's all. Couldn't you manage to come down this Easter ? Tell old Buffle, with my compliments, that I want you. I'll write to him if you like it. I did know him at one time, though I can't say I was ever very fond of him. It stands to reason that you can't get on with Miss Lily without seeing her; unless, indeed, you like better to write to her, which always seems to me to be very poor sort of fun. You'd much better come down, and go a-wooing in the regular old-fashioned way. I need not tell you that Lady Julia will be delighted to see you. You are a prime favourite with her since that affair at the railway station. She thinks a great deal more about that than she does about the bull.

Now, my dear fellow, you know all about it, and I shall take it very much amiss of you if you don't answer my letter soon.

Your-very sincere friend,

DE GUEST.

When Eames had finished this letter, sitting at his office-desk, his surprise and elation were so great that he hardly knew where he was or what he ought to do. Could it be the truth that Lily's uncle had not only consented that the match should he made, but that he had also promised to give his niece a considerable fortune ? For a few minutes it seemed to Johnny as though all obstacles to his happiness were removed, and that there was no impediment between him and an amount of bliss of which he had hitherto hardly dared to dream. Then, when he considered the earl's munificence, he almost cried. He found that he could not compose his mind to think, or even his hand to write. He did not know whether it would be right

in him to accept such pecuniary liberality from any living man, and almost thought that he should feel himself bound to reject the earl's offer. As to the squire's money, that he knew he might accept. All that comes in the shape of a young woman's fortune may be taken by any man.

He would certainly answer the earl's letter, and that at once. He would not leave the office till he had done so. His friend should have cause to bring no further charge against him of that kind. And then again he reverted to the injustice which had been done to him in the matter of letter-writing,— as if that consideration were of moment in such a state of circumstances as was now existing. But at last his thoughts brought themselves to the real question at issue. Would Lily Dale accept him ? After all, the realization of his good fortune depended altogether upon her feelings; and, as he remembered this, his mind misgave him sorely. It was filled not only with a young lover's ordinary doubts,—with the fear and trembling incidental to the bashfulness of hobbledehoyhood,—but with an idea that that affair with Crosbie would still stand in his way. He did not, perhaps, rightly understand all that Lily had suffered, but he conceived it to be probable that there had been wounds which even the last five months might not yet have cured. Could it be that she would allow him to cure these wounds ? As he thought of this he felt almost crushed to the earth by an indomitable bashfulness and conviction of his own unworthiness. What had he to offer worthy of the acceptance of such a girl as Lilian Dale ?

I fear that the Crown did not get out of John Eames an adequate return for his salary on that day. So adequate, however, had been the return given by him for some time past, that promotion was supposed throughout the Income-tax Office to be coming in his way, much to the jealousy of Cradell, Fisher, and others, his immediate compeers and cronies. And the place assigned to him by rumour was one which was generally regarded as a perfect Elysium upon earth in the Civil-Service world. He was, so rumour said, to become private secretary to the First Commissioner. He would be removed by such a change as this from the large uncarpeted room in which he at present sat; occupying the same desk with another man to whom he had felt himself to be ignoniiniously bound, as dogs must feel when they are coupled. This room had been the bear-garden of the office. Twelve or fourteen men sat in it. Large pewter pots were brought into it daily at one o'clock, giving it an air that was not aristocratic. The senior of the room, one Mr. Love, who was presumed to have it under his immediate dominion, was a clerk of the ancient stamp, dull, heavy, unambitious, living out on the farther side of Islington, and unknown beyond the limits of his office to any of his younger brethren. He was generally regarded as having given a bad tone to the room. And then the clerks in this room would not unfrequently be blown up,—with very palpable blowings up,—by an official swell, a certain chief clerk, named Kissing, much higher in standing though younger in age than the gentleman of whom we have before spoken. He would hurry in, out of his own neighbouring chamber, with quick step and nose in the air, shuffling in his office slippers, looking on each occasion as though there were some cause to fear that the whole Civil Service were coming to an abrupt termination, and would lay about him with hard words, which some of those in the big room did not find it very easy to bear. His hair was always brushed straight up, his eyes were always very wide open,—and he usually carried a big letter-book with him, keeping in it a certain place with his finger. This book was almost too much for his strength, and he would flop it down, now on this man's desk and now on that man's, and in a long career of such floppings had made himself to be very much hated. On the score of some old grudge he and Mr. Love did not speak to each other; and for this reason, on all occasions of fault-finding, the blown-up young man would refer Mr. Kissing to his enemy.

" I know nothing about it," Mr. Love would say, not lifting his face from his desk for a moment.

11 I shall certainly lay the matter before the Board," Mr. Kissing would reply, and would then shuffle out of the room with the big book.

Sometimes Mr. Kissing would lay the matter before the Board, and then he, and Mr. Love, and two or three delinquent clerks would be summoned thither. It seldom led to much. The delinquent clerks would be cautioned. One Commissioner would say a word in private to Mr. Love, and another a word in private to Mr. Kissing. Then, when left alone, the Commissioners would have their little jokes, saying that Kissing, they feared, went by favour; and that Love should still be lord of all. But these things were done in the mild days, before Sir Raffle Buffle came to the Board.

There had been some fun in this at first; but of late John Eames had become tired of it. He disliked Mr. Kissing, and the big book out of which Mr. Kissing was always endeavouring to convict him of some official sin, and had got tired of that joke of setting Kissing and Love hy the ears together. When the Assistant Secretary first suggested to him that Sir Raffle had an idea of selecting him as private secretary, and when he remembered the cosy little room, all carpeted, with a leathern arm-chair and a separate washing-stand, which in such case would be devoted to his use, and remembered also that he would be put into receipt of an additional hundred a year, and would stand in the way of still better promotion, he was overjoyed. But there were certain drawbacks. The present private secretary,—who had been private secretary also to the late First Commissioner,—was giving up his Elysium because he could not endure the tones of Sir Raffle's voice. It was understood that Sir Raffle required rather more of a private secretary, in the way of obsequious attendance, than was desirable, and Eames almost doubted his own fitness for the place.

" And why should he choose me ? " he had asked the Assistant Secretary.

" Well, we have talked it over together, and I think that he prefers you to any other that has been named."

" But he was so very hard upon me about the affair at the railway station."

" I think he has heard more about that since; I think that some message has reached him from your friend, Earl De Guest."

" Oh, indeed ! " said Johnny, beginning to comprehend what it was to have an earl for his friend. Since his acquaintance with the nobleman had commenced, he had studiously avoided all mention of the earl's name at his office ; and yet he received almost daily intimation that the fact was well known there, and not a little considered.

" But he is so very rough," said Johnny.

" You can put up with that," said his friend the Assistant Secretary. " His bark is worse than his bite, as you know; and then a hundred a year is worth having." Eames was at that moment inclined to take a gloomy view of life in general, and was disposed to refuse the place, should it be offered to him. He had not then received the earl's letter; but now, as he sat with that letter open before him, lying in the drawer beneath his desk so that he could still read it as he leaned back in his chair, he was enabled to look at things in general through a different atmosphere. In the first place,

Lilian Dale's husband ought to have a room to himself, with a carpet and an arm-chair; and then that additional hundred a year would raise his income at once to the sum as to which the earl had made some sort of stipulation. But could he get that leave of absence at Easter? If he consented to be Sir Baffle's private secretary, he would make that a part of the bargain.

At this moment the door of the big room was opened, and Mr. Kissing shuffled in with very quick little steps. He shuffled in, and coming direct up to John's desk, flopped his ledger down upon it before its owner had had time to close the drawer which contained the precious letter.

" What have you got in that drawer, Mr. Eames ? "

" A private letter, Mr. Kissing."

"Oh;—a private letter!" said Mr. Kissing, feeling strongly convinced there was a novel hidden there, but not daring to express his belief. " I have been half the morning, Mr. Eames, looking for this letter to the Admiralty, and you've put it under S ! " A bystander listening to Mr. Kissing's tone would have been led to believe that the whole Income-tax Office was jeopardized by the terrible iniquity thus disclosed.

"Somerset House," pleaded Johnny.

"Psha;—Somerset House! Half the offices in London "

"You'd better ask Mr. Love," said Eames. "It's all done under his special instructions." Mr. Kissing looked at Mr. Love, and Mr. Love looked steadfastly at his desk. "Mr. Love knows all about the indexing," continued Johnny. "He's index master general to the department."

"No, I'm not, Mr. Eames," said Mr. Love, who rather liked John Eames, and hated Mr. Kissing with his whole heart. " But I believe the indexes, on the whole, are very well done in this room. Some people don't know how to find letters."

"Mr. Eames," began Mr. Kissing, still pointing with a finger of bitter reproach to the misused S, and beginning an oration which was intended for the benefit of the whole room, and for the annihilation of old Mr. Love, " if you have yet to learn that the word Admiralty begins with A and not with S, you have much to learn which should have been acquired before you first came into this office. Somerset House is not a department." Then he turned round to the room at large, and repeated the last words, as though they might become very useful if taken well to heart " Is not a department.

The Treasury is a department; the Home Office is a department ; the India Board is a department—"

"No, Mr. Kissing, it isn't," said a young clerk from the other end of the room.

"You know very well what I mean, sir. The India Office is a department."

"There's no Board, sir."

"Never mind; but how any gentleman who has been in the service three months,—not to say three years,—can suppose Somerset House to be a department, is beyond my comprehension. If you have been improperly instructed " , -

"We shall know all about it another time," said Eames. "Mr. Love will make a memorandum of it."

"I shan't do anything of the kind," said Mr. Love.

"If you have been wrongly instructed,—" Mr. Kissing began again, stealing a glance at Mr. Love as he did so; but at this moment the door was again opened, and a messenger summoned Johnny to the presence of the really great man. "Mr. Eames, to wait upon Sir Raffle." Upon hearing this Johnny immediately started, and left Mr. Kissing and the big book in possession of his desk. How the battle was waged, and how it raged in the large room, we cannot stop to hear, as it is necessary that we should follow our hero into the presence of Sir Baffle Buffle.

"Ah, Eames,—yes," said Sir Raffle, looking up from his desk when the young man entered; "just wait half a minute, will you ? " And the knight went to work at his papers, as though fearing that any delay in what he was doing might be very prejudicial to the nation at large. " Ah, Eames,—well,—yes," he said again, as he pushed away from him, almost with a jerk, the papers on which he had been writing. " They tell me that you know the business of this office pretty well."

"Some of it, sir," said Eames.

"Well, yes; some of it. But you'll have to understand the whole of it if you come to me. And you must be very sharp about it too. You know that FitzHoward is leaving me ? "

"I have heard of it, sir."

"A very excellent young man, though perhaps not But we won't mind that. The work is a little too much for him, and he's going back into the office. I believe Lord De Guest is a friend of yours; isn't he ? "

" Yes ; he is a friend of mine, certainly. He's been very kind to me."

"Ah, well. I've known the earl for many years,—for very many years; and intimately at one time. Perhaps you may have heard him mention my name ? "

"Yes, IJiave, Sir Raffle."

" We were intimate once, but those things go off, you know. He's been the country mouse and I've been the town mouse. Ha, ha, ha! You may tell him that I say so. He won't mind that coming from me."

" Oh, no; not at all," said Eames.

" Mind you tell him when you see him. The earl is a man for whom I've always had a great respect,—a very great respect,—I may say regard. And now, Eames, what do you say to taking Fitz-Howard's place ? The work is hard. It is fair that I should tell you that. The work will, no doubt, be very hard. I take a greater share of what's going than my predecessors have done ; and I don't mind telling you that I have been sent here, because a man was wanted who would do that." The voice of Sir Raffle, as he continued, became more and more harsh, and Eames began to think how wise FitzHoward had been. " I mean to do my duty, and I shall expect that my private secretary will do his. But, Mr. Eames, I never forget a man. Whether he be good or bad, I never forget a man. You don't dislike late hours, I suppose."

" Coming late to the office, you mean ? Oh, no, not in the least."

" Staying late,—staying late. Six or seven o'clock if necessary, —putting your shoulder to the wheel when the coach gets into the mud. That's what I've been doing all my life. They've known what I am very well. They've always kept me for the heavy roads. If they paid, in the Civil Service, by the hour, I believe I should have drawn a larger income than any man in it. If you take the vacant chair in the next room you'll find it's no joke. It's only fair that I should tell you that."

" I can work as hard as any man," said Eames.

" That's right. That's right. Stick to that and I'll stick to you. It will be a great gratification to me to have by me a friend of my old friend De Guest. Tell him I say so. And now you may as well get into harness at once. FitzHoward is there. You can go in to him, and at half-past four exactly ill see you both. I'm very

exact, inincl,—very;—and therefore you must be exact." Then Sir Raffle looked as though he desired to be left alone.

" Sir Raffle, there's one favour I want to ask of you," said Johnny.

" And what's that ?"

" I am most anxious to be absent for a fortnight or three weeks, just at Easter. I shall want to go in about ten days."

" Absent for three weeks at Easter, when the parliamentary work is beginning! That won't do for a private secretary."

" But it's very important, Sir Raffle."

" Out of the question, Eames; quite out of the question."

" It's almost life and death to me."

" Almost life and death. Why, what are you going to do ? " With all his grandeur and national importance, Sir Raffle would be very curious as to little people.

" Well, I can't exactly tell you, and I'm not quite sure myself."

" Then don't talk nonsense. It's impossible that I should spare my private secretary just at that time of the year. I couldn't do it. The service won't admit of it. You're not entitled to leave at that season. Private secretaries always take their leave in the autumn."

" I should like to be absent in the autumn too, but "

"It's out of the question, Mr. Eames."

Then John Eames reflected that it behoved him in such an emergency to fire off his big gun. He had a great dislike to firing this big gun, but, as he said to himself, there are occasions which make a big gun very necessary. " I got a letter from Lord De Guest this morning, pressing me very much to go to him at Easter. It's about business," added Johnny. " If there was any difficulty, he said, he should write to you."

" Write to me," said Sir Raffle, who did not like to be approached too familiarly in his office, even by an earl.

" Of course I shouldn't tell him to do that. But, Sir Raffle, if I remained out there, in the office," and Johnny pointed towards the big room with his head, " I could choose April for my month. And as the matter is so important to me, and to the earl—"

" What can it be ? " said Sir Raffle.

" It's quite private," said John Eames.

Hereupon Sir Raffle became very petulant, feeling that a bargain was being made with him. This young man would fcnly consent to

become his private secretary upon certain terms ! " Well; go in to FitzHoward now. I can't lose all my day in this way."

" But I shall he able to get away at Easter ? "

" I don't know. We shall see about it. But don't stand talking there now." Then John Eames went into FitzHoward's room and received that gentleman's congratulations on his appointment. " I hope you like being rung for, like a servant, every minute, for he's always ringing that bell. And he'll roar at you till you're deaf. You must give up all dinner engagements, for though there is not much to do, he'll never let you go. I don't think anybody ever asks him out to dinner, for he likes being here till seven. And you'll have to write all manner of lies about big people. And, sometimes, when he has sent Rafferty out about his private business, he'll ask you to bring him his shoes." Now Rafferty was the First Commissioner's messenger.

It must be remembered, however, that this little account was given by an outgoing and discomfited private secretary. " A man is not asked to bring another man his shoes," said Eames to himself, 11 until he shows himself fit for that sort of business." Then he made within his own breast a little resolution about Sir Raffle's shoes.

172 THE SMALL HOUSE AT ALLINGTOX.

CHAPTER XVII.

THE NEW PRIVATE SECRETARY.

Income-tax Office, April 8, 18— MY DEAR LORD DE GUEST,

I HARDLY know how to answer your letter, it is so very kind—more than kind. And about not writing before,—I must explain that I have not liked to trouble you with letters. I should have seemed to be encroaching if I had written much. Indeed it didn't come from not thinking about you. And first of all, about the money,— as to your offer, I mean. I really feel that I do not know what I ought to say to you about it, without appearing to be a simpleton. The truth is, I don't know what I ought to do, and can only trust to you not to put me wrong. I have an idea that a man ought not to accept a present of money, unless from his father, or somebody like that. And the sum you mention is so very large that it makes me wish you had not named it. If you choose to be so generous, would it not be better that you should leave it me in your will ?

" So that he might always want me to be dying," said Lord De Guest, as he read the letter out loud to his sister.

" I'm sure he wouldn't want that," said Lady Julia. " But you may live for twenty-five years, you know."

" Say fifty," said the earl. And then he continued the reading of his letter.

But all that depends so much upon another person, that it is hardly worth while talking about it. Of course I am very much obliged to Mr. Dale,—very much indeed,—and I think that he is behaving very handsomely to his niece. But whether it will do me any good, that is quite another thing. However, I shall certainly accept your kind invitation for Easter, and find out whether I have a chance or not. I must tell you that Sir Raffle Buffle has made me his private secretary, by which I get a hundred a year. He says he was a great crony of yours many years ago, and seems to like talking about you very much. You will understand what all that means. He has sent you ever so many messages, but I don't suppose you will care to get them. I am to go to him to-morrow, and from all I hear I shall have a hard time of it.

" By George, he will," said the earl. " Poor fellow ! "

" But I thought a private secretary never had anything to do," said Lady Julia.

" I shouldn't like to be private secretary to Sir Raffle, myself. But he's young, and a hundred a year is a great thing. How we all of us used to hate that man. His voice sounded like a bell with a crack in it. We always used to be asking for some one. to muffle the Buffle. They call him Huffle Scuffle at his office. Poor Johnny ! " Then he finished the letter :—

I told him that I must have leave of absence at Easter, and he at first declared that it was impossible. But I shall cany my point about that. I would not stay away to be made private secretary to the Prime Minister; and yet I almost feel that I might as well stay away for any good that I shall do.

Give my kind regards to Lady Julia, and tell her how. very much obliged to her I am. I cannot express the gratitude which I owe to you. But pray believe me, my dear Lord De Guest, always very faithfully yours,

JOHN EAMES.

It was late before Eames had finished his letter. He had been making himself ready for his exodus from the big room, and preparing his desk and papers for Jiis successor. About half-past five Cradell came up to him, and suggested that they should walk home together.

" What! you here still ? " said Eames. " I thought you always went at four." Cradell had remained, hanging about the office, in order that he might walk home with the new private secretary. But Eames did not desire this. He had much of which he desired to think alone, and would fain have been allowed to walk by himself.

" Yes; I had things to do. I say, Johnny, I congratulate you most heartily ; I do, indeed."

" Thank you, old fellow ! "

" It is such a grand thing, you know. A hundred a year all at once! And then such a snug room to yourself,—and that fellow, Kissing, never can come near you. He has been making himself such a beast all day. But, Johnny, I always knew you'd come to something more than common. I always said so."

11 There's nothing uncommon about this ; except that Fitz says that old Huffle Scuffle makes himself uncommon nasty."

" Never mind what Fitz says. It's all jealousy. You'll have it all your own way, if you look sharp. I think you always do have it all your own way. Are you nearly ready ? "

" Well,—not quite. Don't wait for me, Caudle."

" Oh, I'll wait. I don't mind waiting. They'll keep dinner for us if we both stay. Besides, what matters ? I'd do more than that for you."

11 1 have some idea of working on till eight, and having a chop sent in," said Johnny. " Besides—I've got somewhere to call, by myself."

Then Cradell almost cried. He remained silent for two or three minutes, striving to master his emotion; and at last, when he did speak, had hardly succeeded in doing so. " Oh, Johnny," he said, " I know what that means. You are going to throw me over because you are getting up in the world. I have always stuck to you, through everything ; haven't I ?

" Don't make yourself a fool, Caudle."

" Well; so I have. And if they had made me private secretary, I should have been just the same to you as ever. You'd have found no change in me."

" What a goose you are. Do you say I'm changed, because I want to dine in the city ? "

" It's all because you don't want to walk home with me, as we used to do. I'm not such a goose but what I can see. But, Johnny I suppose I mustn't call you Johnny, now."

" Don't be such a—con-founded " Then Eames got up, and

walked about the room. "Come along," said he, "I don't care about staying, and don't mind where I dine." And he bustled away with his hat and gloves, hardly giving Cradell time to catch him before he got out into the streets. " I tell you what it is, Caudle," said he, " all that kind of thing is disgusting."

" But how would you feel," whimpered Cradell, who had never succeeded in putting himself quite on a par with his friend, even in his own estimation, since that glorious victory at the railway station. If he could only have thrashed Lupex as Johnny had thrashed Crosbie ; then indeed they might have been equal,—a pair of heroes. But he had not done so. He had never told himself that he was a coward, but he considered that circumstances had been specially unkind to him. " But how would you feel," he whimpered, " if the friend whom you liked better than anybody else in the world, turned his back upon you ? "

" I haven't turned my back upon you; except that I can't get you to walk fast enough. Come along, old fellow, and don't talk confounded nonsense. I hate all that kind of thing. You never

ought to suppose that a man will give himself airs, but wait till he does. I don't believe I shall remain with old Scuffles above a month or two. From all that I can hear that's as much as any one can bear."

Then Cradell by degrees became happy and cordial, and during the whole walk flattered Eames with all the flattery of which he was master. And Johnny, though he did profess himself to be averse to " all that kind of thing," was nevertheless open to flattery. When Cradell told him that though FitzHoward could not manage the Tartar knight, he might probably do so; he was inclined to believe what Cradell said. " And as to getting him his shoes," said Cradell, " I don't suppose he'd ever think of asking you to do such a thing, unless he was in a very great hurry, or something of that kind."

" Look here, Johnny," said Cradell, as they got into one of the streets bordering on Burton Crescent, " you know the last thing in the world I should like to do would be to offend you."

" All right, Caudle," said Eames, going on, whereas his companion had shown a tendency towards stopping.

" Look here, now; if I have vexed you about Amelia Roper, I'll make you a promise never to speak to her again."

" D Amelia Roper," said Eames, suddenly stopping himself

and stopping Cradell as well. The exclamation was made in a deep angry voice which attracted the notice of one or two who were passing. Johnny was very wrong,—wrong to utter any curse;— very wrong to ejaculate that curse against a human being; and especially wrong to fulminate it against a woman—a woman whom he had professed to love ! But he did do so, and I cannot tell my story thoroughly without repeating the wicked word.

Cradell looked up at him and stared. "I only meant to say," said Cradell, "I'll do anything you like in the matter."

"Then never mention her name to me again. And as to talking to her, you may talk to her till you're both blue in the face, if you please."

"Oh;—I didn't know. You didn't seem to like it the other day."

"I was a fool the other day,—a confounded fool. And so I have been all my life. Amelia Roper! Look here, Caudle; if she makes up to you this evening, as I've no doubt she will, for she seems to be playing that game constantly now, just let her have her fling. Never mind me; I'll amuse myself with Mrs. Lupex, or Miss Spruce."

"But there'll be the deuce to pay with Mrs. Lupex. She's as cross as possible already whenever Amelia speaks to me. You don't know what a jealous woman is, Johnny." Cradell had got upon what he considered to be his high ground. And on that he felt himself equal to any man. It was no doubt true that Eames had thrashed a man, and that he had not; it was true also that Eames had risen to very high place in the social world, having become a private secretary; but for a dangerous, mysterious, overwhelming, life-enveloping intrigue;—was not he the acknowledged hero of such an affair? He had paid very dearly, both in pocket and in comfort, for the blessing of Mrs. Lupex's society; but he hardly considered that he had paid too dearly. There are certain luxuries which a man will find to be expensive; but, for all that, they may be worth their price. Nevertheless as he went up the steps of Mrs. Roper's house he made up his mind that he would oblige his friend. The intrigue might in that way become more mysterious, and more life-enveloping; whereas it would not become more dangerous, seeing that Mr. Lupex could hardly find himself to be aggrieved by such a proceeding.

The whole number of Mrs. Roper's boarders were assembled at dinner that day. Mr. Lupex seldom joined that festive board, but on this occasion he was present, appearing from his voice and manner to be in high good-humour. Cradell had communicated to the company in the drawing-room the great good fortune which had fallen upon his friend, and Johnny had thereby become the mark of a certain amount of hero-worship.

"Oh, indeed!" said Mrs. Roper. "An 'appy woman 3 r our mother will be when she hears it. But I always said you'd come down right side uppermost."

"Handsome is as handsome does," said Miss Spruce.

"Oh, Mr. Eames!" exclaimed Mrs. Lupex, with graceful enthusiasm, "I wish you joy from the very depth of my heart. It is such an elegant appointment."

"Accept the hand of a true and disinterested friend," said Lupex. And Johnny did accept the hand, though it was very dirty and stained all over with paint.

Amelia stood apart and conveyed her congratulations by a glance,—or, I might better say, by a series of glances. "And now,—now will you not be mine," the glances said; "now that you are rolling in wealth and prosperity?" And then before they went downstairs

she did whisper one word to him. "Oh, I am so happy, John;— so very happy."

"Bother!" said Johnny, in a tone quite loud enough to reach the lady's ear. Then making his way round the room, he gave his arm to Miss Spruce. Amelia, as she walked downstairs alone, declared to herself that she would wring his heart. She had been employed in wringing it for some days past, and had been astonished at her own success. It had been clear enough to her that Eames had been piqued by her overtures to Cradell, and she resolved therefore to play out that game.

"Oh, Mr. Cradell," she said, as she took her seat next to him. "The friends I like are the friends that remain always the same. I hate your sudden rises. They do so often make a man upsetting." " I should like to try, myself, all the same," said Cradell. "Well, I don't think it would make any difference in you; I don't indeed. And of course your time will come too. It's that earl as has done it,—he that was worried by the bull. Since we have known an earl we have been so mighty fine." And Amelia gave her head a little toss, and then smiled archly, in a manner which, to Cradell's eyes, was really very becoming. But he saw that Mrs. Lupex was looking at him from the other side of the table, and he could not quite enjoy the goods which the gods had provided for him. When the ladies left the dining-room Lupex and the two young men drew their chairs near the fire, and each prepared for himself a moderate potation. Eames made a little attempt at leaving the room, but he was implored by Lupex with such earnest protestations of friendship to remain, and was so weakly fearful of being charged with giving himself airs, that he did as he was desired.

" And here, Mr. Eames, is to your very good health," said Lupex, raising to his mouth a steaming goblet of gin-and-water, " and wishing you many years to enjoy your official prosperity."

" Thank ye," said Eames. " I don't know much about the prosperity, but I'm just as much obliged."

"Yes, sir; when I see a young man of your age beginning to rise in the world, I know he'll go on. Now look at me, Mr. Eames. Mr. Cradell, here's your very good health, and may all unkindness

be drowned in the flowing bowl Look at me, Mr. Eames.

I've never risen in the world; I've never done any good in the world, and never shall."

" Oh, Mr. Lupex, don't say that."

" Ah, but I do say it. I've always been pulling the devil by the tail, and never yet got as much as a good hold on to that. And I'll tell you why ; I never got a chance when I was young. If I could have got any big fellow, a star, you know, to let me paint his portrait when I was your age,—such a one, let us say, as your friend Sir Baffle "

" What a star! " said Cradell.

" Well, I suppose he's pretty much known in the world, isn't he ? Or Lord Derby, or Mr. Spurgeon. You know what I mean. If I'd got such a chance as that when I was young, I should never have been doing jobs of scene-painting at the minor theatres at so much a square yard. You've got the chance now, but I never had it." Whereupon Mr. Lupex finished his first measure of gin-and-water.

" It's a very queer thing,—life is," continued Lupex ; and, though he did not at once go to work boldly at the mixing of another glass of toddy, he began gradually, and as if by instinct, to finger the things which would be necessary for that operation. " A very queer thing. Now, remember, young gentlemen, I'm not denying that success in life will depend upon good conduct;—of course it does ; but, then, how often good conduct comes from success! Should I have been what I am now, do you suppose, if some big fellow had taken me by the hand when I was struggling to make an artist of myself? I could have drunk claret and champagne just as well as gin-and-water, and worn ruffles to my shirt as gracefully as many a fellow who used to be very fond of me, and now won't speak to me if he meets me in the streets. I never got a chance,—never."

" But it's not too late yet, Mr. Lupex," said Eames.

" Yes, it is, Eames,—yes, it is." And now Mr. Lupex had grasped the gin-bottle. " It's too late now. The game's over, and the match is lost. The talent is here. I'm as sure of that now as ever I was. I've never doubted my own ability,—never for a moment. There are men this very day making a thousand a year off their easels who haven't so good and true an eye in drawing as I have, or so good a feeling in colours. I could name them; only I won't."

" And why shouldn't you try again ? " said Eames.

" If I were to paint the finest piece that ever delighted the eye of man, who would come and look at it ? Who would have enough belief in me to come as far as this place and see if it were true ? No, Eames; I know my own position and my own ways, and I know my own weakness. I couldn't do a day's work now, unless I were certain of getting a certain number of shillings at the end of it. That's what a man comes to when things have gone against him."

" But I thought men got lots of money by scene-painting ? "

" I don' know what you may call lots, Mr. Cradell; I don't call it lots. But I'm not complaining. I know who I have to thank ; and if ever I blow my own brains out I shan't be putting the blame on the wrong shoulders. If you'll take my advice,"—and now he turned round to Eames,—" you'll beware of marrying too soon in life."

" I think a man should many early, if he marries well," said Eames.

"Don't misunderstand me," continued Lupex. " It isn't about Mrs. L. I'm speaking. I've always regarded my wife as a very fascinating woman."

" Hear, hear, hear ! " said Cradell, thumping the table.

" Indeed she is," said Eames.

" And when I caution you against marrying, don't you misunderstand me. I've never said a word against her to any man, and never will. If a man don't stand by his wife, who will he stand by ? I blame no one but myself. But I do say this ; I never had a chance;—I never had a chance;—never had a chance." And as he repeated the words for the third time, his lips were already fixed to the rim of his tumbler.

At this moment the door of the dining-room was opened, and Mrs. Lupex put in her head.

" Lupex," she said, " what are you doing ? "

" Yes, my dear. I can't say I'm doing anything at the present moment. I was giving a little advice to these young gentlemen." •

" Mr. Cradell, I wonder at you. And, Mr. Eames, I wonder at you, too,—in your position ! Lupex, come upstairs at once." She then stepped into the room and secured the gin-bottle.

" Oh, Mr. Cradell, do come here," said Amelia, in her liveliest tone, as soon as the men made their appearance above. " I've been waiting for you this half-hour. I've got such a puzzle for you." And she made way for him to a chair which was between herself and the wall. Cradell looked half afraid of his fortunes as he took the proffered seat; but he did take it, and was soon secured from any

32—2

positive physical attack by the strength and breadth of Miss Roper's crinoline.

" Dear me! Here's a change," said Mrs. Lupex, out loud.

Johnny Eames was standing close, and whispered into her ear, " Changes are so pleasant sometimes! Don't you think so ? I do."

CHAPTER XVIII.
NEMESIS.

CROSBIE had now settled down to the calm realities of married life, and was beginning to think that the odium was dying away which for a week or two had attached itself to him, partly on account of his usage of Miss Dale, but more strongly in consequence of the thrashing which he had received from John Eames. Not that he had in any way recovered his former tone of life, or that he ever hoped to do so. But he was able to go in and out of his club without embarrassment. He could talk with his wonted voice, and act with his wonted authority at his office. He could tell his friends, with some little degree of pleasure in the sound, that Lady Alexan-drina would be very happy to see them. And he could make himself comfortable in his own chair after dinner, with his slippers and his newspaper. He could make himself comfortable, or at any rate could tell his wife that he did so.

It was very dull. He was obliged to acknowledge to himself, when he thought over the subject, that the life which he was leading was dull. Though he could go into his club without annoyance, nobody there ever thought of asking him to join them at dinner. It was taken for granted that he was going to dine at home ; and in the absence of any provocation to the contrary, he always did dine at home. He had now been in his house for three weeks and had been asked with his wife to a few bridal dinner-parties, given chiefly by friends of the De Courcy family. Except on such occasions he never passed an evening out of his own house, and had not yet, since his marriage, dined once away from his wife. He told himself that his good conduct in this respect was the result of his own resolution; but, nevertheless, he felt that there was nothing else left for him to do. Nobody asked him to go to the theatre. Nobody begged him to drop in of an evening. Men never asked him why he did not play a

rubber. He would generally saunter into Sebright's after he left his office, and lounge about the room for half an hour, talking to a few men. Nobody was uncivil to him. But he knew that the whole thing was changed, and he resolved, with some wisdom, to accommodate himself to his altered circumstances.

Lady Alexandrina also found her new life rather dull, and was sometimes inclined to be a little querulous. She would tell her husband that she never got out, and would declare, when he offered to walk with her, that she did not care for walking in the streets. " I don't exactly see, then, where you are to walk," he once replied. She did not tell him that she was fond of riding, and that the Park was a very fitting place for such exercise; but she looked it, and he understood her. "I'll do all I can for her," he said to himself; "but I'll not ruin myself." " Amelia is coming to take me for a drive," she said another time. " Ah, that'll be very nice," he answered. " No; it won't be very nice," said Alexandrina. " Amelia is always shopping and bargaining with the tradespeople. But it will be better than being kept in the house without ever stirring out."

They breakfasted nominally at half-past nine; in truth, it was always nearly ten, as Lady Alexandrina found it difficult to get herself out of her room. At half-past ten punctually he left his house for his office. He usually got home by six, and then spent the greatest part of the hour before dinner in the ceremony of dressing. He went, at least, into his dressing-room, after speaking a few words to his wife, and there remained, pulling things about, clipping his nails, looking over any paper that came in his way, and killing the time. He expected his dinner punctually at seven, and began to feel a little cross if he were kept waiting. After dinner, he drank one glass of wine in company with his wife, and one other by himself, during which latter ceremony he would stare at the hot coals, and think of the thing he had done. Then he would go upstairs, and have, first a cup of coffee, and then a cup of tea. He would read his newspaper, open a book or two, hide his face when he yawned, and try to make believe that he liked it. She had no signs or words of love for him. She never sat on his knee, or caressed him. She never showed him that any happiness had come to her in being allowed to live close to him. They thought that they loved each other :—each thought so ; but there was no love, no sympathy, no warmth. The very atmosphere was' cold;— so cold that no fire could remove the chill.

In what way would it have been different had Lily Dale sat opposite to him there as his wife, instead of Lady Alexandrina? He told himself frequently that either with one or with the other life would have been the same; that he had made himself for a while unfit for domestic life, and that he must cure himself of that unfit-ness. But though he declared this to himself in one set of half-spoken thoughts, he would also declare to himself in another set, that Lily would have made the whole house bright with her brightness; that had he brought her home to his hearth, there would have been a sun shining on him every morning and every evening. But, nevertheless, he strove to do his duty, and remembered that the excitement of official life was still open to him. From eleven in the morning till five in the afternoon he could still hold a position which made it necessary that men should regard him with respect, and speak to him with deference. In this respect he was better off than his wife, for she had no office to which she could betake herself.

"Yes," she said to Amelia, "it is all very nice, and I don't mind the house being damp; but I get so tired of being alone."

"That must be the case with women who are married to men of business."

"Oh, I don't complain. Of course I knew what I was about. I suppose it won't be so very dull when everybody is up in London."

"I don't find the season makes much difference to us after Christmas," said Amelia; "but no doubt London is gayer in May. You'll find you'll like it better next year; and perhaps you'll have a baby, you know."

"Psha!" ejaculated Lady Alexandrina; "I don't want a baby, and don't suppose I shall have one."

"It's always something to do, you know."

Lady Alexandrina, though she was not of an energetic temperament, could not but confess to herself that she had made a mistake. She had been tempted to marry Crosbie because Crosbie was a man of fashion, and now she was told that the London season would make no difference to her;—the London season which had hitherto always brought to her the excitement of parties, if it had not given her the satisfaction of amusement. She had been tempted to marry at all because it appeared to her that a married woman could enjoy society with less restraint than a girl who was subject to her mother or her chaperon; that she would have more freedom of action as a married woman; and now she was told that she must wait for a baby before she could have anything to do. Courcy Castle was sometimes dull, but Courcy Castle would have been better than this."

When Crosbie returned home after this little conversation about the baby, he was told by his wife that they were to dine with the Gazebees on the next Sunday. On hearing this he shook his head with vexation. He knew, however, that he had no right to make complaint, as he had been only taken to St. John's Wood once since they had come home from their marriage trip. There was, however, one point as to which he could grumble. "Why, on earth, on Sunday?"

"Because Amelia asked me for Sunday. If you are asked for Sunday, you cannot say you'll go on Monday."

"It is so terrible on a Sunday afternoon. At what hour?"

"She said half-past five."

"Heavens and earth! What are we to do all the evening?"

"It is not kind of you, Adolphus, to speak in that way of my relations."

"Come, my love, that's a joke; as if I hadn't heard you say the same thing twenty times. You've complained of having to go up there much more bitterly than I ever did. You know I like your sister, and, in his way, Gazebee is a very good fellow; but after three or four hours, one begins to have had enough of him."

"It can't be much duller than it is ;" but Lady Alexandrina stopped herself before she finished her speech.

"One can always read at home, at any rate," said Crosbie.

"One can't always be reading. However, I have said you would go. If you choose to refuse, you must write and explain."

When the Sunday came the Crosbies of course did go to St. John's Wood, arriving punctually at that door which he so hated at half-past five. One of the earliest resolutions which he made when he first contemplated the De Courcy match, was altogether hostile to the Gazebees. He would see but very little of them. He would shake himself free of that connexion. It was not with that branch of the family that he desired an alliance. But now, as things had gone, that was the only branch of the family with which he seemed to be allied. He was always hearing of the Gazebees. Amelia and Alexandrina were constantly together. He was now dragged there to a Sunday dinner ; and he knew that he should often be dragged there,—that he could not avoid such draggings. He already owed money to Mortimer Gazebee, and was aware that his affairs had been allowed to fall into that lawyer's hands in such a way that he could not take them out again. His house was very thoroughly furnished, and he knew that the bills had been paid; but he had not paid them; every shilling had been paid through Mortimer Gazebee.

"Go with your mother and aunt, De Courcy," the attorney said to the lingering child after dinner; and then Crosbie was left alone with his wife's brother-in-law. This was the period of the St. John's Wood purgatory which was so dreadful to him. With his sister-in-law he could talk, remembering perhaps always that she was an earl's daughter. But with Gazebee he had nothing in common. And he felt that Gazebee, who had once treated him with great deference, had now lost all such feeling. Crosbie had once been a man of fashion in the estimation of the attorney, but that was all over. Crosbie, in the attorney's estimation, was now simply the secretary of a public office,—a man who owed him money. The two had married sisters, and there was no reason why the light of the prosperous attorney should pale before that of the civil servant, who was not very prosperous. All this was understood thoroughly by both the men.

"There's terrible bad news from Courcy," said the attorney, as soon as the boy was gone.

"Why ; what's the matter ?"

"Porlock has married ;—that woman, you know."

"Nonsense."

"He has. The old lady has been obliged to tell me, and she's nearly broken-hearted about it. But that's not the worst of it to my mind. All the world knows that Porlock had gone to the mischief. But he is going to bring an action against his father for some arrears of his allowance, and he threatens to have everything out in court, if he doesn't get his money."

"But is there money due to him ?"

"Yes, there is. A couple of thousand pounds or so. I suppose I shall have to find it. But, upon my honour, I don't know where it's to come from; I don't, indeed. In one way or another, I've paid over fourteen hundred pounds for you."

"Fourteen hundred pounds !"

"Yes, indeed ;—what with the insurance and the furniture, and the bill from our house for the settlements. That's not paid yet, but it's the same thing. A man doesn't get married for nothing, I can tell you."

"But you've got security."

"Oh, yes ; I've got security. But the thing is the ready money. Our house has advanced so much on the Courcy property, that they don't like going any further; and therefore it is that I have to do this myself. They'll all have to go abroad,—that'll be the end of it. There's been such a scene between the earl and George. George lost his temper and told the earl that Porlock's marriage was his fault. It has ended in George with his wife being turned out."

11 He has money of his own."

" Yes, but he won't spend it. He's coming up here, and we shall find him hanging about us. I don't mean to give him a bed here, and I advise you not to do so either. You'll not get rid of him if you do."

" I have the greatest possible dislike to him."

" Yes ; he's a bad fellow. So is John. Porlock was the best, but he's gone altogether to ruin. They've made a nice mess of it between them ; haven't they ? "

This was the family for whose sake Crosbie had jilted Lily Dale ! His single and simple ambition had been that of being an earl's son-in-law. To achieve that it had been necessary that he should make himself a villain. In achieving it he had gone through all manner of dirt and disgrace. He had married a woman whom he knew he did not love. He was thinking almost hourly of a girl whom he had loved, whom he did love, but whom he had so injured, that, under no circumstances, could he be allowed to speak to her again. The attorney there—who sat opposite to him, talking about his thousands of pounds with that disgusting assumed solicitude which such men put on, when they know very well what they are doing—had made a similar marriage. But he had known what he was about. He had got from his marriage all that he had expected. But what had Crosbie got ?

" They're a bad set,—a bad set," said he in his bitterness.

" The men are," said Gazebee, very comfortably.

" H—m," said Crosbie. It was manifest to Gazebee that his friend was expressing a feeling that the women, also, were not all that they should be, but he took no offence, though some portion of the censure might thereby be supposed to attach to his own wife.

" The countess means well," said Gazebee. " But she's had a hard life of it,—a very hard life. I've heard him call her names that would frighten a coalheaver. I have, indeed. But he'll die soon, and then she'll be comfortable. She has three thousand a year jointure."

He'll die soon, and then she'll be comfortable! That was one phase of married life. As Crosbie's mind dwelt upon the words, he remembered Lily's promise made in the fields, that she would do everything for him. He remembered her kisses ; the touch of her fingers; the low silvery laughing voice ; the feel of her dress as she would press close to him. After that he reflected whether it would not be well that he too should die, so that Alexandrina might be comfortable. She and her mother might be very comfortable together, with plenty of money, at Baden Baden!

The squire at Allington, and Mrs. Dale, and Lady Julia De Guest, had been, and still were, uneasy in their minds because no punishment had fallen upon Crosbie,—no vengeance had overtaken him in consequence of his great sin. How little did they know about it! Could he have been prosecuted and put into prison, with hard labour, for twelve months, the punishment would not have been heavier. He would, in that case, at any rate, have been saved from Lady Alexandrina.

" George and his wife are coming up to town ; couldn't we ask them to come to us for a week or so ? " said his wife to him, as soon as they were in the fly together, going home.

" No," shouted Crosbie; " we will do no such thing." There was not another word said on the subject,—nor on any other subject till they got home. When they reached their house Alexandrina had a headache, and went up to her room immediately. Crosbie threw himself into a chair before the remains of a fire in the dining-room, and resolved that he would cut the whole De

Courcy family together. His wife, as his wife, should obey him. She should obey him,—or else leave him and go her way by herself, leaving him to go his way. There was an income of twelve hundred a year. Would it not be a fine thing for him if he could keep six hundred for himself and return to his old manner of life. All his old comforts of course he would not have,—nor the old esteem and regard of men. But the luxury of a club dinner he might enjoy. Unembarrassed evenings might be his,—with liberty to him to pass them as he pleased. He knew many men who were separated from their wives, and who seemed to be as happy as their neighbours. And then he remembered how ugly Alexandrina had been this evening, wearing a great tinsel coronet full of false stones, with a cold in her head which had

reddened her nose. There had, too, fallen upon her in these her married days a certain fixed dreary dowdiness. She certainly was very plain ! So he said to himself, and then he went to hed. I myself am inclined to think that his punishment was sufficiently severe.

The next morning his wife still complained of headache, so that he breakfasted alone. Since that positive refusal which he had given to her proposition for inviting her brother, there had not been much conversation between them. " My head is splitting, and Sarah shall bring some tea and toast up to me, if you will not mind it."

He did not mind it in the least, and ate his breakfast by himself, with more enjoyment than usually attended that meal.

It was clear to him that all the present satisfaction of his life must come to him from his office work. There are men who find it difficult to live without some source of daily comfort, and he was such a man. He could hardly endure his life unless there were some page in it on which he could look with gratified eyes. He had always liked his work, and he now determined that he would like it better than ever. But in order that he might do so it was necessary that he should have much of his own way. According to the theory of his office, it was incumbent on him as Secretary simply to take the orders of the Commissioners, and see that they were executed; and to such work as this his predecessor had strictly confined himself. But he had already done more than this, and had conceived the ambition of holding the Board almost under his thumb. He flattered himself that he knew his own work and theirs better than they knew either, and that by a little management he might be their master. It is not impossible that such might have been the case had there been no fracas at the Paddington station; but, as we all know, the dominant cock of the farmyard must be ever dominant. When he shall once have had his wings so smeared with mud as to give him even the appearance of adversity, no other cock will ever respect him again. Mr. Optimist and Mr. Butterwell knew very well that their secretary had been cudgelled, and they could not submit themselves to a secretary who had been so treated.

" Oh, by-the-by, Crosbie," said Butterwell, coming into his room, soon after his arrival at his office on that day of his solitary breakfast, "I want to say just a few words to you." And Butter-well turned round and closed the door, the lock of which had not previously been fastened. Crosbie, without much thinking, immediately foretold himself the nature of the coming conversation.

" Do you know " said Butterwell, beginning.

" Sit down, won't you ?" said Crosbie, seating bimself as he •spoke. If there was to be a contest, he would make the best fight he could. He would show a better spirit here than he had done on the railway platform. Butterwell did sit down, and felt as he did so, that the very motion of sitting took away some of his power. He ought to have sent for Crosbie into his own room. A man, when he wishes to reprimand another, should always have the benefit of his own atmosphere.

" I don't want to find any fault," Butterwell began.

" I hope you have not any cause," said Crosbie.

"No, no; I don't say that I have. But we think at the Board "

" Stop, stop, Butterwell. If anything unpleasant is coming, it had better come from the Board. I should take it in better spirit; I should, indeed."

" What takes place at the Board must be official." " I shall not mind that in the least. I should rather like it than otherwise."

" It simply amounts to this,—that we think you are taking a little too much on yourself. No doubt, it's a fault on the right side, and arises from your wishing to have the work well done." " And if I don't do it, who will ? " asked Crosbie. " The Board is very well able to get through all that appertains to it. Come, Crosbie, you and I have known each other a great many years, and it would be a pity that we should have any words. I have come to you in this way because it would be disagreeable to you to have any question raised officially. Optimist isn't given to being very angry, but he was downright angry yesterday. You had better take what I say in good part, and go along a little quieter."

But Crosbie was not in a humour to take anything quietly. He was sore all over, and prone to hit out at everybody that he met. " I have done my duty to the best of my ability, Mr. Butterwell," he said, " and I believe I have done it well. I believe I know my duty here as well as any one can teach me. If I have done more than my share of work, it is because other people have done less than theirs." As he spoke, there was a black cloud upon his brow, and the Commissioner could perceive that the Secretary was very wrathful.

" Oh ! very well," said Butterwell, rising from his chair. " I can only, under such circumstances, speak to the Chairman, and ho will tell you what he thinks at the Board. I think you're foolish ; I do, indeed. As for myself, I have only meant to act kindly by you." After that, Mr. Butterwell took himself off.

On the same afternoon, Crosbie was summoned into the Boardroom in the usual way, between two and three. This was a daily occurrence, as he always sat for about an hour with two out of the three Commissioners, after they had fortified themselves with a biscuit and a glass of sherry. On the present occasion, the usual amount of business was transacted, but it was done in a manner which made Crosbie feel that they did not all stand together on their usual footing. The three Commissioners were all there. The Chairman gave his directions in a solemn, pompous voice, which was by no means usual to him when he was in good humour. The Major said little or nothing ; but there was a gleam of satisfied sarcasm in his eye. Things were going wrong at the Board, and he was pleased. Mr. Butterwell was exceedingly civil in his demeanour, and rather more than ordinarily brisk. As soon as the regular work of the day was over, Mr. Optimist shuffled about on his chair, rising from his seat, and then sitting down again. He looked through a lot of papers close to his hand, peering at them over his spectacles. Then he selected one, took off his spectacles, leaned back in his chair, and began his little speech.

" Mr. Crosbie," he said, " we are all very much gratified,— veiy much gratified, indeed,— by your zeal and energy in the service."

" Thank you, sir," said Crosbie; " I am fond of the service."

" Exactly, exactly ; we all feel that. But we think that you,— if I were to say take too much upon yourself, I should say, perhaps, more than we mean."

" Don't say more than you mean, Mr. Optimist." Crosbie's eyes, as he spoke, gleamed slightly with his momentary triumph ; as did also those of Major Fiasco.

" No, no, no," said Mr. Optimist; " I would say rather less than more to so very good a public servant as yourself. But you, doubtless, understand me ? "

" I don't think I do quite, sir. If I have not taken too much on me, what is it that I have done that I ought not to have done ? "

" You have given directions in many cases for which you ought first to have received authority. Here is an instance," and the selected paper was at once brought out.

It was a matter in which the Secretary had been manifestly wrong according to written law, and he could not defend it on its own merits.

" If you wish me," said he, " to confine myself exactly to the positive instructions of the office, I will do so; but I think you will find it inconvenient."

" It will be far the best," said Mr. Optimist.

" Very well," said Mr. Crosbie, " it shall be done." And he at once determined to make himself as unpleasant to the three gentlemen in the room as he might find it within his power to do. He could make himself very unpleasant, but the unpleasantness would be as much to him as to them.

Nothing would now go right with him. He could look in no direction for satisfaction. He sauntered into Sebright's, as he went home, but he could not find words to speak to any one about the little matters of the day. He went home, and his wife, though she was up, complained still of her headache.

" I haven't been out of the house all day," she said, " and that has made it worse."

" I don't know how you are to get out if you won't walk," he answered.

Then there was no more said between them till they sat down to their meal.

Had the squire at Allington known all, he might, I think, have been satisfied with the punishment which Crosbie had encountered.

CHAPTER XIX. PREPARATIONS FOR GOING.

" MAMMA, read that letter."

It was Mrs. Dale's eldest daughter who spoke to her, and they were alone together in the parlour at the Small House. Mrs. Dale took the letter and read it very carefully. She then put it back into its envelope and returned it to Bell.

"It is, at any rate, a good letter, and, as I believe, tells the truth."

" I think it tells a little more than the truth, mamma. As you say, it is a well-written letter. He always writes well when he is in earnest. But yet "

" Yet what, my dear ?"

" There is more head than heart in it."

" If so, he will suffer the less ; that is, if you are quite resolved in the matter."

"I am quite resolved, and I do not think he will suffer much. He would not, I suppose, have taken the trouble to write like that, if he did not wish this thing."

" I am quite sure that he does wish it, most earnestly ; and that he will be greatly disappointed."

"As he would be if any other scheme did not turn out to his satisfaction; that is all."

The letter, of course, was from Bell's cousin Bernard, and containing the strongest plea he was able to make in favour of his suit for her hand. Bernard Dale was better able to press such a plea by letter than by spoken words. He was a man capable of doing anything well in the doing of which a little time for consideration might be given to him ; but he had not in him that power of passion which will force a man to eloquence in asking for that which he desires to obtain. His letter on this occasion was long, and well argued. If

PREPARATIONS FOR GOING.

there was little in it of passionate love, there was much of pleasant flattery. He told Bell how advantageous to hoth their families their marriage would be ; he declared to her that his own feeling in the matter had been rendered stronger by absence; he alluded without boasting to his past career of life as her best guarantee for his future conduct; he explained to her that if this marriage could be arranged there need then, at any rate, be no further question as to his aunt removing with Lily from the Small House; and then he told her that his affection for herself was the absorbing passion of his existence. Had the letter been written with the view of obtaining from a third person a favourable verdict as to his suit, it would have been a very good letter indeed ; but there was not a word in it that could stir the heart of such a girl as Bell Dale.

" Answer him kindly," Mrs. Dale said.

"As kindly as I know how," said Bell. "I wish you would write the letter, mamma."

" I fear that would not do. What I should say would only tempt him to try again."

Mrs. Dale knew very well,—had known for some months past,— that Bernard's suit was hopeless. She felt certain, although the matter had not been discussed between them, that whenever Dr. Crofts might choose to come again and ask for her daughter's hand he would not be refused. Of the two men she probably liked Dr. Crofts the best; but she liked them both, and she could not but remember that the one, in a worldly point of view, would be a very poor match, whereas the other would, in all respects, be excellent. She would not, on any account, say a word to influence her daughter, and knew, moreover, that no word which she could say would influence her ; but she could not divest herself of some regret that it should be so.

" I know what you would wish, mamma," said Bell.

" I have but one wish, dearest, and that is for your happiness. May God preserve you from any such fate as Lily's. When I tell you to write kindly to your cousin, I simply mean that I think him to have deserved a kind reply by his honesty."

" It shall be as kind as I can make it, mamma; but you know what the lady says in the play,—how hard it is to take the sting from that word « no.' " Then Bell walked out alone for a while, and on her return got her desk and wrote her letter. It was very firm and decisive. As for that wit which should pluck the sting VOL.

"from sucli a sharp and waspish word as 'no,'" I fear she had it not. " It will be better to make him understand that I, also, am in earnest," she said to herself; and in this frame of mind she wrote her letter. "Pray do not allow yourself to think that what I have said is unfriendly," she added, in a postscript. " I know how good you are, and I know the great value of what I refuse; but in this matter it must be my duty to tell you the simple truth."

It had been decided between the squire and Mrs. Dale that the removal from the Small House to Guestwick was not to take place till the first of May. When he had been made to understand that Dr. Crofts had thought it injudicious that Lily should be taken out of their present house in March, he had used all the eloquence of which he was master to induce Mrs. Dale to consent to abandon her project. He had told her that he had always considered that house as belonging, of right, to some other of the family than himself; that it had always been so inhabited, and that no squire of Allington had for years past taken rent for it. " There is no favour conferred,—none at all," he had said ; but speaking nevertheless in his usual sharp, ungenial tone.

" There is a favour, a great favour, and great generosity," Mrs. Dale had replied. " And I have never been too proud to accept it; but when I tell you that we think we shall be happier at Guestwick, you will not refuse to let us go. Lily has had a great blow in that house, and Bell feels that she is running counter to your wishes on her behalf,—wishes that are so very kind! "

" No more need be said about that. All that may come right yet, if you will remain where you are."

But Mrs. Dale knew that " all that " could never come right, and persisted. Indeed, she would hardly have dared to tell her girls that she had yielded to the squire's entreaties. It was just then, at that very time, that the squire was, as it were, in treaty with the earl about Lily's fortune; and he did feel it hard that he should be opposed in such a way by his own relatives at the moment when he was behaving towards them with so much generosity. But in his arguments about the house he said nothing of Lily, or her future prospects.

They were to move on the first of May, and one week of April was already past. The squire had said nothing further on the matter after the interview with Mrs. Dale to which allusion has just been made. He was vexed and sore at the separation, thinking that he

was ill-used by the feeling which was displayed by this refusal. He had done his duty by them, as he thought; indeed more than his duty, and now they told him that they were leaving him because they could no longer bear the weight of an obligation conferred^ by his hands. But in truth he did not understand them; nor did they understand him. He had been hard in his manner, and had occasionally domineered, not feeling that his position, though it gave him all the privileges of a near and a dear friend, did not give him the authority of a father or a husband. In that matter of Bernard's proposed marriage he had spoken as though Bell should have considered his wishes before she refused her cousin. He had taken upon himself to scold Mrs. Dale, and had thereby given offence to the girls, which they at the time had found it utterly impossible to forgive.

But they were hardly better satisfied in the matter than was he ; and now that the time had come, though they could not bring themselves to go back from their demand, almost felt that they were treating the squire with cruelty. When their decision had been made,—while it had been making,—he had been stern and hard to them. Since that he had been softened by Lily's misfortune, and softened also by the anticipated loneliness which would come upon him when they should be gone from his side. It was hard upon him that they should so treat him when he was doing his best for them all! And they also felt this, though they did not know the extent to which he was anxious to go in serving them. When they had sat round the fire planning the scheme of their removal, their hearts had been hardened against him, and they had resolved to assert their independence. But now, when the time for action had come, they felt that their grievances against him had already been in a great measure assuaged. This tinged all that they did with a certain sadness ; but still they continued their work.

Who does not know how terrible are those preparations for house-moving;—how infinite in number are the articles which must be packed, how inexpressibly uncomfortable is the period of packing, and how poor and tawdry is the aspect of one's bebngings while they are thus in a state of dislocation ? Now-a-days people who understand the world, and have money commensurate with their understanding, have learned the way of shunning all these disasters, and of leaving the work' to the hands of persons paid for doing it. The crockery is left in the cupboards, the books on the shelves,

the wine in the bins, the curtains on their poles, and the family that is understanding goes for a fortnight to Brighton. At the end of that time the crockery is comfortably settled in other cupboards, the books on other shelves, the wine in other bins, the curtains are hung on other poles, and all is arranged. But Mrs. Dale and her daughters understood nothing of such a method of moving as this. The assistance of the village carpenter in filling certain cases that he had made was all that they knew how to obtain beyond that of their own two servants. Every article had to pass through the hands of some one of the family; and as they felt almost overwhelmed by the extent of the work to be done, they began it much sooner than was necessary, so that it became evident as they advanced in their work, that they would have to pass a dreadfully dull, stupid, uncomfortable week at last, among their boxes and cases, in all the confusion of dismantled furniture.

At first an edict had gone forth that Lily was to do nothing. She was an invalid, and was to be petted and kept quiet. But this edict soon fell to the ground, and Lily worked harder than either her mother or her sister. In truth she was hardly an invalid any longer, and would not submit to an invalid's treatment. She felt herself that for the present constant occupation could alone save her from the misery of looking back,—and she had conceived an idea that the harder that occupation was, the better it would* be for her. While pulling down the books, and folding the linen, and turning out from their old hiding-places the small long-forgotten properties of the household, she would be as gay as ever she had been in old times. She would talk over her work, standing with flushed cheek and laughing eyes among the dusty ruins around her, till for a moment her mother would think that all was well within her. But then at other moments, when the reaction came, it would seem as though nothing were well. She could not sit quietly over the fire, with quiet rational work in her hands, and chat in a rational quiet way. Not as yet could she do so. Nevertheless it was well with her,— within her own bosom. She had declared to herself that she would conquer her misery,—as she had also declared to herself during her illness that'her misfortune should not kill her,—and she was in the way to conquer it. She told herself that the world was not over for her because her sweet hopes had been frustrated. The wound had been deep and very sore, but the flesh of the patient had been sound and healthy, and her blood pure. A physician having knowledge in

such cases would have declared, after long watching of her symptoms, that a cure was probable. Her mother was the physician who watched her with the closest eyes ; and she, though she was sometimes driven to doubt, did hope, with stronger hope from day to day, that her child might live to remember the story of her love without abiding agony.

That nobody should talk to her about it,—that had been the one stipulation which she had seemed to make, not sending forth a request to that effect among her friends in so many words, but showing by certain signs that such was her stipulation. A word to that effect she had spoken to her uncle,—as may be remembered, which word had been regarded with the closest obedience. She had gone out into her little world very soon after the news of Crosbie's falsehood had reached her,—first to church and then among the people of the village, resolving to carry herself as though no crushing weight had fallen upon her. The village people had understood it all, listening to her and answering her without the proffer of any outspoken parley.

" Lord bless 'ee," said Mrs. Crump, the postmistress,and Mrs. Crump was supposed to have the sourest temper in Allington,— " whenever I look at thee, Miss Lily, I thinks that surely thee is the beautifulest young 'ooman in all these parts."

"And you are the Grossest old woman," said Lily, laughing, and giving her hand to the postmistress.

" So I be," said Mrs. Crump. " So I be." Then Lily sat down in the cottage and asked after her ailments. With Mrs. Hearn it. was the same. Mrs. Hearn, after that first meeting which has been already mentioned, petted and caressed her, but spoke no further word of her misfortune. When Lily called a second time upon Mrs. Boyce, which she did boldly by herself, that lady did begin one other word of commiseration. " My dearest Lily, we

have all been made so unhappy " So far Mrs. Boyce got, sitting

close to Lily and striving to look into her face; but Lily, with a slightly heightened colour, turned sharp round upon one of the Boyce girls, tearing Mrs. Boyce's commiseration into the smallest shreds. "Minnie," she said, speaking quite loud, almost with girlish ecstasy, "what do you think Tartar did yesterday? I never laughed so much in my life." Then she told a ludicrous story about a very ugly terrier which belonged to the squire. After that even Mrs. Boyce made no further attempt. Mrs. Dale and Bell both

THE SMALL HOUSE AT ALLINGTON.

understood that such was to be the rule, the rule even to them. Lily would speak to them occasionally on the matter, to one of them at a time, beginning with some almost -single word of melancholy resignation, and then would go on till she opened her very bosom before them; but no such conversation was ever begun by them. But now, in these busy days of the packing, that topic seemed to have been banished altogether.

" Mamma," she said, standing on the top rung of a house-ladder, from which position she was handing down glass out of a cupboard, " are you sure that these things are ours ? I think some of them belong to the house."

" I'm sure about that bowl at any rate, because it was my mother's before I was married."

" Oh, dear, what should I do if I were to break it ? Whenever I handle anything very precious I always feel inclined to throw it down and smash it. Oh ! it was as nearly gone as possible, mamma ; but that was your fault."

" If you don't take care you'll be nearly gone yourself. Do take hold of something."

" Oh, Bell, here's the inkstand for which you've been moaning for three years."

" I haven't been moaning for three years; but who could have put it up there ? "

" Catch it," said Lily ; and she threw the bottle down on to a pile of carpets.

At this moment a step was heard in the hall, and the squire entered through the open door of the room. " So you're all at work," said he.

" Yes, we're at work," said Mrs. Dale, almost with a tone of shame. " If it is to. be done it is as well that it should be got over."

" It makes me wretched enough," said the squire. " But I didn't come to talk about that. I've brought you a note from Lady Julia De Guest, and I've had one from the earl. They want us all to go there and stay the week after Easter."

Mrs. Dale and the girls, when this very sudden proposition was made to them, all remained fixed in their places, and, for a moment, were speechless. Go and stay a week at Guestwick Manor! The whole family! Hitherto the intercourse between the Manor and the Small House had been confined to morning calls, very far between. Mrs. Dale had never dined there, and had latterly even deputed the

"BELT,, HERE'S THE INKSTAND.

calling to her daughters. Once Bell had dined there with her uncle, the squire, and once Lily had gone over with her uncle Orlando. Even this had been long ago, hefore they were quite hrought out, and they had regarded the occasion with the solemn awe of children. Now, at this time of their flitting into some small mean dwelling at Guestwick, they had previously settled among themselves that that affair of calling at the Manor might he allowed to drop. Mrs. Eames never called, and they were descending to the level of Mrs. Eames. 11 Perhaps we shall get game sent to us, and that will be better," Lily had said. And now, at this very moment of their descent in life, they were all asked to go and stay a week at the Manor ! Stay a week with Lady Julia ! Had the Queen sent the Lord Chamberlain down to bid them all go to Windsor Castle it could hardly have startled them more at the first blow. Bell had been seated on the folded carpet when her uncle had entered, and now had again sat herself in the same place. Lily was still standing at the top of the ladder, and Mrs. Dale was at the foot with one hand on Lily's dress. The squire had told his story very abruptly, but he was a man who, having a story to tell, knew nothing better than to tell it out abruptly, letting out everything at the first moment.

" Wants us all! " said Mrs. Dale. " How many does the all mean ? " Then she opened Lady Julia's note and read it, not moving from her position at the foot of the ladder.

"Do let me see, mamma," said Lily; and then the note was handed up to her. Had Mrs. Dale well considered the matter she might probably have kept the note to herself for a while, but the whole thing was so sudden that she had not considered the matter well. Mr DEAR MRS. DALE (the letter ran),

I SEND this inside a note from my brother to Mr. Dale. We particularly want you and your two girls to come to us for a week from the seventeenth of this month. Considering our near connection we ought to have seen more of each other than we have done for years past, and of course it has been our fault. But it is never too late to amend one's ways; and I hope you will receive my confession in the true spirit of affection in which it is intended, and that you will show your goodness by coming to us. I will do all I can to make the house pleasant to your girls, for both of whom I have much real regard.

I should tell you that John Eames will be here for the same week. My brother is very fond of him, and thinks him the best young man of the day. He is one of my heroes, too, I must confess.

Very sincerely yours,
JULIA DE GUEST.

Lily, standing on the ladder, read the letter very attentively. The squire meanwhile stood below speaking a word or two to his sister-in-law and niece. No one could see Lily's face, as it was turned away towards the window, and it was still averted when she spoke. "It is out of the question that we should go, mamma ;— that is, all of us."

" Why out of the question ?" said the squire.

" A whole family! " said Mrs. Dale.

" That is just what they want," said the squire.

"I should like of all things to be left alone for a week," said Lily, " if mamma and Bell would go."

" That wouldn't do at all," said the squire. " Lady Julia specially wants you to be one of the party."

The thing had been badly managed altogether. The reference in Lady Julia's note to John Eames had explained to Lily the whole scheme at once, and had so opened her eyes that all the combined influence of the Dale and De Guest families could not have dragged her over to the Manor.

" Why not do ? " said Lily. " It would be out of the question a whole family going in that way, but it would be very nice for Bell."

" No, it would not," said Bell.

" Don't be ungenerous about it, my dear," said the squire, turning to Bell; "Lady Julia means to be kind. But, my darling," and the squire turned again towards Lily, addressing her, as was his wont in these days, with an affection that was almost vexatious to her; "but, my darling, why should you not go? A change of scene like that will do you all the good in the world, just when you are getting well. Mary, tell the girls that they ought to go."

Mrs. Dale stood silent, again reading the note, and Lily came down from the ladder. When she reached the floor she went directly up to her uncle, and taking his hand turned him round with herself towards one of the windows, so that they stood with their backs to the room. " Uncle," she said, " do not be angry with me. I can't go;" and then she put up her face to kiss him.

He stooped and kissed her and still held her hand. He looked into her face and read it all. He knew well, now, why she could not go; or, rather, why she herself thought that she could not go. " Cannot you, my darling ? " he said.

" No, uncle. It is very kind,—very kind; but I cannot go. I am not fit to go anywhere."

" But you should get over that feeling. You should make a struggle."

" I am struggling, and I shall succeed ; hut I cannot do it all at once. At any rate I could not go there. You must give my love to Lady Julia, and not let her think me cross. Perhaps Bell will go."

What would he the good of Bell's going—or the good of his putting himself out of the way, by a visit which would of itself be so tiresome to him, if the one object of the visit could not be earned out ? The earl and his sister had planned the invitation with the express intention of bringing Lily and Eames together. It seemed that Lily was firm in her determination to resist this intention ; and, if so, it would be better that the whole thing should fall to the ground. He was very vexed, and yet he was not angry with her. Everybody lately had opposed him in everything. All his intended family arrangements had gone wrong. But yet he was seldom angry respecting them. He was so accustomed to be thwarted that he hardly expected success. In this matter of providing Lily with a second lover, he had not come forward of his own accord. He had been appealed to by his neighbour the earl, and had certainly answered the appeal with much generosity. He had been induced to make the attempt with eagerness, and a true desire for its accomplishment ; but in this, as in all his own schemes, he was met at once by opposition and failure.

"'I will leave you to talk it over among yourselves," he said. " But, Mary, you had better see me before you send your answer. If you will come up by-and-by, Ralph shall take the two notes over together in the afternoon." So saying, he left the Small House, and went back to his own solitary home.

" Lily, dear," said Mrs. Dale, as soon as the front door had been closed, " this is meant for kindness to you,—for most affectionate kindness."

" I know it, mamma ; and you must go to Lady Julia, and must tell her that I know it. You must give her my love. And, indeed, I do love her now. But "

" You won't go, Lily? " said Mrs. Dale, beseechingly.

" No, mamma ; certainly I will not go." Then she escaped out of the room by herself, and for the next hour neither of them dared to go to her.

CHAPTER XX.

MRS. DALE IS THANKFUL FOR A GOOD THING.

ON that day they dined early at the Small House, as they had been in the habit of doing since the packing had commenced. And after dinner Mrs. Dale went through the gardens, up to the other house, with a written note in her hand. In that note she had told Lady Julia, with many protestations of gratitude, that Lily was unable to go out so soon after her illness, and that she herself was obliged to stay with Lily. She explained also, that the business of moving was in hand, and that, therefore, she could not herself accept the invitation. But her other daughter, she said, would be very happy to accompany her uncle to Guestwick Manor. Then, without closing her letter, she took it up to the squire in order that it might be decided whether it would or would not suit his views. It might well be that he would not care to go to Lord De Guest's with Bell alone.

" Leave it with me," he said ; " that is, if you do not object."

"Oh dear, no!"

"I'll tell you the plain truth at once, Mary. I shall go over myself with it, and see the earl. Then I will decline it or not, according to what passes between me and him. I wish Lily would have gone."

"Ah! she could not."

"I wish she could. I wish she could. I wish she could." As he repeated the words over and over again, there was an eagerness in his voice that filled Mrs. Dale's heart with tenderness towards him."

"The truth is," said Mrs. Dale, "she could not go there to meet John Eames."

"Oh, I know," said the squire: "I understand it. But that is just what we want her to do. Why should she not spend a week in the same house with an honest young man whom we all like."

"There are reasons why she would not wish it."

"Ah, exactly; the very reasons which should make us induce her to go there if we can. Perhaps I had better tell you all. Lord De Guest has taken him by the hand, and wishes him to marry. He has promised to settle on him an income which will make him comfortable for life."

"That is very generous; and I am delighted to hear it,—for John's sake."

"And they have promoted him at his office."

"Ah! then he will do well."

"He will do very well. He is private secretary now to their head man. And, Mary, so that she, Lily, should not be empty-handed if this marriage can be arranged, I have undertaken ta settle a hundred a year on her,—on her and her children, if she will accept him. Now you know it all. I did not mean to tell you; but it is as well that you should have the means of judging. That other man was a villain. This man is honest. Would it not be well that she should learn to like him? She always did like him, I thought, before that other fellow came down here among us."

"She has always liked him—as a friend."

"She will never get a better lover."

Mrs. Dale sat silent, thinking over it all. Every word that the squire said was true, It would be a healing of wounds most desirable and salutary; an arrangement advantageous to them all; a destiny for Lily most devoutly to be desired,—if only it were possible. Mrs. Dale firmly believed that if her daughter could be made to accept John Eames as her second lover in a year or two all would be well. Crosbie would then be forgotten or thought of without regret, and Lily would become the mistress of a happy home. But there are positions which cannot be reached, though there be no physical or material objection in the way. It is the view which the mind takes of a thing which creates the sorrow that arises from it. If the heart were always malleable and the feelings could be controlled, who would permit himself to be tormented by any of the reverses which affection meets? Death would create no sorrow; ingratitude would lose its sting; and the betrayal of love would do no injury beyond that which it might entail upon worldly circum-stances. But the heart is not malleable; nor will the feelings admit of such control.

"It is not possible for her," said Mrs. Dale. "I fear it is not possible. It is too soon."

"Six months," pleaded the squire.

"It will take years,—not months," said Mrs. Dale.

"And she will lose all her youth."

"Yes; he has done all that by his treachery. But it is done, and we cannot now go back. She loves him yet as dearly as she ever loved him."

Then the squire muttered certain words below his breath,— ejaculations against Crosbie, which were hardly voluntary; but even as involuntary ejaculations were very improper. Mrs. Dale heard them, and was not offended either by their impropriety or their warmth. " But you can understand," she said, " that she cannot bring herself to go there." The squire struck the table with his fist, and repeated his ejaculations. If he could only have known how very disagreeable Lady Alexandrina was making herself, his spirit might, perhaps, have been less vehemently disturbed. If, also, he could have perceived and understood the light in which an alliance with the De Courcy family was now regarded by Crosbie, I think that he would have received some consolation from that consideration. Those who offend us are generally punished for the offence they give ; but we so frequently miss the satisfaction of knowing that we are avenged ! It is arranged, apparently, that the injurer shall be punished, but that the person injured shall not gratify his desire for vengeance.

" And will you go to Guestwick yourself? " asked Mrs. Dale.

" I will take the note," said the squire, " and will let you know to-morrow. The earl has behaved so kindly that every possible consideration is due to him. I had better tell him the whole truth, and go or stay, as he may wish. I don't see the good of going. What am I to do at Guestwick Manor ? I did think that if we had all been there it might have cured some difficulties."

Mrs. Dale got up to leave him, but she could not go without saying some word of gratitude for all that he had attempted to do for them. She well knew what he meant by the curing of difficulties. He had intended to signify that had they lived together for a week at Guestwick the idea of flitting from Allington might possibly have been abandoned. It seemed now to Mrs. Dale as though her

brother-in-law were heaping coals of fire on her head in return for that intention. She felt half-ashamed of what she was doing, almost acknowledging to herself that she should have borne with his sternness in return for the benefits he had done to her daughters. Had she not feared their reproaches she would, even now, have given way.

" I do not know what I ought to say to you for your kindness." 11 Say nothing,—either for my kindness or unkindness ; but stay where you are, and let us live like Christians together, striving to think good and not evil." These were kind, loving words, showing in themselves a spirit of love and forbearance ; but they were spoken in a harsh, unsympathizing voice, and the speaker, as he uttered them, looked gloomily at the fire. In truth the squire, as he spoke^ was half-ashamed of the warmth of what he said.

" At any rate I will not think evil," Mrs. Dale answered, giving him her hand. After that she left him, and returned home. It was too late for her to abandon her project of moving and remain at the Small House; but as she went across the garden she almost confessed to herself that she repented of what she was doing. •

In these days of the cold early spring, the way from the lawn into the house, through the drawing-room window, was not as yet open, and it was necessary to go round by the kitchen-garden on to the road, and thence in by the front door ; or else to pass through the back door, and into the house by the kitchen. This latter mode of entrance Mrs. Dale now adopted; and as she made her way into the hall Lily came upon her, with very silent steps, out from the parlour, and arrested her progress. There was a- smile upon Lily's face as she lifted up her finger as if in caution, and no one looking at her would have supposed that she was herself in trouble. " Mamma," she said, pointing to the drawing-room door, and speaking almost in a whisper, " you must not go in there; come into the parlour."

" Who's there ? Where's Bell ? " and Mrs. Dale went into the parlour as she was bidden. " But who is there ? " she repeated.

" He's there ! "

"Who is he?"

"Oh, mamma, don't be a goose! Dr. Crofts is there, of course. He's been nearly an hour. I wonder how he is managing, for there is nothing on earth to sit upon but the old lump of a carpet. The room is strewed about with crockery, and Bell is such a figure! She has got on your old checked apron, and when he came in she was rolling up the fire-irons in brown paper. I don't suppose she was ever in such a mess before. There's one thing certain,—he can't kiss her hand."

"It's you are the goose, Lily."

"But he's in there certainly, unless he has gone out through the window, or up the chimney."

"What made you leave them?"

"He met me here, in the passage, and spoke to me *ever so seriously. 'Come in,' I said, * and see Bell packing the pokers and tongs.' * I will go in,' he said, ' but don't come with me.' He was ever so serious, and I'm sure he had been thinking of it all the way along."

"And why should he not be serious?"

"Oh, no, of course he ought to be serious; but are you not gla4, mamma? I am so glad. We shall live alone together, you and I; but she will be so close to us! My belief is that he'll stay there for ever unless somebody does something. I have been so tired of waiting and looking out for you. Perhaps he's helping her to p^ck the things. Don't you think we might go in; or would it be ill-natured?"

"Lily, don't be in too great a hurry to say anything. You may be mistaken, you know; and there's many a slip between the cup and the lip."

"Yes, mamma, there is," said Lily, putting her hand inside her mother's arm, "that's true enough."

"Oh, my darling, forgive me," said the mother, suddenly remembering that the use of the old proverb at the present moment had been almost cruel.

"Do not mind it," said Lily, "it does not hurt me, it does me good; that is to say, when there is nobody by except yourself. But, with God's help, there shall be no slip here, and she shall be happy. It is all the difference between one thing done in a hurry, and another done with much thinking. But they'll remain there for ever if we don't go in. Come, mamma, you open the door."

Then Mrs. Bell did open the door, giving some little premonitory notice with the handle, so that the couple inside might be warned of approaching footsteps. Crofts had not escaped, either through the window or up the chimney, but was seated in the middle of the room on an empty box, just opposite to Bell, who was seated upon the lump of carpeting. Bell still wore the checked apron as described by her sister. What might have been the state of her hands I will not pretend to say; but I do not believe that her lover had found anything amiss with them. "How do you do, doctor?" said Mrs. Dale, striving to use her accustomed voice, and to look as though there were nothing of special importance in his visit. "I have just come down from the Great House."

"Mamma," said Bell, jumping up, "you must not call him. doctor any more."

"Must I not? Has any one undoctored him?"

"Oh, mamma, you understand," said Bell.

"I understand," said Lily, going up to the doctor, and giving him her cheek to kiss, "he is to be my brother, and I mean to claim him as such from this moment. I expect him to do everything for us, and not to call a moment of his time his own."

"Mrs. Dale," said the doctor, "Bell has consented that it shall be so, if you will consent."

"There is but little doubt of that," said Mrs. Dale.

"We shall not be rich" began the doctor.

"I hate to be rich," said Bell. "I hate even to talk about it. I don't think it quite manly even to think about it; and I'm sure it isn't womanly."

"Bell was always a fanatic in praise of poverty," said Mrs. Dale.

"No; I'm no fanatic. I'm very fond of money earned. I would like to earn some myself if I knew how."

"Let her go out and visit the lady patients," said Lily. "They do in America."

Then they all went into the parlour and sat round the fire talking as though they were already one family. The proceeding, considering the nature of it,—that a young lady, acknowledged to be of great beauty and known to be of good birth, had on the occasion been asked and given in marriage,—was carried on after a somewhat humdrum fashion, and in a manner that must be called commonplace. How different had it been when Crosbie had made his offer! Lily for the time had been raised to a pinnacle,—a pinnacle which might be dangerous, but which was, at any rate, lofty. With what a pretty speech had Crosbie been greeted! How it had been felt by all concerned that the fortunes of the Small House were v in the ascendant,—felt, indeed, with some trepidation, but still with much inward triumph. How great had been the occasion, forcing Lily

almost to lose herself in wonderment at what had occurred! There was no great occasion now, and no wonderment. No one, unless it was Crofts, felt very triumphant. But they were all very happy, and were sure that there was safety in their happiness. It was hut the other day that one of them had been thrown rudely to the ground through the treachery of a lover, hut yet none of them feared treachery from this lover. Bell was as sure of her lot in life as though she were already being taken home to her modest house in Guestwick. Mrs. Dale already looked upon the man as her son, and the party of four as they sat round the fire grouped themselves as though they already formed one family.

But Bell was not seated next to her lover. Lily, when she had once accepted Crosbie, seemed to think that she could never be too-near to him. She had been in no wise ashamed of her love, and had shown it constantly by some little caressing motion of her hand, leaning on his arm, looking into his face, as though she were continually desirous of some palpable assurance of his presence. It was not so at all with Bell. She was happy in loving and in being loved, but she required no overt testimonies of affection. I do not think it would have made her unhappy if some sudden need had required that Crofts should go to India and back before they were married. The thing was settled, and that was enough for her. But, on the other hand, when he spoke of the expediency of an immediate marriage, she raised no difficulty. As her mother was about to go into a new residence, it might be as well that that residence should be fitted to the wants of two persons instead of three. So they talked about chairs and tables, carpets and kitchens, in a most unromantic, homely, useful manner! A considerable portion of the furniture in the house they were now about to leave belonged to the squire,—or to the house rather, as they were in the habit of saying. The older and more solid things,—articles of household stuff that stand the wear of half a century,—had been in the Small House when they came to it. There was, therefore, a question of buying new furniture for a house in Guestwick,—a question not devoid of importance to the possessor of so moderate an income as that owned by Mrs. Dale. In the first month or two they were to live in lodgings, and their goods were to be stored in some friendly warehouse. Under such circumstances would it not be well that Bell's marriage should be so arranged that the lodging question might not be in any degree complicated by her necessities? This was the last suggestion made by Dr. Crofts, induced no doubt by the great encouragement lie had received.

"That would be hardly possible," said Mrs. Dale. "It only •wants three weeks ;—and with the house in such a condition! " " James is joking," said Bell.

" I was not joking at all," said the doctor.

" Why not send for Mr. Boyce, and cany her off at once on a pillion behind you?" said Lily. "It's just the sort of thing for primitive people to do, like you and Bell. All the same, Bell, I do wish you could have been married from this house."

" I don't think it will make much difference," said Bell.

" Only if you would have waited till summer we would have had such a nice party on the lawn. It sounds so ugly, being married from lodgings ; doesn't it, mamma ? "

"It doesn't sound at all ugly to me," said Bell.

" I shall always call you Dame Commonplace when you're married," said Lily.

Then they had tea, and after tea Dr. Crofts got on his horse and rode back to Guestwick.

" Now may I talk about him ? " said Lily, as soon as the door was closed behind his back.

" No; you may not."

" As if I hadn't known it all along ! And wasn't it hard to bear that you should have scolded me with such pertinacious austerity, and that I wasn't to say a word in answer ! "

" I dont' remember the austerity," said Mrs. Dale.

" Nor yet Lily's silence," said Bell.

" But it's all settled now," said Lily, " and I'm downright happy. I never felt more satisfaction,—never, Bell! "

" Nor did I," said her mother; " I may truly say that I thank God for this good thing."

CHAPTER XXI.

JOHN EAMES DOES THINGS WHICH HE OUGHT NOT TO HAVE DONE.

JOHN EAMES succeeded in making his bargain with Sir Baffle Buffle. He accepted the private-secretaryship on the plainly expressed condition that he was to have leave of absence for a fortnight towards the end of April. Having arranged this he took an affectionate leave of Mr. Love, who was really much affected at parting with him, discussed valedictory pots of porter in the big room, over which many wishes were expressed that he might be enabled to compass the length and breadth of old Huffle's feet, uttered a last cutting joke at Mr. Kissing as he met that gentleman hurrying through the passages with an enormous ledger in his hands, and then took his place in the comfortable arm-chair which FitzHoward had been forced to relinquish.

" Don't tell any of the fellows," said Fitz, " but I'm going to cut the concern altogether. My governor wouldn't let me stop here in any other place than that of private secretary."

" Ah, your governor is a swell," said Eames.

" I don't know about that," said FitzHoward. " Of course he has a good deal of family interest. My cousin is to come in for St. Bungay at the next election, and then I can do better than remain here."

" That's a matter of course," said Eames. " If my cousin were Member for St. Bungay, I'd never stand anything east of Whitehall."

" And I don't mean," said FitzHoward. " This room, you know, is all very nice; but it is a bore coming into the City every day. And then one doesn't like to be rung for like a servant. Not that I mean to put you out of conceit with it."

" It will do very well for me," said Earnes. " I never was very particular." And so they parted, Eames assuming the beautiful arm-chair and the peril of being asked to carry Sir Baffle's shoes, while FitzHoward took the vacant desk in the big room till such time as some member of his family should come into Parliament for the borough of St. Bungay.

But Eames, though he drank the porter, and quizzed FitzHoward, and gibed at Kissing, did not seat himself in his new arm-chair without some serious thoughts. He was aware that his career in London had not hitherto been one on which he could look back with self-respect. He had lived with friends whom he did not esteem; he had been idle, and sometimes worse than idle; and he had allowed himself to be hampered by the pretended love of a woman for whom he had never felt any true affection, and by whom he had been cozened out of various foolish promises which even yet were hanging over his head. As he sat with Sir Baffle's notes before him, he thought almost with horror of the men and women in Burton Crescent. It was now about three years since he had first known Cradell, and he shuddered as he remembered how very poor a creature was he whom he had chosen for his bosom friend. He could not make for himself those excuses which we can make for him. He could not tell himself that he had been driven by circumstances to choose a friend, before he had learned to know what were the requisites for which he should look. He had lived on terms of closest intimacy with this man for three years, and now his eyes were opening themselves to the nature of his friend's character. Cradell was in age three years his senior. " I won't drop him," he said to himself; "but he is a poor creature." He thought, too, of the Lupexes, of Miss Spruce, and of Mrs. Boper, and tried to imagine what Lily Dale would do if she found herself among such people. It would be impossible that she should ever so find herself. He might as well ask her to drink at the bar of a gin-shop as to sit down in Mrs. Boper's drawing-room. If destiny had in store for him such good fortune as that of calling Lily his own, it was necessary that he should altogether alter his mode of life.

In truth his hobbledehoyhood was dropping ofi from him, as its old skin drops from a snake. Much of the feeling and something of the knowledge of manhood was coming on him, and he was beginning to recognize to himself that the future manner of his life must be to him a matter of very serious concern. No such thought had come near him when he first established himself in London. It seems to me that in this respect the fathers and mothers of the present generation understand but little of the inward nature of the young men for whom they are so anxious. They give them credit for so much that it is impossible they should have, and then deny them credit for so much that they possess ! They expect from them when boys the discretion of men,—that discretion which comes from thinking; but will not give them credit for any of that power of thought which alone can ultimately produce good conduct. Young men are generally thoughtful,—more thoughtful than their seniors; but the fruit of their thought is not as yet there. And then so little is done for the amusement of lads who are turned loose into London at nineteen or twenty. Can it be that any mother really expects her son to sit alone evening after evening in a dingy room drinking bad tea, and reading good books ? And yet it seems that mothers do so expect,—the very mothers who talk about the thoughtlessness of youth! 0 ye mothers who from year to year see your sons launched forth upon the perils of the world, and who are so careful with your good advice, with under flannel shirting, with books of devotion and tooth-powder, does it never occur to you that provision should be made for amusement, for dancing, for parties, for the excitement and comfort of women's society? That excitement your sons will have, and if it be not provided by you of one kind, will certainly be provided by themselves of another kind. If I were a mother sending lads out into the world, the matter most in my mind would be this,—to what houses full of nicest girls could I get them admission, so that they might do their flirting in good company.

Poor John Eames had been so placed that he had been driven to do his flirting in very bad company, and he was now fully aware that it had been so. It wanted but two days to his departure for Guestwick Manor, and as he sat breathing a while after the manufacture of a large batch of Sir Raffle's notes, he made up his mind that he would give Mrs. Roper notice before he started, that on his return to London he would be seen no more in Burton Crescent. He would break his bonds altogether asunder, and if there should be any penalty for such breaking he would pay it in what best manner he might be able. He acknowledged to himself that he had been behaving badly to Amelia, confessing, indeed, more sin in that respect than he had in truth committed; but this, at any rate, was clear to him, that he must put himself on a proper footing in that quarter before he could venture to speak to Lily Dale.

As he came to a definite conclusion on this subject the little handbell which always stood on Sir Baffle's table was sounded, and Eanies was called into the presence of the great man. " Ah," said Sir Baffle, leaning back in his arm-chair, and stretching himself after the great exertions which he had been making—" Ah, let me see ? You are going out of town the day after to-morrow."

" Yes, Sir Raffle, the day after to-morrow."

" Ah! it's a great annoyance,— a very great annoyance. But on such occasions I never think of myself. I never have done so, and don't suppose I ever shall. So you're going down to my old friend De Guest ? "

Eanies was always angered when his new patron Sir Baffle talked of his old friendship with the earl, and never gave the Commissioner any encouragement. " I am going down to Guestwick," said he.

"Ah! yes; to Guestwick Manor? I don't remember that I was ever there. I daresay I may have been, but one forgets those things."

" I never heard Lord De Guest speak of it."

" Oh, dear, no. Why should his memory be better than mine ? Tell him, will you, how very glad I shall be to renew our old intimacy. I should think nothing of running down to him for a day or two in the dull time of the year,—say in September or October. It's rather a coincidence our both being interested about you,—isn't it ? "

" I'll be sure to tell him."

" Mind you do. He's one of our most thoroughly independent noblemen, and I respect him very highly. Let me see; didn't I ring my bell ? What was it I wanted ? I think I rang my bell."

" You did ring your bell."

" Ah, yes ; I know. I am going away, and I wanted my

would you tell Baiferty to bring me—my boots?" Whereupon Johnny rang the bell—not the little handbell, but the other bell. " And I shan't be here to-morrow," continued Sir Baffle. "I'll thank you to send my letters up to the square; and if they should send down from the Treasury;—but the Chancellor would write, and in that case you'll send up his letter at once by a special messenger, of course."

" Here's Bafferty," said Eames, determined that he would not even sully his lips with speaking of Sir Baffle's boots.

" Oh, all, yes; Kafferty, bring me my boots."

" Anything else to say ? " asked Eames.

" No, nothing else. Of course you'll be careful to leave everything straight behind you."

" Oh, yes ; I'll leave it all straight." Then Eames withdrew, so that he might not be present at the interview between Sir Baffle and his boots. " He'll not do," said Sir Baffle to himself. " He'U never do. He's not quick enough,—has no go in him. He's not man enough for the place. I wonder why the earl has taken him by the hand in that way."

Soon after the little episode of the boots Eames left his office and walked home alone to Burton Crescent. He felt that he had gained a victory in Sir Baffle's room, but the victory there had been easy. Now he had another battle on his hands, in which, as he believed, the achievement of victory would be much more difficult. Amelia Boper was a person much more to be feared than the Chief Commissioner. He had one strong arrow in his quiver on which he would depend, if there should come to him the necessity of giving his enemy a death-wound. During the last week she had been making powerful love to Cradell, so as to justify the punishment of desertion from a former lover. He would not throw Cradell in her teeth if he could help it; but it was incumbent on him to gain a victory, and if the worst should come to the worst, he must use such weapons as destiny and the chance of war had given him.

He found Mrs. Boper in the dining-room as he entered, and immediately began his work. "Mrs. Boper," he said, "I'm going out of town the day after to-morrow."

" Oh, yes, Mr. Eames, we know that. You're going as a visitor to the noble mansion of the Earl De Guest."

" I don't know about the mansion being very noble, but I'm going down into the country for a fortnight. When I come back "

" When you come back, Mr. Eames, I hope you'll find your room a deal more comfortable. I know it isn't quite what it should be for a gentleman like you, and I've been thinking for some time past "

" But, Mrs. Boper, I don't mean to come back here any more. It's just that that I want to say to you."

" Not come back to the crescent! "

" No, Mrs. Boper. A fellow must move sometimes, you know ; and I'm sure I've been very constant to you for a long time."

" But where are you going, Mr. Eames ? "

"Well; I haven't just made up my mind as yet. That is, it will depend on what I may do,—on what friends of mine may say down in the country. You'll not think I'm quarrelling with you, Mrs. Roper."

"It's them Lupexes as have done it," said Mrs. Roper, in her deep distress.

"No, indeed, Mrs. Roper, nobody has done it."

" Yes, it is; and I'm not going to blame you, Mr. Eames. They've made the house unfit for any decent young gentleman like you. I've been feeling that all along; but it's hard upon a lone woman like me, isn't it, Mr. Eames ? "

" But, Mrs. Roper, the Lupexes have had nothing to do with my going."

" Oh, yes, they have; I understand it all. But what could I do, Mr. Eames ? I've been giving them warning every week for the last six months; but the more I give them warning, the more they won't go. Unless I were to send for a policeman, and have a row in the house "

" But I haven't complained of the Lupexes, Mrs. Roper."

" You wouldn't be quitting without any reason, Mr. Eames. You are not going to be married in earnest, are you, Mr. Eames ? "

" Not that I know of."

" You may tell me ; you may, indeed. I won't say a word,— not to anybody. It hasn't been my fault about Amelia. It hasn't really."

" Who says there's been any fault ? "

" I can see, Mr. Eames. Of course it didn't do for me to interfere. And if you had liked her, I will say I believed she'd have made as good a wife as any young man ever took ; and she can make a few pounds go farther than most girls. You can understand a mother's feelings; and if there was to be anything, I couldn't spoil it; could I, now ? "

" But there isn't to be anything."

" So I've told her for months past. I'm not going to say anything to blame you ; but young men ought to be very particular; indeed they ought." Johnny did not choose to hint to the disconsolate mother that it also behoved young women to be very particular, but he thought it. " I've wished many a time, Mr. Earnes, that she had never come here; indeed I have. But what's a mother to do ? I couldn't put her outside the door." Then Mrs. Roper raised her apron up to her eyes, and began to sob.

" I'm very sorry if I've made any mischief," said Johnny.

" It hasn't been your fault," continued the poor woman, from whom, as her tears became uncontrollable, her true feelings forced themselves and the real outpouring of her feminine nature. " Nor it hasn't been my fault. But I knew what it would come to when I saw how she was going on; and I told her so. I knew you wouldn't put up with the likes of her."

" Indeed, Mrs. Roper, I've always had a great regard for her, and for you too."

" But you weren't going to many her. I've told her so all along, and I've begged her not to do it,—almost on my knees I have ; but she wouldn't be said by me. She never would. She's always been that wilful that I'd sooner have her away from me than with me. Though she's a good young woman in the house,—she is, indeed, Mr.. Eames;—and there isn't a pair of hands in it that works so hard ; but it was no use my talking."

" I don't think any harm has been done."

11 Yes, there has; great harm. It has made the place not respectable. It's the Lupexes is the worst. There's Miss Spruce, who has been with me for nine years,—ever since I've had the house,—she's been telling me this morning that she means to go into the country. It's all the same thing. I understand it. I can see it. The house isn't respectable, as it should be ; and your mamma, if she were to know all, would have a right to be angry with me. I did mean to be respectable, Mr. Eames ; I did indeed."

" Miss Spruce will think better of it."

" You don't know what I've had to go through. There's none of them pays, not regular,—only she and you. She's been like the Bank of England, has Miss Spruce."

",1'm afraid I've not been very regular, Mrs. Roper."

" Oh, yes, you have. I don't think of a pound or two more or less at the end of a quarter, if I'm sure to have it some day. The butcher,—he understands one's lodgers just as well as I do, —if the money's really coming, he'll wait; but he won't wait for such as them Lupexes, whose money's nowhere. And there's Cradell; would you believe it, that fellow owes me eight and twenty pounds!"

" Yes, Mr. Eames, eight and twenty pounds ! He's a fool. It's them Lupexes as have had his money. I know it. He don't talk of paying, and going away. I shall be just left with him and the Lupexes on my hands ; and then the bailiffs may come and sell every stick about the place. I won't say nay to them." Then she threw herself into the old horsehair aim-chair, and gave way to her womanly sorrow.

" I think I'll go upstairs, and get ready for dinner," said Eames.

" And you must go away when you come back ?" said Mrs. PiOper.

" Well, yes, I'm afraid I must. I meant you to have a month's warning from to-day. Of course I shall pay for the month."

" I don't want to take any advantage; indeed, I don't. But I do hope you'll leave your things. You can have them whenever you like. If Chumpend knows that you and Miss Spruce are both going, of course he'll be down upon me for his money." Chumpend was the butcher. But Eames made no answer to this piteous plea. Whether or no he could allow his old boots to remain in Burton Crescent for the next week or two, must depend on the manner in which he might be received by Amelia Eoper this evening.

When he came down to the drawing-room, there was no one there but Miss Spruce. " A fine day, Miss Spruce," said he.

" Yes, Mr. Eames, it is a fine day for London; but don't you think the country air is very nice ? "

" Give me the town," said Johnny, wishing to say a good word for poor Mrs. Koper, if it were possible.

" You're a young man, Mr. Eames ; but I'm only an old woman. That makes a difference," said Miss Spruce.

" Not much," said Johnny, meaning to be civil. " You don't like to be dull any more than I do."

" I like to be respectable, Mr. Eames. I always have been respectable, Mr. Eames." This the old woman said almost in a whisper, looking anxiously to see that the door had not been opened to other listening ears.

" I'm sure Mrs. Roper is very respectable."

" Yes; Mrs. Roper is respectable, Mr. Eames; but there are some here that Hush-sh-sh! " And the old lady put her finger up to her lips, The door opened and Mrs. Lupex swam into the room.

"How d'ye do, Miss Spruce? I declare you're always first.

It's to get a chance of having one of the young gentlemen to yourself, I believe. ^What's the news in the city to-day, Mr. Eames? In your position now of course you hear all the news."

" Sir Raffle Buffle has got a new pair of shoes. I don't know that for certain, but I guess it from the time it took him to put them on."

" Ah! now you're quizzing. That's always the way with you gentlemen when you get a little up in the world. You don't think women are worth talking to then, unless just for a joke or so."

"I'd a great deal sooner talk to you, Mrs. Lupex, than I would to Sir Raffle Buffle."

" It's all very well for you to say that. But we women know what such compliments as those mean;—don't we, Miss Spruce ? A woman that's been married five years as I have,—or I may say six,—doesn't expect much attention from young men. And though I was young when I married,—young in years, that is,—I'd seen too much and gone through too much to be young in heart." This she said almost in a whisper; but Miss Spruce heard it, and was confirmed in her belief that Burton Crescent was no longer respectable.

" I don't know what you were then, Mrs. Lupex," said Eames ; " but you're young enough now for anything."

" Mr. Eames, I'd sell all that remains of my youth at a cheap rate,—at a very cheap rate, if I could only be sure of "

" Sure of what, Mrs. Lupex ? "

"The undivided affection of the one person that I loved. That is all that is necessary to a woman's happiness."

" And isn't Lupex "

" Lupex ! But, hush, never mind. I should not have allowed myself to be betrayed into an expression of feeling. Here's your friend Mr. Cradell. Do you know I sometimes wonder what you find in that man to be so fond of him." Miss Spruce saw it all, and heard it all, and positively resolved upon moving herself to those two small rooms at Dulwich.

Hardly a word was exchanged between Amelia and Eames before dinner. Amelia still devoted herself to Cradell, and Johnny saw that that arrow, if it should be needed, would be a strong weapon. Mrs. Roper they found seated at her place at the dining-table, and Eames could perceive the traces of her tears. Poor woman ! Few positions in life could be harder to bear than hers! To be ever tugging at others for money that they could not pay; to be ever tugged at for money which she could not pay; to desire respectability for its own sake, but to be driven to confess that it was a luxury beyond her means; to put up with disreputable belongings for the sake of lucre, and then not to get the lucre, but be driven to feel that she was ruined by the attempt! How many Mrs. Ropers there are who from year to year sink down and fall away, and no one knows whither they betake themselves! One fancies that one sees them from time to time at the corners of the streets in battered bonnets and thin gowns, with the tattered remnants of old shawls upon their shoulders, still looking as though they had within them a faint remembrance of long-distant respectability. With anxious eyes they peer about, as though searching in the streets for other lodgers. Where do they get their daily morsels of bread, and their poor cups of thin tea,—their cups of thin tea, with perhaps a pennyworth of gin added to it, if Providence be good ! Of this state of things Mrs. Roper had a lively appreciation, and now, poor woman, she feared that she was reaching it, by the aid of the Lupexes. On the present occasion she carved her joint of meat in silence, and sent out her slices to the good guests that would leave her, and to the bad guests that would remain, with apathetic impartiality. What was the use now of doing favour to one lodger or disfavour to another ? Let them take their mutton,—they who would pay for it and they who would not. She would not have the carving of many more joints in that house if Chunipend acted up to all the threats which he had uttered to her that morning.

The reader may, perhaps, remember the little back room behind the dining parlour. A description was given in some former pages of an interview which was held between Amelia and her lover. It was in that room that all the interviews of Mrs. Roper's establishment had their existence. A special room for interviews is necessary in all households of a mixed nature. If a man lives alone with his wife, he can have his interviews where he pleases. Sons and daughters, even when they are grown up, hardly create the necessity of an interview-chamber, though some such need may be felt if the daughters are marriageable and independent in their natures. But when the family becomes more complicated than this, if an extra young man be introduced, or an aunt comes into residence, or grown up children by a former wife interfere with the domestic simplicity, then such accommodation becomes quite indispensable. No woman would think of taking in lodgers without such a room; and this room there was at Mrs. Roper's, very small and dingy, but still sufficient,—just behind the dining parlour and opposite to the kitchen stairs. Hither, after dinner, Amelia was summoned. She had just seated herself between Mrs. Lupex and Miss Spruce, ready to do battle with the former because she would stay, and with the latter because she would go, when she was called out by the servant girl.

"Miss Mealyer, Miss Mealyer,—sh—sh—sh!" And Amelia, looking round, saw a large red hand beckoning to her. "He's down there," said Jemima, as soon as her young mistress had joined her, "and wants to see you most partic'lar."

"Which of 'em?" asked Amelia, in a whisper.

"Why, Mr. Heames, to be sure. Don't you go and have anythink to say to the other one, Miss Mealyer, pray don't; he ain't no good; he ain't indeed."

Amelia stood still for a moment on the landing, calculating whether it would be well for her to have the interview, or well to decline it. Her objects were two;—or, rather, her object was in its nature twofold. She was, naturally, anxious to drive John Eames to desperation; and anxious also, by some slight added artifice, to make sure of Cradell if Eames's desperation did not have a very speedy effect. She agreed with Jemima's criticism in the main, but she did not go quite so far as to think that Cradell was no good at all. Let it be Eames, if Eames were possible; but let the other string be kept for use if Eames were not possible. Poor girl! in coming to this resolve she had not done so without agony. She had a heart, and with such power as it gave her, she loved John Eames. But the world had been hard to her; knocking her about hither and thither unmercifully; threatening, as it now threatened, to take from her what few good things she enjoyed. When a girl is so circumstanced she cannot afford to attend to her heart. She almost resolved not to see Eames on the present occasion, thinking that he might be made the more desperate by such refusal, and remembering also that Cradell was in the house and would know of it.

"He's there a-waiting, Miss Mealyer. Why don't yer come down?" and Jemima plucked her young mistress by the arm.

"I am coming," said Amelia. And with dignified steps she descended to the interview.

"Here she is, Mr. Heames," said the girl. And then Johnny found himself alone with his lady-love.

"You have sent for me, Mr. Eames," she said, giving her head a little toss, and turning her face away from him. "I was engaged upstairs, but I thought it uncivil not to come down to you as you sent for me so special."

"Yes, Miss Roper, I did want to see you very particularly." "Oh, dear!" she exclaimed, and he understood fully that the exclamation referred to his having omitted the customary use of her Christian name.

"I saw your mother before dinner, and I told her that I am going away the day after to-morrow."

"We all know about that;—to the earl's, of course!" And then there was another chuck of her head.

"And I told her also that I had made up my mind not to come back to Burton Crescent."

"What! leave the house altogether!"

"Well; yes. A fellow must make a change sometimes, you know."

"And where are you going, John?" "That I don't know as yet."

"Tell me the truth, John; are you going to be married? Are you—going—to marry—that young woman,—Mr. Crosbie's leavings? I demand to have an answer at once. Are you going to marry her?"

He had determined very resolutely that nothing she might say should make him angry, but when she thus questioned him about "Crosbie's leavings" he found it very difficult to keep his temper. "I have not come," said he, "to speak to you about any one but ourselves."

"That put-off won't do with me, sir. You are not to treat any girl you may please in that sort of way;—oh, John!" Then she looked at him as though she did not know whether to fly at him and cover him with kisses, or to fly at him and tear his hair.

"I know I haven't behaved quite as I should have done," he began.

"Oh, John!" and she shook her head. "You mean, then, to tell me that you are going to marry her?"

"I mean to say nothing of the kind. I only mean to say that I am going away from Burton Crescent."

"John Eames, I wonder what you think will come to you! Will you answer me this; have I had a promise from you,—a distinct promise, over and over again, or have I not?"

"I don't know about a distinct promise"

"Well, well! I did think that you was a gentleman that would not go back from your word. I did think that. I did think that you would never put a young lady to the necessity of bringing forward her own letters to prove that she is not expecting more than she has a right! You don't know! And that, after all that has been between us! John Eames!" And again it seemed to him as though she were about to fly.

"I tell you that I know I haven't behaved well. What more can I say!"

"What more can you say? Oh, John! to ask me such a question! If you were a man you would know very well what more to say. But all you private secretaries are given to deceit, as the sparks fly upwards. However, I despise you,—I do, indeed. I despise you."

"If you despise me, we might as well shake hands and part at once. I daresay that will be best. One doesn't like to be despised, of course; but sometimes one can't help it." And then he put out his hand to her.

"And is this to be the end of all?" she said, taking it.

"Well, yes; I suppose so. You say I'm despised."

"You shouldn't take up a poor girl in that way for a sharp word,—not when she is suffering as I am made to suffer. If you only think of it,—think what I have been expecting!" And now Amelia began to cry, and to look as though she were going to fall into his arms.

"It is better to tell the truth," he said; "isn't it?"

"But it shouldn't be the truth."

"But it is the truth. I couldn't do it. I should ruin myself and you too, and we never should be happy."

"I should be happy,—very happy indeed." At this moment the poor girl's tears were unaffected, and her words were not artful. For a minute or two her heart,—her actual heart,—was allowed to prevail.

"It cannot be, Amelia. Will you not say good-by?"

"Good-by," she said, leaning against him as she spoke.

"I do so hope you will be happy," he said. And then, putting

EAMES DOES THINGS HE OUGHT NOT TO HATE DONE. 223

his arm round her waist, he kissed her; which he certainly ought not to have done.

When the interview was over, he escaped out into the crescent, and as he walked down through the squares,—Woburn Square, and Russell Square, and Bedford Square,—towards the heart of London, he felt himself elated almost to a state of triumph. He had got himself well out of his difficulties, and now he would be ready for his love-tale to Lily.

CHAPTER XXII. THE FIRST VISIT TO THE GUESTWICK BRIDGE.

WHEN John Eames arrived at Guestwick Manor, he was first welcomed by Lady Julia. "My dear Mr. Eames," she said, "I cannot tell you how glad we are to see you." After that she always called him John, and treated him throughout his visit with wonderful kindness. No doubt that affair of the bull had in some measure produced this feeling ; no doubt, also, she was well disposed to the man who she hoped might be accepted as a lover by Lily Dale. But I am inclined to think that the fact of his having beaten Crosbie had been the most potential cause of this affection for our hero on the part of Lady Julia. Ladies,—especially discreet old ladies, such as Lady Julia de Guest,—are bound to entertain pacific theories, and to condemn all manner of violence. Lady Julia would have blamed any one who might have advised Eames to commit an assault upon Crosbie. But, nevertheless, deeds of prowess are still dear to the female heart, and a woman, be she ever so old and discreet, understands and appreciates the summary justice which may be done by means of a thrashing. Lady Julia, had she been called upon to talk of it, would undoubtedly have told Eames that he had committed a fault in striking Mr. Crosbie; but the deed had been done, and Lady Julia became very fond of John Eames.

" Vickers shall show you your room, if you like to go upstairs ; but you'll find my brother close about the house if you choose to go out; I saw him not half an hour since." But John seemed to be well satisfied to sit in the arm-chair over the fire, and talk to his hostess ; so neither of them moved.

" And now that you're a private secretary, how do you like it ?" " I like the work well enough; only I don't like the man, Lady Julia. But I shouldn't say so, because he is such an intimate friend of your brother's."

" An intimate friend of Theodore's!-—Sir Baffle Buffle !" Lady Julia stiffened her back and put on a serious face, not being exactly pleased at being told that the Earl de Guest had any such intimate friend.

" At any rate he tells me so about four times a day, Lady Julia. And he particularly wants to come down here next September."

" Did he tell you that, too ?"

" Indeed he did. You can't believe what a goose he is ! Then his voice sounds like a cracked bell; it's the most disagreeable voice you ever heard in your life. And one has always to be on one's guard lest he should make one do something that is—is—that isn't quite the thing for a gentleman. You understand;—what the messenger ought to do."

" You shouldn't be too much afraid of your own dignity."

" No, I'm not. If Lord de Guest were to ask me to fetch him his shoes, I'd run to Guestwick and back for them and think nothing of it,—-just because I know he's my friend. He'd have a right to send me. But I'm not going to do such things as that for Sir Baffle Buffle."

" Fetch him his shoes !"

" That's what FitzHoward had to do, and he didn't like it."

" Isn't Mr. FitzHoward nephew to the Duchess of St. Bungay ?"

" Nephew, or cousin, or something."

" Dear me!" said Lady Julia, "what a horrible man !" And in this way John Eames and her ladyship became very intimate.

There was no one at dinner at the Manor that day but the earl and his sister and their single guest. The earl when he came in was very warm in his welcome, slapping his young friend on the back, and poking jokes at him with a good-humoured if not brilliant pleasantry.

" Thrashed anybody lately, John ?"

" Nobody to speak of," said Johnny.

" Brought your nightcap down for your out-o'-doors nap ?"

" No ; but I've got a grand stick for the bull," said Johnny.

" Ah ! that's no joke now, I can tell you," said the earl. " We had to sell him, and it half broke my heart. We don't know what had come to him, but he became quite unruly after that;—

knocked Darvell down in the straw-yard! It was a very bad business,—a very bad business, indeed! Come, go and dress. Do you remember how you came down to dinner that day? I shall never forget how

Crofts stared at you. Come, you've only got twenty minutes, and you London fellows always want an hour."

"He's entitled to some consideration now lie's a private secretary," said Lady Julia.

"Bless us all! yes; I forgot that. Come, Mr. Private Secretary, don't stand on the grandeur of your neck-tie to-day, as there's nobody here but ourselves. You shall have an opportunity tomorrow."

Then Johnny was handed over to the groom of the chambers, and exactly in twenty minutes he re-appeared in the drawing-room.

As soon as Lady Julia had left them after dinner, the earl began to explain his plan for the coming campaign. "I'll tell you now what I have arranged," said he. "The squire is to be here tomorrow with his eldest niece,—your Miss Lily's sister, you know."

"What, Bell?"

"Yes, with Bell, if her name is Bell. She's a very pretty girl, too. I don't know whether she's not the prettiest of the two, after all."

"That's a matter of opinion."

"Just so, Johnny; and do you stick to your own. They're coming here for three or four days. Lady Julia did ask Mrs. Dale and Lily. I wonder whether you'll let me call her Lily?"

"Oh, dear! I wish I might have the power of letting you."

"That's just the battle that you've got to fight. But the mother and the younger sister wouldn't come. Lady Julia says it's all right;—that, as a matter of course, she wouldn't come when she heard you were to be here. I don't quite understand it. In my days the young girls were ready enough to go where they knew they'd meet their lovers, and I never thought any the worse of them for it."

"It wasn't because of that," said Eames.

"That's what Lady Julia says, and I always find her to be right in things of that sort. And she says you'll have a better chance in going over there than you would here, if she were in the same house with you. If I was going to make love to a girl, of course I'd sooner have her close to me,—staying in the same house. I should think it the best fun in the world. And we might have had a dance, and all that kind of thing. But I couldn't make her come, you know."

"Oh, no; of course not."

"And Lady Julia thinks that it's best as it is. You must go over, you know, and get the mother on your side, if you can. I take it, the truth is this;—you mustn't he angry with me, you know, for saying it."

"You may be sure of that."

"I suppose she was fond of that fellow, Croshie. She can't be very fond of him now, I should think, after the way he has treated her; but she'll find a difficulty in making her confession that she really likes you better than she ever liked him. Of course that's what you'll want her to say."

"I want her to say that she'll be my wife,—some day."

"And when she has agreed to the some day, then you'll begin to press her to agree to your day;—eh, sir? My belief is you'll bring her round. Poor girl! why should she break her heart when a decent fellow like you will only be too glad to make her a happy woman?" And in this way the earl talked to Eames till the latter almost believed that the difficulties were vanishing from out of his path. " Could it be possible," he asked himself, as he went to bed, " that in a fortnight's time Lily Dale should have accepted him as her future husband ?" Then he remembered that day on which Crosbie, with the two girls, had called at his mother's house, when, in the bitterness of his heart, he had sworn to himself that he would always regard Crosbie as his enemy. Since then the world had gone well with him; and he had no longer any very bitter feeling against Crosbie. That matter had been arranged on the platform of the Paddington Station. He felt that if Lily would now accept him he could almost shake hands with Crosbie. The episode in his life and in Lily's would have been painful; but he would learn to look back upon that without regret, if Lily could be taught to believe that a kind fate had at last given her to the better of her two lovers. " I'm afraid she won't bring herself to forget him," he had said to the earl. " She'll only be too happy to forget him," the earl had answered, " if you can induce her to begin the attempt. Of course it is very bitter at first;—all the world knew about it; but, poor girl, she is not to be wretched for ever, because of that. Do you go about your work with some little confidence, and I don't doubt but what you'll have your way. You have everybody in your favour,—the squire, her mother, and all." While such words as these were in his ears how could he fail to hope and to be confident ? While he was sitting cozily over his bedroom fire he resolved that it should be as the earl had said. But when he got up on the following morning, and stood

shivering as lie came out of his bath, he could not feel the same confidence. " Of course I shall go to her," he said to himself, " and make a plain story of it. But I know what her answer will he. She will tell me that she cannot forget him." Then his feelings towards Crosbie were not so friendly as they had been on the previous evening.

He did not visit the Small House on that, his first day. It had been thought better that he should first meet the squire and Bell at Guestwick Manor, so he postponed his visit to Mrs. Dale till the next morning.

" Go when you like," said the earl. " There's the brown cob for you to do what you like with him while you are here."

" I'll go and see my mother," said John; " but I won't take the cob to-day. If you'll let me have him to-morrow, I'll ride to Ailing-ton." So he walked off to Guestwick by himself.

He knew well every yard of the ground over which he went, remembering every gate and stile and greensward from the time of his early boyhood. And now as he went along through his old haunts, he could not but look back and think of the thoughts which had filled his mind in his earlier wanderings. As I have said before, in some of these pages, no walks taken by the man are so crowded with thought as those taken by the boy. He had been early taught to understand that the world to him would be very hard; that he had nothing to look to but his own exertions, and that those exertions would not, unfortunately, be backed by any great cleverness of his own. I do not know that anybody had told him that he was a fool ; but he had come to understand, partly through his own modesty, and partly, no doubt, through the somewhat obtrusive diffidence of his mother, that he was less sharp than other lads. It is probably true that he had come to his sharpness later in life than is the case with many young men. He had not grown on the sunny side of the wall. Before that situation in the Income-tax Office had fallen in his way, very humble modes of life had offered themselves,—or, rather, had not offered themselves for his acceptance. He had endeavoured to become an usher at a commercial seminary, not supposed to be in a very thriving condition; but he had been, luckily, found deficient in his arithmetic. There had been some chance of his going into the leather-warehouse of Messrs. Basil and Pigskin, but those gentlemen had required a premium, and any payment of that kind had been quite out of his mother's power. A country attorney, who had

known the family for years, had been humbly solicited, the widow almost kneeling before him with tears, to take Johnny by the hand and make a clerk of him; but the attorney had discovered that Master Johnny Eames was not supposed to be sharp, and would have none of him. During those days, those gawky, gaiuless, unadmired days, in which he had wandered about the lanes of Guestwick as his only amusement, and had composed hundreds of rhymes in honour of Lily Dale which no human eye but his own had ever seen, he had come to regard himself as almost a burden upon the earth. Nobody seemed to want him. His own mother was very anxious; but her anxiety seemed to him to indicate a continual desire to get rid of him. For hours upon hours he would fill his mind with castles in 'the air, dreaming of wonderful successes in the midst of which Lily Dale always reigned as a queen. He would carry on the same story in his imagination from month to month, almost contenting himself with such ideal happiness. Had it not been for the possession of that power, what comfort could there have been to him in his life? There are lads of seventeen who can find happiness in study, who can busy themselves in books and be at their ease among the creations of other minds. These are they who afterwards become well-informed men. It was not so with John Eames. He had never been studious. The perusal of a novel was to him in those days a slow affair; and of poetry he read but little, storing up accurately in his memory all that he did read. But he created for himself his own romance, though to the eye a most unromantic youth; and he wandered through the Guest-wick woods with many thoughts of which they who knew him best knew nothing. All this he thought of now as, with devious steps, he made his way towards his old home; — with very devious steps, for he went backwards through the woods by a narrow path which led right away from the town down to a little water-course, over which stood a wooden foot-bridge with a rail. He stood on the centre of the plank, at a spot which he knew well, and rubbing his hand upon the rail, cleansed it for the space of a few inches of the vegetable growth produced by the spray of the water. There, rudely carved in the wood, was still the word LILY. When he cut those letters she had been almost a child. " I wonder whether she will come here with me and let me show it to her," he said to himself. Then he took out his knife and cleared the cuttings of the letters, and having done so, leaned upon the rail, and looked down upon the running water. How well things in the world had gone for him! How well! And

yet what would it all be if Lily would not come to him? How well the world had gone for him! In those days when he stood there carving the girl's name everybody had seemed to regard him as a heavy burden, and he had so regarded himself. Now he was envied by many, respected by many, taken by the hand as a friend by those high in the world's esteem. When he had come near the Guestwick Mansion in his old walks,—always, however, keeping at a great distance lest the grumpy old lord should be down upon him and scold him,—he had little dreamed that he and the grumpy old lord would ever be together on such familiar terms, that he would tell to that lord more of his private thoughts than to any other living being; yet it had come to that. The grumpy old lord had now told him that that gift of money was to be his whether Lily Dale accepted him or no. " Indeed, the thing's done," said the grumpy lord, pulling out from his pocket certain papers, " and you've got to receive the dividends as they become due." Then, when Johnny had expostulated, — as, indeed, the circumstances had left him no alternative but to expostulate,—the earl had roughly bade him hold his tongue, telling him that he would have to fetch Sir Baffle's boots directly he got back to London. So the conversation had quickly turned itself away to Sir Kaffle, whom they had both ridiculed with much satisfaction. " If he finds his way down here in September, Master Johnny, or in any other month either, you may fit my head with a foolscap.

Not remember, indeed! Is it not wonderful that any man should make himself so mean a fool ?" All this was thought over again, as Eames leaned upon the bridge. He remembered every word, and remembered many other words,—earlier words, spoken years ago, filling him with desolation as to the prospects of his life. It had seemed that his friends had united in prophesying that the outlook into the world for him was hopeless, and that the earning of bread must be for ever beyond his power. And now his lines had fallen to him in very pleasant places, and he was among those whom the world had determined to caress. And yet, what would it all be if Lily would not share his happiness ? When he had carved that name on the rail, his love for Lily had been an idea. It had now become a reality which might probably be full of pain. If it were so,—if such should be the result of his wooing, — would not those old dreamy days have been better than these—the days of his success ?

It was one o'clock by the time that he reached his mother's house, and he found her and his sister in a troubled and embarrassed state. " Of course you know, John," said his mother, as soon as their first embraces were over, " that we are going to dine at the Manor this evening ?" But he did not know it, neither the earl nor Lady Julia having said anything on the subject. " Of course we are going," said Mrs. Eames, " and it was so very kind. But I've never been out to such a house for so many years, John, and I do feel in such a twitter. I dined there once, soon after we were married; but I never have been there since that."

" It's not the earl I mind, but Lady Julia," said Mary Eames.

" She's the most good-natured woman in the world," said Johnny.

"Oh, dear ; people say she is so cross !"

" That's because people don't know her. If I was asked who is the kindest-hearted woman I know in the world, I think I should say Lady Julia de Guest. I think I should."

" Ah ! but then they're so fond of you," said the admiring mother. " You saved his lordship's life,—under Providence."

" That's all bosh, mother. You ask Dr. Crofts. He knows them as well as I do."

" Dr. Crofts is going to marry Bell Dale," said Mary; and then the conversation was turned from the subject of Lady Julia's perfections, and the awe inspired by the earl.

" Crofts going to marry Bell! " exclaimed Eames, thinking almost with dismay of the doctor's luck in thus getting himself accepted all at once, while he had been suing with the constancy almost of a Jacob.

"Yes," said Mary; "and they say that she has refused her cousin Bernard, and that, therefore, the squire is taking away the house from them. You know they're all coming into Guestwick."

" Yes, I know they are. But I don't believe that the squire is taking away the house."

" Why should they come then ? Why should they give up such a charming place as that ?"

" Rent-free ! " said Mrs. Eames.

" I don't know why they should come away, but I can't believe the squire is turning them out; at any rate not for that reason." The squire was prepared to advocate John's suit, and therefore John was bound to do battle on the squire's behalf.

"He is a very stem man," said Mrs. Eames, "and they say that since that affair of poor Lily's he has been more cross than ever with them. As far as I know, it was not Lily's fault."

" Poor Lily! " said Mary. " I do pity her. If I was her I should hardly know how to show my face ; I shouldn't, indeed."

" And why shouldn't she show her face ?" said John, in an angry tone. "What has she done to be ashamed of? Show her face indeed! I cannot understand the spite which one woman will sometimes have to another."

" There is no spite, John; and it's very wrong of you to say so," said Mary, defending herself. " But it is a very unpleasant thing for a girl to be jilted. All the world knows that she was engaged to him."

" And all the world knows " But he would not proceed to declare that all the world knew also that Crosbie had been well thrashed for his baseness. It would not become him to mention that even before his mother and sister. All the world did know it; all the world that cared to know anything of the matter;—except Lily Dale herself. Nobody had ever yet told Lily Dale of that occurrence at the Paddington Railway Station, and it was well for John that her friends and his had been so discreet.

"Oh, of course you are her champion," said Mary. "And I didn't mean to say anything unkind. Indeed I didn't. Of course it was a misfortune."

" I think it was the best piece of good fortune that could have happened to her, not to marry a d scoundrel like "

" Oh, John !" exclaimed Mrs. Eames.

" I beg your pardon, mother. But it isn't swearing to call such a man as that a d scoundrel." And he particularly emphasized the naughty word, thinking that thereby he would add to its import, and take away from its naughtiness. " But we won't talk any more about him. I hate the man's very name. I hated him the first moment that I saw him, and knew that he was a blackguard from his look. And I don't believe a word about the squire having been cross to them. Indeed I know he h!ts been the reverse of cross. So Bell is going to many Dr. Crofts ! "

"There is no doubt on earth about that," said Mary. "And they say that Bernard Dale is going abroad with his regiment."

Then John discussed with his mother his duties as private secretary, and his intention of leaving Mrs. Roper's house. " I suppose it isn't nice enough for you now, John," said his mother.

" It never was very nice, mother, to tell you the truth. There were people there . But you mustn't think I am turning up iny nose because I'm getting grand. I don't want to live any better than we all lived at Mrs. Eoper's; but she took in persons that were not agreeable. There is a Mr. and Mrs. Lupex there." Then he described something of their life in Burton Crescent, but did not say much about Amelia Roper. Amelia Roper had not made her appearance in Guestwick, as he had once feared that she would do; and therefore it did not need that he should at present make known to his mother that episode in his life.

When he got back to the Manor House he found that Mr. Dale and his niece had arrived. They were both sitting with Lady Julia when he went into the morning room, and Lord de Guest was standing over the fire talking to them. Eames as he came among them felt terribly conscious of his position, as though all there were aware that he had been brought down from London on purpose to make a declaration of love ;—as, indeed, all of them were aware of that fact. Bell, though no one had told her so in direct words, was as sure of it as the others.

" Here comes the prince of matadores," said the earl.

" No, my lord; you're the prince. I'm only your first follower." Though he could contrive that his words should be gay, his looks were sheepish, and when he gave his hand to the squire it was only by a struggle that he could bring himself to look straight into the old man's face.

" I'm very glad to see you, John," said the squire, " very glad indeed."

" And so am I," said Bell. " I have been so happy to hear that you have been promoted at your office, and so is mamma."

"I hope Mrs. Dale is quite well," said he ;—" and Lily." The word had been pronounced, but it had been done with so manifest an effort that all in the room were conscious of it, and paused as Bell prepared her little answer.

"My sister has been very ill," you know,—with scarlatina. But she has recovered with wonderful quickness, and is nearly well again now. She will be so glad to see you if you will go over."

"Yes; I shall certainly go over," said John.

"And now shall I show you your room, Miss Dale?" said Lady Julia. And so the party was broken up, and the ice had been broken.

CHAPTER XXIII. LOQUITUR HOPKINS.

THE squire had been told that his niece Bell had accepted Dr. Crofts, and he had signified a sort of acquiescence in the arrangement, saying that if it were to be so, he had nothing to say against Dr. Crofts. He spoke this in a melancholy tone of voice, wearing on his face that look of subdued sorrow which was now almost habitual to him. It was to Mrs. Dale that he spoke on the subject. "I could have wished that it might have been otherwise," he said, "as you are well aware. I had family reasons for wishing that it might be otherwise. But I have nothing to say against it. Dr. Crofts, as her husband, shall be welcome to my house." Mrs. Dale, who had expected much worse than this, began to thank him for his kindness, and to say that she also woul'd have preferred to see her daughter married to her cousin. "But in such a matter the decision should be left entirely to the girl. Don't you think so?"

"I have not a word to say against her," he repeated. Then Mrs. Dale left him, and told her daughter that her uncle's manner of receiving the news had been, for him, very gracious. "You were his favourite, but Lily will be so now," said Mrs. Dale.

"I don't care a bit about that;—or, rather, I do care, and think it will be in every way better. But as I, who am the naughty one, will go away, and as Lily, who is the good one, will remain with you, doesn't it almost seem a pity that you should be leaving the house?"

Mrs. Dale thought it was almost a pity, but she could not say so now. "You think Lily will remain," she said.

"Yes, mamma; I feel sure she will."

"She was always very fond of John Earnes;—and he is doing so well."

"It will be of no use, mamma. She is fond of him,—very fond. In a sort of a way she loves him—so well, that I feel sure she never mentions his name without some inward reference to her old childish thoughts and fancies. If he had come before Mr. Crosbie it would have all been well with her. But she cannot do it now. Her pride would prevent her, even if her heart permitted it. Oh! dear; it's very wrong of me to say so, after all that I have said before; but I almost wish you were not going. Uncle Christopher seems to be less hard than he used to be; and as I.was the sinner, and a's I am disposed of "

"It is too late now, my dear."

"And we should neither of us have the courage to mention it to Lily," said Bell.

On the following morning the squire sent for his sister-in-law, as it was his wont to do when necessity came for any discussion on matters of business. This was perfectly understood between them, and such sending was not taken as indicating any lack of courtesy on the part of Mr. Dale. "Mary," he said, as soon as Mrs. Dale was seated, "I shall do for Bell exactly what I have proposed to do for Lily. I had intended more than that once, of course. But then it would all have gone into Bernard's pocket; as it is, I shall make no difference between them. They shall each have a hundred a year,—that is, when they marry. You had better tell Crofts to speak to me."

" Mr. Dale, he doesn't expect it. He does not expect a penny."

" So much the better for him; and, indeed, so much the better for her. He won't make her the less welcome to his home because she brings some assistance to it."

" We have never thought of it,—any of us. The offer has come so suddenly that I don't know what I ought to say."

" Say—nothing. If you choose to make me a return for it—; but I am only doing what I conceive to be my duty, and have no right to ask for a kindness in return."

" But what kindness can we show you, Mr. Dale ?"

" Remain in that house." In saying these last words he spoke as though he were again angry,—as though he were again laying down the law to them,—as though he were telling her of a duty which was due to him and incumbent on her. His voice was as stern and his face as acid as ever. He said that he was asking for a kindness; but surely no man ever asked for kindness in a voice

so peremptory. " Remain in that house." Then he turned himself in towards his table as though he had no more to say.

But Mrs. Dale was beginning, now at last, to understand something of his mind and real character. He could be affectionate and forbearing in his giving; but when asking, he could not be otherwise than stem. Indeed, he could not ask; he could only demand.

" We have done so much now," Mrs. Dale began to plead.

" Well, well, well. I did not mean to speak about that. Things

are unpacked easier than they are packed. But, however

Never mind. Bell is to go with me this afternoon to Guestwick Manor. Let her be up here at two. Grimes can bring her box round, I suppose."

11 Oh, yes : of course."

" And don't be talking to her about money before she starts. I had rather you didn't;—you understand. But when you see Crofts, tell him to come to me. Indeed, he'd better come at once, if this thing is to go on quickly."

It may easily be understood that Mrs. Dale would " disobey the injunctions contained in the squire's last words. It was quite out of the question that she should return to her daughters and not tell them the result of her morning's interview with their uncle, A hundred a year in the doctor's modest household would make all the difference between plenty and want, between modest plenty and endurable want. Of course she told them, giving Bell to understand that she must dissemble so far as to pretend ignorance of the affair.

"I shall thank him at once," said Bell; "and tell him that I did not at all expect it, but am not too proud to accept it."

"Pray don't, my dear; not just now. I am breaking a sort of promise in telling you at all,— only I could not keep it to myself. And he has so many things to worry him ! Though he says nothing about it now, he has half broken his heart about you and Bernard." Then, too, Mrs. Dale told the girls what request the squire had just made, and the manner in which he had made it. " The tone of his voice as he spoke brought tears into my eyes. I almost wish we had not done anything."

"But, mamma," said Lily, "what difference can it make to him? You know that our presence near him was always a trouble to him. He never really wanted us. He liked to have Bell there when he thought that Bell would marry his pet."

" Don't be unkind, Lily."

"I don't mean to be unkind. Why shouldn't Bernard be his pet? I love Bernard dearly, and always thought it the best point in uncle Christopher that he was so fond of him. I knew, you know, that it was no use. Of course I knew it, as I understood all about somebody else. But Bernard is his pet."

"He's fond of you all, in his own way," said Mrs. Dale.

"But is he fond of you?—that's the question," said Lily. *' We could have forgiven him anything done to us, and have put up with any words he might have spoken to us, because he regards us as children. His giving a hundred a year to Bell won't make you comfortable in this house if he still domineers over you. If a neighbour be neighbourly, near neighbourhood is very nice. But uncle Christopher has not been neighbourly. He has wanted to be more than an uncle to us, on condition that he might be less than a brother to you. Bell and I have always felt that his regard on such terms was not worth having."

"I almost feel that we have been wrong," said Mrs. Dale; "but in truth I never thought that the matter would be to him one of so much moment."

When Bell had gone, Mrs. Dale and Lily were not disposed to continue with much energy the occupation on which they had all been employed for some days past. There had been life and excitement in the work when they had first commenced their packing, but now it was grown wearisome, dull, and distasteful. Indeed so much of it was done that but little was left to employ them, except those final strappings and fastenings, and that last collection of odds and ends which could not be accomplished till they were absolutely on the point of starting. The squire had said that unpacking would be easier than packing, and Mrs. Dale, as she wandered about among the hampers and cases, began to consider whether the task of restoring all the things to their old places would be very disagreeable. She said nothing of this to Lily, and Lily herself, whatever might be her thoughts, made no such suggestion to her mother.

"I think Hopkins will miss us more than any one else," she said. "Hopkins will have no one to scold."

Just at that moment Hopkins appeared at the parlour window, and signified his desire for a conference.

"You must come round," said Lily. "It's too cold for the window to be opened. I always like to get him into the house, because he feels himself a little abashed by the chairs and tables; or, perhaps, it is the carpet that is too much for him. Out on the gravel-walks he is such a terrible tyrant, and in the greenhouse he almost tramples upon one!"

Hopkins, when he did appear at the parlour door, seemed by his manner to justify Lily's discretion. He was not at all masterful in his tone or bearing, and seemed to pay to the chairs and tables all the deference which they could have expected.

"So you be going in earnest, ma'am," he said, looking down at Mrs. Dale's feet.

As Mrs. Dale did not answer him at once, Lily spoke:—"Yes, Hopkins, we are going in a very few days, now. We shall see you sometimes, I hope, over at Guestwick."

"Humph!" said Hopkins. "So you be really going! I didn't think it'd ever come to that, miss; I didn't indeed,—and no more it oughtn't; but of course it isn't for me to speak."

"People must change their residence sometimes, you know," said Mrs. Dale, using the same argument by which Eames had endeavoured to excuse his departure to Mrs. Koper.

"Well, ma'am; it ain't for me to say anything. But this I will say, I've lived here about t' squire's place, man and boy, jist all my life, seeing I was born here, as you knows, Mrs. Dale; and of all the bad things I ever see come about the place, this is a sight the worst."

"Oh, Hopkins!"

"The worst of all, ma'am; the worst of all! It'll just kill t' squire! There's ne'ery doubt in the world about that. It'll be the very death of t' old man."

"That's nonsense, Hopkins," said Lily.

"Very well, miss. I don't say but what it is nonsense; only you'll see. There's Mr. Bernard,—he's gone away; and by all accounts he never did care very much for the place. They all say he's a-going to the Hingies. And Miss Bell is going to be married,—which is all proper, in course : why shouldn't she ? And why shouldn't you, too, Miss Lily ? "

"Perhaps I shall, some day, Hopkins."

"There's no day like the present, Miss Lily. And I do say this, that the man as pitched into him would be the man for my money." This, which Hopkins spoke in the excitement of the moment, was perfectly unintelligible to Lily, and Mrs. Dale, who shuddered as she heard him, said not a word to call for any explanation. "But," continued Hopkins, "that's all as it may be, Miss Lily, and yon be in the hands of Providence,—as is others."

"Exactly so, Hopkins."

"But why should your mamma be all for going away ? She ain't going to marry no one. Here's the house, and there's she, and there's t' squire ; and why should she be for going away ? So much going away all at once can't be for any good. It's just a breaking up of everything, as though nothing wasn't good enough for nobody. I never went away, and I can't abide it."

"Well, Hopkins; it's settled now," said Mrs. Dale, "and I'm afraid it can't be unsettled."

"Settled;—well. Tell me this : do you expect, Mrs. Dale, that he's to live there all alone by hisself without any one to say a cross word to,—unless it be me or Dingles; for Jolliffe's worse than nobody, he's so mortial cross hisself. Of course he can't stand it. If you goes away, Mrs. Dale, Mister Bernard, he'll be squire in less than twelve months. He'll come back from the Hinges, then, I suppose ? "

"I don't think my brother-in-law will take it in that way, Hopkins."

"Ah, ma'am, you don't know him,—not as I knows him ;—all the ins and outs and crinks and crannies of him. I knows him as I does the old apple-trees that I've been a-handling for forty year. There's a deal of bad wood about them old cankered trees, and some folk say they ain't worth the ground they stand on; but I know where the sap runs, and when the fruit-blossom shows itself I know where the fruit will be the sweetest. It don't take much to kill one of them old trees,—but there's life in 'm yet if they be well handled."

"I'm sure I hope my brother's life may be long spared to him," said Mrs. Dale.

"Then don't be taking yourself away, ma'am, into them gashly lodgings at Guestwick. I says they are gashly for the likes of a Dale. It is not for me to speak, ma'am, of course. And I only came up now just to know what things you'd like with you out of the greenhouse."

"Oh, nothing, Hopkins, thank you," said Mrs. Dale.

"He told me to put up for you the best I could pick, and I means to do it;" and Hopkins, as he spoke, indicated by a motion of his head that he was making reference to the squire.

"We shan't have any place for them," said Lily. "I must send a few, miss, just to cheer you up a bit. I fear you'll be very clolesome there. And the doctor,—he ain't got what you can call a regular garden, but there is a bit of a place behind." "But we wouldn't rob the dear old place," said Lily. "For the matter of that what does it signify ? T' squire'll be that wretched he'll turn sheep in here to destroy the place, or he'll have the garden ploughed. You see if he don't. As for the place, the place is clean done for, if you leave it. You don't suppose he'll go and let the Small House to strangers. T' squire ain't one of that sort any ways."

" Ah me ! " exclaimed Mrs. Dale, as soon as Hopkins had taken himself off.

" What is it, mamma ? He's a dear old man, but surely what he says cannot make you really unhappy."

" It is so hard to know what one ought to do. I did not mean to be selfish, but it seems to me as though I were doing the most selfish thing in the world."

" Nay, mamma ; it has been anything but selfish. Besides, it is we that have done it; not you."

" Do you know, Lily, that I also have that feeling as to breaking up one's old mode of life of which Hopkins spoke. I thought that I should be glad to escape from this place, but now that the time has come I dread it."

" Do you mean that you repent ? "

Mrs. Dale did not answer her daughter at once, fearing to commit herself by words which could not be retracted. But at last she said, " Yes, Lily ; I think I do repent. I think that it has not been well done."

" Then let it be undone," said Lily.

The dinner-party at Guestwick Manor on that day was not very bright, and yet the earl had done all in his power to make his guests happy. But gaiety did not come naturally to his house, which, as will have been seen, was an abode very unlike in its nature to that of the other earl at Courcy Castle. Lady de Courcy at any rate understood how to receive and entertain a housefull of people, though the practice of doing so might give rise to difficult questions in the privacy of her domestic relations. Lady Julia did not understand it; but then Lady Julia was never called upon to answer for the expense of extra servants, nor was she asked about twice a week who the

LOQUITUR HOPKINS.

was to pay the wine-merchant's bill ? As regards Lord de

Guest and the Lady Julia themselves, I think they had the best of it; but I am bound to admit, with reference to chance guests, that the house was dull. The people who were now gathered at the earl's table could hardly have been expected to be very sprightly when in company with each other. The squire was not a man much given to general society, and was unused to amuse a table full of people. On the present occasion he sat next to Lady Julia, and from time to time muttered a few words to her about the state of the country. Mrs. Eames was terribly afraid of everybody there, and especially of the earl, next to whom she sat, and whom she continually called " my lord," showing by her voice as she did so that she was almost alarmed by the sound of her own voice. Mr. and Mrs. Boyce were there, the parson sitting on the other side of Lady*Julia, and the parson's wife on the other side of the earl. Mrs. Boyce was very studious to show that she was quite at home, and talked perhaps more than any one else; but in doing so she bored the earl most exquisitely, so that he told John Eames the next morning that she was worse than the bull. The parson ate his dinner, but said little or nothing between the two graces. He was a heavy, sensible, slow man, who knew himself and his own powers. " Uncommon good stewed beef," he said, as he went home ; " why can't we have our beef stewed like that ? " " Because we don't pay our cook sixty pounds a year," said Mrs. Boyce. "A woman with sixteen pounds can stew beef as well as a woman with sixty," said he ; " she only wants looking after." The earl himself was possessed of a sort of gaiety. There was about him a lightness of spirit which often made him an agreeable companion to one single person. John Eames conceived him to be the most sprightly old man of his day,—an old man with the fun and frolic almost of a boy. But this spirit, though it would show itself before John Eames, was not up to the entertainment of John Eames's mother and sister, together with the squire, the parson, and the parson's wife of Allington. So that the earl was overweighted and did not shine on this occasion at his own dinner-table. Dr. Crofts, who had also been invited, and who had secured the place which was now peculiarly his 'own, next to Bell Dale, was no doubt happy enough ; as, let us hope, was the young lady also; but they added very little to the general hilarity of the company. John Eames was seated between his own sister and the parson, and did not at all enjoy his position. He had a full view of the doctor's felicity, as the happy pair sat opposite to him, and conceived himself to be hardly treated by Lily's absence.

The party was certainly very dull, as were all such dinners at Guestwick Manor. There are houses, which, in their every-day course, are not conducted by any means in a sad or unsatisfactory manner,—in which life, as a rule, runs along merrily enough; but which cannot give a dinner-party; or, I might rather say, should never allow themselves to be allured into the attempt. The owners of such houses are generally themselves quite aware of the fact, and dread the dinner which they resolved to give quite as much as it is dreaded by their friends. They know that they prepare for their guests an evening of misery, and for themselves certain long hours of purgatory which are hardly to be endured. But they will do it. Why that long table, and all those supernumerary glasses and knives and forks, if they are never to be used? That argument produces all this misery; that and others cognate to it. On the present occasion, no doubt, there were excuses to be made. The squire and his niece had been invited on special cause, and their presence would have been well enough. The doctor added in would have done no harm. It was good-natured, too, that invitation given to Mrs. Eames and her daughter. The error lay in the parson and his wife. There was no necessity for their being there, nor had they any ground on which to stand, except the party-giving ground. Mr. and Mrs. Boyce made the dinner-party, and destroyed the social circle. Lady Julia knew that she had been wrong as soon as she had sent out the note.

Nothing was said on that evening which has any bearing on our story. Nothing, indeed, was said which had any bearing on anything. The earl's professed object had been to bring the squire and young Eames together; but people are never brought together on such melancholy occasions. Though they sip their port in close contiguity, they are poles asunder in their minds and feelings. When the Guestwick fly came for Mrs. Eames, and the parson's pony phaeton came for him and Mrs. Boyce, a great relief was felt ; but the misery of those who were left had gone too far to allow of any reaction on that evening. The squire yawned, and the earl yawned, and then there was an end of it for that night.

CHAPTER XXIV. THE SECOND VISIT TO THE GUESTWICK BRIDGE.

BELL had declared that her sister would be very happy to see John Eames if he would go over to Allington, and he had replied that of course he would go there. So much having been, as it were, settled, he was able to speak of his visit as a matter of course at the breakfast table, on the morning after the earl's dinner-party. " I must get you to come round with me, Dale, and see what I am doing to the land," the earl said. And then he proposed to order saddle-horses. But the squire preferred walking, and in this way they were disposed of soon after breakfast.

John had it in his mind to get Bell to himself for half an hour, and hold a conference with her; but it either happened that Lady Julia was too keen in her duties as a hostess, or else, as was more possible, Bell avoided the meeting. No opportunity for such an interview offered itself, though he hung about the drawing-room all the morning. " You had better wait for luncheon, now," Lady Julia said to him about twelve. But this he declined ; and taking himself away hid himself about the place for the next hour and a half. During this time he considered much whether it would be better for him to ride or walk. If she should give him any hope, he could ride back triumphant as a field-marshal. Then the horse would be delightful to him. But if she should give him no hope,—if it should be his destiny to be rejected utterly on that morning,—then the horse would be terribly in the way of his sorrow. Under such circumstances what could he do but roam wide about across the fields, resting when he might choose to rest, and running when it might suit him to run. "And she is not like other girls," he thought to himself. " She won't care for my boots being dirty." So at last he elected to walk.

"Stand up to her boldly, man," the earl had said to him. " By George, what is there to he afraid of? It's my belief they'll give most to those who ask for most. There's nothing sets 'em against a man like being sheepish." How the earl knew so much, seeing that he had not himself given signs of any success in that walk of life, I am not prepared to say. But Eames took his advice as being in itself good, and resolved to act upon it. " Not that any resolution will be of any use," he said to himself, as he walked along. " When the moment comes I know that I shall tremble before her, and I know that she'll see it; but I don't think it will make any difference in her."

He had last seen her on the lawn behind the Small House, just at that time when her passion for Crosbie was at the strongest. Eames had gone thither impelled by a foolish desire to declare to her his hopeless love, and she had answered him by telling him that she loved Mr. Crosbie better than all the world besides. Of course she had done so, at that time ; but, nevertheless, her manner of telling him had seemed to him to be cruel. And he had also been cruel. He had told her that he hated Crosbie,—calling him " that man," and assuring her that no earthly consideration should induce him to go into " that man's house." Then he had walked away moodily wishing him all manner of evil. Was it not singular that all the evil things which he, in his mind, had meditated for the man, had fallen upon him. Crosbie had lost his love! He had so proved himself to be a villain that his name might not be so much as mentioned ! He had been ignominiously thrashed ! But what good would all this be if his image were still dear to Lily's heart. " I told her that I loved her then," he said to himself, " though I had no right to do so. At any rate I have a right to tell her now."

When he reached Allington he did not go in through the village and up to the front of the Small House by the cross street, but turned by the church gate and passed over the squire's terrace, and by the end of the Great House through the garden. Here he encountered Hopkins. " Why, if that b'aint Mr. Eames! " said the gardener. " Mr. John, may I make so bold! " and Hopkins held out a very dirty hand, which Eames of course took, unconscious of the cause of this new affection.

" I'm just going to call at the Small House, and I thought I'd come this way."

"To be sure; this way, or that way, or any way, who's so

welcome, Mr. John ? I envies you; I envies you more than I envies any man. If I could a got him by the scuff of the neck, I'd a treated him jist like any wermin ;—I would, indeed ! He was wermin! I ollays said it. I hated him ollays; I did indeed, Mr. John, from the first moment when he used to be nigging away at them foutry balls, knocking them in among the rhododendrons, as though there weren't no flower blossoms for next year. He never looked at one as though one were a Christian ; did he, Mr. John ? "

" I wasn't very fond of him myself, Hopkins."

" Of course you weren't very fond of him. Who was ?—only she, poor young lady. She'll be better now, Mr. John, a deal better. He wasn't a wholesome lover,—not like you are. Tell me, Mr. John, did you give it him well when you got him ? I heard you did;—two black eyes, and all his face one mash of gore !" And Hopkins, who was by no means a young man, stiffly put himself into a fighting attitude.

Eames passed on over the little bridge, which seemed to be in a state of fast decay, unattended to by any friendly carpenter, now that the days of its use were so nearly at an end; and on into the garden, lingering on the spot where he had last said farewell to Lily. He looked about as though he expected still to find her there; but there was no one to be seen in the garden, and no sound to be heard. As every step brought him nearer to her whom he was seeking, he became more and more conscious of the hopelessness of his errand. Him she had never loved, and why should he venture to hope that she would love him now ? He would have turned back had he not been aware -that his promise to others required that he should persevere. He had said that he would do this thing, and he would be as good as his word. But he hardly ventured to hope that he might be successful. In this frame of mind he slowly made his way up across the lawn.

" My dear, there is John Eames," said Mrs. Dale, who had first seen him from the parlour window.

" Don't go, mamma."

" I don't know ; perhaps it will be better that I should."

"No, mamma, no; what good can it do ? It can do no good. I like him as well as I can like any one. I love him dearly. But it can do no good. Let him come in here, and be very kind to him; but do not go away and leave us. Of course I knew he would come, and I shall be very glad to see him."

Then Mrs. Dale went round to the other room, and admitted her visitor through the window of the drawing-room. " We are in terrible confusion, John, are we not ? "

" And so you are really going to live in G-uestwick ? " " Well, it looks like it, does it not ? But, to tell you a secret,— only it must be a secret; you must not mention it at Guestwick Manor; even Bell does not know;—we have half made up our minds to unpack all our things and stay where we are."

Eames was so intent on his own purpose, and so fully occupied with the difficulty of the task before him, that he could hardly receive Mrs. Dale's tidings with all the interest which they deserved. " Unpack them all again," he said. " That will be very troublesome. Is Lily with you, Mrs. Dale ? "

" Yes, she is in the parlour. Come and see her." So he followed Mrs. Dale through the hall, and found himself in the presence of his love.

" How do you do, John ? " " How do you do, Lily ? " We all know the way in which such meetings are commenced. Each longed to be tender and affectionate to the other,—each in a different way; but neither knew how to throw any tenderness into this first greeting. " So you're staying at the Manor House," said Lily.

" Yes; I'm staying there. Your uncle and Bell came yesterday afternoon."

" Have you heard about Bell ? " said Mrs. Dale. " Oh, yes; Mary told me. I'm so glad of it. I always liked Dr. Crofts very much. I have not congratulated her, because I didn't know whether it was a secret. But Crofts was there last night, and if it is a secret he didn't seem to be very careful about keeping it."

"It is no secret," said Mrs. Dale. " I don't know that I am fond of such secrets." But as she said this, she thought of Crosbie's engagement, which had been told to every one, and of its consequences.

" Is it to be soon ?" he asked.

" Well, yes ; we think so. Of course nothing is settled." " It was such fun," said Lily. "

James, who took, at any rate, a year or two to make his proposal, wanted to be married the next day afterwards."

" No, Lily; not quite that."

" Well, mamma, it was very nearly that. He thought it could all be done this week. It has made us so happy, John! I don't know anybody I should so much like for a brother. I'm very glad you like him ;—very glad. I hope you'll be friends always." There was some little tenderness in this,—as John acknowledged to himself.

" I'm sure we shall,—if he likes it. That is, if I ever happen to see him. I'll do anything for him I can if he ever comes up to London. Wouldn't it be a good thing, Mrs. Dale, if he settled himself in London?"

" No, John; it would be a very bad thing. Why should he wish to rob me of my daughter ? "

Mrs. Dale was speaking of her eldest daughter ; but the very allusion to any such robbery covered John Eames's face with a blush, made him hot up to the roots of his hair, and for the moment silenced him.

" You think he would have a better career in London ? " said Lily, speaking under the influence of her superior presence of mind.

She had certainly shown defective judgment in desiring her mother not to leave them alone; and of this Mrs. Dale soon felt herself aware. The thing had to be done, and no little precautionary measure, such as this of Mrs. Dale's enforced presence, would prevent it. Of this Mrs. Dale was well aware; and she felt, moreover, that John was entitled to an opportunity of pleading his own cause. It might be that such opportunity would avail him nothing, but not the less should he have it of right, seeing that he desired it. But yet Mrs. Dale did not dare to get up and leave the room. Lily had asked her not to do so, and at the present period of their lives all Lily's requests were sacred. They continued for some time to talk of Crofts and his marriage ; and when that subject was finished, they discussed their own probable,—or, as it seemed now, improbable,— removal to Guestwick. "It's going too far, mamma," said Lily, " to say that you think we shall not go. It was only last night that you suggested it. The truth is, John, that Hopkins came in and discoursed with the most wonderful eloquence. Nobody dared to oppose Hopkins. He made us almost cry ; he was so pathetic."

" He has just been talking to me, too," said John, " as I came through the squire's garden."

" And what has he been saying to you ? " said Mrs. Dale.

"Oh, I don't know; not much." John, however, remembered well, at this moment, all that the gardener had said to him. Did she know of that encounter between him and Croshie ? and if she did know of it, in what light did she regard it ?

They had sat thus for an hour together, and Eames was not as yet an inch nearer to his object. He had sworn to himself that he would not leave the Small House without asking Lily to be his wife. It seemed to him as though he would be guilty of falsehood towards the earl if he did so. Lord De Guest had opened his house to him, and had asked all the Dales there, and had offered himself up as a sacrifice at the cruel shrine of a serious dinner-party, to say nothing of that easier and lighter sacrifice which he had made in a pecuniary point of view, in order that this thing might be done. Under such circumstances Eames was too honest a man not to do it, let the difficulties in his way be what they might.

He had sat there for an hour, and Mrs. Dale still remained with her daughter. Should he get up boldly and ask Lily to put on her bonnet and come out into the garden ? As the thought struck him, he rose and grasped at his hat. " I am going to walk back to Guestwick," said he.

" It was very good of you to come so far to see us."

" I was always fond of walking," he said. " The earl wanted me to ride, but I prefer being on foot when I know the country, as I do here."

" Have a glass of wine before you go."

" Oh, dear, no. I think I'll go back through the squire's fields, and out on the road at the white gate. The path is quite dry now."

" I dare say it is," said Mrs. Dale.

" Lily, I wonder whether you would come as far as that with me." As the request was made Mrs. Dale looked at her daughter almost beseechingly. " Do, pray do," said he ; " it is a beautiful day for walking."

The path proposed lay right across the field into which Lily had taken Crosbie when she made her offer to let him off from his engagement. Could it be possible that she should ever walk there again with another lover ? " No, John," she said; "not to-day, I think. I am almost tired, and I had rather not go out."

" It would do you good," said Mrs. Dale.

" I don't want to be done good to, mamma. Besides, I should have to come back by myself."

" I'll come back with you," said Johnny.

" Oh, yes; and then I should have to go again with you. But, John, really I don't wish to walk to-day." Whereupon John Eames again put down his hat.

" Lily," said he; and then he stopped. Mrs. Dale walked away to the window, turning her hack upon her daughter and visitor. " Lily, I have come over here on purpose to speak to you. Indeed, I have come down from London only that I might see you."

"Have you, John?"

" Yes, I have. You know well all that I have got to tell you. I loved you hefore he ever saw you ; and now that he has gone, I love you better than I ever did. Dear Lily!" and he put out his hand to her.

" No, John; no," she answered,

11 Must it be always no ? "

" Always no to that. How can it be otherwise ? You would not have me marry you while I love another! "

" But he is gone. He has taken another wife."

" I cannot change myself because 'he is changed. If you are kind to me you will let that be enough."

" But you are so unkind to me ! "

" No, no ; oh, I would wish to be so kind to you ! John, here; take my hand. It is the hand of a friend who loves you, and will always love you. Dear John, I will do anything,—everything for you but that."

" There is only one thing," said he, still holding her by the hand, but with his face turned from her.

" Nay ; do not say so. Are you worse off than I am ? I could not have that one thing, and I was nearer to my heart's longings than you have ever been. I cannot have that one thing; but I know that there are other things, and I will not allow myself to be brokenhearted."

" You are stronger than I am," he said.

"Not stronger, but more certain. Make yourself as sure as I am, and you, too, will be strong. Is it not so, mamma ? "

" I wish it could be otherwise ;—I wish it could be otherwise ! If you can give him any hope "

" Mamma! "

" Tell me that I may come again,—in a year," he pleaded.

" I cannot tell you so. You may not come again,—not in this way. Do you remember what I told you before, in the garden; that I loved him better than all the world besides ? It is still the same.

I still love him better than all the world. How, then, can I give you any hope ? "

" But it will not be so for ever, Lily."

" For ever ! "Why should he not be mine as well as hers when that for ever comes ? John, if you understand what it is to love, you will say nothing more of it. I have spoken to you more openly about this than I have ever done to anybody, even to mamma, because I have wished to make you understand my feelings. I should be disgraced in my own eyes if I admitted the love of another

man, after—after . It is to me almost as though I had married

him. I am not blaming him, remember. These things are different with a man."

She had not dropped his hand, and as she made her last speech was sitting in her old chair with her eyes fixed upon the ground. She spoke in a low voice, slowly, almost with difficulty; but still the words came very clearly, with a clear, distinct voice which caused them to be remembered with accuracy, both by Eames and Mrs. Dale. To him it seemed to be impossible that he should continue his suit after such a declaration. To Mrs. Dale they were terrible words, speaking of a perpetual widowhood, and telling of an amount of suffering greater even than that which she had anticipated. It was true that Lily had never said so much to her as she had now said to John Eames, or had attempted to make so clear an exposition of her own feelings. " I should be disgraced in my own eyes if I admitted the love of another man!" They were terrible words, but very easy to be understood. Mrs. Dale had felt, from the first, that Eames was coming too soon, that the earl and the squire together were making an effort to cure the wound too quickly after its infliction ; that time should have been given to her girl to recover. But now the attempt had been made, and words had been forced from Lily's lips, the speaking of which would never be forgotten by herself.

" I knew that it would be so," said John.

" Ah, yes ; you know it, because your heart understands my heart. And you will not be angry with me, and say naughty, cruel words, as you did once before. We^will think of each other, John, and pray for each other; and will always love one another. When we do meet let us be glad to see each other. No other Mend shall ever be dearer to me than you are. You are so true and honest! When you marry I will tell your wife what an infinite blessing God has given her."

" You shall never do that."

" Yes, I will. I understand what you mean ; but yet I will."

" Good-by, Mrs. Dale," he said.

" Good-by, John. If it could have been otherwise with her, you should have had all my best wishes in the matter. I would have loved you dearly as my son ; and I will love you now." Then she put up her lips and kissed his face.

" And so will I love you," said Lily, giving him her hand again. He looked longingly into her face as though he had thought it possible that she also might kiss him : then he pressed her hand to his lips, and without speaking any further farewell, took up his hat and left the room.

" Poor fellow! " said Mrs. Dale.

"They should not have let him come," said Lily. "But they don't understand. They think that I have lost a toy, and they mean to be good-natured, and to give me another." Very shortly after that Lily went away by herself, and sat alone for hours; and when she joined her mother again at tea-time, nothing further was said of John Eames's visit.

He made his way out by the front door, and through the churchyard, and in this way on to the field through which he had asked Lily to walk with him. He hardly began to think of what had passed till he had left the squire's house behind him. As he made his way through the tombstones he paused and read one, as though it interested him. He stood a moment under the tower looking up at the clock, and then pulled out his own watch, as though to verify the one by the other. He made, unconsciously, a struggle to dr.ve away from his thoughts the facts of the late scene, and for some ave or ten minutes he succeeded. He said to himself a word or two about Sir Raffle and his letters, and laughed inwardly as he remembered the figure of Rafierty bringing in the knight's shoes. He had gone some half mile upon his way before he ventured to stand still and tell himself that he had failed in the great object of his life.

Yes; he had failed: and he acknowledged to himself, with bitter reproaches, that he had failed, now and for ever. He told himself that he had obtruded upon her in her sorrow with an unmannerly love, and rebuked himself as having been not only foolish but ungenerous. His friend the earl had been wont, in his waggish way, to call him the conquering hero, and had so talked him out of his common sense as to have made hir? almost think that he would be successful in his suit. Now, as he told himself that any such success must have been impossible, he almost hated the earl for having brought him to this condition. A conquering hero, indeed! How should he manage to sneak back among them all at the Manor House, crestfallen and abject in his misery? Everybody knew the errand on which he had gone, and everybody must know of his failure. How could he have been such a fool as to undertake such a task under the eyes of so many lookers-on? Was it not the case that he had so fondly expected success, as to think only of his triumph in returning, and not of his more probable disgrace? He had allowed others to make a fool of him, and had so made a fool of himself that now all hope and happiness were over for him. How could he escape at once out of the country,—back to London? How could he get away without saying a word further to any one? That was the thought that at first occupied his mind.

He crossed the road at the end of the squire's property, where the parish of Allington divides itself from that of Abbot's Guest in which the earl's house stands, and made his way back along the copse which skirted the field in which they had encountered the bull, into the high woods which were at the back of the park. Ah, yes; it had been well for him that he had not come out on horseback. That ride home along the high road and up to the Manor House stables would, under his present circumstances, have been almost impossible to him. As it was, he did not think it possible that he should return to his place in the earl's house. How could he pretend to maintain his ordinary demeanour under the eyes of those two old men? It would be better for him to get home to his mother,—to send a message from thence to the Manor, and then to escape back to London. So thinking, but with no resolution made, he went on through the woods, and down from the hill back towards the town till he again came to the little bridge over the brook. There he stopped and stood a while with his broad hand spread over the letters which he had cut in those early days, so as to hide them from his sight. "What an ass I have been,—always and ever!" he said to himself.

It was not only of his late disappointment that he was thinking, but of his whole past life. He was conscious of his hobbledehoy-hood,—of that backwardness on his part in assuming manhood which had rendered him incapable of making himself acceptable to Lily before she had fallen into the clutches of Crosbie. As he thought of this he

"SHE HAS REFUSED ME, AND IT IS ALL

THE SECOND VISIT TO THE GUESTWICK BRIDGE. 253

declared to himself that if he could meet Crosbie again he would again thrash him,—that he would so belabour him as to send him out of the world, if such sending might possibly be done by fair beating, regardless whether he himself might be called upon to follow him. Was it not hard for the two of them,—for Lily and for him also,—there should be such punishment because of the insincerity of that man? When he had thus stood upon the bridge for some quarter of an hour, he took out his knife, and, with deep, rough gashes in the wood, cut out Lily's name from the rail.

He had hardly finished, and was still looking at the chips as they were being earned away by the stream, when a gentle step came close up to him, and turning round, he saw that Lady Julia was on the bridge. She was close to him, and had already seen his handiwork. " Has she offended you, John ? " she said.

" Oh, Lady Julia ! "

"Has she offended you ?"

" She has refused me, and it is all over."

" It may be that she has refused you, and that yet it need not be all over. I am sorry that you have cut out the name, John. Do you mean to cut it out from your heart ? "

" Never. I would if I could, but I never shall."

" Keep to it as to a great treasure. It will [be a joy to you in after years, and not a sorrow. To have loved truly, even though you shall have loved in vain, will be a consolation when you are as old as I am. It is something to have had a heart."

" I don't know. I wish that I had none."

" And, John ;—I can understand her feeling now ; and, indeed, I thought all through that you were asking her too soon; but the time may yet come when she will think better of your wishes."

" No, no; never. I begin to know her now."

" If you can be constant in your love you may win her yet. Remember how young she is ; and how young you both are. Come again in two years' time, and then, when you have won her, you shall tell me that I have been a good old woman to you both."

" I shall never win her, Lady Julia." As he spoke these last words the tears were running down his cheeks, and he was weeping openly in the presence of his companion. It was well for him that she had come upon him in his sorrow. When he once knew that she had seen his tears, he could pour out to her the whole story of his grief; and as he did so she led him back quietly to the house.

(254)

CHAPTER XXV. NOT VERY FIE FEE AFTER ALL.

IT will perhaps be remembered that terrible things had been foretold as about to happen between the Hartletop and Omnium families. Lady Dumbello had smiled whenever Mr. Plantagenet Palliser had spoken to her. Mr. Palliser had confessed to himself that politics were not enough for him, and that Love was necessary to make up the full complement of his happiness. Lord Dumbello had frowned laterly when his eyes fell on the tall figure of the duke's heir; and the duke himself,—that potentate, generally so mighty in his silence, —the duke himself had spoken. Lady De Courcy and Lady Clandid-lem were, both of them, absolutely certain that the thing had been fully arranged. I am, therefore, perfectly justified in stating that the world was talking about the loves,—the illicit loves,—of Mr. Palliser and Lady Dumbello.

And the talking of the world found its way down to that respectable country parsonage in which Lady Dumbello had been born, and from which she had been taken away to those noble halls which she now graced by her presence. The talking of the world was heard at Plumstead Episcopi, where still lived Archdeacon Grantly, the lady's father ; and was heard also at the deanery of Barchester, where lived the lady's aunt and grandfather. By whose ill-mannered tongue the rumour was spread in these ecclesiastical regions it boots not now to tell. But it may he remembered that Courcy Castle was not far from Barchester, and that Lady De Courcy was not given to hide her lights under a bushel.

It was a terrible rumour. To what mother must not such a rumour respecting her daughter be very terrible ? In no mother's ears could it have sounded more frightfully than it did in those of Mrs. Grantly. Lady Dumbello, the daughter, might be altogether worldly ; but Mrs. Grantly had 'never'been'more than half worldly. In one moiety of her character, her habits, and her desires, she had been wedded to things good in themselves,—to religion, to charity, and to honest-hearted uprightness. It is true that the circumstances of her life had induced her to serve both God and Mammon, and that, therefore, she had gloried greatly in the marriage of her daughter with the heir of a marquis. She had revelled in the aristocratic elevation of her child, though she continued to dispense books and catechisms with her own hands to the children of the labourers of Plumstead Episcopi. When Griselda first became Lady Dumbello the mother feared somewhat lest her child should find herself unequal to the exigencies of her new position. But the child had proved herself more than equal to them, and had mounted up to a dizzy height of success, which brought to the mother great glory and great fear also. She delighted to think that her Griselda was great even among the daughters of marquises ; but she trembled as she reflected how deadly would be the fall from such a height—should there ever be a fall!

But she had never dreamed of such a fall as this ! She would have said,—indeed, she often had said,—to the archdeacon that Griselda's religious principles were too firmly fixed to be moved by outward worldly matters; signifying, it may be, her conviction that that teaching of Plumstead Episcopi had so fastened her daughter into a groove, that all the future teaching of Hartlebury would not suffice to undo the fastenings. When she had thus boasted no such idea as that of her daughter running from her husband's house had ever come upon her; but she had alluded to vices of a nature kindred to that vice,—to vices into which other aristocratic ladies sometimes fell, who had been less firmly grooved; and her boastings had amounted to this,—that she herself had so successfully served God and Mammon together, that her child might go forth and enjoy all worldly things without risk of damage to things heavenly. Then came upon her this rumour. The archdeacon told her in a hoarse whisper that he had been recommended to look to it, that it was current through the world that Griselda was about to leave her husband.

" Nothing on earth shall make me believe it," said Mrs. Grantly. But she sat alone in her drawing-room afterwards and trembled. Then came her sister, Mrs. Arabin, the dean's wife, over to the parsonage, and in half-hidden words told the same story. She had

heard it from Mrs. Proudie, the bishop's wife. " That woman is as false as the father of falsehoods," said Mrs. Grantly. But she trembled the more; and as she prepared her parish work, could think of nothing but her child. What would be all her life to come, what would have been all that was past of her life, if this thing should happen to her ? She would not believe it; but yet she trembled the more as she thought of her daughter's exaltation, and remembered that such things had been done in that world to which Griselda now belonged. Ah ! would it not have been better for them if they had not raised their heads so high ! And she walked out alone among the tombs of the neighbouring churchyard, and stood over the grave in which had been laid the body of her other daughter. Could it be that the fate of that one had been the happier.

Very few words were spoken on the subject between her and the archdeacon, and yet it seemed agreed among them that something should be done. He went up to London, and saw his daughter,—not daring, however, to mention such a subject. Lord Dumbello was cross with him, and very uncommunicative. Indeed both the archdeacon and Mrs. Grantly had found that their daughter's house was not comfortable to them, and as they were sufficiently proud among their own class they had not cared to press themselves on the hospitality of their son-in-law. But he had been able to perceive that all was not right in the house in Carlton Gardens. Lord Dumbello was not gracious with his wife, and there was something in the silence, rather than in the speech, of men, which seemed to justify the report which had reached him.

"He is there oftener than he should be," said the archdeacon. "And I am sure of this, at least, that Dumbello does not like it."

"I will write to her," said Mrs. Grantly at last. "I am still her mother;—I will write to her. It may be that she does not know what people say of her."

And Mrs. Grantly did write.

Plumstead, April, 186— DEAREST GRISELDA,

IT seems sometimes that you have been moved so far away from me that I have hardly a right to concern myself more in the affairs of your daily life, and I know that it is impossible that you should refer to me for advice or sympathy, as you would have done had you married some gentleman of our own standing. But I am quite sure that my child does not forget her mother, or fail to look back upon her mother's love ; and that she will allow me to speak to her if she be in trouble, as I would to any other child whom I

had loved and cherished. I pray God that I may be wrong in supposing that such trouble is near you. If I am so you will forgive me my solicitude.

Rumours have reached us from more than one quarter that Oh ! Griselda,

I hardly know in what words to conceal and yet to declare that which I have to write. They say that you are intimate with Mr. Palliser, the nephew of the duke, and that your husband is much offended. Perhaps I had better tell you all, openly, cautioning you not to suppose that I have believed it. They say that it is thought that you are going to put yourself under Mr. Palliser's protection. My dearest child, I think you can imagine with what an agony I write these words,—with what terrible grief I must have been oppressed before I could have allowed myself to entertain the thoughts which have produced them. Such things are said openly in Barchester, and your father, who has been in town and has seen you, feels himself unable to tell me that my mind may be at rest.

I will not say to you a word as to the injury in a worldly point £of view which would come to you from any rupture with your husband. I believe that you can see what would be the effect of so terrible a step quite as plainly as I can show it you. You would break the heart of your father, and send your mother to her grave;—but it is not even on that that I may most insist. It is this,—that you would offend your God by the worst sin that a woman can commit, and cast yourself into a depth of infamy in which repentance before God is almost impossible, and from which escape before man is not permitted.

I do not believe it, my dearest, dearest child,—my only living daughter; 1 do not believe what they have said to me. But as a mother I have not dared to leave the slander unnoticed. If you will write to me and say that it is not so, you will make me happy again, even though you should rebuke me for my suspicion.

Believe that at all times and under all circumstances, I am still your loving mother, as I was in other days. SUSAN GRANTLY.

We will now go back to Mr. Palliser as he sat in his chambers at the Albany, thinking of his love. The duke had cautioned him, and the duke's agent had cautioned him; and he, in spite of his high feeling of independence, had almost been made to tremble. All his thousands a year were in the balance, and perhaps everything on which depended his position before the world. But, nevertheless, though he did tremble, he resolved to persevere. Statistics were becoming dry to him, and love was very sweet. Statistics, he thought, might be made as enchanting as ever, if only they could be mingled with love. The mere idea of loving Lady Dumbello had seemed to give a salt to his life of which he did not now know how to rob himself. It is true that he had not as yet enjoyed many of the absolute blessings of love, seeing that his conversations with Lady Dumbello had never been warmer than those which have been repeated in these pages ; VOL ii.

but his imagination had been at work ; and now that Lady Dumbello was fully established at her house in Carlton Gardens, he was determined to declare his passion on the first convenient opportunity. It was sufficiently manifest to him that the world expected him to do so, and that the world was already a little disposed to find fault with the slowness of his proceedings.

He had been once at Carlton Gardens since the season had commenced, and the lady had favoured him with her sweetest smile. But he had only been half a minute alone with her, and during that half-minute had only time to remark that he supposed she would now remain in London for the season.

" Oh, yes," she had answered, " we shall not leave till July." Nor could he leave till July, because of the exigencies of his statistics. He therefore had before him two, if not three, clear months in which to manoeuvre, to declare his purposes, and prepare for the future events of his life. As he resolved on a certain morning that he would say his first tender word to Lady Dumbello that very night, in the drawing-room of Lady De Courcy, where he knew that he should meet her, a letter came to him by the post. He well knew the hand and the intimation which it would contain. It was from the duke's agent, Mr. Fothergill, and informed him that a certain sum of money had been placed to his credit at his banker's. But the letter went further, and informed him also that the duke had given his agent to understand that special instructions would be necessary before the next quarterly payment could be made. Mr. Fothergill said nothing further, but Mr. Palliser understood it all. He felt his blood run cold round his heart; but, nevertheless, he determined that he would not break his word to Lady De Courcy that night.

And Lady Dumbello received her letter also on the same morning. She was being dressed as she read it, and the maidens who attended her found no cause to suspect that anything in the letter had excited her ladyship. Her ladyship was not often excited, though she was vigilant in exacting from them their utmost cares. She read her letter, however, very carefully, and as she sat beneath the toilet implements of her maidens thought deeply of the tidings which had been brought to her. She was angry with no one;—she was thankful to no one. She felt no special love for any person concerned in the matter. Her heart did not say, " Oh, my lord and husband! " or, " Oh, my lover !" or, "Oh, my mother, the friend of my childhood ! " But she became aware that matter for thought had been brought

before her, and she did think. " Send my love to Lord Dumbello," she said, when the operations were nearly completed, " and tell him that I shall be so glad to see him if he will come to me while I am at breakfast."

" Yes, my lady." And then the message came back: " His lordship would be with her ladyship certainly."

" Gustavus," she said, as soon as she had seated herself discreetly in her chair, " I have had a letter from my mother, which you had better read ; " and she handed to him the document. " I do not know what I have done to deserve such suspicions from her ; but she lives in the country, and has probably been deceived by ill-natured people. At any rate you must read it, and tell me what I shall do."

We may predicate from this that Mr. Palliser's chance of being able to shipwreck himself upon that rock was but small, and that he would, in spite of himself, be saved from his uncle's anger. Lord Dumbello took the letter and read it very slowly, standing, as he did so, with v his back to the fire. He read very slowly, and his wife, though she never turned her face directly upon his, could see that he became very red, that he was fluttered and put beyond himself, and that his answer was not ready. She was well aware that his conduct to her during the last three months had been much altered from his former usages; that he had been rougher with her in his speech when alone, and less courteous in his attention when in society; but she had made no complaint or spoken a word to show him that she had marked the change. She had known, moreover, the cause of his altered manner, and having considered much,*had resolved that she would live it down. She had declared to herself that she had done no deed and spoken no word that justified suspicion, and therefore she would make no change in her ways, or show herself to be conscious that she was suspected. But now,—having her mother's letter in her hand,—she could bring him to an explanation without making him aware that she had ever thought that he had been jealous of her. To her, her mother's letter was a great assistance. It justified a scene like this, and enabled her to fight her battle after her own fashion. As for eloping with any Mr. Palliser, and giving up the position which she had won;—no, indeed! She had been fastened in her grooves too well for that! Her mother, in entertaining any fear on such a subject, had shown herself to be ignorant of the solidity of her daughter's character.

"Well, Gustavus," she said at last. "You must say what

THE SMALL HOUSE AT ALLINGTON.

answer I shall make, or whether I shall make any answer." But he was not even yet ready to instruct her. So he unfolded the letter and read it again, and she poured out for herself a cup of tea.

" It's a very serious matter," said he.

" Yes, it is serious; I could not but think such a letter from my mother to be serious. Had it come from any one else I doubt whether I should have troubled you; unless, indeed, it had been from any as near to you as she is to me. As it is, you cannot but feel that I am right."

" Right! Oh, yes, you are right,—quite right to tell me ; you should tell me everything. D them ! " But whom he meant to condemn he did not explain.

"I am above all things averse to cause you trouble," she said. " I have seen some little things of late "

" Has he ever said anything to you ? "

" Who,—Mr. Palliser ? Never a word."

" He has hinted at nothing of this kind ? "

" Never a word. Had he done so, I must have made you understand that he could not have -been allowed again into my drawing-room." Then again he read the letter, or pretended to do so.

" Your mother means well," he said.

" Oh, yes, she means well. She has been foolish to believe the tittle-tattle that has reached her,—very foolish to oblige me to give you this annoyance."

" Oh, as for that, I'm not annoyed. By Jove, no. Come, Griselda, let us have it all out; other people have said this, and I have been unhappy. Now, you know it all."

" Have I made you unhappy ? "

" Well, no; not you. Don't be hard upon me when I tell you the whole truth. Fools and brutes have whispered things that have vexed me. They may whisper till the devil fetches them, but they shan't annoy me again. Give me a kiss, my girl." And he absolutely put out his arms and embraced her. " Write a good-natured letter to your mother, and ask her to come up for a week in May. That'll be the best thing ; and then she'll understand. By Jove, it's twelve o'clock. Good-by."

Lady Dumbello was well aware that she had triumphed, and that her mother's letter had been invaluable to her. But it had been used, and therefore she did not read it again. She ate her breakfast in quiet comfort, looking over a milliner's French circular as she did

so; and then, when the time for such an operation had fully come, she got to her writing-table and answered her mother's letter.

DEAR MAMMA (she said),

I THOUGHT it best to show your letter at once to Lord Dumbello. He said that people would be ill-natured, and seemed to think that the telling of such stories could not be helped. As regards you, he was not a bit angry, but said that you and papa had better come^to us for a week about the end of next month. Do come. We are to have rather a large dinner-party on the 23rd. His Koyal Highness is coming, and I think"papa would like to meet him. Have you observed that those very high bonnets have all gone out: I never liked them ; and as I had got a hint from Paris, I have been doing my best to put them down. I do hope nothing will prevent your coming.

Your affectionate daughter, Carlton Gardens, Wednesday. G. DUMBELLO.

Mrs. Grantly was aware, from the moment in which she received the letter, that she had wronged her daughter hy her suspicions. It did not occur to her to disbelieve a word that was said in the letter, or an inference that was implied. She had been wrong, and rejoiced that it was so. But nevertheless there was that in the letter which annoyed and irritated her, though she could not explain to herself the cause of her annoyance. She had thrown all her heart into that which she had written, but in the words which her child had written not a vestige of heart was to be found. In that reconciling of God and Mammon which Mrs. Grantly had carried on so successfully in the education of her daughter, the organ had not been required, and had become withered, if not defunct, through want of use.

" We will not go there, I think," said Mrs. Grantly, speaking to her husband.

" Oh dear, no ; certainly not. If you want to go to town at all,

I will take rooms for you. And as for his Royal Highness !

I have a great respect for his Royal Highness, but I do not in the least desire to meet him at Dumbello's table."

And so that matter was settled, as regarded the inhabitants of Plumstead Episcopi.

And whither did Lord Dumbello betake himself when he left his wife's room in so great a hurry at twelve o'clock ? Not to the Park, nor to Tattersall's, nor to a Committee-room of the House of Commons, nor yet to the bow-window of his club. But he went straight to a great jeweller's in Ludgate-hill, and there purchased a wonderful green necklace, very rare and curious, heavy with green sparkling

THE SMALL HOUSE AT ALLINGTON.

drops, with three rows of shining green stones embedded in chaste gold,—a necklace amounting almost to a jewelled cuirass in weight and extent. It had been in all the exhibitions, and was very costly and magnificent. While Lady Dumbello was dressing in the evening this was brought to her with her lord's love, as his token of renewed confidence ; and Lady Dumbello, as she counted the sparkles, triumphed inwardly, telling herself that she had played her cards well.

But while she counted the sparkles produced by her full reconciliation with her lord, poor Plantagenet Palliser was still trembling in his ignorance. If only he could have been allowed to see Mrs. Grantly's letter, and the lady's answer, and the lord's present! But no such seeing was vouchsafed to him, and he was carried off in his brougham to Lady De Courcy's house, twittering with expectant love, and trembling with expectant ruin. To this conclusion he had come at any rate, that if anything was to be done, it should be done now. He would speak a word of love, and prepare his future in accordance with the acceptance it might receive.

Lady De Courcy's rooms were very crowded when he arrived there. It was the first great crushing party of the season, and all the world had been collected into Portman Square. Lady De Courcy was smiling as though her lord had no teeth, as though her eldest son's condition was quite happy, and all things were going well with the De Courcy interests. Lady Margaretta was there behind her, bland without and bitter within; and Lady Rosina also, at some further distance, reconciled to this world's vanity and finery because there was to be- no dancing. And the married daughters of the house were there also, striving to maintain their positions on the strength of their undoubted birth, but subjected to some snubbing by the lowness of their absolute circumstances. Gazebee was there, happy in the absolute fact of his connection with an earl, and blessed with the consideration that was extended to him as an earl's son-in-law. And Crosbie, also, was in the rooms,—was present there, though he had sworn to himself that he would no longer dance attendance on the countess, and that he would sever himself away from the wretchedness of the family. But if he gave up them and their ways, what else would then be left to him ? He had come, therefore, and now stood alone, sullen, in a corner, telling himself that all was vanity. Yes; to the vain all will be vanity; and to the poor of heart all will be poor.

Lady Dumbello was there in a small inner room, seated on a

couch to which she had heen brought on her first arrival at the house, and on which she would remain till she departed. From time to time some very noble or very elevated personage would come before her and say a word, and she would answer that elevated personage with another word; but nobody had attempted with her the task of conversation. It was understood that Lady Dumbello did not converse,—— unless it were occasionally with Mr. Palliser.

She knew well that Mr. Palliser was to meet her there. He had told her expressly that he should do so, having inquired, with much solicitude, whether she intended to obey the invitation of the countess. " I shall probably be there," she had said, and now had determined that her mother's letter and her husband's conduct to her should not cause her to break her word. Should Mr. Palliser " forget" himself, she would know how to say a word to him as she had known how to say a word to her husband. Forget himself! She was very sure that Mr. Palliser had been making up his mind to forget himself for some months past.

He did come to her, and stood over her, looking unutterable things. His unutterable things, however, were so looked, that they did not absolutely demand notice from the lady. He did not sigh like a furnace, nor open his eyes upon her as though there were two suns in the firmament above her head, nor did he beat his breast or tear his hair. Mr. Palliser had been brought up in a school which delights in tranquillity, and never allows its pupils to commit themselves either to the sublime or to the ridiculous. He did look an unutterable thing or two; but he did it with so decorous an eye, that the lady, who was measuring it with great accuracy, could not, as yet, declare that Mr. Palliser had " forgotten himself."

There was room by her on the couch, and once or twice, at Hartle-bury, he had ventured so to seat himself. On the present occasion, however, he could not do so without placing himself manifestly on her dress. She would have known how to fill a larger couch even than that,—as she would have known, also, how to make room,—had it been her mind to do so. So he stood still over her, and she smiled at him. Such a smile ! It was cold as death, flattering no one, saying nothing, hideous in its unmeaning, unreal grace. Ah! how I hate the smile of a woman who smiles by rote! It made Mr. Palliser feel very uncomfortable;—but he did not analyze it, and persevered.

" Lady Dumbello," he said, and his voice was very low, " I have been looking forward to meeting you here."

" Have you, Mr. Palliser ? Yes; I remember that you asked me whether I was coming."

" I did. Hm— Lady Dumbello !" and he almost trenched upon the outside verge of that schooling which had taught him to avoid both the sublime and the ridiculous. But he had not forgotten himself as yet, and so she smiled again.

" Lady Dumbello, in this world in which we live, it is so hard to get a moment in which we can speak." He had thought that she would move her dress, but she did not.

" Oh, I don't know," she said; "one doesn't often want to say very much, I think."

" Ah, no; not often, perhaps. But when one does want! How I do hate these crowded rooms! " Yet, when he had been at Hartle-bury he had resolved that the only ground for him would be the crowded drawing-room of some large London house. "I wonder whether you ever desire anything beyond them ?"

"Oh, yes," said she; " but I confess that I am fond of parties."

Mr. Palliser looked round and thought that he saw that he was unobserved. He had made up his mind as to what he would do, and he was determined to do it. He had in him none of that readiness which enables some men to make love and carry off their Dulcineas at a moment's notice, but he had that pluck which would have made himself disgraceful in his own eyes if he omitted to do that as to the doing of which he had made a solemn resolution. He would have preferred to do it sitting, but, faute de mieux, seeing that a seat was denied to him, he would do it standing.

" Griselda," he said,—and it must be admitted that his tone was not bad. The word sank softly into her ear, like small rain upon moss, and it sank into no other ear. " Griselda !"

"Mr. Palliser!" said she; —and though she made no scene, though she merely glanced upon him once, he could see that he was wrong.

" May I not call you so ? "

" Certainly not. Shall I ask you to see if my people are there?" He stood a moment before her hesitating. " My carriage, I mean." As she gave the command she glanced at him again, and then he obeyed her orders.

When he returned she had left her seat; but he heard her name announced on the stairs, and caught a glance of the back of her head as she made her way gracefully down through the crowd. He never attempted to make love to her again, utterly disappointing the hopes of Lady De Courcy, Mrs. Proudie, and Lady Clandidlem.

As I would wish those who are interested in Mr. Palliser's fortunes to know the ultimate result of this adventure, and as we shall not have space to return to his affairs in this little history, I may, perhaps, be allowed to press somewhat forward, and tell what Fortune did for him before the close of that London season. Everybody knows that in that spring Lady Glencora MacCluskie was brought out before the world, and it is equally well known that she, as the only child of the late Lord of the Isles, was the great heiress of the day. It is true that the hereditary possession of Skye, Staffa, Mull, Arran, and Bute went, with the title, to the Marquis of Auldreekie, together with the counties of Caithness and Eoss-shire. But the property in Fife, Aberdeen, Perth, and Kincardineshire, comprising the greater part of those counties, and the coal-mines in Lanark, as well as the enormous estate within the city of Glasgow, were unentailed, and went to the Lady Glencora. She was a fair girl, with bright blue eyes and short wavy flaxen hair, very soft to the eye. The Lady Glencora was small in stature, and her happy round face lacked, perhaps, the highest grace of female beauty. But there was ever a smile upon it, at which it was very pleasant to look; and the intense interest with which she would dance, and talk, and follow up every amusement that was offered her, was very charming. The horse she rode was the dearest love;— oh ! she loved him so dearly ! And she had a little dog that was almost as dear as the horse. The friend of her youth, Sabrina Scott, was—oh, such a girl! And her cousin, the little Lord of the Isles, the heir of the marquis, was so gracious and beautiful that she was always covering him with kisses. Unfortunately he was only six, so that there was hardly a possibility that the properties should be brought together.

But Lady Glencora, though she was so charming, had even in this, her first outset upon the world, given great uneasiness to her friends, and caused the Marquis of Auldreekie to be almost wild with dismay. There was a terribly handsome man about town, who had spent every shilling that anybody would give him, who was very fond of brandy, who was known, but not trusted, at Newmarket, who was said to be deep in every vice, whose father would not speak to him;— and with him the Lady Glencora was never tired of dancing. One

266 THE SMALL HOUSE AT ALLINGTON.

morning she had told her cousin the marquis, with a flashing eye,— for the round blue eye could flash,—that Burgo Fitzgerald was more sinned against than sinning. Ah me ! what was a guardian marquis, anxious for the fate of the family property, to do under such circumstances as that ?

But before the end of the season the marquis and the duke were both happy men, and we will hope that the Lady Glencora also was satisfied. Mr. Plantagenet Palliser had danced with her twice, and had spoken his mind. He had an interview with the marquis, which was pre-eminently satisfactory, and everything was settled. Glencora no doubt told him how she had accepted that plain gold ring from Burgo Fitzgerald, and how she had restored it; but I doubt whether she ever told him of that wavy lock of golden hair which Burgo still keeps in his receptacle for such treasures.

" Plantagenet," said the duke, with quite unaccustomed warmth, " in this, as in all things, you have shown yourself to be everything that I could desire. I have told the marquis that Matching Priory, with the whole estate, should be given over to you at once. It is the most comfortable country-house I know. Glencora shall have The Horns as her wedding present."

But the genial, frank delight of Mr. Fothergill pleased Mr. Palliser the most. The heir of the Pallisers had done his duty, and Mr. Fothergill was unfeignedly a happy man.

(267)

CHAPTER XXVI. SHOWING HOW MR. CROSBIE BECAME AGAIN A HAPPY MAN.

IT has been told in the last chapter how Lady De Courcy gave a great party in London in the latter days of April, and it may therefore be thought that things were going well with the De Courcys; but I fear the inference would be untrue. At any rate, things were not going well with Lady Alexandrina, for she, on her mother's first arrival in town, had rushed to Portman-square with a long tale of her sufferings.

"Oh, mamma! you would not believe it; but he hardly ever speaks to me."

" My dear, there are worse faults in a man than that."

" I am alone there all the day. I never get out. He never offers to get me a carriage. He asked me to walk with him once last week, when it was raining. I saw that he waited till the rain began. Only think, I have not been out three evenings this month,—except to Amelia's; and now he says he won't go there any more, because a fly is so expensive. You can't believe how uncomfortable the house is."

" I thought you chose it, my dear."

" I looked at it, but, of course, I didn't know what a house ought to be. Amelia said it wasn't nice, but he would have it. He hates Amelia. I'm sure of that, for he says everything he can to snub her and Mr. Gazebee. Mr. Gazebee is as good as he, at any rate. What do you think ? He has given Richard warning to go. You never saw him, but he was a very good servant. He has given him warning, and he is not talking of getting another man. I won't live with him without somebody to wait upon me."

" My dearest girl, do not think of such a thing as leaving him."

" But I will think of it, mamma. You do not know what my life is in that house. He never speaks to me,—never. He comes home before dinner at half-past six, and when he has just shown himself he goes to his dressing-room. He is always silent at dinner-time, and after dinner he goes to sleep. He breakfasts always at nine, and goes away at half-past nine, though I know he does not get to his office till eleven. If I want anything, he says that it cannot be afforded. I never thought before that he was stingy, but I am sure now that he must be a miser at heart."

"It is better so than a spendthrift, Alexandrina."

" I don't know that it is better. He could not make me more unhappy than I am. Unhappy is no word for it. What can I do, shut up in such a house as that by myself from nine o'clock in the morning till six in the evening ? Everybody knows what he is, so that nobody will come to see me. I tell you fairly, mamma, I will not stand it. If you cannot help me, I will look for help elsewhere."

It may, at any rate, be said that things were not going well with that branch of the De Courcy family. Nor, indeed, was it going well with some other branches. Lord Porlock had married, not having selected his partner for life from the choicest cream of the aristocratic circles, and his mother, while endeavouring to say a word in his favour, had been so abused by the earl that she had been driven to declare that she could no longer endure such usage. She had come up to London in direct opposition to his commands, while he was fastened to his room by gout; and had given her party in defiance of him, so that people should not say, when her back was turned, that she had slunk away in despair.

"I have borne it," she said to Margaretta, "longer than any other woman in England would have done. While I thought that any of you would marry "

" Oh, don't talk of that, mamma," said Margaretta, putting a little scorn into her voice. She had not been quite pleased that even her mother should intimate that all her chance was over, and yet she herself had often told her mother that she had given up all thought of marrying.

" Rosina will go to Amelia's," the countess continued; "Mr. Gazebee is quite satisfied that it should be so, and he will take care that she shall have enough to cover her own expenses. I propose that you and I, dear, shall go to Baden-Baden."

" And about money, mamma ? "

" Mr. Gazebee must manage it. In spite of all that your father says, I know that there must be money. The expense will be much less so than in our present way."

" And what will papa do himself?"

" I cannot help it, my dear. No one knows what I have had to bear. Another year of it would kill me. His language has become worse and worse, and I fear every day that he is going to strike me with his crutch."

Under all these circumstances it cannot be said that the De Courcy interests were prospering.

But Lady De Courcy, when she had made up her mind to go to Baden-Baden, had by no means intended to take her youngest daughter with her. She had endured for years, and now Alexandrina was unable to endure for six months. Her chief grievance, moreover, was this,—that her husband was silent. The mother felt that no woman had a right to complain much of any such sorrow as that. If her earl had sinned only in that way, she would have been content to have remained by him till- the last!

And yet I do not know whether Alexandria's life was not quite as hard as that of her mother. She barely exceeded the truth when she said that he never spoke to her. The hours with her in her new comfortless house were very long,—very long and very tedious. Marriage with her had by no means been the thing that she had expected. At home, with her mother, there had always been people around her, but they had not always been such as she herself would have chosen for her companions. She had thought that, when married, she could choose and have those about her who were congenial to her; but she found that none came to her. Her sister, who was a wiser woman than she, had begun her married life with a definite idea, and had carried it out; but this poor creature found herself, as it were, stranded. When once she had conceived it in her heart to feel anger against her husband,—and she had done so before they had been a week together,—there was no love to bring her back to him again. She did not know that it behoved her to look pleased when he entered the room, and to make him at any rate think that his presence gave her happiness. She became gloomy before she reached her new house, and never laid her gloom aside. He would have made a struggle for some domestic comfort, had any seemed to be within his reach. As it was, he struggled for domestic propriety, believing that he might so best bolster up his present lot in life. But the task became harder and harder to him, and the

gloom became denser and more dense. He did not think of her unhappiness, but of his own; as she did not think of his tedium, but of hers. " If this be domestic felicity! " he would say to himself, as he sat in his arm-chair, striving to fix his attention upon a book.

" If this be the happiness of married life! " she thought, as she remained listless, without even the pretence of a book, behind her teacups. In truth she would not walk with him, not caring for such exercise round the pavement of a London square; and he had resolutely determined that she should not run into debt for carriage hire. He was not a curmudgeon with his money ; he was no miser. But he had found that in marrying an earl's daughter he had made himself a poor man, and he was resolved that he would not also be an embarrassed man.

When the bride heard that her mother and sister were about to escape to Baden-Baden, there rushed upon her a sudden hope that she might be able to accompany the flight. She would not be parted from her husband, or at least not so parted that the world should suppose that they had quarrelled. She would simply go away and make a long visit,—a very long visit. Two years ago a sojourn with her mother and Margaretta at Baden-Baden would not have offered to her much that was attractive; but now, in her eyes, such a life seemed to be a life in Paradise. In truth, the tedium of those hours in Princess Eoyal Crescent had been very heavy.

But how could she contrive that it should be so ? That conversation with her mother had taken place on the day preceding the party, and Lady De Courcy had repeated it with dismay to Margaretta.

" Of course he would allow her an income," Margaretta had coolly said.

" But, my dear, they have been married only ten weeks."

"I don't see why anybody is to be made absolutely wretched because they are married," Margaretta answered. " I don't want to persuade her to leave him, but if what she says is true, it must be very uncomfortable."

Crosbie had consented to go to the party in Portman-square, but had not greatly enjoyed himself on that festive occasion. He had stood about moodily, speaking hardly a word to any one. His whole aspect of life seemed to have been altered during the last few months. It was here, in such spots as this that he had been used to find his glory. On such occasions he had shone with peculiar light, making envious the hearts of many who watched the brilliance of his career as they stood around in dull quiescence. But now no one in those rooms had been more dull, more silent, or less courted than he ; and yet he was established there as the son-in-law of that noble house. " Rather slow work; isn't it ? " Gazebee had said to him, having, after many efforts, succeeded in reaching his brother-in-law in a corner. In answer to this Crosbie had only grunted. " As for myself," continued Gazebee, "I would a deal sooner be at home with my paper and slippers. It seems to me these sort of gatherings don't suit married men." Crosbie had again grunted, and had then escaped into another corner.

Crosbie and his wife went home together in a cab,—speechless both of them. Alexandrina hated cabs,—but she had been plainly told that in such vehicles, and in such vehicles only, could she be allowed to travel. On the following morning he was at the breakfast-table punctually by nine, but she did not make her appearance till after he had gone to his office. Soon after that, however, she was away to her mother and her sister; but she was seated grimly in her drawing-room when he came in to see her, on his return to his house. Having said some word which might be taken for a greeting, he was about to retire ; but she stopped him with a request that he would speak to her.

" Certainly," said he. " I was only going to dress. It is nearly the half-hour."

" I won't keep you very long, and if dinner is a few minutes late it won't signify. Mamma and Margaretta are going to Baden-Baden."

" To Baden-Baden, are they ? "

"Yes; and they intend to remain there—for a considerable time." There was a little pause, and Alexandrina found it necessary to clear her voice and to prepare herself for further speech by a little cough. She was determined to make her proposition, but was rather afraid of the manner in which it might be first received.

" Has anything happened at Courcy Castle ? " Crosbie asked.

" No; that is, yes; there may have been some words between papa and mamma; but I don't quite know. That, however, does not matter now. Mamma is going, and purposes to remain there for the rest of the year."

" And the house in town will be given up."

" I suppose so, but that will be as papa chooses. Have you any objection to my going with mamma ? "

What a question to be asked by a bride of ten weeks' standing !

She had hardly been a month with her husband in her new house, and she was now asking permission to leave it, and to leave him also, for an indefinite number of months,—perhaps for ever. But she showed no excitement as she made her request. There was neither sorrow, nor regret, nor hope in her face. She had not put on half the animation which she had once assumed in asking for the use, twice a week, of a carriage done up to look as though it were her own private possession. Crosbie had then answered her with great sternness, and she had wept when his refusal was made certain to her. But there was to be no weeping now. She meant to go,—with his permission if he would accord it, and without if he should refuse it. The question of money was no doubt important, but Gazebee should manage that,—as he managed all those things.

" Going with them to Baden-Baden ? " said Crosbie. " For how long ?"

" Well; it would be no use unless it were for some time." " For how long a time do you mean, Alexandrina ? Speak out what you really have to say. For a month ? " "Oh, more than that."

" For two months, or six, or as long as they may stay there ? " " We could settle that afterwards, when I am there." During all this time she did not once look into his face, though he was looking hard at her throughout.

" You mean," said he, " that you wish to go away from me." " In one sense it would be going away, certainly." " Bat in the ordinary sense ? is it not so ? When you talk of going to Baden-Baden for an unlimited number of months, have you any idea of coming back again ? " " Back to London, you mean ? "

" Back to me,—to my house,—to your duties as a wife ! Why cannot you say at once what it is you want ? You wish to be separated from me ? "

" I am not happy here,—in this house."

" And who chose the house ? Did I want to come here ? But it is not that. If you are not happy here, what could you have in any other house to make you happy ? "

" If you were left alone in this room for seven or eight hours at a time, without a soul to come to you, you would know what I mean. And even after that, it is not much better. You never speak to me when you are here."

" Is it my fault that nobody comes to you ? The fact is, Alexandrina, that you will not reconcile yourself to the manner of life which is suitable to my income. You are wretched because you cannot have yourself driven round the Park. I cannot find you a carriage, and will not attempt to do so. You may go to Baden-Baden, if you please;—that is, if your mother is willing to take you."

" Of course I must pay my own expenses," said Alexandrina. But to this he made no answer on the moment. As soon as he had given his permission he had risen from his seat and was going, and her last words only caught him in the doorway. After all, would not this be the cheapest arrangement that he could make ? As he went through his calculations he stood up with his elbow on the mantelpiece in his dressing-room. He had scolded his wife because she had been unhappy with him ; but had he not been quite as unhappy with her ? Would it not be better that they should part in this quiet, half-unnoticed way;—that they should part and never again come together ? He was lucky in this, that hitherto had come upon them no prospect of any little Crosbie to mar the advantages of such an arrangement. If he gave her four hundred a year, and allowed Gazebee two more towards the paying off encumbrances, he would still have six on which to enjoy himself in London. Of course he could not live as he had lived in those happy days before his marriage, nor, independently of the cost, would such a mode of life be within his reach. But he might go to his club for his dinners ; he might smoke his cigar in luxury; he would not be bound to that wooden home which, in spite of all his resolutions, had become almost unendurable to him. So he made his calculations, and found that it would be well that his bride should go. He would give over his house and his furniture to Gazebee, allowing Gazebee to do as he would about that. To be once more a bachelor, in lodgings, with six hundred a year to spend on himself, seemed to him now such a prospect of happiness that he almost became light-hearted as he dressed himself. He would let her go to Baden-Baden.

There was nothing said about it at dinner, nor did he mention the subject again till the servant had left the tea-things on the drawing-room table. " You can go with your mother if you like it," he then said.

" I think it will be b2st," she answered.

" Perhaps it will. At any rate you shall suit yourself."

" And about money ? "

" You had better leave me to speak to Gazebee about that."

" Very well. Will you have some tea ? " And then the whole thing was finished.

On the next day she went after lunch to her mother's house, and never came back again to Princess Eoyal Crescent. During that morning she packed up those things which she cared to pack herself, and sent her sisters there, with an old family servant, to bring away whatever else might be supposed to belong to her. " Deai% dear," said Amelia, " what trouble I had in getting these things together for them, and only the other day. I can't but think she's wrong to go away."

"I don't know," said Margaretta. " She has not been so lucky as you have in the man she has married. I always felt that she would find it difficult to manage him."

" But, my dear, she has not tried. She has given up at once. It isn't management that was wanting. The fact is that when Alexandrina began she didn't make up her mind to the kind of thing she was coming to. I did. I knew it wasn't to be all party-going and that sort of thing. But I must own that Crosbie isn't the same sort of man as Mortimer. I don't think I could have gone on with him. You might as well have those small books put up ; he won't <;are about them." And in this way Crosbie's house was dismantled.

She saw him no more, for he made no farewell visit to the house in Portman Square. A note had been brought to him at his office: "I am here with mamma, and may as well say good-by now. We start on Tuesday. If you wish to write, you can send your letters to the housekeeper here. I hope you will make yourself comfortable, and that you will be well. Yours affectionately, A. C." He made no answer to it, but went that day and dined at his club.

" I haven't seen you this age," said Montgomerie Dobbs.

" No. My wife is going abroad with her mother, and while she is away I shall come back here again."

There was nothing more said to him, and no one ever made any inquiry about his domestic affairs. It seemed to him now as though he had no friend sufficiently intimate with him to ask him after his wife or family. She was gone, and in a month's time he found himself again in Mount Street,—beginning the world with five hundred a year, not six. For Mr. Gazebee, when the reckoning

came, showed him that a larger income, at the present moment was not possible for him. The countess had for a long time refused to let Lady Alexandrina go with her on so small a pittance as four hundred and fifty;—and then were there not the insurances to he maintained ?

But I think he would have consented to accept his liberty with three hundred a year,—so great to him was the relief.

CHAPTER XXVII. LILIAN DALE VANQUISHES HER MOTHER.

MBS. DALE had been present during the interview in which John Eames had made his prayer to her daughter, hut she had said little or nothing on that occasion. All her wishes had been in favour of the suitor, but she had not dared to express them, neither had she dared to leave the room. It had been hard upon him to be thus forced to declare his love in the presence of a third person, but he had done it, and had gone away with his answer. Then, when the thing was over,

Lily, without any communion with her mother, took herself off, and was no more seen till the evening hours had come on, in which it was natural that they should be together again. Mrs. Dale, when thus alone, had been able to think of nothing but this new suit for her daughter's hand. If only it might be accomplished ! If any words from her to Lily might be efficacious to such an end! And yet, hitherto, she had been afraid almost to utter a word.

She knew that it was very difficult. She declared to herself over and over that he had come too soon,—that the attempt had been made too quickly after that other shipwreck. How was it possible that the ship should put to sea again at once, with all her timbers so rudely strained ? And yet, now that the attempt had been made, now that Eames had uttered his request and been sent away with an answer, she felt that she must at once speak to Lily on the subject, if ever she were to speak upon it. She thought that she understood her child and all her feelings. She recognized the violence of the shock which must be encountered before Lily could be brought to acknowledge such a change in her heart. • But if the thing could be done, Lily would be a happy woman. When once done it would be in all respects a blessing. And if it were not done, might not Lily's life be blank, lonely, and loveless to the end ? Yet when Lily came down in the evening, with some light, half-joking word on her lips, as was usual to her, Mrs. Dale was still afraid to venture upon her task.

"I suppose, mamma, we may consider it as a settled thing that everything must be again unpacked, and that the lodging scheme "will be given up."

" I don't know that, my dear."

"Oh, but I do—after what you said just now. What geese everybody will think us ! "

"I shouldn't care a bit for that, if we didn't think ourselves geese, or if your uncle did not think us so."

" I believe he would think we were swans. If I had ever thought he would be so much in earnest about it, or that he would ever have cared about our being here, I would never have voted for going. But he is so strange. He is affectionate when he ought to be angry, and ill-natured when he ought to be gentle and kind."

"He has, at any rate, given us reason to feel sure of his affection."

" For us girls I never doubted it. But, mamma, I don't think I could face Mrs. Boyce. Mrs. Hearn and Mrs. Crump would be very bad, and Hopkins would come down upon us terribly when he found that we had given way. But Mrs. Boyce would be worse than any of them. Can't you fancy the tone of her congratulations ? "

"I think I should survive Mrs. Boyce."

" Ah, yes ; because we should have to go and tell her. I know your cowardice of old, mamma ; don't I ? And Bell wouldn't care a bit, because of her lover. Mrs. Boyce will be nothing to her. It is I that must bear it all. Well, I don't mind; I'll vote for staying if you will promise to be happy here. Oh, mamma, I'll vote for anything if you will be happy."

" And will you be happy ? "

" Yes, as happy as the day is long. Only I know we shall never see Bell. People never do see each other when they live just at that distance. It's too near for long visits, and too far for short visits. I'll tell you what; we might make arrangements each to walk halfway, and meet at the corner of Lord De Guest's wood. I wonder whether they'd let us put up a seat there. I think we might have a little house and carry sandwiches and a bottle of beer. Couldn't we see something of each other in that way? "

Thus it came to be the fixed idea of both of them that they would abandon their plan of migrating to Guestwick, and on this subject they continued to talk over their tea-table; but on that evening Mrs. Dale ventured to say nothing about John Eames.

But they did not even yet dare to commence the work of reconstructing their old home. Bell must come back before they would do that, and the express assent of the squire must be formally obtained. Mrs. Dale must, in a degree, acknowledge herself to have been wrong, and ask to be forgiven for her contumacy.

" I suppose the three of us had better go up in sackcloth, and throw ashes on our foreheads as we meet Hopkins in the garden," said Lily, "and then I know he'll heap coals of fire on our heads by sending us an early dish of peas. And Dingles would bring us in a pheasant, only that pheasants don't grow in May."

"If the sackcloth doesn't take an unpleasanter shape than that, I shan't mind it."

"That's because you've got no delicate feelings. And then uncle Christopher's gratitude ! "

" Ah ! I shall feel that."

" But, mamma, we'll wait till Bell comes home. She shall decide. She is going away, and therefore she'll be free from prejudice. If uncle offers to paint the house,—and I know he will,—then I shall be humbled to the dust."

But yet Mrs. Dale had said nothing on the subject which was nearest to her heart. When Jjily in pleasantry had accused her of cowardice, her mind had instantly gone off to that other matter, and she had told herself that she was a coward. Why should she be afraid of offering her counsel to her own child ? It seemed toner as though she had neglected some duty in allowing Crosbie's conduct to have passed away without hardly a word of comment on it between herself and Lily. Should she not have forced upon her daughter's conviction the fact that Crosbie had been a villain, and as such should be discarded from her heart ? As it was, Lily had spoken the simple truth when she told John Eames that she was dealing more openly with him on that affair of her engagement than she had ever dealt, even with her mother. Thinking of this as she sat in her own room that night, before she allowed herself to rest, Mrs. Dale resolved that on the next morning she would endeavour to make Lily see as she saw and think as she thought.

She let breakfast pass by before she began her task, and even then she did not rush at it at once. Lily sat herself down to her work when the teacups were taken away, and Mrs. Dale went down to her kitchen as was her wont. It was nearly eleven before she seated herself in the parlour, and even then she got her work-box before her and took out her needle.

" I wonder how Bell gets on with Lady Julia," said Lily.

" Very well, I'm sure."

" Lady Julia won't bite her, I know, and I suppose her dismay at the tall footmen has passed off by this time."

" I don't know that they have any tall footmen."

" Short footmen then,—you know what I mean ; all the noble belongings. They must startle one at first, I'm sure, let one determine ever so much not to be startled. It's a very mean thing, no doubt, to be afraid of a lord merely because he is a lord; yet I'm sure I should be afraid at first, even of Lord De Guest, if I were staying in the house."

" It's well you didn't go then."

" Yes, I think it is. Bell is of a firmer mind, and I dare say she'll get over it after the first day. But what on earth does she do there ? I wonder whether they mend their stockings in such a house as that."

" Not in public, I should think."

" In very grand houses they throw them away at once, I suppose. I've often thought about it. Do you believe the Prime Minister ever has his shoes sent to a cobbler ? "

" Perhaps a regular shoemaker will condescend to mend a Prime Minister's shoes."

"You do think they are mended then? But who orders it? Does he see himself when there's a little hole coming, as I do? Does an archbishop allow himself so many pairs of gloves in a year?"

"Not very strictly, I should think."

"Then I suppose it comes to this, that he has a new pair whenever he wants them. But what constitutes the want? Does he ever say to himself that they'll do for another Sunday? I remember the bishop coming here once, and he had a hole at the end of his thumb. I was going to be confirmed, and I remember thinking that he ought to have been smarter."

"Why didn't you offer to mend it?"

"I shouldn't have dared for all the world."

The conversation had commenced itself in a manner that did not promise much assistance to Mrs. Dale's project. When Lily got upon any subject, she was not easily induced to leave it, and when her mind had twisted itself in one direction, it was difficult to untwist it. She was now bent on a consideration of the smaller social habits of the high and mighty among us, and was asking her mother whether she supposed that the royal children ever carried halfpence in their pockets, or descended so low as fourpenny-bits.

"I suppose they have pockets like other children," said Lily.

But her mother stopped her suddenly,—

"Lily, dear, I want to say something to you about John Eames."

"Mamma, I'd sooner talk about the Eoyal Family just at present."

"But, dear, you must forgive me if I persist. I have thought much about it, and I'm sure you will not oppose me when I am doing what I think to be my duty."

"No, mamma; I won't oppose you, certainly."

"Since Mr. Crosbie's conduct was made known to you, I have mentioned his name in your hearing very seldom."

"No, mamma, you have not. And I have loved you so dearly for your goodness to me. Do not think that I have not understood and known how generous you have been. No other mother ever was so good as you have been. I have known it all, and thought of it every day of my life, and thanked you in my heart for your trusting silence. Of course, I understand your feelings. You think him bad and you hate him for what he has done."

"I would not willingly hate any one, Lily."

"Ah, but you do hate him. If I were you, I should hate him; but I am not you, and I love him. I pray for his happiness every night and morning, and for hers. I have forgiven him altogether, and I think that he was right. When I am old enough to do so without being wrong, I will go to him and tell him so. I should like to hear of all his doings and all his success, if it were only possible. How, then, can you and I talk about him? It is impossible. You have been silent and I have been silent,—let us remain silent."

"It is not about Mr. Crosbie that I wish to speak. But I think you ought to understand that conduct such as his will be rebuked by all the world. You may forgive him, but you should acknowledge"

"Mamma, I don't want to acknowledge anything;—not about him. There are things as to which a person cannot argue." Mrs. Dale felt that this present matter was one as to which she could not argue. "Of course, mamma," continued Lily, "I don't want to oppose you in anything, but I think we had better be silent about this."

"Of course I am thinking only of your future happiness."

"I know you are; but pray believe me that you need not be alarmed. I do not mean to be unhappy. Indeed, I think I may say I am not unhappy; of course I have been unhappy,—very unhappy. I did think that my heart would break. But that has passed away, and I believe I can be as happy as my neighbours. We're all of us sure to have some troubles, as you used to tell us when we were children."

Mrs. Dale felt that she had begun wrong, and that she would have been able to make better progress had she omitted all mention of Crosbie's name. She knew exactly what it was that she wished to say,—what were the arguments which she desired to expound before her daughter; but she did not know what language to use, or how she might best put her thoughts into words. She paused for a while, and Lily went on with her work as though the conversation was over. But the conversation was not over.

" It was about John Eames, and not about Mr. Crosbie, that I wished to speak to you."

" Oh, mamma !"

" My dear, you must not hinder me in doing what I think to be a duty. I heard what he said to you and what you replied, and of course I cannot but have my mind full of the subject. Why should you set yourself against him in so fixed a manner ? "

" Because I love another man." These words she spoke out loud, in a steady, almost dogged tone, with a certain show of audacity,— as though aware that the declaration was unseemly, but resolved that, though unseemly, it must be made.

" But, Lily, that love, from its very nature, must cease; or, rather, such love is not the same as that you felt when you thought that you were to be his wife."

" Yes, it is. If she died, and he came to me in five years' time, I would still take him. I should think myself constrained to take him."

" But she is not dead, nor likely to die."

" That makes no difference. You don't understand me, mamma."

" I think I do, and I want you to understand me also. I know, how difficult is your position ; I know what your feelings are; but I know this also, that if you could reason with yourself, and bring yourself in time to receive John Eames as a dear friend "

"I did receive him as a dear friend. Why not ? He is a dear friend. I love him heartily,— as you do."

" You know what I mean ? "

" Yes, I do; and I tell you it is impossible."

" If you would make the attempt, all this misery would soon be forgotten. If once you could bring yourself to regard him as a friend, who might become your husband, all this would be changed,—and I should see you happy !"

" You are strangely anxious to be rid of me, mamma !"

" Yes, Lily;—to be rid of you in that way. If I could see you put your hand in his as his promised wife, I think that I should be the happiest woman in the world."

" Mamma, I cannot make you happy in that way. If you really understood my feelings, my doing as you propose would make you very unhappy. I should commit a great sin,—the sin against which women should be more guarded than against any other. In my heart I am married to that other man. I gave myself to him, and loved him, and rejoiced in his love. When he kissed me I kissed him again, and I longed for his kisses. I seemed to live only that he might caress me. All that time I never felt myself to be wrong,— because he was all in all to me. I was his own. That has been changed,—to my great misfortune; but it cannot be undone or forgotten. I cannot be the girl I was before he came here. There are things that will not have themselves buried and put out of sight, as though they had never been. I am as you are, mamma,—widowed. But you have your daughter, and I have my mother. If you will be contented, so will I." Then she got up and threw herself on her mother's neck.

Mrs. Dale's argument was over now. To such an appeal as that last made by Lily no rejoinder on her part was possible. After that she was driven to acknowledge to herself that she must be silent. Years as they rolled on might make a change, but no reasoning could be of avail. She embraced her daughter, weeping over her,— whereas Lily's eyes were dry. " It shall be as you will," Mrs. Dale murmured.

" Yes, as I will. I shall have my own way; shall I not ? That is all I want; to be a tyrant over you, and make you do my bidding in everything, as a well-behaved mother should do. But I won't be stern in my orderings. If you will only be obedient, I will be so gracious to you! There's Hopkins again. I wonder whether he has come to knock us down and trample upon us with another speech."

Hopkins knew very well to which window he must come, as only one of the rooms was at the present time habitable. He came up to the dining-room, and almost flattened his nose against the glass.

" Well, Hopkins," said Lily, " here we are." Mrs. Dale had turned her face away, for she knew that the tears were still on her cheek.

" Yes, miss, I see you. I want to speak to your mamma, miss."

" Come round," said Lily, anxious to spare her mother the necessity of showing herself at once. " It's too cold to open the window; come round, and I'll open the door."

" Too cold!" muttered Hopkins, as he went. " They'll find it a deal colder in lodgings at Guestwick." However, he went round through the kitchen, and Lily met him in the hall.

" Well, Hopkins, what is it? Mamma has got a headache."

" Got a headache, has she ? I won't make her headache no worse. It's my opinion that there's nothing for a headache so good as fresh air. Only some people can't abear to be blowed upon, not for a minute. If you don't let down the lights in a greenhouse more or less every day, you'll never get any plants,—never;—and it's just the same with the grapes. Is I to go back and say as how I couldn't see her?"

" You can come in if you like; only be quiet, you know."

"Ain't I ollays quiet, miss ? Did anybody ever hear me rampage ? If you please, ma'am, the squire's come home."

" What, home from Guestwick ? Has he brought Miss Bell ? "

"He ain't brought none but hisself, 'cause he come on horseback ; and it's my belief he's going back almost immediate. But he wants you to come to him, Mrs. Dale."

" Oh, yes, I'll come at once."

" He bade me say with his kind love. I don't know whether that makes any difference."

" At any rate, I'll come, Hopkins."

" And I ain't to say nothing about the headache ?"

" About what ?" said Mrs. Dale.

" No, no, no," said Lily. " Mamma will be there at once. Go and tell my uncle, there's a good man," and she put up her hand and backed him out of the room.

" I don't believe she's got no headache at all," said Hopkins, grumbling, as he returned through the back premises. " What lies gentlefolks do tell! If I said I'd a headache when I ought to be out among the things, what would they say to me ? But a poor man mustn't never lie, nor yet drink, nor yet do nothing." And so lie went back with his message.

" What can have brought your uncle home ? " said Mrs. Dale.

" Just to look after the cattle, and to see that the pigs are not all dead. My wonder is that he should ever have gone away."

" I must go up to him at once."

" Oh, yes, of course."

" And what shall I say about the house ?"

" It's not about that,—at least I think not. I don't think he'll speak about that again till you speak to him."

"But if he does?"

" You must put your trust in Providence. Declare you've got a bad headache, as I told Hopkins just now ; only you would throw me over by not understanding. I'll walk with you down to the bridge." So they went off together across the lawn.

But Lily was soon left alone, and continued her walk, waiting for her mother's return. As she went round and round the gravel paths, she thought of the words that she had said to her mother. She had declared that she also was widowed. "And so it should be," she said, debating the matter with herself. " What can a heart be worth if it can be transferred hither and thither as circumstances and convenience and comfort may require ? When he held me here in his arms"—and,.as the thoughts ran through her brain, she remembered the very spot on which they had stood—" oh, my love!" she had said to him then as she returned his kisses—" oh, my love, my love, my love!" " When he held me here in his arms, I told myself that it was right, because he was my husband. He has changed, but I have not. It might be that I should have ceased to love him, and then I should have told him so. I should have done as he did." But, as she came to this, she shuddered, thinking of the Lady Alexaudrina. " It was very quick," she said, still speaking to herself; "very, very. But then men are not the same as women." And she walked on eagerly, hardly remembering where she was, thinking over it all, as she did daily; remembering every little thought and word of those few eventful months in which she had learned to regard Crosbie as her husband and master. She had declared that she had conquered her unhappiness; but there were moments in which she was almost wild with misery. " Tell me to forget him!" she said. "It is the one thing which will never be forgotten."

At last she heard her mother's step coming down across the squire's garden, and she took up her post at the bridge.

" Stand and deliver," she said, as her mother put her foot upon the plank. " That is, if you've got anything worth delivering. Is anything settled?"

" Come up to the house," said Mrs. Dale, " and I'll tell you all."

CHAPTER XXVIII. THE FATE OF THE SMALL HOUSE.

THERE was something in the tone of Mrs. Dale's voice, as she desired her daughter to come up to the house, and declared that her budget of news should be opened there, which at once silenced Lily's assumed pleasantry. Her mother had been away fully two hours, during which Lily had still continued her walk round the garden, till at last she had become impatient for her mother's footstep. Something serious must have been said between her uncle and her mother during those long two hours. The interviews to which Mrs. Dale was occasionally summoned at the Great House did not usually exceed twenty minutes, and the upshot would be communicated to the girls in a turn or two round the garden; but in the present instance Mrs. Dale positively declined to speak till she was seated within the house.

" Did he come over on purpose to see you, mamma ?"

" Yes, my dear, I believe so. He wished to see you, too; but I asked his permission to postpone that till after I had talked to you."

" To see me, mamma ? About what ? "

" To kiss you, and bid you love him; solely for that. He has not a word to say to you that will vex you."

" Then I will kiss him, and love him, too."

" Yes, you will when I have told you all. I have promised him solemnly to give up all idea of going to Guestwick. So that is over."

" Oh, oh ! And we may begin to unpack at once ? What an episode in one's life!"

" We may certainly unpack, for I have pledged myself to him; and he is to go into Guestwick himself and arrange about the

" Does Hopkins know it ? "

" I should think not yet."

" Nor Mrs. Boyce ! Mamma, I don't believe I shall be able to survive this next week. We shall look such fools ! I'll tell you what we'll do;—it will be the only comfort I can have;—we'll go to work and get everything back into its place before Bell comes home, so as to surprise her."

"What! in two days?"

" Why not ? I'll make Hopkins come and help, and then he'll not be so bad. I'll begin at once and go to the blankets and beds, because I can undo them myself."

" But I haven't half told you all; and, indeed, I don't know how to make you understand what passed between us. He is very unhappy about Bernard; Bernard has determined to go abroad, and may be away for years."

" One can hardly blame a man for following up his profession."

" There was no blaming. He only said that it was very sad for him that, in his old age, he should be left alone. This was before there was any talk about our remaining. Indeed he seemed determined not to ask that again as a favour. I could see that in his eye, and I understood it from his tone. He went on to speak of you and Bell, saying how well he loved you both; but that, unfortunately, his hopes regarding you had not been fulfilled."

" Ah, but he shouldn't have had hopes of that sort."

" Listen, my dear, and I think that you will not feel angry with him. He said that he felt his house had never been pleasant to you. Then there followed words which I could not repeat, even if I could remember them. He said much about myself, regretting that the feeling between us had not been more kindly. ' But my heart,' he said, * has ever been kinder than my words.' Then I got up from where I was seated, and going over to him, I told him that we would remain here."

" And what did he say ? "

" I don't know what he said. I know that I was crying, and that he kissed me. It was the first time in his life. I know that he was pleased,—beyond measure pleased. After a while he became animated, and talked of doing ever so many things. He promised that very painting of which you spoke."

" Ah, yes, I knew it; and Hopkins will be here-with the peas before dinner-time to-morrow, and Dingles with his shoulders smothered with rabbits. And then Mrs. Boyce ! Mamma, he didn't

think of Mrs. Boyce; or, in very charity of heart, he would still have maintained his sadness."

" Then he did not think of her; for when I left him he was not at all sad. But I haven't told you half yet."

" Dear me, mamma; was there more than that ? "

" And I've told it all wrong; for what I've got to tell now was said before a word was spoken about the house. He brought it in just after what he said about Bernard. He said that Bernard would, of course, be his heir."

" Of course he will."

" And that he should think it wrong to encumber the property with any charges for you girls."

" Mamma, did any one ever "

" Stop, Lily, stop; and make your heart kinder towards him if you can."

" It is kind; only I hate to be told that I'm not to have a lot of money, as though I had ever shown a desire for it. I have never envied Bernard his man-servant, or his maid-servant, or his ox, or his ass, or anything that is his. To tell the truth I didn't even wish it to be Bell's, because I knew well that there was somebody she would like a great deal better than ever she could like Bernard."

" I shall never get to the end of my story."

" Yes, you will, mamma, if you persevere."

" The long and the short of it is this, that he has given Bell three thousand pounds, and has given you three thousand also."

" But why me, mamma ? " said Lily, and the colour of her cheeks became red as she spoke. There should if possible be nothing more said about John Eames; but whatever might or might not be the necessity of speaking, at any rate, let there be no mistake. " But why me, mamma ? "

" Because, as he explained to me, he thinks it right to do the same by each of you. The money is yours at this moment,—to buy hair-pins with, if you please. I had no idea that he could command so large a sum."

"Three thousand pounds! The last money he gave me was half-a-crown, and I thought that he was so stingy! I particularly wanted ten shillings. I should have liked it so much better now if he had given me a nice new five-pound note."

" You'd better tell him so."

" No; because then he'd give me that too. But with five pounds I should have the feeling that I might do what I liked with it;— buy a dressing-case, and a thing for a squirrel to run round in. But nobody ever gives girls money like that, so that they can enjoy it."

" Oh, Lily; you ungrateful child ! "

" No, I deny it. I'm not ungrateful. I'm very grateful, because his heart was softened—and because he cried and kissed you. I'll be aver so good to him ! But how I'm to thank him for giving me three thousand pounds, I cannot think. It's a sort of thing altogether beyond my line of life. It sounds like something that's to come to me in another world, but which I don't want quite yet. I am grateful, but with a misty, mazy sort of gratitude. Can you tell me how soon I shall have a new pair of Balmoral boots because of this money ? If that were brought home to me I think it would enliven my gratitude."

The squire, as he rode back to Guestwick, fell again from that animation, which Mrs. Dale had described, into his natural sombre mood. He thought much of his past life, declaring to himself the truth of those words in which he had told his sister-in-law that his heart had ever been kinder than his words. But the world, and all those nearest to him in the world, had judged him always by his words rather than by his heart. They had taken the appearance, which he could not command or alter, rather than the facts, of which he had been the master. Had he not been good to all his relations ?—and yet was there one among them that cared for him ? " I'm almost sorry that they are going to stay," he said to himself;—" I know that I shall disappoint them." Yet when he met Bell at the Manor House he accosted her cheerily, telling her with much appearance of satisfaction that that flitting into Guestwick was not to be accomplished.

" I am so glad," said she. " It is long since I wished it."

" And I do not think your mother wishes it now."

" I am sure she does not. It was all a misunderstanding from the first. When some of us could not do all that you wished, we thought it better " Then Bell paused, finding that she would get herself into a mess if she persevered.

"We will not say anymore about it," said the squire. "The thing is over, and I am very glad that it should be so pleasantly settled. I was talking to Dr. Crofts yesterday."

" Were you, uncle ? "

" Yes; and he is to come and stay with me the day before he is married. We have arranged it all. And we'll have the breakfast up at the Great House. Only you must fix the day. I should say some time in March. And, my dear, you'll want to make yourself fine ; here's a little money for you. You are to spend that before your marriage, you know." Then he shambled away, and as soon as he was alone, again became sad and despondent. He was a man for whom we may predicate some gentle sadness and continued despondency to the end of his life's chapter.

We left John Eames in the custody of Lady Julia, who had overtaken him in the act of erasing Lily's name from the railing which ran across the brook. He had been premeditating an escape home to his mother's house in Guestwick, and thence back to London, without making any further appearance at the Manor House. But as soon as he heard Lady Julia's step, and saw her figure close upon him, he knew that his retreat was cut off from him. So he allowed himself to be led away quietly up to the house. With Lady Julia herself he openly discussed the whole matter,—telling her that his hopes were over, his happiness gone, and his heart half-broken. Though he would perhaps have cared but little for her congratulations in success, he could make himself more amenable to consolation and sympathy from her than from any other inmate in the earl's house. " I don't know what I shall say to your brother," he whispered to her, as they approached the side door at which she intended to enter.

" Will you let me break it to him ? After that he will say a few words to you of course, but you need not be afraid of him."

" And Mr. Dale ?" said Johnny. " Everybody has heard about it. Everybody will know what a fool I have made myself." She suggested that the earl should speak to the squire, assured him that nobody would think him at all foolish, and then left him to make his way up to his own bedroom. When there he found a letter from Cradell, which had been delivered in his absence; but the contents of that letter may best be deferred to the next chapter. They were not of a nature to give him comfort or to add to his sorrow.

About an hour before dinner there was a knock at his door, and the earl himself, when summoned, made his appearance in the room. He was dressed in his usual farming attire, having been caught by Lady Julia on his first approach to the house, and had come away direct to his young friend, after having been duly trained in what he ought to say by his kind-hearted sister. I am not, however, prepared to declare that lie strictly followed his sister's teaching in all that he said upon the occasion.

"Well, my boy," he began, "so the young lady has been perverse."

"Yes, my lord. That is, I don't know about being perverse. It is all over."

"That's as may be, Johnny. As far as I know, not half of them accept their lovers the first time of asking."

"I shall not ask her again."

"Oh, yes, you will. You don't mean to say you are angry with her for refusing you."

"Not in the least. I have no right to be angry. I am only angry with myself for being such a fool, Lord De Guest. I wish I had been dead before I came down here on this errand. Now I think of it, I know there are so many things which ought to have made me sure how it would be."

"I don't see that at all. You come down again,—let me see,— it's May now. Say you come when the shooting begins in September. If we can't get you leave of absence in any other way, we'll make old Buffle come too. Only, by George, I believe he'd shoot us all. But never mind; we'll manage that. You keep up your spirits till September, and then we'll fight the battle another way. The squire shall get up a little party for the bride, and my lady Lily must go then. You shall meet her so ; and then we'll shoot over the squire's land. We'll bring you together so ; you see if we don't. Lord bless me ! Refused once ! My belief is, that in these days a girl thinks nothing of a man till she has refused him half-a-dozen times."

"I don't think Lily is at all like that."

"Look here, Johnny. I have not a word to say against Miss Lily. I like her very much, and think her one of the nicest girls I know. When she's your wife, I'll love her dearly, if she'll let me. But she's made of the same stuff as other girls, and will act in the same way. Things have gone a little astray among you, and they won't right themselves all in a minute. She knows now what your feelings are, and she'll go on thinking of it, till at last you'll be in her thoughts more than that other fellow. Don't tell me about her becoming an old maid, because at her time of life she has been so unfortunate as to come across a false-hearted man like that. It may take a little time; but if you'll carry on and not be down-hearted, you'll find it will all come right in the end. Everybody doesn't get

all that they want in a minute. How I shall quiz you about all this when you have been two or three years married ! "

"I don't think I shall ever be able to ask her again ; and I feel sure, if I do, that her answer will be the same. She told me in so many words- ; but never mind, I cannot repeat her words."

"I don't want you to repeat them ; nor yet to heed them beyond their worth. Lily Dale is a very pretty girl; clever, too, I believe, and good, I'm sure; but her words are not more sacred than those of other men or women. What she has said to you now, she means, no doubt; but the minds of men and women are prone to change, especially when such changes are conducive to their own happiness."

"At any rate I'll never forget your kindness, Lord De Guest."

"And there is one other thing I want to say to you, Johnny. A man should never allow himself to be cast down by anything,—not outwardly, to the eyes of other men."

"But how is he to help it ?"

"His pluck should prevent him. You were not afraid of a roaring bull, nor yet of that man when you thrashed him at the railway station. You've pluck enough of that kind. You must now show that you've that other kind of pluck. You know the story of the boy who would not cry though the wolf was gnawing him underneath his frock. Most of us have some wolf to gnaw us somewhere; but we are generally gnawed beneath our clothes, so that the world doesn't see ; and it behoves us so to bear it that the world shall not suspect. The man who goes about declaring himself to be miserable will be not only miserable, but contemptible as well."

" But the wolf hasn't gnawed me beneath my clothes; everybody knows it."

" Then let those who do know it learn that you are able to bear such wounds without outward complaint. I tell you fairly that I cannot sympathize with a lackadaisical lover."

" I know that I have made myself ridiculous to everybody. I wish I had never come here. I wish you had never seen me."

" Don't say that, my dear boy ; but take my advice for what it is worth. And remember what it is that I say; with your grief I do sympathize, but not with any outward expression of it;— not with melancholy looks, and a sad voice, and an unhappy gait. A man should always be able to drink his wine and seem to enjoy it. If he can't, he is so much less of a man than he would be otherwise,—not so much more, as some people seem to think. Now get yourself dressed, my dear fellow, and conte down to dinner as though nothing had happened to you."

As soon as the earl was gone John looked at his watch and saw that it still wanted some forty minutes to dinner. Fifteen minutes would suffice for him to dress, and therefore there was time sufficient for him to seat himself in his arm-chair and think over it all. He had for a moment been very angry when his friend had told him that he could not sympathize with a lackadaisical lover. It was an ill-natured word. He felt it to be so when he heard it, and so he continued to think during the whole of the half-hour that he sat in that chair. But it probably did him more good than any word that the earl had ever spoken to him,—or any other word that he could have used. " Lackadaisical! I'm not lackadaisical," he said to himself, jumping up from his chair, and instantly sitting down again. " I didn't say anything to him. I didn't tell him. Why did he come to me?" And yet, though he endeavoured to abuse Lord De Guest in his thoughts, he knew that Lord De Guest was right, and that he was wrong. He knew that he had been lackadaisical, and was ashamed of himself; and at once resolved that he would henceforth demean himself as though no calamity had happened to him. " I've a good mind to take him at his word, and drink wine till I'm drunk." Then he strove to get up his courage by a song.

If she be not fair for me, What care I how

" But I do care. What stuff it is a man writing poetry and putting into it such lies as that! Everybody knows that he did care, —that is, if he wasn't a heartless beast."

But nevertheless, when the time came for him to go down into the drawing-room he did make the effort which his friend had counselled, and walked into the room with less of that hang-dog look than the earl and Lady Julia had expected. They were both there, as was also the squire, and Bell followed him in less than a minute.

"You haven't seen Crofts to-day, John, have you?" said the earl.

'* No ; I haven't been anywhere his way !"

" His way! His ways are every way, I take it. I wanted him to come and dine, but he seemed to think it improper to eat two dinners in the same house two days running. Isn't that his theory, Miss Dale ?"

" I'm sureldon't know, Lord De Guest. At any rate, it isn't mine."

So they went to their feast, and before his last chance was over John Eames found himself able to go through the pretence of enjoying his roast mutton. *

There can, I think, be no doubt that in all such calamities as that which he was now suffering, the agony of the misfortune is much increased by the conviction that the facts of the case are known to those round about the sufferer. A most warm-hearted and intensely-feeling young gentleman might, no doubt, eat an excellent dinner after being refused by the girl of his devotions, provided that he had reason to believe that none of those in whose company he ate it knew anything of his rejection. But the same warm-hearted and intensely-feeling young gentleman would find it very difficult to go through the ceremony with any appearance of true appetite or gastronomic enjoyment, if he were aware that all his convives knew all the facts of his little misfortune. Generally, we may suppose, a man in such condition goes to his club for his dinner, or seeks consolation in the shades of some adjacent Richmond or Hampton Court. There he meditates on his condition in silence, and does ultimately enjoy his little plate of whitebait, his cutlet and his moderate pint of sherry. He probably goes alone to the theatre, and, in his stall, speculates with a somewhat bitter sarcasm on the vanity of the world. Then he returns home, sad indeed, but with a moderated sadness, and as he puffs out the smoke of his cigar at the open window,—with perhaps the comfort of a little brandy-and-water at his elbow,—swears to himself that, " By Jove, he'll have another try for it." Alone, a man may console himself, or among a crowd of unconscious mortals; but it must be admitted that the position of John Eames was severe. He had been invited down there to woo Lily Dale, and the squire and Bell had been asked to be present at the wooing. Had it all gone well, nothing could have been nicer. He would have been the hero of the hour, and everybody would have sung for him his song of triumph. But everything had not gone well, and he found it very difficult to carry himself otherwise than lackadaisically. On the whole, however, his effort was such that the earl gave him credit for his demeanour, and told him when parting with him for the night that he was a fine fellow, and that everything should go right with him yet.

" And you mustn't be angry with me for speaking harshly to you," he said.

" I wasn't a bit angry."

" Yes, you were; and I rather meant that you should be. But you mustn't go away in dudgeon."

He stayed at the Manor House one day longer, and then he returned to his room at the Income-tax Office, to the disagreeable sound of Sir Raffle's little bell, and the much more disagreeable sound of Sir Raffle's big voice.

CHAPTER XXIX. JOHN EAMES BECOMES A MAN.

EAMES, when he was half way up to London in the railway carriage took out from his pocket a letter and read it. During the former portion of his journey he had been thinking of other things; but gradually he had resolved that it would be better for him not to think more of those other things for the present, and therefore he had recourse to his letter by way of dissipating his thoughts. It was from Cradell, and ran as^ follows :—

Income-Tax Office, May,— 186-.

MY DEAR JOHN,—I hope the tidings which I have to give you will not make you angry, and that you will not think I am untrue to the great friendship which I have for you because of that which I am now going to tell you. There is no man —[and the word man was underscored]—there is no man whose regard I value so highly as I do yours ; and though I feel that you can have no just ground to be displeased with me after all that I have heard you say on many occasions, nevertheless, in matters of the heart it is very hard for one person to understand the sentiments of another, and when the affections of a lady are concerned, I know what quarrels will sometimes arise.

Eames, when he had got so far as this, on the first perusal of the letter, knew well what was to follow. " Poor Caudle !" he said to himself; " he's hooked, and he'll never get himself off the hook again."

But let that be as it may, the matter has now gone too far for any alteration to be made by me ; nor would any mere earthly inducement suffice to change me. The claims of friendship are very strong, but those of love are paramount. Of course I know all that has passed between you and Amelia Koper. Much of this I had heard from you before, but the rest she has now told me with that pure-minded honesty which is the most remarkable feature in| her character. She has confessed that at one time she felt attached to you, and that she was induced by your perseverance to allow you to regard her as your fiancy. [Fancy-girl he probably conceived to be the vulgar English for the elegant term which he used.] But all that must be over between you now. Amelia has promised

to be mine —[this also was underscored]—and mine I intend that she shall be. That you may find in the kind smiles of L. D. consolation for any disappointment which this may occasion you, is the ardent wish of your true friend,

JOSEPH CRADELL.

P.S—Perhaps I had better tell you the whole. Mrs. Eoper has been in some trouble about her house. She is a little in arrears with her rent, and some bills have not been paid. As she explained that she has been brought into this by those dreadful Lupexes I have consented to take the house into my own hands, and have given bills to one or two tradesmen for small amounts. Of course she will take them up, but it was the credit that was wanting. She will carry on the house, but I shall, in fact, be the proprietor. I suppose it will not suit you now to remain here, but don't you think I might make it comfortable enough for some of our fellows; say half-a-dozen, or so ? That is Mrs. Roper's idea, and I certainly think it is not a bad one. Our first efforts must be to get rid of the Lupexes. Miss Spruce goes next week. In the meantime we are all taking our meals up in our own rooms, so that there is nothing for the Lupexes to eat. But they don't seem to mind that, and still keep the sitting-room and best bedroom. We mean to lock them out after Tuesday, and send all their boxes to the public-house.

Poor Cradell! Eames, as he threw himself back upon his seat and contemplated the depth of misfortune into which his friend had fallen, began to be almost in love with his own position. He himself was, no doubt, a very miserable fellow. There was only one thing in life worth living for, and that he could not get. He had been thinking for the last three days of throwing himself before a locomotive steam-engine, and was not quite sure that he would not do it yet; but, nevertheless, his place was a place among the gods as compared to that which poor Cradell had selected for himself. To be not only the husband of Amelia Roper, but to have been driven to take upon himself as his bride's fortune the whole of his future mother-in-law's debts ! To find himself the owner of a very indifferent lodging-house;—the owner as regarded all responsibility, though not the owner as regarded any possible profit! And then, above and almost worse than all the rest, to find himself saddled with the Lupexes in the beginning of his career! Poor Cradell indeed!

Eames had not taken his things away from the lodging-house before he left London, and therefore determined to drive to Burton Crescent immediately on his arrival, not with the intention of remaining there, even for a night, but that he might bid them farewell, speak his congratulations to Amelia, and arrange for his final settlement with Mrs. Roper. It should have been explained in the

last chapter that the earl had told him before parting with him that his want of success with Lily would make no difference as regarded money. John had, of course, expostulated, saying that he did not want anything, and would not, under his existing circumstances, accept anything; but the earl was a man who knew how to have his own way, and in this matter did have it. Our friend, therefore, was a man of wealth when he returned to London, and could tell Mrs. Eoper that he would send her a cheque for her little balance as soon, as he reached his office.

He arrived in the middle of the day,—not timing his return at all after the usual manner of Government clerks, who generally manage to reach the metropolis not more than half an hour before the moment at which they are bound to show themselves in their seats. But he had come back two days before he was due, and had run away from the country as though London in May to him were much pleasanter than the woods and fields. But neither had London nor the woods and fields any influence on his return. He had gone down that he might throw himself at the feet of Lily Dale,—gone down, as he now confessed to himself, with hopes almost triumphant, and he had returned because Lily Dale would not have him at her feet. " I loved him,—him, Crosbie,—better than all the world besides. It is still the same. I still love him better than all the world." Those were the words which had driven him back to London; and having been sent away with such words as those, it was little matter to him whether he reached his office a day or two sooner or later. The little room in the city, even with the accompaniment of Sir Raffle's bell and Sir Raffle's voice, would be now more congenial to him than Lady Julia's drawing-room. He would therefore present himself to Sir Raffle on that very afternoon, and expel some interloper from his seat. But he would first call in Burton Crescent and say farewell to the Ropers.

The door was opened for him by the faithful Jemima. "Mr. Heames, Mr. Heames! ho dear, ho dear! " and the poor girl, who had always taken his side in the adventures of the lodging-house, raised her hands on high and lamented the fate which had separated her favourite from its fortunes. " I suppose you knows it all, Mister Johnny ? " Mister Johnny said that he believed he did know it all, and asked for the mistress of the house. " Yes, sure enough, she's at home. She don't dare stir out much, 'cause of them Lupexes. Ain't this a pretty game ? No dinner and no nothink! Them boxes is Miss Spruce's. She's agoing now, this minute. You'41 find 'em all upstairs in the drawen-room." So upstairs into the drawing-room he went, and there he found the mother and daughter, and with them Miss Spruce, tightly packed up in her bonnet and shawl. "Don't, mother," Amelia was saying ; " what's the good of going on in that way ? If she chooses to go, let her go."

" But she's heen with me now so many years," said Mrs. Roper, sobbing; "and I've always done everything for her ! Haven't I, now, Sally Spruce ? " It struck Eames immediately that, though he had been an inmate in the house for two years, he had never before heard that maiden lady's Christian name. Miss Spruce was the first to see Eames as he entered the room. It is probable that Mrs. Roper's pathos might have produced some answering pathos on her part had she remained unobserved, but the sight of a young man brought her back to her usual state of quiescence. " I am only an old woman," said she; " and here's Mr. Eames come back again."

"How d'ye do, Mrs. Roper? how d'ye do, Amelia? how d'ye do, Miss Spruce ? " and he shook hands with them all.

"Oh, laws," said Mrs. Roper, " you have given me such a start!"

" Dear me, Mr. Eames ; only think of your coming back in that way," said Amelia.

"Well, what way should I come back? You didn't hear me knock at the door, that's all. So Miss Spruce is really going to leave you ? "

"Isn't it dreadful, Mr. Eames? Nineteen years we've been together;—taking both houses together, Miss Spruce, we have, indeed." Miss Spruce, at this point, struggled very hard to convince John Eames that the period in question had in truth extended over only eighteen years, but Mrs. Roper was authoritative, and would not permit it. " It's nineteen years if it's a day. No one ought to know dates if I don't, and there isn't one in the world understands her ways unless it's me. Haven't I been up to your bedroom every night, and with my own hand given you " But she stopped herself, and was too good a woman to declare before a young man what had been the nature of her nightly ministrations to her guest.

"I don't think you'll be so comfortable anywhere else, Miss Spruce," said Eames.

" Comfortable ! of course she won't," said Amelia. " But if I was mother I wouldn't have any more words about it."

" It isn't the money I'm thinking of, but the feeling of it," said Mrs. Roper. "The house will be so lonely like. I shan't know myself; that I shan't. And now that things are all settled so pleasantly, and that the Lupexes must go on Tuesday I'll tell you what, Sally; I'll pay for the cab myself, and I'll start off to Dulwich by the omnibus to-morrow, and settle it all out of my own pocket. I will indeed. Come ; there's the cab. Let me go down, and send him away."

" I'll do that," said Eames. " It's only sixpence, off the stand," Mrs. Roper called to him as he left the room. But the cabman got a shilling, and John, as he returned, found Jemima in the act of carrying Miss Spruce's boxes back to her room. " So much the better for poor Caudle," said he to himself. "As he has gone into the trade it's well that he should have somebody that will pay him."

Mrs. Roper followed Miss Spruce up the stairs and Johnny was left with Amelia. " He's written to you, I know," said she, with her face turned a little away from him. She was certainly very handsome, but there was a hard, cross, almost sullen look about her, which robbed her countenance of all its pleasantness. And yet she had no intention of being sullen with him.

" Yes," said John. " He has told me how it's all going to be."

"Well?" she said.

1 'Well? "said he.

" Is that all you've got to say ? "

" I'll congratulate you, if you'll let me."

" Psha ;—congratulations ! I hate such humbug. If you've no feelings about it, I'm sure that I've none. Indeed I don't know what's the good of feelings. They never did me any good. Are you engaged to marry L. D.? "

"No, I am not."

"And you've nothing else to say to me ? "

"Nothing,—except my hopes for your happiness. What else can I say ? You are engaged to many my friend Cradell, and I think it will be a happy match."

She turned away her face further from him, and the look of it became even more sullen. Could it be possible that at such a moment she still had a hope that he might come back to her ?

" Good-by, Amelia," he said, putting out his hand to her.

" And this is to be the last of you in this house ! "

"Well, I don't know about that. I'll come and call upon you, if you'll let me, when you're married."

"Yes," she said, "that there may be rows in the house, and noise, and jealousy,—as there have been with that wicked woman upstairs. Not if I know it, you won't! John Eames, I wish I'd never seen you. I wish we might have both fallen dead when we first met. I didn't think ever to have cared for a man as I have cared for you. It's all trash and nonsense and foolery; I know that. It's all very well for young ladies as can sit in drawing-rooms all their lives, but when a woman has her way to make in the world it's all foolery. And such a hard way too to make as mine is!"

"But it won't be hard now."

"Won't it? But I think it will. I wish you would try it. Not that I'm going to complain. I never minded work, and as for company, I can put up with anybody. The world's not to be all dancing and fiddling for the likes of me. I know that well enough. But ," and then she paused.

"What's the 'but' about, Amelia?"

"It's like you to ask me; isn't it ?" To tell the truth he should not have asked her. " Never mind. I'm not going to have any words with you. If you've been a knave I've been a fool, and that's worse."

"But I don't think I have been a knave."

"I've been both," said the girl; "and both for nothing. After that you may go. I've told you what I am, and I'll leave you to name yourself. I didn't think it was in me to have been such a fool. It's that that frets nie. Never mind, sir ; it's all over now, and I wish yen goodnbry.^

I do not think that there was the slightest reason why John should have again kissed her at parting, but he did so. She bore it, not struggling with him ; but she took his caress with sullen endurance. " It'll be the last," she said. " Good-by, John Eames."

" Good-by, Amelia. Try to make him a good wife and then you'll be happy." She turned up her nose at this, assuming a look of unutterable scorn. But she said nothing further, and then he left the room. At the parlour door he met Mrs. Koper, and had his parting words with her.

"I am so glad you came," said she. "It was just that word you said that made Miss Spruce stay. Her money is so ready, you know! And so you've had it all out with her about Cradell. She'll make him a good wife, she will indeed;—much better than you've been giving her credit for."

" I don't doubt she'll be a very good wife."

"You see, Mr. Eames, it's all over now, and we understand each other; don't we ? It made me very unhappy when she was setting her cap at you ; it did indeed. She is my own daughter, and I couldn't go against her;—could I ? But I knew it wasn't in any way suiting. Laws, I know the difference. She's good enough for him any day of the week, Mr. Eames."

"That she is,—Saturdays or Sundays," said Johnny, not knowing exactly what he ought to say.

"So she is ; and if he does his duty by her she won't go astray in hers by him. And as for you, Mr. Eames, I am sure I've always felt it an honour and a pleasure to have you in the house; and if ever you could use a good word in sending to me any of your young men, I'd do by them as a mother should; I would indeed. I know I've been to blame about those Lupexes, but haven't I suffered for it, Mr. Eames ? And it was difficult to know at first; wasn't it ? And as to you and Amelia, if you would send any of your young men to try, there couldn't be anything more of that kind, could there ? I know it hasn't all been just as it should have been;—that is as regards you; but I should like to hear you say that you've found me honest before you went. I have tried to be honest, I have indeed."

Eames assured her that he was convinced of her honesty, and that he had never thought of impugning her character either in regard to those unfortunate people, the Lupexes, or in reference to other matters. " He did not think," he said, " that any young men would consult him as to their lodgings; but if he could be of any service to her, he would." Then he- bade her good-by, and having bestowed half-a-sovereign on the faithful Jemima, he took a long farewell of Burton Crescent. Amelia had told him not to come and see her when she should be married, and he had resolved that he would take her at her word. So he walked off from the Crescent, not exactly shaking the dust from his feet, but resolving that he would know no more either of its dust or of its dirt. Dirt enough he had encountered there certainly, and he was now old enough to feel that the inmates of Mrs. Roper's house had not been those among whom a resting-place for his early years should judiciously have been sought. But he had come out of the fire comparatively unharmed, and I regret to say that he felt but little for the terrible scorchings to which his friend had been subjected and was about to subject himself. He was quite content to look at the matter exactly as it was looked at by Mrs. Roper. Amelia was good enough for Joseph Craclell—any day of the week. Poor Cradell, of whom in these pages after this notice no more will be heard! I cannot but think that a hard measure of justice was meted out to him, in proportion to the extent of his sins. More weak and foolish than our friend and hero he had been, but not to my knowledge more wicked. But it is to the vain and foolish that the punishments fall;—and to them they fall so thickly and constantly that the thinker is driven to think that vanity and folly are of all sins those which may be the least forgiven. As for Cradell I may declare that he did marry Amelia, that he did, with some pride, take the place of master of the house at the bottom of Mrs. Roper's table, and that he did make himself responsible for all Mrs. Roper's debts. Of his future fortunes there is not space to speak in these pages.

Going away from the Crescent Eames had himself driven to his office, which he reached just as the men were leaving it, at four o'clock. Cradell was gone, so that he did not see him on that afternoon ; but he had an opportunity of shaking hands with Mr. Love, who treated him with all the smiling courtesy due to an official bigwig,—for a private secretary, if not absolutely a big-wig, is seimVbig, and entitled to a certain amount of reverence;—and he passed Mr. Kissing in the passage, hurrying along as usual with a huge book under his arm. Mr. Kissing, hurried as he was, stopped his shuffling feet; but Eames only looked at him, hardly honouring him with the acknowledgment of a nod of his head. Mr. Kissing, however, was not offended; he knew that the private secretary of the First Commissioner had been the guest of an earl; and what more than a nod could be expected from him ? After that John made his way into the august presence of Sir Raffle, and found that great man putting on his shoes in the presence of FitzHoward. FitzHoward blushed; but the shoes had not been touched by him, as he took occasion afterwards to inform John Eames.

Sir Raffle was all smiles and civility. " Delighted to see you back, Eames : am, upon my word ; though I and FitzHoward have got on capitally in your absence; haven't we, FitzHoward ?"

" Oh, yes,"* drawled FitzHoward. " I haven't minded it for a time, just while Eames has been away."

" You're much too idle to keep at it, I know; but your bread will be buttered for you elsewhere, so it doesn't signify. My compliments to the duchess when you see her." Then FitzHoward went. "And how's my dear old friend?" asked Sir Raffle, as though of all men living Lord De Guest were the one for whom he had the strongest and the oldest love. And yet he must have known that John Eames knew as much about it as he did himself. But there are men who have the most lively gratification in calling lords and marquises their friends, though they know that nobody believes a word of what they say,—even though they know how great is the odium they incur, and how lasting is the ridicule which their vanity produces. It is a gentle insanity which prevails in the outer courts of every aristocracy; and as it brings with itself considerable annoyance and but a lukewarm pleasure, it should not be treated with too keen a severity.

" And how's my dear old friend ? " Eames assured him that his dear old friend was all right, that Lady Julia was all right, that the dear old place was all right. Sir Raffle now spoke as though the " dear old place " were quite well known to him. " Was the game doing pretty well ? Was there a promise of birds ?" Sir Raffle's anxiety was quite intense, and expressed with almost familiar affection. " And, by-the-by, Eames, where are you living at present ? "

"Well, I'm not settled. I'm at the Great Western Railway Hotel at this moment."

" Capital house, very ; only it's expensive if you stay there the whole season." Johnny had no idea of remaining there beyond one night, but he said nothing as to this. " By-the-by, you might as well come and dine with us to-morrow. Lady Buffle is most anxious to know you. There'll be one or two with us. I did ask my friend Dumbello, but there's some nonsense going on in the House, and he thinks that he can't get away." Johnny was more gracious than Lord Dumbello, and accepted the invitftion. " I wonder what Lady Buffle will be like ?" he said to himself, as he walked away from the office.

He had turned into the Great Western Hotel, not as yet knowing where to look for a home ; and there we will leave him, eating his solitary mutton-chop at one of those tables which are so comfortable to the eye, but which are so comfortless in reality. I speak not now with reference to the excellent establishment which has been named, but to the nature of such tables in general. A solitary mutton-chop in an hotel coffee-room is not a banqi .et to be envied by any god ; and if the mutton-chop be converted into soup, fish, little dishes, big dishes, and the rest, the matter becomes worse and not better. What comfort are you to have, seated alone on that horsehair chair,

staring into the room and watching the waiters as they whisk about their towels ? No one but an Englishman has ever yet thought of subjecting himself to such a position as that I But here we will leave John Eames, and in doing so I must be allowed to declare that only now, at this moment, has he entered on his manhood. Hitherto he has been a hobbledehoy,—a calf, as it were, who had carried his calfishness later into life than is common with calves; but who did not, perhaps, on that account, give promise of making a worse ox than the rest of them. His life hitherto, as recorded in these pages, had afforded him no brilliant success, had hardly qualified him for the r61e of hero which he has been made to play. I feel that I have been in fault in giving such prominence to a hobbledehoy, and that I should have told my story better had I brought Mr. Crosbie more conspicuously forward on my canvas. He at any rate has gotten to himself a wife,—as a hero always should do; whereas I must leave my poor friend Johnny without any matrimonial prospects.

It was thus that he thought of himself as he sat moping over his solitary table in the hotel coffee-room. He acknowledged to himself that he had not hitherto been a man ; but at the same time he made some resolution which, I trust, may assist him in commencing his manhood from this date.

CHAPTER XXX. CONCLUSION,

It was early in June that Lily went up to her uncle at the Great House, pleading for Hopkins,—pleading that to Hopkins might he restored all the privileges of head gardener at the Great House. There was some absurdity in this, seeing that he had never really relinquished his privileges; but the manner of the quarrel had been in this wise.

There was in those days, and had been for years, a vexed question between Hopkins and Jolliffe the bailiff on the matter of

stable manure. Hopkins had pretended to the right of taking what he required from the farmyard, without asking leave of any one. Jolliffe in return had hinted, that if this were so, Hopkins would take it all. " But I can't eat it," Hopkins had said. Jolliffe merely grunted, signifying by the grunt, as Hopkins thought, that though a gardener couldn't eat a mountain of manure fifty feet long and fifteen high,—couldn't eat in the body,-—he might convert it into things edible for his own personal use. And so there had been a great feud. The unfortunate squire had of course been called on to arbitrate, and having postponed his decision by every contrivance possible to him, had at last been driven by Jolliffe to declare that Hopkins should take nothing that was not assigned to him. Hopkins, when the decision was made known to him by his master, bit his old lips, and turned round upon his old heel, speechless. " You'll find it's so at all other places," said the squire, apologetically. " Other places I" sneered Hopkins. Where would he find other gardeners like himself? It is hardly necessary to declare that from that moment he resolved that he would abide by no such order. Jolliffe on the next morning informed the squire that the order had been broken, and the squire fretted and fumed, wishing that Jolliffe were well buried under the mountain in question. " If they all is to do as

they like," said Jolliffe, " then nobody won't care for nobody." The squire understood that an order if given must be obeyed, and therefore, with many inner groanings of the spirit, resolved that war must be waged against Hopkins.

On the following morning he found the old man himself wheeling a huge barrow of manure round from the yard into the kitchen-garden. Now, on ordinary occasions, Hopkins was not required to do with his own hands work of that description. He had a man under him who hewed wood, and carried water, and wheeled barrows,—one man always, and often two. The squire knew when he saw him that he was sinning, and bade him stop upon his road.

" Hopkins," he said, " why didn't you ask for what you wanted, before you took it ?" The old man put down the barrow on the ground, looked up in his master's face, spat into his hands, and then again resumed his barrow. " Hopkins, that won't do," said the squire. " Stop where you are."

" What won't do ?" said Hopkins, still holding the barrow from the ground, but not as yet progressing.

" Put it down, Hopkins," and Hopkins did put it down. " Don't you know that you are flatly disobeying my orders ?"

" Squire, I've been here about this place going on nigh seventy years."

" If you've been going on a hundred and seventy it, wouldn't do that there should be more than one master. I'm the master here, and I intend to be so to the end. Take that manure back into the yard."

" Back into the yard ?" said Hopkins, very slowly.

" Yes; back into the yard."

" What,—afore all their faces ? "

11 Yes ; you've disobeyed me before all their faces ?"

Hopkins paused a moment, looking away from the squire, and shaking his head as though he had need of deep thought, but by the aid of deep thought had come at last to a right conclusion. Then he resumed the barrow, and putting himself almost into a trot, carried away his prize into the kitcheng-arden. At the pace which he went it would have been beyond the squire's power to stop him, nor would Mr. Dale have wished to come to a personal encounter with his servant. But he called after the man in dire wrath that if he were not obeyed the disobedient servant should rue the consequences for ever. Hopkins, equal to the occasion, shook his head as he trotted

40—2

on, deposited his load at the foot of the cucumber-frames, and then at once returning to his master, tendered to him the key of the greenhouse.

" Master," said Hopkins, speaking as best he could with his scanty breath, " there it is;—there's the key; of course I don't want no warning, and doesn't care about my week's wages. I'll be out of the cottage afore night, and as for the work'us, I suppose they'll let me in at once, if your honour'll give 'em a line."

Now as Hopkins was well known by the squire to be the owner of three or four hundred pounds, the hint about the workhouse must be allowed to have been melo-dramatic.

." Don't be a fool," said the squire, almost gnashing his teeth.

" I know I've been a fool," said Hopkins, " about that 'ere doong; my feelings has been too much for me. When a man's feelings has been too much for him, he'd better just take hisself off, and lie in the work'us till he dies." And then he again tendered the key. But the squire did not take the key, and so Hopkins went on. " I s'pose I'd better just see to the lights and the like of that, till you've suited yourself, Mr. Dale. It 'ud be a pity all them grapes should go off, and they, as you may say, all one as fit for the table. It's a long way the best crop I ever see on 'em. I've been that careful with 'em that I haven't had a natural night's rest, not since February. There ain't nobody about this place as understands grapes, nor yet anywhere nigh that could be got at. My lord's head man is wery ignorant; but even if he knew ever so, of course he couldn't come here. I suppose I'd better keep the key till you're suited, Mr. Dale."

Then for a fortnight there was an interregnum in the gardens, terrible in the annals of Allington. Hopkins lived in his cottage indeed, and looked most sedulously after the grapes. In looking after the grapes, too, he took the greenhouses under his care; but he would have nothing to do with the outer gardens, took no wages, returning the amount sent to him back to the squire, and insisted with everybody that he had been dismissed. He went about with some terrible horticultural implement always in his hand, with which it was said that he intended to attack Jolliffe ; but Jolliffe prudently kept out of his way.

As soon as it had been resolved by Mrs. Dale and Lily that the flitting from the Small House at Allington was not to be accomplished, Lily communicated the fact to Hopkins.

" Miss," said he, " when I said them few words to you and your mamma, I knew that you would listen to reason."

This was no more than Lily had expected; that Hopkins should claim the honour of having prevailed by his arguments was a matter of course.

" Yes," said Lily ; " we've made up our minds to stay. Uncle wishes it."

' ' Wishes it! Laws, miss; it ain't only wishes. And we all wishes it. Why, now, look at the reason of the thing. Here's this here house "

" But, Hopkins, it's decided. We're going to stay. What I want to know is this; can you come at once and help me to unpack ? "

" What! this very evening, as is "

" Yes, now; we want to have the things about again before they come back from Guestwick."

Hopkins scratched his head and hesitated, not wishing to yield to any proposition that could be considered as childish; but he gave way at last, feeling that the work itself was a good work. Mrs. Dale also assented, laughing at Lily for her folly as she did so, and in this way the things were unpacked very quickly, and the alliance between Lily and Hopkins became, for the time, very close. This work of unpacking and resettling was not yet over, when the battle of the manure broke out, and therefore it was that Hopkins, when his feelings had become altogether too much for him " about the doong," came at last to Lily, and laying down at her feet all the weight and all the glory of his sixty odd years of life, implored her to make matters straight for him. " It's been a killing me, miss, so it has; to see the way they've been a cutting that 'sparagus. It ain't cutting at all. It's just hocking it up;—what is fit, and what isn't, all together. And they've been a-putting the plants in where I didn't mean 'em, though they know'd I didn't mean 'em. I've stood by, miss, and said never a word. I'd a died sooner. But, Miss Lily, what my sufferings have been, 'cause of my feelings getting the better of me about that—you know, miss — nobody will ever tell;—nobody — nobody—nobody." Then Hopkins turned away and wept.

"Uncle," said Lily, creeping close up against his chair, " I want to ask you a great favour."

" A great favour. Well, I don't think I shall refuse you anything at present. It isn't to ask another earl to the house,—is it ? "

" Another earl! " said Lily.

" Yes; haven't you heard ? Miss Bell has been here this morning, insisting that I should have over Lord De Guest and his sister for the marriage. It seems that there was some scheming between Bell and Lady Julia."

" Of course you will ask them."

" Of course I must. I've no way out of it. It'll be all very well for Bell, who'll be off to Wales with her lover; but what am I to do with the earl and Lady Julia, when they're gone ? Will you come and help me?"

In answer to this, Lily of course promised that she would come and help. "Indeed," said she, "I thought we were all asked up for the day. And now for my favour. Uncle, you must forgive poor Hopkins."

" Forgive a "fiddlestick !" said the squire. " No, but you must. You can't think how unhappy he is." " How can I forgive a man who won't forgive me. He goes prowling about the place doing nothing; and he sends me back his wages, and he looks as though he were going to murder some one; and all because he wouldn't do as he was told. How am I to forgive such a man as that ? "

"But, uncle, why not?"

" It would be his forgiving me. He knows very well that he may come back whenever he pleases; and, indeed, for the matter of that he has never gone away.

" But he is so very unhappy." " What can I do to make him happier ?"

" Just go down to his cottage and tell him that you forgive him." " Then he'll argue with me."

"No; I don't think he will. He is too much down in the world for arguing now."

" Ah! you don't know him as I do. All the misfortunes in the world wouldn't stop that man's conceit. Of course I'll go if you ask me, but it seems to me that I'm made to knock under to everybody. I hear a great deal about other people's feelings, but I don't know that mine are very much thought of." He was not altogether in a happy mood, and Lily almost regretted that she had persevered; but she did succeed in carrying him off across the garden to the cottage, and as they went together she promised him that she would think of him always,always. The scene with Hopkins cannot be described now, as it would take too many of our few remaining pages. It resulted,

I am. afraid I must confess, in nothing more triumphant to the squire than a treaty of mutual forgiveness. Hopkins acknowledged, with much self-reproach, that his feelings had been too many for him ; but then, look at his provocation ! He could not keep his tongue from that matter, and certainly said as much in his own defence as he did in confession of his sins. The substantial triumph was altogether his, for nobody again ever dared to interfere with his operations in the farmyard. He showed his submission to his master mainly by consenting to receive his wages for the two weeks which he had passed in idleness.

Owing to this little accident, Lily was not so much oppressed by Hopkins as she had expected to be in that matter of their altered plans; but this salvation did not extend to Mrs.

Hearn, to Mrs. Crump, or, above all, to Mrs. Boyce. They, all of them, took an interest more or less strong in the Hopkins controversy; but their interest in the occupation of the Small House was much stronger, and it was found useless to put Mrs. Hearn off with the gardener's persistent refusal of his wages, when she was big with inquiry whether the house was to be painted inside, as well as out. " Ah," said she, " I think I'll go and look at lodgings at Guestwick myself, and pack up some of my beds." Lily made no answer to this, feeling that it was a part of that punishment which she had expected. " Dear, dear," said Mrs. Crump to the two girls; "well, to be sure, we should a been lone without 'ee, and mayhap we might a got worse in your place; but why did 'ee go and fasten up all your things in them big boxes, just to unfasten 'em all again ? "

" We changed our minds, Mrs. Crump," said Bell, with some severity.

" Yees, I know ye changed your mindses. Well, it's all right for loiks o' ye, no doubt; but if we changes our mindses, we hears of it."

"So, it seems, do we!" said Lily. "But never mind, Mrs. Crump. Do you send us our letters up early, and then we won't quarrel."

" Oh, letters! Drat them for letters. I wish there weren't no sich things. There was a man here yesterday with his imperence. I don't know where he come from,—down from Lun'on, I b'leeve : and this was wrong, and that was wrong, and everything was wrong ; and then he said he'd have me discharged the sarvice."

" Dear me, Mrs. Crump; that wouldn't do at all."

" Discharged the sarvice ! Tuppence farden a day ! So I toM 'un to discharge hisself, and take all the old bundles and things away upon his shoulders. Letters indeed! What business have they with post-missusses, if they cannot pay 'em better nor tuppence farden a day ?" And in this way, under the shelter of Mrs. Crump's storm of wrath against the inspector who had visited her, Lily and Bell escaped much that would have fallen upon their own heads; but Mrs. Boyce still remained. I may here add, in order that Mrs. Crump's history may be carried on to the farthest possible point, that she was not " discharged the sarvice," and that she still receives her twopence farthing a day from the Crown. " That's a bitter old lady," said the inspector to the man who was driving him. " Yes, sir; they all says the same about she. There ain't none of 'em get much change out of Mrs. Crump."

Bell and Lily went together also to Mrs. Boyce's. " If she makes herself very disagreeable, I shall insist upon talking of your marriage," said Lily.

" I've not the slightest objection," said Bell; " only I don't know what there can be to say about it. Marrying the doctor is such a very commonplace sort of thing."

" Not a bit more commonplace than marrying the parson," said Lily.

" Oh, yes, it is. Parsons' marriages are often very grand affairs. They come in among county people. That's their luck in life. Doctors never do; nor lawyers. I don't think lawyers ever get married in the country. They're supposed to do it up in London. But a country doctor's wedding is not a thing to be talked about much."

Mrs. Boyce probably agreed in this view of the matter, seeing that she did not choose the coming marriage as her first subject of conversation. As soon as the two girls were seated she flew away immediately to the house, and began to express her very great surprise,—her surprise and her joy also,—at the sudden change which had been made in their plans. " It is so much nicer, you know," said she, " that things should be pleasant among relatives."

" Things always have been tolerably pleasant with us," said Bell.

" Oh, yes; I'm sure of that. I've always said it was quite a pleasure to see you and your uncle together. And when we heard about your all having to leave "

" But we didn't have to leave, Mrs. Boyce. We were going to leave because we thought mamma would be more comfortable in Guestwick; and now we're not going to leave, because we've all 'changed our mindses,' as Mrs. Crump calls it."

" And is it true the house is going to be painted ?" asked Mrs. Boyce.

" I believe it is true," said Lily.

" Inside and out ?"

" It must be done some day," said Bell.

" Yes, to be sure; but I must say it is generous of the squire. There's such a deal of woodwork about your house. I know I wish the Ecclesiastical Commissioners would paint ours ; but nobody ever does anything for the clergy. I'm sure I'm delighted you're going to stay. As I said to Mr. Boyce, what should we ever have done without you ? I believe the squire had made up his mind that he would not let the place."

" I don't think he ever has let it."

" And if there was nobody in it, it would all go to rack and ruin ; wouldn't it ? Had your mamma to pay anything for the lodgings she engaged at Guestwick ?"

" Upon my word, I don't know. Bell can tell you better about that than I, as Dr. Crofts settled it. I suppose Dr. Crofts tells her everything." And so the conversation was changed, and Mrs. Boyce was made to understand that whatever further mystery there might be, it would not be unravelled on that occasion.

It was settled that Dr. Crofts and Bell should be married about the middle of June, and the squire determined to give what grace he could to the ceremony by opening his own house on the occasion. Lord De Guest and Lady Julia were invited by special arrangement between her ladyship and Bell, as has been before explained. The colonel also with Lady Fanny came up from Torquay on the occasion, this being the first visit made by the colonel to his paternal roof for many years. Bernard did not accompany his father. He had not yet gone abroad, but there were circumstances which made him feel that he would not find himself comfortable at the wedding. The service was performed by Mr. Boyce, assisted, as the County Chronicle very fully remarked, by the Reverend John Joseph Jones, M.A., late of Jesus College, Cambridge, and curate of St. Peter's, Northgate, Guestwick ; the fault of which little advertisement was this,—that as none of the readers of the paper had patience to get beyond the Reverend John Joseph Jones, the fact of Bell's marriage with Dr. Crofts was not disseminated as widely as might have been wished.

The marriage went off very nicely. The squire was upon his very best behaviour, and welcomed his guests as though he really enjoyed their presence there in his halls. Hopkins, who was quite aware that he had been triumphant, decorated the old rooms with mingled flowers and greenery with an assiduous care which pleased the two girls mightily. And during this work df wreathing and decking there was one little morsel of feeling displayed which may as well be told in these last lines. Lily had been encouraging the old man while Bell for a moment had been absent.

" I wish it had been for thee, my darling! " he said ; " I wish it had been for thee ! "

'* It is much better as it is, Hopkins," she answered, solemnly.

" Not with him, though," he went on, " not with him. I wouldn't a hung a bough for him. But with t'other one."

Lily said no word further. She knew that the man was expressing the wishes of all around her. She said no word further, and then Bell returned to them.

But no one at the wedding was so gay as Lily,—so gay, so bright, and so wedding-like. She flirted with the old earl till he declared that he would many her himself. No one seeing her that evening, and knowing nothing of her immediate history, would have imagined that she herself had been cruelly jilted some six or eight months ago. And those who did know her could not imagine that what she then suffered had hit her so hard, that no recovery seemed possible for her. But though no recovery, as she herself believed, was possible for her,—though she was as a man whose right arm had been taken from him in the battle, still all the world had not gone with that right arm. The bullet which had maimed her sorely had not touched her life, and she scorned to go about the world complaining either by word or look of the injury she had received. " Wives when they have lost their husbands still eat and laugh," she said to herself, " and he is not dead like that." So she resolved that she would be happy, and I here declare that she not only seemed to carry out her resolution, but that she did carry it out in very truth. " You're a dear good man, and I know you'll be good to her," she said to Crofts just as he was about to start with his bride.

" I'll try, at any rate," he answered.

" And I shall expect you to be good to me too. Remember you have married the whole family; and, sir, you mustn't believe a word of what that bad man says in his novels about mothers-in-law. He

has done a great deal of harm, and shut half the ladies in England out of their daughters' houses."

" He shan't shut Mrs. Dale out of mine."

" Remember he doesn't. Now, good-by." So the bride and bridegroom went off, and Lily was left to flirt with Lord De Guest.

Of whom else is it necessary that a word or two should be said before I allow the weary pen to fall from my hand ? The squire, after much inward straggling on the subject, had acknowledged to himself that his sister-in-law had not received from him that kindness which she had deserved. He had acknowledged this, purporting to do his best to amend his past errors; and I think I may say that his efforts in that line would not be received ungraciously by Mrs. Dale. I am inclined therefore to think that life at Allington, both at the Great House and at the Small, would soon become pleasanter than it used to be in former days. Lily soon got the Balmoral boots, or, at least, soon learned that the power of getting them as she pleased had devolved upon her from her uncle's gift; so that she talked even of buying the squirrel's cage; but I am not aware that her extravagance led her as far as that.

Lord De Courcy we left suffering dreadfully from gout and ill-temper at Courcy Castle. Yes, indeed ! To him in his latter days life did not seem to offer much that was comfortable. His wife had now gone from him, and declared positively to her son-in-law that no earthly consideration should ever induce her to go back again;— " not if I were to starve! " she said. By which she intended to signify that she would be firm in her resolve, even though she should thereby lose her carriage and horses. Poor Mr. Gazebee went down to Courcy, and had a dreadful interview with the earl; but matters were at last arranged, and her ladyship remained at Baden-Baden in a state of semi-starvation. That is to say, she had but one horse to her carriage.

As regards Crosbie, I am inclined to believe that he did again recover his power at his office. He was Mr. Butterwell's master, and the master also of Mr. Optimist, and the major. He knew his business, and could do it, which was more, perhaps, than might fairly be said of any of the other three. Under such circumstances he was sure to get in his hand, and lead again. But elsewhere his star did not recover its ascendancy. He dined at his club almost daily, and there were those with whom he habitually formed some little circle. But he was not the Crosbie of former days,the

Crosbie known in Belgravia and in St. James's Street. He had taken his little vessel bravely out into the deep waters,'and had sailed her well while fortune stuck close to him. But he had forgotten his nautical rules, and success had made him idle. His plummet and lead had not been used, and he had kept no look-out ahead. Therefore the first rock he met shivered his bark to pieces His wife, the Lady Alexandrina, is to be seen in the one-horse carriage with her mother at Baden-Baden.

THE END. VOLUME 2

Printed in Great Britain
by Amazon